SEVEN DAYS
DEAD

SEVEN DAYS DEAD

The Storm Murders Trilogy

JOHN FARROW

MINOTAUR BOOKS
A Thomas Dunne Book
New York

A THOMAS DUNNE BOOK FOR MINOTAUR BOOKS.
An imprint of St. Martin's Publishing Group.

SEVEN DAYS DEAD. Copyright © 2016 by John Farrow Mysteries, Inc. All rights reserved. Printed in the United States of America. For information, address St. Martin's Press, 175 Fifth Avenue, New York, N.Y. 10010.

www.thomasdunnebooks.com
www.minotaurbooks.com

Library of Congress Cataloging-in-Publication Data

Names: Farrow, John, 1947– author.
Title: Seven days dead / John Farrow.
Description: First edition. | New York : Minotaur Books, 2016. | Series: The storm murders trilogy ; 2 | "A Thomas Dunne book."
Identifiers: LCCN 2015050065| ISBN 9781250057693 (hardcover) | ISBN 9781250086594 (e-book)
Subjects: LCSH: Police—Québec (Province)—Montréal—Fiction. | Murder—Investigation—Fiction. | BISAC: FICTION / Mystery & Detective / Police Procedural. | GSAFD: Mystery fiction.
Classification: LCC PR9199.3.F455 S49 2016 | DDC 813/.54—dc23
LC record available at http://lccn.loc.gov/2015050065

Our books may be purchased in bulk for promotional, educational, or business use. Please contact your local bookseller or the Macmillan Corporate and Premium Sales Department at 1-800-221-7945, extension 5442, or by e-mail at MacmillanSpecialMarkets@macmillan.com.

First Edition: May 2016

10 9 8 7 6 5 4 3 2 1

For Lynne

ACKNOWLEDGMENTS

The author is abundantly grateful to his editor, Marcia Markland, at Thomas Dunne Books, for her commitment to this project, and to Quressa Robinson for her quick and courteous responses to every request. You rock!

PART 1

ONE

Time and tide wait for no man and no woman.

And here, she reminds herself again, the tide is swift.

All day, waves kicked up across the Gulf of Maine, out to the Atlantic and into the Bay of Fundy, a waterway shaped like the opening jaws of a shark. Winds staggered ships. Surprised by a whole gale expected to track south but veering north instead, fishermen yearn for safe harbor, the family table, a lover's nudge. Yet no boat attempts landfall tonight, the tempest too wicked against these craggy shores, the combination a treachery.

Boats wait this one out at sea.

Ashore, deeper inside the bay, sirens wail to warn of the sea's return. A seventy-foot range in depth is a danger to the unwary. The story goes that a champion Thoroughbred with a top-notch jockey on its back cannot outrun this tidal bore. Not that any horse is out on the flats tonight. A sleek gray Porsche, though, running down a highway parallel to the inflow, also fails to maintain Fundy's relentless clip. The driver's vision is reduced by the deluge and ponds pooling on the road further impede the car's progress. Yet she accepts the challenge, her speed limited by the dark of the gale, the barreling funnels of wind, occasional hairpin turns, and sudden blind dips that in these conditions are life-threatening. Spurred on by the likelihood of an imminent death in her family, the night traveler perseveres and, against her better judgment, presses on.

Time will not wait for anyone, she knows, and certainly not for her.

Nor will the tide.

Nor will her dying father.

Bastard.

Yet the race to arrive before his death is on.

A man familiar with the driver's father, acquainted with his idio-syncrasies and failings—if not the depths of his depravity—endures the storm in the comfort of a church manse, his home. Rain pelts down on the rooftop and windows, forlorn hounds bay in the stovepipe, gusts clatter the shingles and shake the doors. Yet for all the commotion on the exterior walls of this old wooden cottage, inside, the Reverend Simon Lescavage feels quite snug. He sips a cup of English Breakfast. In the light of a frizzy oil lamp he's reading a book on cosmology. Complicated stuff. Hours ago the electricity went down and it's not likely to be up anytime soon, so lamps and candles are lit, a flashlight is handy, his tea is quite soothing, and the small fire in the hearth—not necessary in summer but needed to heat a beverage tonight—burns cozily, crackles. His book, a challenge, surely is just the ticket for the solitary evening.

Theories on the origins of the universe fascinate him. He reads more about quantum mechanics these days than about theology, and revels in the study of black holes and star formations. Not long ago, in grap-pling with notions concerning miracles in a sermon, he tripped up and embarked on a tangent that gave a nod to string theory and dark energy. His congregation was baffled. In his current phase, the minister neglects Biblical homilies, and reserves his adoration for scientific inquiries into the cosmos.

Not that a snippet of that expanse is viewed from his island home tonight.

Out there in the deeper blackness, islands stand as guardians to the Bay of Fundy. A few are rarely inhabited: Kent, Sheep and Hay, and Machias, where the puffins roost, and farther north there's White Head, Cheney, and Ross, the wee sisters of Great Duck, Gulf Islet, and a more northern, less well-known Nantucket. All of them, and Grand Manan, the largest and most populated of the scattering, where Lescavage is comfortably lodged, are being slammed without any echo of mercy. Waves roil also across the salmon farms. From near space, they appear as crop circles in neat, tight rows upon the sea, each wide enough to harbor a battleship as well as three-quarters of a million fish. Yet the salmon are secure within their cages tonight, and Lescavage assumes that across the Isle of Grand Manan everyone is secure enough as well, doing what he's doing, if not reading then huddling close, under a blanket or wearing earbuds to listen to music that mutes the bedlam of the storm.

He assumes that in nine months' time babies will bob to the surface, the final flotsam blown ashore by this wind and sea. Other wives, bereft of companionship tonight, fret about their men upon the deep, and Lescavage worries along with them.

Silently, secretly, he prays for their lives.

Old habits, as the adage goes, and he concurs, die hard.

His head is bowed when the phone rings, disrupting his peace. Tempted not to answer, he accepts that on a night such as this no one will believe that he's not home, so in that sense he has little choice. The phone goes on ringing. A persistence that's annoying, as it invokes his servitude.

Simon Lescavage maintains only one telephone in his dwelling. It squats on a small table in the kitchen, buried beneath a newspaper and packaging for spaghetti noodles he's neglected to toss into the recycling bin. He gets rid of the debris first, compressing into a plastic bag what he'll transfer outside later, then shifts the *Telegraph Journal* to one side and picks up the receiver after a dozen rings. He does not intend to sound gruff, but promptly betrays himself with his tone.

"Yeah?"

Rain, at that instant, drums more violently on the windowpanes.

He recognizes the woman's voice, as she's his housekeeper every second Tuesday and on Sunday afternoons sweeps out the church. She's explaining her situation at some length, with urgency but with no attempt to be concise.

He finally interrupts the spiel. "What is it this time, really?"

She continues to vent.

Grumpily, Lescavage interrupts, "I'm not all that impressed. Are you?"

She hardly takes a breath, and the pastor finds himself distracted by the beat of rain on the glass while she follows through on her rant. He already knows that if this conversation continues in its present vein, he's likely to be out in the weather himself momentarily. He's a slight man who at first glance looks unduly fit for fifty-seven. His 142 pounds comes across to most people as trim, yet five years ago he was 124, which had been his average for decades. The additional weight suits him. He's rarely called scrawny anymore. Women no longer shout at him from their doorways commanding that he enter their homes and eat something, to fatten up, although they may have stopped all that because he's older now. Or they are. Or because when he did eat in their homes, little came of it, he did nothing more than chow down. He's no longer quite so skinny, has never thought of himself as short and has refused to gauge his height as merely average. He hates that designation, a nod to vanity that in the overall scheme of his life is rare for him—although it's true that a buzz cut is meant to preempt impending baldness. Lescavage has never tried to pass himself off as tall, that would be absurd, yet along with his self-consciousness about being diminutive he's compounded the matter by denying what any tape measure and the attitudes of others contend. He flies in the face of that logic. Once only he put up a description of his attributes on an online Christian dating site, choosing to describe himself as "well-proportioned," which in his mind covered both his exceptional skinniness back then and a general lack of tallness. Otherwise, he's not notably vain.

"All right," he says, ceding to the housekeeper's request. Always the pushover, and perhaps resenting that about himself, his response to her next suggestion is strident. "No, Ora! Not a chance! I'll arrive in a huff. That's it, that's all. I reserve the right to be my petulant self. Tell him that. Say it to his face. Tell him—" Lescavage weighs what pithy remark he might charge the housekeeper to pass along to her current employer, a man on his last legs if that impression is to be believed, although Lescavage doesn't. "Ora, sorry, never mind. I'll tell him myself."

He nods, as if she can see the gesture through the phone line, and adds after she states some further opinion, "I agree with you. It is better this way."

She hangs up without a subsequent word. The Reverend Lescavage follows suit. For a moment he reads from the newspaper—a headline has grabbed his attention—but, disappointed in the story, he puts it down and blows out the wall lamp in the kitchen. In dimmer light he strides through to the front door.

The pastor snuffs a pair of candles and lowers the wicks on oil lamps.

In the vestibule, Lescavage lifts rain pants off a hook and bends to retrieve his boots. He's seated upon an antique pine bench, one that might have served a shoemaker eons ago or supported the ample backside of a fisherman repairing a net. Pausing, he considers that he may have been summoned out tonight to slog through the wet for another man's amusement, but he pulls the rain pants on over his trousers anyway and works his feet into the boots. He is the son of a clergyman, his mother a fisherman's daughter, and he takes particular pride in the maternal side of his lineage. He knows that the nuance has held him in good stead among his flock. His people, as he calls them, have generally been fond of him, even though lately they're not sure what to make of a pastor who's lost his faith yet still enjoys, and wants to keep, his job. When he explains himself, it's all so complicated. He stands, adjusts the pants' suspenders over his shoulders, slips on his slicker and rain hat, and braces himself for the wild, warm wind and the fearsome onslaught of the torrent.

He's unwilling to drive in this weather, or in this dark. Not on these roads. No matter, it's a short distance, and initially trees protect him from a portion of the bluster, their tops swaying, branches flailing the air. He's stunned by the volume of the wind's roaring. Away from his house, everything is so dark that he can't see the trees anymore, and when he holds a hand up, he can't make out his fingers. His feet barely discern the pavement. Like stepping on stones in a fast-flowing stream.

Lescavage walks up Old Airport Road, then turns right onto Light-house Road, a simple intersection that tonight is maddening to locate. With a bend in direction, the wind hits hardest. He dares not open both eyelids in the gusts. His face stings. The Orrock mansion is farther along, but while the distance is not far—an uphill walk he's done a thousand times, often to take in the vista from the lighthouse—on this trek the required effort in the teeth of the gale is immense.

He leaves the lighthouse and its muted lamp behind.

Thanks to a generator, lights are on in Alfred Orrock's big house and across his yard, and Lescavage easily finds his way up the long, winding path. Standing under the porch light and a protective over-hang, he shakes the rain off in a style not dissimilar to a dog's. He rings the bell, then readies himself for anything.

The young housekeeper has the door open in a wink and bounds outside.

"Whoa, whoa, Ora! Where's the fire?"

She's a step past him, but as he clutches her arm, she retreats. Al-though well dressed for the weather, she takes another look at the night. Hers will be a longer hike home than the distance Lescavage just cov-ered, and the weather is more wicked than it appeared while she was safely ensconced indoors. The way the wind bellows over the cliffs and how the rain slams down from one direction, then another, give her pause. Protected by the porch overhang, she pulls her rain hat over her ears, holds it there with both hands. She crinkles her nose and, with her mouth in some odd contortion, remarks, "I don't need to watch him die, do I? I'm not paid for that."

Ora is pleasantly chubby, with a drooping nose, and quite a tall forehead above a round face the world regards as plain. She's a bright-cheeked young lady. Lescavage finds her cute in her way.

"I put in my hours. Anyway, I'm not a freaking nurse."

"Ora, he's not dying. Ask yourself, since when are we ever that lucky?"

Her eyes asquint, she retorts, "He says he is! Doesn't he? I wouldn't put it past the old prick bugger anyway. Sorry for my language there,

Rev, but I've had it up to here with him." She frees up a hand to measure to the height of her scalp.

Lescavage removes his rain hat under the protection of the overhang, lets the water pour off. "Yeah, well," he concedes, "if the shoe fits."

"What's that supposed to mean? What shoe?"

"It's an expression."

"So aren't I the stupid mutt."

"It's a very common expression."

"So now I'm dumber than the dumb asses."

"Ora." He sighs. "You called him a 'prick bugger.' I've not heard that one before. All I'm saying is, I don't think it's unfair to call him that."

"Watch your language there, Rev."

She pulls her hat more tightly down her cheeks. An umbrella would not survive two seconds out here except in a lull, so the strategy of clamping both hands to her rain hat is wise.

"You won't stay?" His voice has gone falsely plaintive, coaxing, a plea.

"I'm gonzo, Revy. He's all yours. See ya on the flip!"

True to her word, she splashes down into the broad puddle at the base of the steps, cocks her head to the right and into her shoulder against the wind, and stomps through an enveloping blackness beyond the fringe of walkway lamps. Lescavage watches her go for longer than he can actually make out her form, but he knows what this caring gesture really means. He's putting off the inevitable. He goes inside through the open door, then shuts it tightly.

Amazing, he thinks, how much quieter this house is than his own in the midst of an onslaught.

He sticks his rain hat on the top hook of a shiny aluminum wall-mounted rack. His jacket, stuck to him by the wet, peels off slowly, like skin, and while trying to be free of it, he calls into the house. "Alfred! Upstairs or down?" He stays quiet, awaiting a response, but receives none. No sound is apparent other than the faint hum of the backyard generator and the underlying chant of the rain. "I know you can hear me!" he attests. "You might be dead but you're not deaf!"

An insult might shake loose a reaction, but not this time. He continues to strip off his outerwear and wedges the boots from his feet, dries his face on a sleeve, then admits himself to the house and stands there in his socks.

In the living room off the grand foyer, the La-Z-Boy is vacant. A snack that Ora Matheson threw together for either her employer or herself—cheeses and an assortment of crackers, bread slices, preserves, and a few green grapes—has gone largely untouched. Lescavage is instantly aware of his own desire for a nosh. He cracks a scone in half, slathers on butter and raspberry jam, and has a nibble. Before finishing, he prepares a second scone then carries his snack deeper into the house.

"Alfred? Anywhere?"

Opulence abounds, but he's used to all that and pays it no mind. Outside these walls, the house is legendary and valued to be more glamorous than it actually is. He and Ora entertained themselves one time by repeating stories they'd overheard glorifying Alfred Orrock's home. They are among a select few to be admitted, and due to the proprietor's frailty, both have been entrusted with keys. Yet their opinion of the place is never believed. Most islanders, preferring the imaginative tales, presume they've been intimidated into keeping mum, that they probably live under threat of retaliation if they speak. The stair railing is made of gold, so it's been reported. The chandelier of diamonds. A subterranean wine cellar the size of a submarine will double as a bomb shelter at the world's end. The upstairs master bedroom has its own indoor swimming pool, and when Ora scoffed at the idea, saying, "That's ridiculous!" she was informed about secret doors to secret chambers, and, of course, the secret pool. "You don't know more than nothing, do you? You're just the hired help. Billy Kerr's uncle worked on that house, it wasn't all mainlanders." She was excoriated for being dim, so unaware of the obvious. She simply didn't have a head for the plain facts, people scolded.

One plain fact that the Reverend Lescavage knows, because he asked Billy Kerr's uncle who was aging badly in Dark Harbour, is that the man helped build the chimney. Only that. No secret rooms. He never stepped inside the house while it was under construction, but he did see a floor plan. The layout for massive rooms. Only mainlanders built the interior, and what they said about it during the process was never believed, and, after they'd gone home, soon forgotten. The sadness of the rooms—the absence of life, of ceremony, of tradition, of *people*—leaves the more prevalent impression on the minister every time he visits, so all that is quite fancy here strikes him as unimpressive.

He climbs the wide staircase. Halfway up, it turns. If this were a daytime sojourn, or a moonlit night, the full-height window at this landing would show a seascape of shining beauty. The waves undoubtedly crash way below, unseen in the dark, their roar obliterated by the rain, wind, and, to a lesser extent, the generator.

The visitor goes straight on through to Alfred Royce Orrock's bedroom.

Why anyone would need a space this massive just to sleep in baffles him always. Now, a space to die in. But Lescavage rejects that bit about death's door being ajar. Just another Orrock ploy. A way to get something nobody wants to give him. Another craven extortion. Probably, anyway.

And yet, Lescavage admits, seeing the man under the fluffy duvet, partially propped up by pillows and sleeping rather peacefully, he looks barely alive. He observes the man in his slumber and finishes the last scone. Slaps his hands together to rid himself of the crumbs, then pulls up the bedside chair put there for the convenience of visitors like him, or only for him, and sits down.

The tyrant does seem sound asleep.

An occasional splutter indicates that he remains among the living.

"Alfred," the pastor says gently, quietly, "it's me. Simon." Orrock does not stir. Yet Lescavage remains unconvinced by this evidence of nocturnal bliss. "Don't invite me over here to tell me you're asleep."

The man's eyelids flicker, the lips move, and for a moment the minister accepts that the other man is indeed frail. When he speaks, the voice is dry, a scratchiness in the tone, but the attitude, the *attitude*, remains pure Orrock.

"It wasn't a goddamned invitation," the ailing man decrees.

He seems to be waking up to his visitor's presence, his eyes straining to stay open, and he adjusts his weight and straightens his back. By her own claim, Ora Matheson is his housekeeper and not a nurse, but Lescavage gives credit where it's due—she's done a fine job looking after the old geezer. One minor stain on the lapel of his pajamas, but otherwise he looks tidy. His thin gray hair has been combed. He's clean-shaven. The spaces around him are in order and the bed is neat except for where he's lying under the covers. Even at that he doesn't disturb the duvet very much, having gone thin. Suddenly, the old patriarch winces and holds his eyes shut, waiting for a marauding affliction to pass.

"You told Ora to ask me here," Lescavage points out to him.

"A command," the man qualifies. "I ordered you to get your ass up here. On the double. Obedient puppy that you are, you obeyed. As you should." He swallows, and moistens his lips with his tongue. "I'm reasonably satisfied, but you could have been quicker about it. You wouldn't have had to wake me then."

Lescavage stares at him awhile, noticing the scalloped cheeks, the desiccated skin around his eyes, nose, and mouth, the exaggerated wrinkling at the base of his neck. Ironic, the dismissive, autocratic words mated to the scratchy, failing voice. He gazes upon him long enough that he's able to get the man's attention, and Orrock fully opens his eyes to look back at him.

"What?" Orrock asks.

"Fuck you," the minister says.

"Excuse me? Is that any way for my spiritual adviser to talk? Especially now."

"What's so special about now?"

"I'm on the brink of fucking death. I'm about to meet your goddamned saints. Do you want me to put in a good word for you or what?"

Lescavage stretches in his chair, then clasps a wrist and rests his head back against his hands. He's willing to warm to this joust. "Your spiritual adviser is the devil himself. Doesn't he swear?"

"Not like a sailor, no," Orrock maintains, "and never at me. Give him half a chance, you'll find out he has the soul of a poet. As do I."

The pastor isn't certain, but detects the hint of a smile on the faded, drawn visage. "Right. Poet. How are you anyway?"

On a dime, Orrock turns on him again. "Ah, you sweet *bitch*, how do you think I am? I'm dying. Just because you're too scrawny to squeeze out a decent turd, Lescavage, doesn't mean you're not pure shit on a stick to me."

The minister looks away in anger a moment. "Then why ask me over, Alf? Or *command* me? How can I help? Do I look like some sort of grave digger to you?"

"You stink. You're putrid," Orrock mutters aimlessly, adding, "I need a drink."

"Ora could've made you a drink."

"Or you can," the old man asserts.

Lescavage is up for this battle. "Or not."

Alfred Orrock gathers his energy. He indicates his water glass with a jut of his chin, a request Lescavage is willing to entertain. He helps hold the glass for him as the old man quenches his thirst.

"Whiskey," he demands when finished, "with a dash of water and one cube."

"Fuck you, Alfred."

"Stop with the language. I'm not saying you can't serve yourself."

"I'm good, thanks." Lescavage, though, does not sound convinced.

"All right." The old man paces himself, the words emerging slowly. Perhaps affected by that rhythm, they gain a measure of gravity. "Truth is, there's more to it."

"That's always the case with you."

"I need more than a drink. I need one righteous piss."

"Ora could've passed you the bedpan. You don't need to drag me out here on a night like this so you can take a flying leak."

"And—" He coughs, then uses the back of his hand to clean off a dab of spittle. "I'm not walking too good today, Simon. Feet like lead. My back's in a vise. I need you to escort me to the can, then pull my pants down so I can take a crap. How do you like that?" He wipes some nastiness from his lips with the back of his hand. "I can't ask that young thing with the cute titties to help me shit twice on the same day. It's not dignified. As she reminds me so bloody often, she's not a nurse." He might be smiling, although it's hard to tell as his facial muscles haven't so much as twitched while holding his visitor's steady gaze. One frail finger points at the minister, an implied accusation. "You, Simon," he says, "will help me with that."

Lescavage blows air from his lungs, looks away, and crosses his arms as though to indicate defiance. But he doesn't find much of an argument for mutiny. "This has nothing to do with your dignity or your despicable bowels. All you care about is humiliating the other person."

Orrock's smile is quite evident now. "Not the other person, Lescavage. In my prime, maybe. Maybe. Now? I only have it in for you."

The minister thinks the matter through. In so many elderly people, he's noticed that their gentle failings—frights, regrets, grievances, revolving patterns—all come home to roost in their dotage and grow exaggerated as the person's capabilities and faculties fade. Orrock is a mean man at heart, who is not about to reform at this stage of his life, not unless a few ghosts from decades and centuries past and future suddenly elect to haunt him.

"Seriously? Alfred? You can't shit on your own?"

"I would if I could. Too long a hike across this floor. It's a god-damn expedition. I refuse to use a bedpan for that, or shit where I sleep. I don't own a walker. Here's the kicker. I need assistance to squat down."

Standing, the visitor peels back the duvet and reveals the skeletal form of the island patriarch. He looks shockingly frail in his too-large pajamas. At least two sizes too big for him now. A hip bone juts out, lacking flesh. Over the last couple of months, including just two days ago, Lescavage has seen the man only in street clothes, which apparently camouflaged his deterioration.

"I don't know," the minister remarks quietly, "if you've heard about a novel idea. It's called a hospital?"

"Yeah, where at my age they force you to wear diapers. They never come when you call. Then bill you a mint. When they know you're rich, they bill for all the poor who can't pay. And don't talk to me about nurses. Pack of thieves, the lot."

"We have health care now. We've had it for your entire adult life."

"I'll die at home, thanks."

"Yeah," Lescavage murmurs, "about that. Dying. Promises, promises."

Any such discussion will have to wait, as the men fall to the logistics of their procedure. The minister criticizes the ailing patient for not buying a wheelchair. "Lord knows you can afford one."

"I never foresaw the need. Anyway, when I die, it ends up in a junkyard."

"Donate it to the needy."

"Socialism. Forget it."

"Actually, it's called charity."

"Same difference."

"Bullshit," the minister sums up.

"Wash out. Your mouth. With soap."

They must coordinate their movements. Orrock shows determination, but he also wails when a leg or a hip twists. Lescavage is shocked by the man's weightlessness. He's probably dipped below 150 pounds, when not so long ago he was at least forty more than that. Even his remaining weight somehow feels as though it's composed of air. Or of dust.

"Up," Lescavage instructs him.

The old man still has drive. With one arm slung over the pastor's shoulders, Orrock hobbles off across the carpeted floor to the bathroom. Entwined in that embrace, he intones, "Sweetheart, after I piss and shit and you make me a drink—if you're lucky, my last—I shall grant you the honor of hearing my confession."

Lescavage shortens his gait to suit the other's man's ministeps. "We've been through this. I'm not Catholic, neither are you. I don't do confession."

"You're not even a believer! So don't tell me what you do or don't do. You're a fraud. But you will hear my confession."

In the past, he's advised him to call in a Roman Catholic priest if he's so hell-bent on confessing before his death, but he lost that debate then and presumes he'll lose it again. Still, he insists, grumbling, "I don't hear confessions."

"You'll hear mine," Orrock tells him, a tone that sounds like a warning.

"By the way, Ora wanted out tonight. That's why you're here. I've been working her too hard. The poor girl needs to get laid. Not that you don't, but for her it's an option."

The bathroom, the minister once remarked, is as large as his own living room, and he might not be wrong. Perhaps this is where the idea of a swimming pool comes from, as there's nearly enough room for one, and the spa tub is huge. The reverend assists the man to the toilet and gets him turned around. They both work to aim his bum above the bowl. Lescavage tugs the pajama bottoms down, exposing his skinny legs. With his arms wrapped around his nurse for the evening, Orrock lowers himself. A difficult descent. His legs provide only wobbly scaffolding. Seated, he bends forward, which strikes the minister as an act of modesty as the pajama shirt flops over his privates. He's not surprised when the old man retaliates, for this is humiliating to him, and he will not go through it without inflicting damage on his only witness.

"First, sniff my poop, Simon Lescavage. Then wipe my ass. Don't forget to flush. Next, fix me a drink. After that, have the decency to hear my confession."

Neither man speaks as they listen to the tinkle of urine.

"I'll fix that drink now. While I'm waiting."

"Sure. Go ahead. Pour a stiff one for yourself. You're going to need it."

Suddenly, Orrock is interrupted by a pain across his belly. He jerks forward and cries out, an involuntarily reflex as he clutches his helper and hangs on.

"You all right?" Lescavage immediately regrets his words. He expects Orrock to lash back at him for the inane comment. Of course he's not all right. But the man is in too much agony to ridicule him just yet.

"Christ, that hurt," he whispers.

His skin color seems more pale now, washed out. Lescavage observes him as the man releases his grip and eases back down on the toilet seat. "At least it doesn't stink so bad," the minister says.

Orrock accepts the kindness. "Small mercies, hey. Small mercies."

He needs a minute to recover.

Toilet paper is stacked on a portable stake. People in town would probably say it's pure silver, but it's polished aluminum, standard fare. Orrock removes the top roll from the column, then holds it out to his helper. He gazes up at him.

"Now wipe," he says.

The two men have locked eyes. Neither moves.

"I can't bend around," Orrock explains.

Still, Lescavage stands still. He feels like a man being tested who does not understand the rules of engagement, or the possible outcome or the repercussions.

"I can't reach," the man on his humble throne stipulates.

Lescavage looks away, across the marble floor, over the spa tub to the window, where the wind and rain fiercely pound, then back at him.

That peculiar smile appears again, the one for which there is no evidence. He's not pleading, Alfred Orrock is only being contemptuous, when he adds, "Please."

The minister takes the paper roll in hand. Unwinds a section. He has a sudden desire to tell this man that he's done this before. He suffers a need to share that experience, but at the same moment he knows he won't, for that would be breaking an unspoken pact, so he stifles the impulse. Still, he wants to explain that he's not mortified, because once he wiped his own mother's bottom when she was at a similar stage in her life and the nurse was absent. Like Orrock, she had every speck of her wits about her, but unlike him, she worked to mollify his trepidation.

"After what I've been through, dear," she said, "with physicians and the nurses—some of them look like mere kids to me—all their awful tests, oh, after those intrusions, these silly indignities don't matter much anymore."

What he wanted to share, and oddly, with Orrock, was that the intimacy of the act, of wiping his mother's bottom as she had done endlessly for him as a babe, invoked such tenderness in both of them, such a sense of love and sadness, that the act itself didn't vex him and never stuck with him. He's forgotten about it until now. In a way, mother and son recognized that these failing bodies did not constitute their lives. The act was a mere trifling, and did not prove to be an indignity for either of them, certainly not a humiliation. Perhaps the contrary. He was not anticipating a similar reaction in this instance, except that in invoking the previous experience he discovered himself inoculated against Orrock's contempt and his effort to mock him, so that he could deny the pleasure the other man derived from his intended insult.

He finishes with a last full swipe, flushes, and shows Orrock no glimmer of distress.

The man grunts. Lescavage waits to be told what to do next.

"Don't just stand there, you gutless jellyfish," the old man gripes, by way of thanks, but his voice reflects his defeat. "Haul me up."

They manage the slow shuffle across the floor, although pain accompanies Orrock's repositioning upon the bed. Sweat breaks out across his brow and he succumbs to a dry wheeze and hacking.

"That drink," he commands. "You know where I keep my liquor. You've raided the shelf often enough, with and without my permission."

That's something townsfolk never think to exaggerate. They'd be impressed with the extravagance of his bar. Enough to make the entire island tipsy.

"I don't mind if I do help myself," Lescavage remarks.

"Make mine a double. Then you'll hear my bloody confession."

Lescavage looks at him. At the skin pulled across the old man's cheekbones and jaw, at the slack mouth. The dull pallor of impending death. He supposes that his reluctance to hear this man's confession derives less from his pastoral tradition than from his interest in what the vile man might have to say. He actually *wants* to know what's on Orrock's mind at the hour of his death, if this is that hour, after a lifetime of subterfuge and villainy. What really counts, now that nothing is left in this world to be gained? For the clergyman, the prurient impulse is not something he welcomes in himself. Clearly unprofessional, not in the least ministerial. He feels himself a helpless gossip about to hang on to each syllable of a red-hot rumor. He's hopelessly and, he concludes, *morbidly* curious. For that reason alone, he feels ashamed. He does not want to hear this man's confession precisely because he so very much desires to absorb every detail.

"Don't get your knickers in a twist," Orrock says, as if reading his mind. "I know you're a fraud. That's not news to me. Just remember, we're not hearing *your* confession tonight, simple Simon. Only mine."

Lescavage lowers his head, then shakes it slowly. He whispers, "You're the devil himself, Alfred. Incarnate. I'm about to hear the devil's own confession."

"Whatever," murmurs Orrock. His eyelids flutter. He licks his chapped lips. "Something like that anyway. If you're lucky. Fetch the whiskey, you wormy slime bucket. You shit wiper, you. Loosen my tongue."

As always, Lescavage yields ground. "Sure. I'll make mine a double as well."

TWO

Falling off the shoulder of the road, the sleek gray Porsche skims across a rapid series of shallow potholes, causing the undercarriage—the shocks in need of repair—to sound like an old-fashioned Gatling gun. Then the car bucks out of a deeper puddle sending a whole other cascade of water up and over the vehicle. Barely hanging on, the driver steers back onto the road, or what she thinks is the road, and taps the brakes gently. Wipers fight against the wet but the windshield takes its own sweet time to clear. When she can peer through the opaque smudges again, she sees lights. She's arriving in a town, the only one left before the land drops into the Bay of Fundy and the sea.

The town's name is Blacks Harbour, commonly referred to as Blacks. Any apostrophe has been lost to time or never existed.

Crossing the border from Maine into New Brunswick, she stopped for a pee, but otherwise it's been straight through from Portland, where she gassed up and grabbed a coffee and doughnut, and before that, Boston, where she took the call from her father's maid. Or whatever she is. Whore, perhaps. With him, you never knew. In a bout of honesty one time (who could tell if that's what it was or if he was ever close to speaking the truth), or if not honesty, then at a moment when he appeared to have no particular agenda and no special grudge, her father mentioned in passing that he never found himself interested in women who were, in his words, *difficult.* He said, "When the nitty gets down to the gritty, everybody has their thing. My thing is, I'm only attracted to promiscuous women. If they're not sleeping around, they're not sleeping with me." He was explaining why he'd never remarried. At the time, she didn't know what to make of his *thing.* The peccadillo seemed unique, she'd give him that, but it also kept him safe from marriage, for what man married a woman with that proclivity? If real, his preference dovetailed with his nature—was he not being cruel? Did he not just call every woman he ever slept with a whore, by virtue of his *thing*? And didn't that include her own mother? And wasn't that just the cat's meow?

During her drive, she'd been doing this, chewing the cud of her past, regurgitating old debates and conversations as though she might masticate history until it became something quite different. She could scarcely believe it, but on occasion the water on the windshield was less of a problem than the tears in her eyes, but she *could* believe it when she assessed that she was not grieving for *him,* but for all the old gripes and the nasty memories and for what caused them, and she grieved for the life that might have been yet never had a snowball's chance in a pizza oven. He was not a man she'd ever want to know yet knew him to be her father. That thought dredged up a well-worn anxiety—namely, how much of him existed in her?

Blacks is not a large town, although the drive in from the outskirts takes a while. The homes spread out, then a lengthy stretch of woodland returns, followed by shopping areas and more bungalows. Finally, the road dips to a mere smidge above sea level and a big arrow rears up on the right, indicating Grand Manan. The ferry won't be running at this hour. She carries in her purse a phone number passed along by her father's maid. A while back, she made the call, which gave her an address. She remembers the town well enough that she finds the street without too much difficulty, missing her turn once on account of the rain, but she circles back and finds it on the next pass and drives slowly along, checking numbers. Seeing anything is virtually impossible in these conditions. She gets out once and is soaked in an instant. She runs to a door and checks the civic address, then counts houses after that to hopefully land at the right one. She gets out again and gets soaked again. Some numbers were skipped so she's gone too far, but on her third attempt at walking up to a door she's right on the money.

She rings the bell and hears chimes.

The man's been waiting for her. He lets her in as far as his vestibule and shuts the door behind her. They don't know each other. Suspicious, his wife hangs back in the hallway and two small kids gape up at the visitor from behind their father's thighs. She supposes that on a night like this she might resemble a feral cat.

A very wet feral cat.

From her eyes she clears hair away that feels knotted and pasted on her skin.

"Hi," she says. Often the tallest in the room, she's a head above him.

"You're wet," he says.

"It's raining," she replies.

"I believe you," he says.

"Are you Mr. McCarran?" She tries to smile, first at him, then at his kids, but gives up when she receives no similar expression in return. She won't bother trying her act on the man's wife. The two women are about the same age. The man is much older.

"Sticky," he says.

"Ah, excuse me?"

"My name. It's Sticky."

Perfect, she thinks. "Ah, okay. Sticky. Sticky McCarran? I'm the one who called. I need to get to Grand Manan."

"In this weather? You don't mean tonight." When she does not answer promptly, he thinks that she just might. "Don't you know how bad it is out there?"

"I'm led to believe that you own a good boat. I understand that you're a pretty good skipper."

"That doesn't make him stupid," his wife says from fifteen feet away.

The man doesn't turn his head when she speaks. He continues to study the new arrival.

"I'll pay four times your usual rate," she says. "A fair price, times four. On account of the hour and the storm, and everything."

He's not a large man, but by the way he carries himself she can tell that he's as strong as a bear. Being a fisherman, he would be. He seems to mull over her offer, then points out to her, "There's a ferry in the morning. Usually that's how people go. Plus, you can take your car."

She nods, to accept his reasoning, and returns the gaze of the little girl on his left side. The boy seems the shier of the two, and looks back to his mom often, as though to make sure that she's still there. Someone to run to should things get scary. Or more puzzling. The girl is waiting with bated breath.

"Mr. McCarran, it's my father. He's dying. Maybe tonight. This might be my last chance to see him alive."

She notices now that he was quite determined when she first showed up, although she hadn't noticed then, to dismiss her request. Now that he's hesitating, she can spot the difference in his attitude. Almost like his son, he glances back slightly toward his wife, who takes a step forward and clutches her left elbow in her opposite hand.

"Sticky," he corrects her.

For a moment, she's perplexed, then acknowledges her mistake. "Yes. Of course. Pardon me. Sticky."

"I'm sorry to hear that," he says. He's thinking to himself for a moment, then adds, "It's a brute nasty storm, isn't it?"

"It's . . ." She begins as though she has something critical on her mind, then forgets what it is and starts over on a different tack. "He's Orrock—my dad—he's Alfred Orrock. You must have worked for him at some point. He gave me your number. I'm not from around here. At least, not anymore. I'm up from Boston. I'm his daughter." She pokes her hand out. "Madeleine. Friends call me Maddy."

He shakes the proffered hand, and she's right. He's strong. After they disengage, he stares at her silently for a moment, then checks back with his wife, who takes another step forward. This seems meaningful somehow. Maddy Orrock feels that she's winning them both over, and the daughter is looking up at her dad as though urging him to go along with this drenched late-night visitor. This feral cat. The little girl is giving him her okay.

"Being an Orrock, you been on boats before," he says.

"Sticky, trust me, I've been on boats smaller than yours in storms bigger than this. I won't be a liability."

When he shrugs, it's not to fully concur. "A woman on a boat is automatic bad luck."

She checks how that line is going down with his wife, and is surprised to see that she also seems to object. "Who says?" Maddy asks him.

"Everybody knows," he answers.

"An ancient superstition, Mr. McCarran. Sticky! Sorry. You're a more modern man than that, I'm sure."

He appears to concede as much. "I'll tell you how modern I am. I will take you across to Grand Manan for six times my going rate."

She looks at him intently. Her glance skids across to his wife, but she's holding firm also, no help there, then she looks back at him. "Six times. What's that, a special tax for being an Orrock?"

He shakes his head, and his big right hand touches the cheek of his daughter with such tenderness that Maddy Orrock wants to weep again, although she doesn't know why. He says, "The high cost of fuel is all. In a storm like this, we'll burn triple to make headway. The tide's running foul. The waves. I'm sympathetic to your situation, Maddy. A death in the family is a hard thing. Doesn't matter the family."

"Thank you, Sticky. For your sympathy. Six times the rate, then, because of the hour, the risk, the inconvenience, the cost of fuel, my family name, my gender, and my general desperation, I suppose." She tries to laugh off her own animosity, but he's still looking at her intently.

"You don't get seasick at all?" he asks. "My wife, she gets seasick herself."

"I didn't say that."

"It'll be a black and rolling night. No fun to be had out there."

"I expect to be sick. In rolling seas, I usually am."

His look conveys a mixture of sympathy and admiration. "You go to sea still?"

She gives the question more attention than perhaps it deserves. "You know that my name is Orrock. Do you think I've had much choice?"

He goes on staring at her. "You have a choice right now tonight, you do."

She agrees. "I want to cross to Grand Manan tonight, Sticky."

He seems to be consulting his daughter when he looks down at her, then back up again. "Okay," he says. "I'll get my gear. We've done this before."

While he's gone, Maddy finds herself exchanging a long gaze with his wife, then asks, "What did he mean by that?"

"He's peculiar."

"Your husband?"

"Peculiar." Then she emerges from something, adding, "There's tea. In the kitchen. Come through. A warm cup to send you on your way. You'll be miserable through the night, might as well start out warm. I'll make sandwiches, put hot soup in the thermos."

The kids run through the house ahead of them as they go.

Maddy asks, "Can I leave my car in your driveway while I'm gone?"

"Off to the far right side will be fine. Don't let the storm scare you. Stick will get you home all right."

"Oh," Maddy says quietly, "I'm not sure I'd call it that."

"Mmm," the woman says, as if she knows what she's talking about, but that cannot possibly be true.

THREE

Lescavage stands by the window, where he views his own reflection in the dark glass. In his king-size bed, under the duvet, Alfred Orrock observes him.

A sheet of paper lies beside the old man.

The minister, as though addressing his own image, remarks, "All the dirt you dredge up in a lifetime"—he turns to confront his adversary and longtime friend before continuing—"all the harm you do to others, the mendacity you set loose upon the world just for the hell of it, for the fun of it—"

"How lovely. I'm getting a sermon."

"—or because it's in your foul nature, and yet, Alfred, you save the worst of it to the bitter end. I once thought that evil was an outmoded concept in the modern world. A relic of the past. Now I don't doubt its presence anymore."

That bare hint of an insipid grin radiates off him again. "Simon, Simon, Simon, this is why I chose you for the job! For your bons mots. Your gift of gab! I'm departing in style, but all this is nothing without your fine words. I'm privileged to be attending my own wake. But I also chose you, Simon, because you're a weakling. You know that, right? Though it's beside the point now. I appreciate what you bring to the table. So do it, Simon. Do as I ask."

They stare across the room at each other, a broad gap.

Lamplight gleams on the windows.

"Right now?" Lescavage whispers.

"No time like the present. So what's your decision?" Orrock inquires calmly.

"You bastard," Lescavage responds.

"Like I said, I'll put in a good word for you with the marching saints. If I get to see any, of course. I presume there's some doubt that I'll be in that parade. I keep my promises when I can, if I can, Lescavage. That's one thing to be said about me when you're standing over my grave. Or dancing on it. Dust to dust and all that, but I'm true to my word. Remind people. I don't make many promises, but the ones I make, I keep, if I can."

"Up yours."

"Simon, you can do better than that, can't you? Now's your chance."

Still, the minister does not move. He's not sure that he can do this, only that he has no choice. A tremor traces a line up his left arm, and in a moment of paralysis, of internal panic, he thinks that he might be the first to die here. But no. He no longer believes in a God so kind. He won't be delivered from this darkness.

"Do it, Simon," the old man taunts him. "Don't even think about it. Just do it quickly and it's done. Then walk away. Out of the goodness of my heart, I've offered you more incentive than anyone can possibly need. I've given you no alternative, no way out. Put your silly conscience and your half-assed petty pride aside. Do it now. My daughter, you should know, is on her way. She'll be here by morning—"

"You bastard."

"Yes. I'm a bastard. That's not news. Do it because you hate me. Do it out of rage—haven't I made you mad enough? Or do it for mercy—who cares? Do it *because it's the right thing to do*. Just do it. If you don't, Simon, the consequences will fall on your head like a plague. You see? I have my own bons mots. Me and my devil poet. Oh, think of others, you limp prick. You know you have to. You're that weak. Do what's right for *them*."

Fingers trembling, he gestures to the sheet of paper on the bed.

Lescavage, hands on his hips, bends forward at the waist. A kind of retch, partially a gasp, escapes him.

"Good. Good. It's real for you now. Don't hesitate. Don't be a fool, Simon. Don't talk yourself out of it now. Just go ahead and do it. Come over here. One step at a time. Come."

The minister buries his mouth in the crook of his elbow as though to stifle further involuntary emissions from his diaphragm. Still, he half-bursts into tears and his torso rocks.

"Come. Come here. Come on."

"You're getting stronger. You don't need to die tonight," the minister protests.

"Hardly the point. If I don't die tonight, you know what I'll do next."

Lescavage goes over. He won't look directly at the man, but in his peripheral vision he sees him remove a pillow from under his head, then hold it up. He looks at the pillow now. It blocks his view of him. The man, this demon, sight unseen, is still whispering the same desolate encouragement to the tempo of a lover's urgency. Lescavage knows he must do this, that somehow he must find the strength or the courage as he takes the pillow in both his hands.

He has no choice.

Orrock whispers, "Yes. Yes, Simon. Now. Yes. Now, Simon."

That's the hardest part, now done. Just to hold the pillow in his hands.

"Dear, sweet Simon. My sweet bitch. Do it."

Lescavage whispers back, "Shut the fuck up."

Then he raises the pillow high over his head while letting loose a guttural roaring, which evokes even in Orrock a fright, a joy, a change to his complexion. The old man's eyes expand. The minister thrusts the pillow down across the man's face and climbs upon him and mounts him as a lover might, except that he presses his body over the pillow on the man's face and feels him buck beneath his stomach. The Reverend

Lescavage cries out again, as though he is the one at his life's end and who wants to stop this but he does not. He wants God to strike him dead for it, but He does not, and Lescavage releases another violent roaring to shut out the storm and the night and his own life even as the life beneath him finally ceases to respond. Orrock succumbs to death with no further objection, going all quiet and limp. The reverend continues to embrace him, to lie perfectly still over him, pressing his stomach upon the pillow and the man's face as a lover spent, now, the reckless deed accomplished.

A further minute as long as an hour passes before his own breathing subsides, and he rises.

He stands over the dead man.

He knows that if he could not have killed him before, if he were still alive, he could kill him now. He'd kill him now for what he just made him do, the bastard.

Orrock denies him that privilege, as he no longer has breath.

Lescavage suffers a rash of self-pity rather than remorse.

Then gets himself under control.

Then gets to work.

First, he removes the sheet of paper from the bed and places it on the nearby bureau. He leans over the body and removes the pillow from the man's face, although he's thinking that the bastard doesn't deserve this dignity. He returns the pillow to underneath the man's head, and makes the corpse conform to a relaxed posture beneath the duvet. A body now that looks undisturbed, committed to an undeserved rest. "Your damned confession," he complains to the corpse, and turns back the duvet and adjusts it comfortably below the man's chin. He leaves both arms outside the covering and crosses them over his chest. He wishes his eyes would shut and the mouth also. Placing a hand on top of Orrock's head, the other under his chin, he presses the mouth closed. But when he shuts the eyelids they draw open again.

He'll let some coroner glue them permanently shut. In the mean-time, he does this the old-fashioned way, fishing two coins from his pocket and using them to keep the man's eyes closed.

"I guess you got your last wish, Orrock," he whispers to the corpse, bending over him, as though he might be heard and this is a secret that they might share. "Robbed me of my soul. Anyway, these are the last two nickels you make on earth."

Lescavage takes the handwritten paper from the bureau and reads it, not for the first time. When he's done, he folds it in half, then quarters, and slides it into his hip pocket. He buttons the pocket's flap to keep the document safe. He then opens the bureau's top drawer. A different handwritten sheet rests there amid facecloths and fresh underwear, socks and pills. He reads over this one as well, then restores it to its place.

He checks around the room for any evidence of what has occurred, for anything he might have overlooked, or for any echo of his spasmodic bellowing. He knows that no one could have heard him above the storm, but he strained his throat at one point and feels as though he can still hear himself, still see himself, as if overwhelmed by lust in the violent throes of a paroxysm. Gone mad. If what he did can be proved by an outsider, he believes that it cannot be proved by anyone living or working on this island. He is not afraid of discovery, only of what comes next. Of living with this secret. Of dealing with the consequences. Of living with himself.

Damn this man, to defeat him so cruelly, to induce him to carry out such a bestial act against all that he's believed and cared about, against all that he's thought and upheld about himself. To dash his sense of himself to ruins.

A crime against the quirks and quarks, the quantum mechanics he's come to take refuge in, a violation the cosmos might not notice yet may never forgive, either.

He's still feeling adrenaline snap through him, not so gently easing him back down to what will be his new condition. He can't yet fathom this knowledge of himself. *I'm a killer. A murderer now. Oh God.* Worse, he fears he may be exactly what Orrock charged—a weakling. At a moment that counted, he took an action, and yet he had been nothing but indecisive. He had succumbed to coercion. Did he fail or succeed in his time of testing? He doesn't know, and that forms a measure of his dismay. He takes a few deeper breaths. Tries to find a balance. A part of him wants to find God again, but he's too overwhelmed by self-recrimination to commence to do so or even think about that. The God he once knew would want him found, but he cannot permit himself to believe that, especially not now, not after what he's done.

He dare not confess his sins. His *sin*. This particular sin.

No one will ever know, but *I'm a killer now. A murderer. Oh God.*

Lescavage turns off the light and departs the room.

He does not leave the house.

He wants no one to inadvertently find the body, and wants to be there when the word gets out. The night is too far gone and he's too shaken to alert anyone yet. So the Reverend Lescavage takes a throw blanket from off a downstairs sofa and loosely wraps himself in it upon the La-Z-Boy, and there he chooses to spend the night. First, he finishes the grapes on the plate beside him, then draws the blanket tighter around himself, cocoonlike, and although a few lights remain on throughout the house, he closes his eyes. He must will his eyelids to stay shut. His impulse is to stare out into these empty rooms, into the storm of this night. But he must deny himself that indulgence. He must refuse to succumb to shock. Nor can he allow his gaze or his mind to fall away, or he might lose himself entirely. He wills his eyes to remain closed, he commands his body to rest, to suck it up, to carry on, and whatever else he thinks he might do to correct his sinfulness on this awful night, he must resist that temptation, now and forevermore.

He dare not even pray.

If he prays, he knows, he'll be lost. Remorse will overwhelm him. That will lead to confession. And any confession now will lead to disaster.

FOUR

In a motel along the New Brunswick coast, an establishment that tries valiantly to maintain a decent standard despite an impossibly short tourist season, this one a quick jaunt north of the Maine border on a picturesque cove off the Bay of Fundy, retired Montreal detective Émile Cinq-Mars sleeps soundly beside his wife.

In the midst of the storm's bluster, she stirs.

Sandra Cinq-Mars listens awhile to the wind, the rain, and her husband's even breathing, and while she can barely make out his form in the dark, she discerns that he's sleeping deeply and comfortably tonight. A sleep not agitated by nerves or stress or an onerous to-do list. For a change, there's no such list. Slammed by the gale, they endured a strenuous drive through the North Maine Woods from their Quebec farm. Normally, they might not have persevered through weather fit for Noah's Ark, but hotel reservations and a set time for a ferry crossing struck them as being as absolute as a sailor's embarkation orders. Miss the boat, and their island summer vacation—their *first ever* summer holiday—might be lost. En route, they did cancel one mainland hotel reservation and booked another, shaving a half hour or so off the first leg of the trip to add it on to the next, but still they arrived frayed, exhausted, hungry, and generally done-in. Through dinner, Émile could barely keep his eyes open. Once back at the motel they had nothing to do. Even watching television was a pain as the electricity intermittently went off. So they tucked in early, and while it's still only the middle of the night, they've been sleeping for a solid seven hours.

Sandra rises and tosses a flimsy robe over her silky sleepwear and finds her way around the bed to the bathroom without banging her knees in the dark. She closes the door and flicks the switch from habit, only to discover that the power is out again. After her tinkle and a quick wash of her hands, she returns to the room but not to bed. Instead, she sits in one of two cushiony armchairs that front the broad window overlooking a small harbor and the sea. Boats moored in the bay, a few with a light on, bob in the waves. She curls her legs up under herself, then just about jumps out of her skin when her husband, invisibly seated in the companion chair, reaches out and touches her hand.

"Oh my God!"

"What?"

"I thought you were in bed! Alert a girl before creeping up on her! Émile!"

He laughs. "I wasn't creeping. I was just sitting here."

"No but I—Jesus! Your icy fingers, man. So creepy!"

He tests his fingers against his own skin. If anything, they're warm. "I thought that's why you sat here. What do you mean 'icy'?"

"Excuse me? What do you mean, why I sat here?"

"Because I was sitting here."

"I can't see in the dark. Émile! I thought you were asleep!"

"I was."

"Good for you. I may never sleep again, however."

She laughs, too, now.

They're quiet awhile, mesmerized by the wind and the rain on the big picture window. Outside, waves break below their room. These are not the great waves marauding across the bay tonight, as the harbor is well protected by an isthmus. Yet the lesser waves still chuck stones on a beach, and drum a steady cadence.

"Actually," Émile states, "I had my best sleep in months. Maybe we should risk our lives driving through a storm more often."

"Sure thing, for eleven hours straight. Do that too often, it'll put you to sleep permanently."

"Worth it, no?"

They share another quiet interlude, then Sandra interrupts. "It's so dark out. The power's still off."

"Romantic. I was sitting here thinking that before tonight, I've never slept by the seaside in my entire life." Given that he's nineteen years older than she is, they've shared less time together than strangers meeting them might assume. A later-in-life marriage not only for him but, in a way, for her as well. "Farm boy. Then big-city cop. No life by the sea. But the sound of the waves is mesmerizing. What about you, time by the ocean–wise?"

Sandra straightens a leg out, holds it in midair, stretching, rotating the foot. "For a farm girl I'm pretty familiar with the coast. From the mountains of New Hampshire to the shore is a short hop. My parents made the trip most summers. Good memories. A kid on the sand. Body-surfing. Collecting shells. Then, my first summer out of college, I headed straight for Hampton Beach. Freedom! Waited tables by night, showed off my bikini bod all day long."

"If I knew you were exhibiting, I would've made the trip down."

"Perv."

They hold hands in the dark awhile, their fingers mildly attentive.

"Where we're going isn't beach country," Émile mentions.

"Thank goodness. My bikini days are ancient history."

"I don't know why."

"Thank you, sir. But the skin cancer scare took away the appeal of spending whole summers on a beach."

"Maybe, but I'm thinking of you in a bikini. I'd risk skin cancer for that. You could stay under an umbrella, no? With me?"

"Oh shut up. But thanks. This is something though, isn't it? Émile?

Us? On vacation. The winter ones are fine but, I don't know, a summer one feels decadent."

"Get used to them."

"Okay. I will. But do I have it in me? Do you? Those are big questions."

Émile laughs lightly again, flits a few fingers up the column of her forearm. "We're workaholics?"

She laughs, too. "Okay, if we both go out of our minds walking around the cliffs of Grand Manan, then, yes, that's who we are. Workaholics. If we go back home and find out that we're anxious to get back here again, or anywhere else, then, no, we don't qualify. But I think I'll pass the test. I've done summer before. But you, sir. You're the villain of the piece. I think you're doomed to fail, Émile. If there aren't any local bank robberies, you might arrange for one just to go investigate."

"As long as there are no more dead bodies, thank you very much."

"With you around, Émile, they'll fall out of the trees."

"Don't say that. That's one part of my retirement I'm happy about. The total absence of cadavers falling out of trees."

A spasm of laughter bursts from her.

"What?" Émile asks in mock alarm.

"Émile, true or false? You were never a homicide detective."

"Okay, okay. I know."

"True or false, Émile?"

"Okay. I was not in Homicide."

"And—" she needles him.

"And what?"

"And—"

Reluctantly, he owns up to his record. "I spent my career solving murders anyway. But!" he fires back.

"But what?"

"I'm retired, but not only that, I'm taking time off for the first time ever in the summer. I can learn to relax. I'm a quick study, no? I can definitely learn to ignore bodies falling out of trees. Let them drop. I'll show you."

They squeeze hands, enjoying this nocturnal tease, and they're quiet awhile again, as though anticipating the marvel of this experiment, the two of them off on their own in the summertime, responsibilities set aside. All has not been sweetness and light between them. They've had their tussles, a few vague issues that have proven difficult to get at or define, so that even in a moment of happy expectation they are both fraught with a dose of worry. Perhaps that's why Sandra adds a touch of the sultry to her voice when she suggests, "Maybe there's another part of your retirement you'll be happy about, Émile. Besides the absence of corpses. Maybe I can teach you a few tricks. To relax."

"Meaning?"

She unwinds from her chair. The flimsy outer robe falls off. She's standing in the dark, but his eyes have adjusted. He sees her lower a thin strap on her nightdress and coyly lift a shoulder.

"Ah, sweetie, you know that I'm an old man. I need a pill first. Then a short time for it to take effect."

"You're in your prime with me, Mr. Man. But take the pill. I've leased the farm, you're retired, so go slow, Émile. We have all the time in the world."

Cinq-Mars stands, although it takes a bit of a shove to get him up and out of his chair. Not the most elegant approach. Next to her, he's impressively tall, even in the dark, and by comparison she is small as she drops her nightie to the floor and steps free of the garment to slip wholly naked into his loving arms. She kisses his chest. His right hand rises up her rib cage to rest under her left breast and he loves its weight over the length of his fingers, time's delicate, beautiful *sag*, which might keep her off a beach in her bikini but inspires this intimacy in him every time. As deep as his sleep has been, he's that calm, that quiet, yet in another way he's equally as tempestuous as the wind outside. When he touches her chin, she opens her lips and presses the whole of her strong form against him to receive and return their first kiss by the sea.

FIVE

When asked, she prefers to reply that she's five foot eleven. She'll say, "Around five eleven, give or take," sometimes adding that she's earned every inch. Yet Madeleine Orrock knows that she's a mere eighth of an inch less than six feet. That eighth gives her license, she believes, but either way she finds herself crouching in the wheelhouse of a lobster boat, the *Donna Beth*. She tests whether or not she can stand upright without cracking her noggin on the ceiling, and she can, easily, yet in the rise and fall and crash through the waves of this small, stout boat and in the ominous dark she feels the ceiling loom as near, ready to conk her cranium. When standing and lifted by the momentum of the boat dropping off a wave, she bends at the waist, tilts her neck down, and cramps her shoulders to avoid being knocked out—scrunching up, a reflex tall girls are taught to avoid in the proper care of their posture. At times, the wheelhouse feels as though it is compressing around her.

Once more, Maddy ventures back through the cabin and out the stern door to the aft deck. The sea is rollicking. Rain and salt water slosh underfoot. Salty spindrift mingles with the sideways deluge as she keeps one hand on the boat and backs her way to the railing to up-chuck whatever remains in her belly.

After extraordinary retching to regurgitate a smidgen of fluid, she has the dry heaves awhile, her stomach squeezing as though she's bound in a constrictor's grip. As the spasms subside, and they don't go gently, she meanders back into the warmth of the cabin, mindful of the slippery footing and her rampant dizziness, and climbs up into Sticky McCarran's diving, dipping, spinning wheelhouse.

She's mildly embarrassed. Being sick on a boat is an indignity she's loath to suffer, in part because it's too girlie for her nature and an affront to her background, although intellectually she knows that it can happen to anyone unaccustomed to the motion. In the lights reflected off his instruments, the captain of the *Donna Beth* notices that she's upset.

"I'll say this for you, Miss Orrock."

"Maddy."

"You're no landlubber. You remember the difference between the weather rail and the lee."

"That's not saying much."

"More than you think. You'd be surprised how many go to the weather side first, because it's higher, feels a bit safer. Until they try vomiting into the wind."

"We all do that once. But once only."

"You're not used to the sea no more is all. Weather like this, not many are."

"Christ, it's lumpy," she says, knowing that it's way more than that.

"Freaking A," he agrees.

She's curious if he'd use a different word if she weren't a woman.

They have close to eighteen nautical miles to cross and their pro-gress against wind and current has been reduced to less than five over the ground per hour. The boat handles the conditions well enough, and early on Maddy is confident in that aspect. All things considered, the passage is safe and straightforward. If only her stomach would settle, or, more particularly, the gyrating toss and swing of the mechanisms of her inner ear, which seek a balance, some level plane, finding none.

"When I was kid," she says, "I was taught to keep one hand on the boat and, if I felt nauseous, an eye on the horizon. That works. But only if there's a horizon. That advice doesn't do much good tonight."

"It's black out," Sticky concurs.

"Pitch."

"Turn around?" he asks her quietly. Blacks Harbour remains closer than Grand Manan, and the weather will be easier to ride in that direction.

Maddy shakes her head. She won't tolerate retreat.

Seated alongside Sticky McCarran at the wheel, she must hang on as the boat spills off the back of a tall crest and careens down a nearly vertical descent. The bow rears up slightly toward the base of the wave, but what's coming next is familiar yet always exciting as the bow buries itself and hard water surges across the deck to slam against the windows with all the violence of an automotive collision. She might well be driving her Porsche on a Ferris wheel through a car wash. In the darkness under so much water, one degree of blindness compounds another. The wipers swish uselessly a while, and as the buoyancy of the widely flared bow lifts the *Donna Beth* out of the sea again and they rise, the diesel never breaks its steady muttering pace, unperturbed by the matter. Maddy shakes her head as though washing the sea off herself, as though pushing squid and sardines and plankton back out of her ears and nostrils and larynx, as if during those many seconds while the boat is at its nadir she's in a whale's dark belly and now, as they scale the next roller, she's spewed out the blowhole into the black sky again, afloat above it all momentarily.

She fears smacking her head.

Similar scenes from childhood wash back over her, not unlike the water that rushes off the deck, and she feels a strange release and expiation, as though this limited and probably safe ordeal is a debt she pays, something she just has to get through, a way of making amends. But for what, and why does she feel so guilty? Because her father is dying? Old age does that to people. Because they've been estranged for so long? Whose fault is that, pray tell? she argues to the sea and to the blackness beyond the wheelhouse. Not mine. Yet she agrees with herself that she may not be the guilty party here, but neither is she free of her past, and especially not on this rambunctious crossing.

Maddy feels the need to break out of herself a little. Not only is she road-weary from the day and now storm-tossed, plagued by guilt and a lurking, impending grief that she cannot wholly understand or even begin to accept, but she's feeling claustrophobic and torn, and not a speck of her malaise, she fears, is related to being seasick. Yet being seasick is bad enough.

Being seasick is the worst thing there is or can be at the moment.

She turns to Sticky to see if they can talk, deflect the gloom, get something going to release her from a battery of complaints and afflictions.

"Have you worked for my dad, Sticky? Over the years? He gave me your number—I presume you know him."

"You don't remember me?"

"Should I?"

He shrugs off the question. "When I got my first boat, he helped me out."

"My father helped you out." If she weren't a seasick dog, she'd laugh. He had to be telling a joke.

"Sure he did. I got my boat young. It's not easy being a young fellow carrying that kind of bank loan, interest what it was back in the day. I had the experience, with my old guy, you know. I was at his knee nearly from the day I was born, so I knew I could fish or catch lobster or pull up whatever the sea was willing to provide. The bank seemed to agree with me, too, on account of my family. There's six of us boys and five of us got our own boats. I got mine at a younger age than any of them, and that's a risk. A so-so year early on and the whole idea is doomed. Your dad was a big help to me with that."

So this is no joke. "Sticky, I'm sorry, but my dad doesn't go around helping people out. What did he get out of it?"

At least, given his expression, he seems to understand her objection. He isn't living in some alternative world. "I know what people say. Your old man's a hard crust. But you ever deal with the folks in Dark Harbour? Some are good people, most are, but if it's not a harpoon between your ribs from a few of the men living there, it's a shiv. There's lunatics in that crowd, in my opinion."

"Maybe. But they might also have justification for their grievances. Some do. Anyway, what do you know about Dark Harbour? You're a mainlander."

"When I started with your father, I used to pick him up there."

Again, similar to his remark about her father's helpfulness, this makes no sense.

"Sticky, what are you talking about? My dad never lived in Dark Harbour."

"Of course not. But he'd like to go there. Down to that beach. He had business with the people harvesting dulse, for one thing."

"That's true, but why would you *pick him up*? He could drive himself."

"He liked to walk."

"What? He didn't." This she cannot believe.

"Sometimes you came with him."

"I did not. You must be thinking of someone else."

"You were a babe in arms, Maddy. He liked to hike there. Across the back of Seven Days Work, over the Whistle, on along that escarpment. He'd take you on his back. You in a pack. Then the long descent on the trail to Dark Harbour, and after he did his business there, I'd pick him up and take both of you home by boat."

Maddy goes quiet. She can remember something like that. Not as a babe in arms or as a toddler, but perhaps later? As a child? "Sticky, did you pick my dad and me up when I was a bit older?"

"Sure did. He loved his hikes. Loved bringing his little girl along, too."

No, he didn't, Maddy's insisting to herself, but she questions how much she really knew about it back then. Perhaps less than Sticky McCarran does.

"So, you were like a water taxi for him? Is that right?"

This time, he takes a turn at being silent. Maddy holds her stomach as a bad moment passes, then suddenly she's rapt, astounded by the steepness of their descent down a wave. She'd scream if she hadn't taught herself not to do that, to bear through the fright and the wild-ness of the sea. This time when the hull slams hard, the impact jars her teeth and bones.

"Ooompf." Maddy's expiration vocalizes what the boat feels.

"Sorry," Sticky says, but it's no fault of his that they're out on this night.

Perhaps he's forgotten her question as the boat begins to rise again, but momentarily he adds, "In the early days, me not much more than a kid, and your dad becoming a successful man, from the fishery. He started with dulse when it was small potatoes."

"It's still small potatoes."

Sticky isn't willing to concede that. "He did well with it. He saw the potential, your old man. Him and me, we hauled the dulse that he reduced down to powder into the United States. Totally legal now. I'm not saying it was then."

"Pulverized dulse isn't alcohol. It's not a drug. When was it not legal?"

"It's an importation. Subject to taxes, rules and regulations. People ingest it. That's a whole other book of forms you need to fill out, and a bunch of tests, not to mention pay the fees, the fines, and, like I said, the taxes."

"So you smuggled dulse powder so my dad could avoid taxes."

"He was just starting out and I had big payments on the boat. The risk was worth it back then."

Maddy looks more closely at Sticky this time. Something makes sense to her. If someone on the island worked with her father to illegally smuggle dulse into the United States, then someone else on the island would have found out about it and reported him. Few would have had any compunction against betraying him. So he contracted with some-one off-island to help keep an illicit enterprise secret.

"He arranged it for you, didn't he?" Maddy asks him.

"Arranged?" McCarran asks in turn.

"Your boat loan. He got it for you." That way, he could own him.

Sticky nods.

"It all worked out," he says. "I did those shipments. Didn't like it much, but bills got paid. A few good years and your dad's powder business prospers, he can go legit, bring it aboveboard. My loan on the boat is under control, that puts my fishing life in half-decent shape. Until the cod ran out so now it's lobster. A short season here, not like in the States. So I still run errands for him. I like your father. He's been fair to me. He's a good one."

Run errands. She knows a euphemism when she hears one.

In her lifetime, no one has ever called her father good or fair within Maddy's earshot. She just can't believe this guy, or these other aspects about her dad. A hiker? He did something for recreation that he enjoyed? He took along his daughter? The news strikes her as incomprehensible, and coming while she is on her way to hear his last words before his death, she scarcely believes her own ears.

"My father," she says. "You're not describing him in terms I usually hear."

Sticky spins the wheel to cross a wave. Hard to see in the dark, though, and they bury the bow again.

"I know what you're saying," he tells her. "I know how people talk about him. Maybe they have reason. He's a hard crust. But with me, at sea, I think he was more himself. I tell people that, they doubt what I say. But when it was just the two of us out on the water, Mr. Orrock was a contented man. I'll tell you what—always, he was fair and good to me."

In a way, hearing these words about her father makes her angrier still. If he was capable of being fair and good, then why wasn't he that way more often? Or once in a while at least? Or all the time? Or with her? In the past, she bolstered her morale by reminding herself that her father was not capable of normal, kind behavior. She is discovering now that that might not be true, which means that when he was being unkind, it was not merely a consequence of his nature, but a conscious choice. He made it his business to be unkind. That makes everything worse.

She won't attempt to explain any of it to Sticky, and after their talk they brave the night in a silence that is rarely interrupted. For no reason that she can fathom, Maddy is not violently ill again. Instead, she suffers a different sort of misery.

SIX

On the steep, dark embankment that descends into Dark Harbour along the high western shore of Grand Manan, among the trees and rocks where the ragged homes are embedded in the forest and permanently manage without electricity, as the residents prefer it that way and shun most modern accoutrements, one man rises from his lair just as the storm is on the verge of abating. He stretches and yawns mightily, as though emerging from the maw of the earth after a lengthy hibernation. He does not intend to fling open his door, but the wind catches it by surprise on his way out and he's thrown back a step before regaining both his footing and a firmer hold on the handle. Impenetrable at its peak, the wind has calmed enough now that a man can stand upright without being blown down, yet it perseveres with sufficient force that he desires to walk in the storm awhile, to witness the gale's denouement. Not on his rickety front porch, either, sheltered by the trees, but out on some wild bluff where it's impossible to distinguish sky from sea or where the wind touches down on land. Something in the air has announced the weather's impending diminishment, a lessening of the roar and whistling, a quarter turn of the tap to reduce the velocity of precipitation. In such a tempest, a man might assume that he won't be lifted up in a swirl and tossed out to sea, although he'll take the risk, and anyway it's the sea that he wants to observe, that restless convulsion.

Although familiar with such storms throughout his life, and his lodging offers only rudimentary refuge, he has never grown weary of their might.

He returns indoors a minute, dressing properly in outdoor garb that's more sophisticated than what his neighbors might wear, then embarks upon a hike. He will stroll through the utter darkness across the cliffs of Grand Manan while the wind whips the island's back and rain pelts down and the waves below crash and crash again in beautiful and ferocious rhythm. Dawn will surely find him upon some rock above the seascape, content in his tribute to this wild season, exhausted in his jubilation, the whales content in their travels below, as fishermen return or those who are safe in their harbors tonight venture out.

The man plants food in his coat's big pockets and is on his way.

Madeleine Orrock steps from the *Donna Beth* onto a floating dock in North Head Harbour on the island of Grand Manan. She takes a moment to locate her footing, to be sure she's steady. Her body feels as though it's still moving, even when her mind is reasonably certain that she's standing still. Following this internal contest of wills, she knows that she's all right, no longer seasick, and fit to stroll down the dock and up the gangway even as they sway to the motions of the disturbed water. All is dark in town. Indeed, all is blackness, with no more than an occasional candle flickering in a window. A power failure again. Too well she remembers them from childhood. She and the skipper have concluded their business—Sticky will wait for daylight before returning to Blacks, sleeping on the boat in the interim—but before departing she has a final question for him.

"Stick, you mentioned six brothers. Four, plus you, have boats. What does the other one do? Does he fish?"

"He's a chartered account," the captain of the *Donna Beth* deadpans. He speaks in a sly way, before checking her reaction. She expects a further punch line, but Sticky only shrugs, as though to suggest that life at times is incomprehensible.

They repeat their good-byes a few times and Maddy, happy with her balance, walks down the dock and heads up the gangway. She calls back to him while he's giving his dock lines a final inspection, "Hey, Sticky! Was I bad luck for ya?"

He returns her smile. "Not yet."

So much standing water to slog through once she's on hard land, puddles everywhere, and in the dark the size and depth of them is difficult to determine. The hard ground seems to sway as her inner ear settles. Overhead, clouds rampage past, and the moon, while never visible, casts an occasional glow, so at least the cloud cover is thinning and breaking up. Climbing the hill to her ancestral home feels akin to landing on Mars without the prerequisite buggy. In the dark and the rain and against the backdrop of a random shambles of memory, the place comes across to her as both eerily remote and colossally alien.

She strides on.

Of course. Her dad's house is lit up. The rest of the island sleeps in the dark.

Just like her father to always assert his status.

Maddy doesn't quite know what to do, how to effect this entry, and feeling awkward about her homecoming rings the doorbell. Bright, tinny, silly chimes ring out. She preferred Sticky's. She lingers a few moments on the stoop but quickly grows irritated and enters. This is, after all, as she reminds herself, or tries to convince herself, her home, too. In a way, it is. At the very least, it's the one she grew up in. She believes that she has a key for the door on her chain, but in any case, it's not locked. This was never a policy her father endorsed—an unlocked door—so she blames the help.

She blames them as well for no one being on hand to greet her. A dying old man might be bedridden, for all she knows, but surely the help—a maid, a favorite bimbo, or whatever she might be, not to mention an attending medical staff, for surely her father hired *someone*—would at least answer the door. But nothing.

"Wakey wakey," she warns as she checks out the lower rooms, but after sloughing off her rain gear and wandering around downstairs, she fails to locate anyone. Going by the leftovers on a plate, the La-Z-Boy was occupied in recent hours, and several lights are on, but no one's about. She hopes she won't find that maid/whore sleeping in her old bed. Or worse, sleeping in her father's.

She climbs the broad staircase.

Maddy chooses to look into her old room first—it's not occupied, and hasn't been. On first glance, it gives her the willies. Nothing in there, nor the room itself, reminds her of herself or of childhood. A foreign place now. Her father's room, she's already noticed, is in the dark, lights out, and she doesn't know how to proceed. Enter and wake him, then suffer his rebuke for doing so? Or let him sleep and risk finding out tomorrow that he isn't even home, that he's been hospitalized, and get chewed out for that, too.

Without much delay, she decides that she didn't drive all this way and cross rough water to ignore her father before he dies, so she might as well screw up her courage and get this over with. Her compromise is to step through the dark to the far side of his room, where she's close enough to discern by the faint yard lights that the old guy is securely under the covers, and appears to be sleeping comfortably.

The experience is a new one. She's never observed him sleeping before. Somehow this strikes her as astonishing. The sight seems weird. Otherworldly. As her eyes adjust, she has the impression that he's quickly gotten very old, an impression that drains her, and she feels, although not quite seasick again, wobbly on her feet.

Or, she tries to tell herself, she's still getting used to a surface underfoot that's motionless. Her feet haven't adjusted, she keeps sensing waves.

Tiptoeing to his bedside, Maddy sits in the chair next to him and waits for her father to awaken.

She recalls him advising her one time when she was home for the summer from graduate school to get over herself, that worse fathers exist in the world. *Did I ever abuse you? Hit you? Deny you anything that wasn't in your best interest? Did I ever wrongfully scold you?* His litany went on, and and to every question he forced her to answer honestly, the reply was always *no.* But that was the thing. He didn't get how *mean* it was to be asking all those questions to which the answer was always *no* and yet at the same time be totally unaware of the harm he'd committed without ever abusing her, or striking her, or ignoring her, or any of the other *legitimate complaints,* in his words, that other children had about their parents all over the island. For that matter, throughout the world. He was so damn right but he was so totally in the wrong to imply that her complaints, by comparison to sordid stories, were rendered illegitimate. The cruelty of bestial parents, his argument seemed to be, dismissed his own. *Really, you're just a spoiled rich girl brat, and if that's your only problem, then for God's sakes don't complain. Enjoy it. Didn't I send you off to the university of your choice, which just happens to be to a school as far away from me as you could possibly find? What dad does that?* And finally she could say yes, and she admitted, "Yes, you're paying for Stanford."

"Eight years of it," he pointed out.

"Seven," she corrected him. That's about all that she had on him at the time of the discussion, that her seven years of university tuition felt like eight to him.

"Just seven years," she repeats quietly now, her first words since entering the bedroom. Her first words spoken in person to him in three years. And having spoken, she suddenly detects his silence. Not only the still, interior quiet of the night, amid the diminishing rain and the generator going on outside, but the interior dead silence of this intimate space.

Suddenly, it feels expansive, as if it's swallowing her up.

Maddy touches his wrist then. Her hand, that instantly, snaps back.

She feels her breath trapped in her lungs, as though they can no longer inflate nor contract.

And wills herself to touch him again.

He's cold.

Cold, she confirms. Her father is cold.

Not *mean* cold. Stone cold.

She says what she never would have imagined saying. "Daddy."

And flicks on the bedside lamp. Sees the nickels on his eyes.

The sight of him shocks her. The bright, sparkling money for eyes.

She's stunned.

He did not wait for her. He's dead.

Of course, when did he ever wait for her?

That quickly, her anger returns.

"You never, ever waited for me, not ever," she remarks, as though the words constitute a formal complaint. Maddy sits back in the chair again, not knowing what to do, thinking that she is supposed to react a certain way, but she doesn't know how. She may feel disconnected from this man, but death appalls her, and he is someone she has always known. Probably they were close once, a long, long time ago. She's surprised by the anger rising through her bloodstream. When she was first alerted to the impending death of her father, she thought only, So? It's about time. Good riddance. Yet a minute later she wanted nothing more than to get here before he passed away. She wanted to know what he'd say, and wonders now if anyone did get to talk to him. She expects that her one old friend on the island, and her father's, the Reverend Lescavage, would have been here, but who knows whom her father let in the door these days? Could be anyone. Could be no one. Probably his whore/maid, the one who phoned, but where is she now?

Who was with him when he died, or was he alone then, too?

Who put the nickels on his eyes?

Suddenly, she feels the emptiness of the house, the loneliness of this death. Not that he deserved better, but had anyone been with him before he died, they promptly abandoned him, leaving him there.

Oh, probably to go party. Celebrate.

Thoughts boomerang in her head. She feels sorry for herself one second, angry the next, and all of it yields to regret, dismay, confusion, until she pities herself again. She senses a rising august hopelessness. For the very first time she understands that her race to arrive here derived from one lingering aspect to her nature—that she felt a lurking, private, provocative *hopefulness* swimming in her bloodstream. Her father must come clean, they must arrive at an understanding, a resolution. If she recognized it earlier she'd have done a number on herself to get rid of the whole ridiculous notion, but it crept upon her unannounced, like a flu bug, to take hold, tricking her defenses. Now that she sees it for what it is, it's all too foreign and too late. Some deep residual *hope* has been dashed. She feels done in. As though she'll never know that resident *hopefulness* again, only this sudden hopelessness, for now she can never know what her father was unable to touch upon in an endless litany of foul deeds, the ones he righteously claimed he never inflicted upon her, as if that absence of overt cruelty somehow negates the inexplicable, intangible, indestructible cruelty she breathed from the moment of her birth. Now that he's dead, an inert, motionless, unrepentant *nothing,* no contrite act of repentance or fulsome admission of guilt or a complex explanation of *why* can save her, and her hope for that release is now extinguished with him.

He's dead. That's it, that's all. He won't say a word now.

His body's not worth the ten cents that rest on his eyes.

She feels neither grief nor remorse.

Or what she feels she does not know to be either grief or remorse.

He's been left alone, and no one on the entire island that he so dominated for half a century gave enough of a damn to do more for this defeated old man than fold his hands over his chest, give him a couple of nickels, and leave a few lights on.

A neglect that he deserves, she remits to herself.

But this dreadful silence she does not comprehend. This vacancy in her now. So she grieves, actually grieves, for words unknown that she has secretly coveted but knows now were never meant to summon more than an abject silence.

For that reason and that reason alone, Maddy, quietly, briefly, and in a way that a stranger might comprehend no more than she does, lets loose a few tears.

Then she shakes off the mood. Gets up and goes downstairs. She uses the bathroom, munches a few leftovers from the fridge, binds herself in a blanket on the La-Z-Boy, and commits herself to sleep. She'll be surprised if sleep does overcome her, so is taken by surprise when eventually she awakens.

SEVEN

Police are outside. Men from the funeral home go about their work indoors, murmuring in low, bloodless voices, as if to ensure that the dead won't hear. Madeleine Orrock leans against the front doorjamb to her family home, taking on the responsibility of being its gatekeeper. Down the road, a smattering of local folks, who noticed the Mounties and the undertaker's van at the mansion, engage in repartee, generally jovial. No respectful solemnity in evidence there. A few venture onto the property to pick up a pertinent detail or two from the police, then serve as sentries, tipping off new arrivals about the goings-on. Often they speak for less than thirty seconds before the people receiving the report scurry back into town like excited chipmunks to broadcast the news farther afield. Maddy expects a marching band in a jiff, banners raised, the mayor to drop by to declare a civic holiday and a week's festivities.

In her head, children will be singing, "Ding-dong! The prick is dead. The wicked prick is dead!" She's not sure that she won't want to join in.

When the housekeeper shows up on her doorstep, Maddy puts a

face to her name, remembering her from previous visits, although the woman didn't work for her dad back then. Not a bimbo, and nothing about her appearance qualifies as whorish. Maddy is secretly embarrassed by her previous harsh judgment of this rather dowdy girl. At times, her father's influence insinuates itself in her own character and opinions. She might disapprove, yet she feels powerless to behave differently. The housekeeper desires access to the mansion. She seems to think that she has every right to be admitted. And why not? Maddy asks herself. Let her in. But she sees things differently also.

"You were close to my father?" She really wants to ask, Did he say anything?

"People say the wickedest things, don't they? Yes, they do. I kept the house tidy-o. I got paid for that. Every once in a while he tried to cop a feel, but I never let him. When he got sicker I cleaned up his dribbles. I was never paid a fat penny for that. So no. We weren't *close*."

"I didn't mean it that way."

The housekeeper knows a bald-faced lie when she hears one. Maddy can tell.

"I'm sorry," Maddy tacks on. "It's just that—"

"No worries. He was your dad," Ora remarks. "You knew what to expect, am I right? Anyway, what people say. They're all stupid in the head if you ask me."

"I apologize for being one of the dumb ones."

"No worries! There's only one Einstein, right? So, can I come in?"

"Why?"

"Why?" She looks as though she's fishing for a fib to answer the question. Ora Matheson is an island girl who lives where people are welcome at every door and to be refused entry is outside her personal experience. Maddy suffers a doubt. Perhaps she's lived too long in Boston. "To clean the house up," the younger woman attests. "People will be coming over, no? The house was squeaky clean when I left it, but I want to finish the job, not that you can make everything tidy-o and perfect every minute of every day, although he used to think so, your dad did. There'll be visitors, no? How many, do you think? What's your best guesstimate on that?"

"Probably none. Look, the house is as tidy as it will ever be. Thanks for that." Maddy gazes out across the yard. More folks are attracted to the fuss as the day's good news makes the rounds. "You left him alone," she brings up, and means it as an accusation, but she's already been corrected by this woman once and shown to be mistaken, so adds, "Didn't you?"

"Seriously? You ask me that? Oh, hardly! I left him with Reverend Lescavage. He came over during the storm to spell me off, and because your daddy asked him to. I mean, he commanded him to come over, put it that way. So Revy came over."

"I see." Maddy's eyes soften. She has no particular grievance against the island, at least not outside her family home. She feels at odds, though, as if she's partially to blame for her father's life, and fears that others think so. A perpetual fear. "Thanks for taking care of him," she says. "That couldn't've been easy."

Some weird sound is released by the housekeeper, one that, while not attributable to any known language, manages to sum up Maddy's assumption more emphatically. Looking after her father had definitely not been easy.

"Ora, I think we'll just let the undertaker's men do their thing and take my father out. We won't need any cleaning, okay? I'll let you know if that changes."

"Oh, all righty," the younger woman agrees, "but if I'm not full-time I charge more for cleaning up after a party, just so you know." Quickly, she skips away and bolts off to join the company of the two officers from the Royal Canadian Mounted Police.

Maddy watches her go while scarcely moving herself, then continues to survey the activity in her front yard. Overhead, clouds scud. The wind is no longer a maelstrom but is still brisk. Below the cliff that the house is situated on, waves crash ashore. Power on the island remains off and the house generator ran out of fuel an hour ago, so she's living like everyone else and is content with that. If he were already buried, her father would be rolling over in his grave, but instead he's subject to the ministrations of the undertaker's crew rolling him over into a body bag. She ponders what her father's housekeeper can be saying to the

Mounties, so blithely chatting away, and why do they go on talking to her, and for so long?

Ora says, "He was here when I left. Put that in your pipe. Or don't you smoke?"

"You're sure?"

"In the flesheroo. If he was a ghost, he wasn't good at it."

He has to think what that means, then gives up. The senior officer remarks, "If you see him before I do, Ora, ask him to give me a buzz, okay? Thanks."

The policeman is silver-haired and large, imposing and authoritative even out of his uniform, doubly so when dressed. He's always known that he looks especially good when suited up. He envies his partner at the moment, who has successfully made a break for it, heading off the property to a cruiser, while he's been snared by Ora, her fingers gripping the sleeve of his jacket. He's prying her fingers off one at a time, although she doesn't seem to notice, when suddenly she gets his attention.

"Hey hey hey," Ora whispers. "The rats are climbing over the wall. Can you believe what my eyes are seeing here?"

Checking the direction of her interest the officer spots a man striding up the hill from town. A rain jacket is strapped around his waist, the sleeves knotted together at his hips. The rain pants he wears indicate that he began the walk in earlier weather, or that he's expecting more of the same. What makes him distinctive is not so much his clothing as his posture and bearing. A march-like swing to his arms seems to impart balance to his uphill stride, virtually military in its precision, while seemingly unnatural. Nobody walks like that, elbows rising up and out. The stride might seem laughable on a different body type or on anyone lacking self-confidence, but the man's demeanor defrays any such slight. He not only commands and sustains attention—Ora Matheson's, and everyone else's—but respect as well. Or so the policeman surmises in the moment before he gathers that the new arrival has chosen a destination, and he is it. Ora notices that, too.

"Oh my brown shit, he's coming straight here!" She seems in a sudden and inexplicable panic.

"Who is he?"

"That's Roadcap, you dumb twist!"

"Mind your manners, Miss Matheson."

"Don't be so sensitive. I call everybody names."

"What name do you call him?"

She doesn't hesitate a second. "Scary wacko dreamboat dude."

The cop eyes him more closely, and draws a conclusion from a previous encounter, a long while back. He fears that she might have a comparable phrase for him, apart from "dumb twist," but decides that he's better off not asking. "Tell me his real name again."

"Roadcap."

He's heard that name mentioned. He knows of him.

"News travels fast," the cop calls.

"Why's that?" The man stops fifteen feet away, which seems an odd distance for a conversation he's evidently intent on having.

"All the way to Dark Harbour."

"Okay. I'm from there. But I heard no news lately. What's up?"

The policeman looks away, a fake pause for dramatic effect perhaps, and in that moment notices that Maddy Orrock is paying attention. She's crossed her arms and stepped to the rim of the mansion's porch to observe the man facing the policeman. "Orrock's dead," the cop tells him. "If that's news to you, then you're probably last on the island to hear." When the man does not seem to react immediately, he adds, "Is that why you're up here for some reason?"

"I didn't know. Sorry to hear that. But no, I don't walk across the island because somebody dies. Doesn't matter who it is. How'd he die anyhow?"

"Old age," Ora pipes up. She tucks herself in slightly behind the policeman, as if for her protection. "People die that way. Maybe not in your family, but . . ."

The man looks at her then, and while his choice of words is challenging, his tone remains flat and cordial, his gaze level. "You know nothing about my family."

"Not if you don't say so," she replies.

The officer notices a look of puzzlement cross the man's brow, and sees him choose not to bother decoding her remark. "She's got a mouth on her," the cop points out.

"My way to keep your eyes up that high, copper man."

"All right," the officer says, clearly irritated now.

"All right what?"

The Mountie feels that she might be sassing him to make him look bad in front of their visitor.

"Enough of that."

"Of what?"

"Of that. Will you excuse us, please?" He does a quarter turn to exclude her from further conversation, and as he makes that motion sees Madeleine Orrock come down the stairs. She's casually sauntering toward him. "Can we help you with something, sir?" he asks the man called Roadcap.

"*Sir?*" Ora complains at his back. "*Sir?* Don't call him that. Not him."

Roadcap ignores her but answers the Mountie. "The other way around maybe. I can help you out, I think."

"How so?"

Ora butts in. "I thought Dark Harbour people got nothing to do with cops."

"Maybe for good reason," Roadcap suggests.

"No argument there."

"Ora," the cop says, "will you please be quiet?"

"Dark Harbour guys never date us local girls. Ever notice?"

The officer sees that Maddy is curious enough to come closer, but she has stopped along the way and stands observing them, listening in. That's not difficult given the extended range Roadcap has deployed to talk to him, and his voice carries.

"Sir?" the policeman asks, and he must also raise his voice a trifle to speak across the gulf between them. "How can we help you? Or you help us, as the case may be?"

"Like I said, I came across the island. Overnight. Through the storm. I met Reverend Lescavage along the way."

"Oh I know," Ora pipes up from behind the officer's back, "he's got a thing for you Dark Harbour thugs. His flock gone astray or something like that. Pretty funny when you think about it. I mean, he's the one astray, right?"

"Maybe we can talk about this in private?" Roadcap suggests.

"Is there a problem?" the Mountie inquires, finally alert.

"You can say that."

The Mountie gestures with his chin and the two men stroll farther uphill while remaining in the front yard of the Orrock mansion. They finally come within a conversational distance of each other. Maddy takes advantage of their departure to step forward herself, and comes up alongside Ora Matheson.

"What are they talking about?" Maddy asks.

Ora looks her over, exactly as she did when she first arrived, a kind of up-and-down assessment. "Not what," she says. "Who."

"Then who?"

"Reverend Lescavage. You know him, right?"

"Family friend, yeah. I've known him all my life."

"Me, too. All my life. But it's been a shorter life for me."

"So far," Maddy tacks on.

Ora agrees with that. "Yeah. Right. So far."

They see the Mountie extract his notebook and start to scribble things down.

"So what are they talking about?" Maddy asks again.

"That's for them to know and for us to go find out," Ora tells her.

EIGHT

Officer Wade Louwagie of the Royal Canadian Mounted Police has made it through a third year on the island of Grand Manan. Coming off a lengthy stint with post-traumatic stress disorder, he's taken to the place, and credits the island with his salvation. The Mounties have declined to take a page from their sister police organizations across the continent to provide expert counsel for officers with PTSD symptoms, partially believing in the mythic power of their famous tunic to hide what's going on beneath the skin—and in an officer's discombobulated head—but mainly convinced that the best therapy, perhaps the only therapy, is to get back to work. Officer Louwagie's attempts to get back to work failed repeatedly, his anxiety clouded by alcoholism, leading to drug addiction, which wound up in long bouts of tearfulness and inadvertent panics, night sweats, the shakes, violent headaches, two attempted suicides, weeks of mulling over shooting himself, and one admission to a rehab center. Since the Mounties' hierarchy contends, perhaps as a remnant from their horse-and-rider heritage, that the only way to deal with a fall is to get back in the saddle, Louwagie was given one last assignment, a do-or-die posting, where to everyone's surprise he made significant progress. Given his success on Grand Manan, he's been left in place and finds himself in command. If he's never posted elsewhere again, he's fine with that.

He credits the sea. Arriving on Grand Manan, he did what tourists do, only in all seasons, walking the cliff trails and the forest loops, spending time on rocky beaches. The ocean seemed to soothe his inner panic, alleviate a deep malaise, and him a prairie boy whose only sense of water growing up was found in sloughs. He's not fond of being in a boat and on the water—that doesn't work for him—but the shoreline, the breadth of sea and sky, this foreign geography, helps his head. He doesn't do drugs anymore, he's not on the wagon but he drinks sparingly. He's doubled down on cigarettes, although on the scale of things it's a vice that might kill him, but slowly. The other options can be quicker. He also talks to Ora Matheson a lot, and to a few other young working women around the island. Only talk, but all of it is a comfort.

What he's seen, what led him to descend from being an idealistic recruit with a prizefighter's physique to become an alcoholic basket case, is not something he's willing to talk about, although the events are sufficiently torturous on his psyche that HQ cut him more than the usual slack, and is content now to cut their losses and leave him right where he is. Out of the way, doing himself some good.

So he does not like hearing what he's now being told, and must ask the man from Dark Harbour to repeat himself more than once to get his point across. He's written his name down as Aaron Oscar Roadcap, a man who, he recalls hearing, derives from a criminal background and possesses a shadowy past. People whisper about him among themselves but say nothing openly to Louwagie, as if afraid to do so.

"What were you doing out in the storm, exactly?" he inquires again.

"I told you, I—"

"You were walking out in the rain, in the wind, in the dark. You enjoy that sort of thing. Okay, I get that. I don't understand it, but I'm taking you at your word here. But what were you actually *doing*?"

"I wasn't doing anything. Except for what I said. Walking. Sometimes I was sitting. I was lying on my back when the sun came up."

"The sun came up."

"Yeah, it did, actually."

"That's not what I meant," Officer Louwagie attests. He's feeling lost.

"Then what did you mean?"

"I mean, who goes out and lies on their back, probably on wet ground, when the sun comes up after a rainstorm?"

"Besides me? I can't say. But I do it, Officer. It's a free country."

"Yeah," Louwagie concedes. "It is." In truth, he isn't finding the idea so strange. Whatever floats your boat, he wants to tell the man, but doesn't. He even thinks that he might try it himself sometime, just go out into the wind and the roar. "Was anyone else with you? Besides you and Reverend Lescavage?"

"Yeah. A bunch of people. Not with me, but out there on their own."

"Out in the rain? Really? A bunch? What were they doing?"

"Beats me. They had tents. They were camping."

"That's not allowed up there."

"I'm not the police. You are. So I didn't arrest anybody."

"Don't be a smartass, all right?"

"All right."

"So who were they? These campers. Are they still there?"

"Can't say. We didn't stop for a chat. It was my impression that they were packing up."

"Your impression. Okay. Did you meet them before or after?"

"You mean—before," Roadcap concludes. "A bit before. They were in the vicinity."

"Okay." Louwagie writes that down. "What word, sir, exactly what word did you use again? You know, to describe—"

"Reverend Lescavage?"

"Yes, Reverend Lescavage."

"Eviscerated. I could have said gutted. Or filleted. His entrails are all over the ground."

"Jesus H—Okay. A big word. An educated man's word, if I may say so."

Roadcap does not rise to the bait.

"And you can take me to see him now?"

"If you're driving, the shortest way up is via the Whistle. We can walk in from there."

"*Via.* That's another word. Although a short one. You didn't come down here by that way, did you? You didn't take the Whistle Road into town."

"No, sir. I came in over Seven Days Work."

"Why?"

"Why? Because that's the way I was already going. It's what I planned to do."

"But it was shorter if you backtracked and came down from the Whistle, no?"

"Sure. Shorter. That would be shorter."

"Then why not—"

"He was already dead, sir. Reverend Lescavage. I couldn't do anything for him by taking the shorter route."

"Then why not take it anyway, is what I'm asking."

"That's not the way I was walking. I just came in the way I was coming in. And—"

"Go on."

"I suppose. Did I really want to walk back through the campers? They might've done it, right? Eviscerated that man. Did I really want to walk back through them?"

The officer puts his book away. He's not sure how he's going to handle this, how his internal system will react—what the experts on the subject call his "psyche." He has qualms about his nerves, his endurance, the side-swiping impact of an unforeseen depression. What memories might be evoked by all this? An evisceration. Will everything he's gained over the last three years be sabotaged in the blink of an eye, in a glimpse of a man's entrails? He wants to just go and sit by the sea instead. Maybe like this man does sometimes, out in a storm. He could send his partner in his place, but he's in command here with a job to do, and perhaps this is a test. Get back on the job, Mounties say. This is his chance to find out if he can really do that.

"All right," he tells Roadcap. "Take me up there. Just let me have a word with my partner."

"Sure thing, Corporal. Whenever you're ready."

He doesn't know if the man is being sarcastic with him, but he might be.

Officer Wade Louwagie speaks to his constable, Réjean Methot, and the two agree to separate. Louwagie is giving the order but the leadership style he's been trying to nurture requires him to consult first. Methot offers to remain at the Orrock place and keep the peace, given the public's interest. They don't want anyone scrawling graffiti on the walls, that's one thing, but worse than that is also a concern. Worse than that means arson. In recent months, islanders have been enduring a spate of fires, and they don't particularly want the mansion turned into flames on its fine overlook above the Bay of Fundy in retribution for fifty years of island dominance. The king is dead, and neither officer wants anyone celebrating. Experience has taught that celebration means drinking, and that brings on an excess of exuberance, and after that, just about anything can go down. Louwagie listens, consistent with his new leadership style, but he has a different task in mind. When Methot hears what Roadcap has reported, he accepts the urgency of his next job. If the Orrock home needs protecting, the current occupant will have to provide it on her own.

Louwagie glances up. He sees that Maddy Orrock has moved off several yards. She is engaged now in a staring contest with Roadcap, who returns her steady gaze without blinking. Corporal Louwagie walks over to her, then past her, then turns to virtually whisper in her ear. He's secretly fantasizing about what it might be like to make love to a woman so tall who is, for him, quite young. Then he wonders what it might be like to make love to a woman so rich. And what it might be like to make love to any woman again. It's been a while. Such thoughts wing past him before he asks, "Miss Orrock, do you know this man?"

"What does he want?" She also whispers.

She possesses the same internal authority her father possessed.

"Miss, he has information about Reverend Simon Lescavage. Do you know him, this man?"

"His father," she says, then finally breaks from her spell and looks at the Mountie rather than at Roadcap. "A long time ago, his father murdered my mother."

Ten seconds tick by before Louwagie even thinks to react. He says, "Bugger," and walks over to the man from Dark Harbour to lead him to the dead body of one of the town's many pastors. He knows that if the town has an overabundance of professions, they are, in no particular order, layabouts, fishermen, and clergy, but apparently the latter group has just been diminished by one. He's thinking also that if Maddy Orrock's mother was slain by Aaron Roadcap's dad, then a little bad blood might flow between them. But he doesn't think it's worthwhile to ask about that on the drive up to the Whistle, nor does he believe that it serves a useful purpose to revisit the bad blood of the past. He's mulling things over and advising himself to keep his mouth shut for now when they climb into the squad car, yet the moment the doors slam shut, Louwagie blurts out, in a casual tone that suggests his question has no bearing on anything, "Did your father go to prison, sir?"

The man seems nonplussed, not in the least put out by the question. "As a matter of fact, he did. Why do you ask?"

"Is he out now?" If a convicted killer is living on the island and a murder has taken place, he might wrap this crime up in no time flat.

Aaron Roadcap deflates that ambition. "No, sir. My father never got out. He died in prison."

Corporal Louwagie murmurs that he's sorry. He doesn't know what to say. He starts up the car. Sadness, he's thinking, lies all around. Some days it's inescapable. Inside, outside, on the skin, under it. He's hoping that he will be able to cope, with both the sadness to come, and with what he must now see—the entrails of the poor Reverend Lescavage spilled upon the morning's sodden earth, high above the sea. Driving up to the Whistle, he's thinking less about the crime on his doorstep than about the woman, the rich one, the tall drink of water, and he does feel sorry for her, for losing her father, but he really can't help his idle mind. He ponders again what it might be like to kiss and touch someone like her, that tall, that rich, or even, he admits to himself, what it might be like to kiss and touch someone not *like* her, but her.

———————

Over the hump of the Whistle, after its long climb, the road descends a short distance to butt up against a homemade, yet well-made, wooden barricade. After that, the drop is sheer off the towering cliff into the bright blue bay below. Clouds are clearing out nicely and the sea is continuing to settle. Having initially pulled over to the side, Louwagie changes his mind. He performs a three-point turn, switching off the motor only when the Dodge is pointed straight back uphill. A clever move, to prepare for a quick getaway, as though he knows what to do at this place. He and his witness disembark.

"Come here often, do you?" Aaron Roadcap kids him, and slams the side door shut.

"Not if I can help it."

In a sense, the island is dry, as no bars exist. Yet the government-run liquor store sells more booze than any in all of New Brunswick. This despite an impossibly small population. So the people themselves are not dry, they simply choose to drink in their own places, be it in their homes, or on their boats, or out here in the wild. The Whistle is a favorite hangout. On any given summer evening, folks gather in numbers. A barrier has been built to prevent the most inebriated from tumbling over the ledge, probably laughing all the way to the ground and creating a thud so distant as to be silent, unnoticed. So the regulars look out for one another. Anyone becoming too tipsy is required to stand on the safe side of the barrier, while only the more sober among them may enjoy a front-row seat to observe the setting sun. The vantage is due west, and from this height the view is all that it's cracked up to be in the tourist brochures. West lies the continent, and between that huge landmass and this mere dot of one, various species of whale—humpback and minke, finback and right whales, who breed here—break the Bay of Fundy's glimmering surface. All come for the nutrients carried in on a tide so powerful that the volume of water every twelve and a half hours all but equals the daily flow of every river on the planet. No surprise, then, that even lost and wandering orcas from the Pacific have found their way to this feeding ground.

"Do you?" the cop inquires of Roadcap. They haven't shared a word for over a minute, both losing themselves in the vista, so he adds, "Come here often?"

"I'm not a drinking man. Once in a while I drop by for the stories."

Louwagie makes a sound, as though wishing he could do the same. Cops aren't welcome. "So which way?" the officer asks.

They follow a trail along the ridge, not one that's well known, as it's hazardous to tourists with their kids in tow, but the most dedicated and athletic of hikers can follow it across the Bishop. The policeman can scarcely believe that this man passed through here at night, in a storm, with scant, if any, moonlight, although he learned that Roadcap did carry a flashlight.

"Still," the officer points out, "dangerous."

"Not if you're used to it. Not if you know it well."

"No. Still dangerous."

On second thought, the man agrees. Yet he knows the trail intimately, and has the sense to be careful even in daylight. They tramp across the Bishop until he encounters what he believes to be the camping area for a group of men and women the night before.

"How did you see them here if they were sleeping in the dark?"

"I heard them. They didn't come here to sleep."

"I see. How do you know what they came here for?"

"I don't. But in the dark, over the storm, they had to shout to communicate."

In departing, the unknown strangers left little trace of their trespass. Grass lies matted in patches where tents were pitched, and the remains of a small cooking fire demonstrates that it was never lit for long. A near-impossible task in the torrential rain. Neophyte campers. Today they are probably drying out somewhere. A broken tent peg was left behind, and Roadcap points out where another is stuck in rock, unwilling to be extracted.

"And you have no idea who they were or why they were here?"

"How should I know? They weren't my people."

To the Mountie's mind, that doesn't sound like an honest answer, but for now he doesn't push him. Instead, they amble on across the

meadows and into the woods of Ashburton Head. Corporal Louwagie, in this pastoral, can forget from one moment to the next the
purpose of this trek, and what awaits him. He is hardly paying attention when his guide pipes up, "There." And the cop stops walking and
cranes his neck up.

There.

He was supposed to prepare himself. But how does he prepare for
this?

A shock.

Louwagie is overcome by a maze of reactions, both familiar and
strange, immediate and distant. As if he himself has fallen away from
here and into a dream. He feels both dizzy and ill, which he can handle,
but he's also suddenly disoriented, and Louwagie is not confident he
can deal with that part. Or with any of this. As though a physical
switch has been flicked in his brain, admitting the dreaded serum of
depression and entanglement, confusion and remorse, that has nagged
him for much of his career. His guide kindly waits and makes no
comment while he vomits over a cairn of stones probably placed there
decades ago by travelers who wanted to express their appreciation of
the surrounds and to welcome future lovers of nature. Wade Louwagie
wipes the foul spillage from his lips on the back of his hand, then
coughs more up, then rubs the hand through the grass. When he thinks
he's done, he goes back and has another good look, but it's as though
he can't see what is plainly before his eyes. Rather, he's witnessing what
resides at the bottom of his mind like a fermenting rot. Another time
and place is evoked, another foul brutality he wishes he'd never seen.
Then he stumbles forward and challenges himself to do his job, to take
a hard look.

He does so. He takes a hard look. And remains standing. Though
he wobbles.

The Reverend Simon Lescavage's body is strapped with twine to the
bark of a dead tree, one burned by a lightning stroke perhaps a decade
previously. Lightning has struck twice in the same place, for the man's
stomach has burst and emptied as though scorched by a bolt, the remains
of his intestines and organs a dire and foul mess upon the ground. Birds

hunker in the trees, waiting to resume their morning feast. The corpse shows no outward signs of further violation, although what's been done to him is bestial. What killed him was this devouring—no kind bullet to the head or slash of the man's throat. He endured an agony, forsaken by life and any sense of decent humanity before death mercifully took him.

No evidence presents itself. No weapon has been left behind, and if anyone tossed it over the cliff, it's not likely to be located. The only possible suspect is the man who has led him here. That fellow knows the way in like no other, and the way back out again. Which can't be said of too many people, especially when a storm at night increases the challenges.

"Would you mind putting your raincoat on, sir?"

"Excuse me?"

"Humor me."

Roadcap does so. The officer examines it quite closely, making no attempt to conceal his suspicion.

"Anything?" Roadcap asks.

"Nothing," Louwagie admits. "Of course, in that storm, that rain, that deluge, it was like walking through a car wash several miles long. I can't expect to see blood or guts or anything of that nature even if you are the guilty party. You see my dilemma."

"I suppose I do."

The officer knows he should have asked before they left North Head, but he asks him now. "Do you have any knives on you, sir?"

"I never carry more than one," Roadcap says.

"Why carry one at all?"

"I harvest dulse for a living."

"So you don't leave home without it, huh?"

"I didn't say that."

"Is it on you now?"

"Yup."

Their mutual stare goes on a short while.

"May I have it, sir?"

"Will I get it back?"

"May I have it, sir?"

Roadcap hesitates, then opens his raincoat and reaches around to the side of his waist under the tail of his shirt. He extracts a knife of some heft and length—the blade runs to six, six and a half inches— and passes it to the policeman properly, the handle offered first.

"Thank you. I'm taking this in as evidence."

"That's not evidence."

"Our experts will decide on that."

"You don't have experts," Roadcap scoffs. Then he adds, "Not on this island."

"They can travel. Purely precautionary, sir. You understand."

Roadcap declines to reply, looking away and out to sea through the trees.

"Do you carry a gun?" Louwagie challenges him.

The man stares back at him, then asks, "Are you going to search me?"

"Only if I feel the need. Any guns?"

"Nope," Roadcap responds.

"Now we have a problem," Louwagie shares with him.

"What's that?"

"We can't leave the corpse like this. The carrion will get at it while we're gone. They already have. I don't know if there are any relatives. But just in case, we want to protect the eyes at least."

"Do you want me to walk into town again for help?"

"I have my phone."

"So what's the problem?"

"I can't leave the scene here. But the undertaker, my partner, our experts who will probably fly in, on account of the outdoor circum- stances they will need to be guided here. It's not going to be easy, either examining the body here or when we carry it out. So."

"So," Roadcap repeats.

"Could I ask you to walk back to the Whistle, then guide these other people here?"

"I'm not saying no, but isn't that a lot to ask of somebody under suspicion?"

"It sure is," Louwagie agrees. "But maybe not so much to ask of an innocent man." He's a handsome man, Louwagie notes. That's always something to overcome. People, himself included, are always less suspicious of the handsome or the pretty. He warns himself to be vigilant. The guy is also an intelligent man, and that's the more difficult hurdle here.

"Or of a man, guilty or innocent," Roadcap interjects, "who wants to pass himself off as innocent."

Louwagie can't dispute that. Still, he persists. "Will you help me out here, sir? I can ask people to come on their own, but it'll slow down our procedures."

"Sure," Roadcap says without hesitating further. "Why not? I'd do it for anybody, but Simon Lescavage was someone I liked. You see? I'm not doing it to indicate my innocence. I don't care what you think of me. I'm doing it for him."

If the man is trying to prove his innocence, Louwagie grants that he's doing a good job. He doesn't seem to be acting as a guilty man might, at least according to his own speculations. In any case, he is not free to trust him on this, he just needs him to do this one huge favor.

The man strikes off, back to the Whistle, and before Louwagie gets on the phone to call for help, he studies the body again. He can scarcely bear a glance, yet sticks with it and observes the man's face. The wide-open eyes. The gaping mouth, as though he's been caught in mid-scream. His hair is cut short. Strands are flattened by the wind and rain against his scalp, and what hits the corporal then is what has felt odd from the moment of his arrival. The stark eyes, the flat hair, the slack jaw—it's as though he's not looking at the man he knew as Reverend Lescavage, or even at his corpse. For some reason, out here on the edge of this field, it feels as though he's looking at his skeletal remains. At his skull. As though the man's been dead for a week. The pestering birds may have created that effect, but hanging on a tree trunk that way, he more closely resembles a scarecrow than a man. A thought that both creeps the officer out and causes him to feel particularly unnerved.

Perhaps it's a good thing, he thinks, that the minister's internal organs and intestines are strewn on the ground. Crows and animals unknown have had plenty to feast on, and have left his face intact. For now. Louwagie gets on his phone, as he needs to protect the corpse from further carnage, then begin the hunt for the brutal murderer of this gentle soul.

NINE

The call for passengers on the ferry to return to their vehicles below-decks is repeated over the loudspeaker, but neither Sandra nor Émile Cinq-Mars is budging. Let others answer the cattle call to crowd below, to sit in the cave of the hold while waiting for the ship to dock and the great steel doors to crank wide open. They will not easily be removed from their rapt attention of the view from the ship's topmost deck.

As the vessel steams to the harbor at North Head, they pass Long Eddy Point, the northern tip of the island. The whole of Grand Manan is shaped not unlike a cow's carcass prepped for seasoning, wide in the flanks and narrowing at the base. The upper shoulder, then, is where a hook garrotes the beef for hanging in a meat locker. By consulting a tourist chart, Émile Cinq-Mars determines that above the jut of Long Eddy Point at sea level, way up high, in essence where the hook would emerge in his imaginative rendering, is a lookout known as the Whistle, at the end of Whistle Road. The sunset views from there, he's told, are extraordinary.

The Bishop is the next section of promontory as the boat travels nearly due south, slightly easterly, followed by the solid rock of Ashburton Head. A sailing ship from another era sank on that stark shore, leaving behind nothing but its name. Then rising from the sea comes next the sheer cliff pegged as Seven Days Work, where the whole of creation is said to be etched in the massive rock borne to a sheer and impressive height. From that aerie, it's a dizzying drop below. They catch a last glimpse into Whale Cove, where they'll be staying, when the peninsula that's shaped something like a jigsaw puzzle piece, and which guards the cove on one side and on its opposite the harbor and town of North Head, juts into view and blocks their line of sight. As the boat bears around Swallowtail Light, and the loudspeakers again beg them below, Sandra and Émile curl into each other and dream of summer, of this time away. Hard to believe that it's upon them now.

A man of forty or so who's wearing big canvas gloves, as if he's intent on harvesting honey from hives, stands next to them, places his wrists comfortably on the ship's railing, and gives them an appraising eye. They look back at him. He smiles. He's more than a foot shorter than Émile Cinq-Mars, big-boned, with wide, expressive ears and full lips. In an astonishing way, he projects the kind of face and disposition another man can trust in virtually an instant.

"Hi," he says.

"Hi," Sandra says, and smiles back. She can't help herself, he seems so jolly.

"I'm Raymond, myself."

"Hello, Raymond," Émile says, and offers his first name in return.

"Good to meet you, Émile. Listen up. You have a car. That fact cannot be hidden from me. I remember you coming aboard. Sometimes I notice tall people, I don't know why. Anyway, I noticed you."

"Okay," Émile says, not yet cognizant of where this might be going.

"Okay," Raymond explains. "So now it's time for you to get below, like it or not, and sit in your vehicle. If you don't, I will have no choice but to kick your butt—your wife gets a pass on this, I'm a gentleman— but I'll kick your butt, Émile, right on down the stairs. No matter what you do or don't do, you are going to find yourself down below in your car. You might as well go voluntarily, no?"

Not many people could issue such a threat, even in jest, and still come across as friendly. Raymond succeeds. Émile relaxes his grip on the rail.

"Nice talking to you, Raymond. I have to go now."

"Yes! You do. Nice talking to you, too."

They find their way down the echoing chamber of the stairwell, happy that they remained on deck for the best of the island views, that they halved their time in the boring, dank hold.

Disembarking, they spot Raymond, this time waving cars off and cordially keeping them in straight lines, a bright grin on his face, a man in love with his work. The oversized gloves flash instructions to stop, go forward, or slow down, and as they pass him by he gives Émile and Sandra a wink. They both feel formally welcomed onto the island.

The tide's gone low again, making for a steep climb out of the hold and up the docking ramp to ground level. Drivers are moving more slowly than necessary, in Émile's estimation, their progress herky-jerky, but once he gains the higher ground he identifies the issue. A squad car bearing the buffalo-head emblem of the Royal Canadian Mounted Police has positioned itself with its cherries flashing to block cars about to load onto the ferry for the trip back to the mainland. Disembarking cars are not directly affected, but rubbernecking drivers slow down to see what there is to see—not much really—and the vehicles jam up in the arrival lanes.

Émile rubbernecks as well, although he convinces himself that his interest is professional rather than idle curiosity.

"Émile," Sandra chastises him.

"Just looking," he says.

"Forget it, chum."

An officer is snapping a photo of every license plate and quickly sharing a word with each driver.

"They're looking for somebody," Émile remarks.

"Cops are always looking for somebody. But you, you only have eyes for me."

"This is different."

"How so?"

"Whoever it is, they don't want that person to leave the island."

"Which is," Sandra warns him, "just so we're clear on this, absolutely none of your business."

"Absolutely," he agrees, but he must slow down for the cars ahead of him, which are bunching up at a stop sign. After that some go left and some veer right, and Cinq-Mars is guessing that he wants the left lane, but he isn't really sure. He tries to recapture a glimpse of the tourist map in his head. Other first-time visitors are also confused and that slows the entire process. "I'm just thinking how convenient it would be to work on an island. Makes it tough for the bad guys to get away if all they can do is swim."

"You worked on an island, Émile. Montreal," she deadpans.

"We have bridges. And a tunnel. Here, there's only one way to drive or walk off—via the ferry. You're trapped if you don't own your own boat."

"Which still makes it none of your beeswax, darling."

"Absolutely. No argument. But I'm saying, these are lucky cops. I hope they appreciate that."

"I only see one."

Émile hazards a further look. "You're right. They're short-staffed."

"Which shows you that it's not that big a case. You don't need to enlist."

He keeps one hand on the wheel but raises the other to acknowledge both her point and her humor. "I'm not enlisting. Have no fear. I'm just saying—"

Looking back at the policemen going through the line of cars, he feels something ominous in the air. An instinct perhaps, but he figures that even on a small and presumably peaceful island the police don't investigate every car leaving and take a photograph of its license plate if some guy shoplifted a screwdriver. He disagrees with his wife. Asking only one guy to do this job doesn't diminish the necessity or importance.

"What are you saying, Émile? May I remind you? Dear? Sweetie? A, you're retired, and B, we're on vacation. C, I repeat, this is not your affair."

"I'm just saying, something must have spooked them to go to all this trouble."

"Drive, Émile. The coast is clear."

She no sooner speaks than the car behind them honks, and Émile scoots out and turns left. They're immediately in the heart of North Head. A preponderance of ferry vehicles creates congestion in the village. Émile pulls off to check his bearings, congratulates himself on choosing the appropriate direction for their destination, memorizes a couple of coordinates, and merges his Jeep back into traffic. He's going at a snail's pace until he splits off from the main artery onto an inland roadway and is making good progress when he spies trouble ahead.

Sandra sees it, too. "Other cars aren't stopping," she mentions.

"Tourists," Émile responds.

"We're tourists, too," Sandra protests, even while she agrees. Certain troubles you don't drive by whether you're a local resident or not, even if it is your time for leisure.

In the oncoming lane, a battered, rusty old pickup, which looks as though it has always been battered and rusty, has been further beaten up by virtue of being down in a shallow ditch, mostly on its side, with no way of extricating itself. The driver, a woman, is still behind the wheel, although she hangs on to the door frame through the open window to keep from sliding down to the lower side of the truck. She is being assisted, more or less, by a man who is probably the driver of the Audi A8 parked farther along and pointed in the same direction Cinq-Mars is headed. Émile parks his Jeep behind the Audi and slides out.

The man on the pavement throws up his hands.

"She doesn't want to get out!" he shouts as Émile comes closer, almost as though he expects to be accused of something and needs to shift the blame.

Almost as though, Cinq-Mars is thinking, my old badge shows. If not his badge, then perhaps his demeanor. The man appears to be treating him as though he's a cop in a uniform. "Why not?"

"A bump on the head perhaps. She might've knocked herself senseless."

"You're the nutcase!" the woman hollers out.

"Is she badly hurt?" Cinq-Mars asks.

"She's bleeding."

Cinq-Mars discovers that the man is wrong on one account, for the woman seems very keen on escaping her vehicle. She just can't. She looks strong, but she lacks the purchase to push her front door upward and open, in part because the gravitational pull of the door angling down into the ditch is too much for her, and in part because she won't let go of it. Her own weight thwarts her from pushing the door open. She's also too large a person to easily slide out the open window, although that's also a question of her footing. He gets her to switch her grip to the steering wheel, then pulls on the door and holds it open as Sandra assists the woman—it's a struggle—to squeeze herself out. Essentially, she has to squirm uphill out of the vehicle as it's way over on a tilt. She's no sooner on her feet on solid ground than she lights into the man from the Audi.

"All over the road you drive!"

"Listen, lady." He's cross, but she overrides him.

"I know, Mr. Fancy Car, you think you own the highway. But I pay my taxes, too, year-round, not like you summer folk with your fancy cars and honking horns and *pedal to the metal*." She waves her hands in the air to make her final point.

"I *had* to honk my horn. You were way over the line! Like by six feet!"

"Just to show I won't be pushed around by the likes of you. I was making a point! I'm sick and tired of being pushed off the road because you think it's a racetrack. Now look what you've done!"

"If you didn't crawl like a tortoise, I might not appear to be going so fast. Why don't you walk? For you, it would be quicker."

"You see?" the woman asks Émile, and in the wink of an eye she's calm. She poses the same question to Sandra. "You see? He wants me off the road. He wants me to *walk*, so he can use the road as his personal racetrack."

"I don't want you to walk—"

"You'd run me down if I did. At least I'm safer in my truck."

"You call that a truck?"

Both faces are red, their minds made up, but they take a break, as if a bell to end round one has sounded. The abrasion over the woman's left eye where she banged off the steering wheel is nasty enough, and Sandra manages to soothe her sufficiently to have a closer look. A number of cuts and bruises are across her face, a little blood, and Cinq-Mars concludes that perhaps she is a drinker. Given the evidence of her wreck of a pickup and the marks on her face, she's been in fender benders previously. He makes a mental note to drive way over to one side if he sees her coming.

"It's not deep," Sandra assures her, "but it's ugly. You'll probably need stitches on your forehead. These other cuts could use some help, too. Disinfectant." Her polite way of calling her dirty. "Let's get you to a hospital." Then she rethinks. "Is there a hospital on the island?"

"You bet." The woman's tone is mildly scolding now. "It's a fine hospital. Ten beds!"

Émile has a suggestion. "Sir?" he asks the Audi guy. "Would you care to take her there? You probably know the way."

First he says, "It's not like I don't have other matters to attend to," but when Émile continues to gaze at him, a gentle look, nothing overly accusatory, he relents to a degree. He's a tall man with blond locks showing under a baseball cap that advertises a company that manufacturers shock absorbers, and he has a rosiness to his complexion and clear pores. He exudes affluence, a member in good standing of the leisure class, as much an effect of the monocle he's sporting on a dangling string as the Audi. "Yes indeed, I will take her should she choose to go. I put in a call to the police, but no one is answering in person at the moment."

"All right. Why don't you take her in, then? Will that be okay, ma'am?"

She bristles and scoffs but slowly comes around. "No speeding," she stipulates.

"I'm sure he'll take it nice and slow. Won't you, sir?"

Conceding to such a demand is against his nature, he lets that be known, but eventually consents. The two move off toward the Audi, and Sandra and Émile follow behind.

"Fancy car," the woman says as she gets close to it. Émile skips on ahead and opens the front passenger door for the injured woman. She examines the interior before climbing in. "Fancy leather," she says, still making nice.

"Yes, well," the man replies, the best that he can do to acknowledge her compliment. "If you don't mind, try not to bleed all over it, okay?"

Émile nearly reprimands him, but lets it go and so does the woman. The two buckle up and the Audi makes a U-turn. Watching the car drive off, Émile Cinq-Mars notices the Massachusetts plates.

"Good save," Sandra compliments him. "Okay, Émile, you did your good deed for the day and police work all in one fell swoop. You should be done for the next two weeks, minimum. Let's get on with this vacation thing. Figure out how it's supposed to go."

He kisses her then, right on the highway, and a different pickup coming down the road rewards them with an exuberant honk. That breaks them up and, smiling, they tramp back to the Jeep and carry on up the road to find their cabin.

TEN

Despite the hiccup of encountering a road accident along the way, their holiday could not be getting off to a better start for Sandra and Émile Cinq-Mars. Having booked a cabin built in the 1920s that's described by its proprietor as rustic, they were never certain if the charm depicted in online photographs might be duplicated upon close inspection. The claim to be *charming* could cover a plethora of sins, such as musty, damp, drafty, mouse-ridden, and leaky, with lousy plumbing, a filthy kitchen, a plugged toilet, a smoky fireplace, and dismal views of a parking lot or a construction site. *Rustic* could be deployed to dignify a dump. The ocean view depicted on the Internet might have been superseded by a condominium development a week earlier, or years ago. One never knows.

All such fears are summarily allayed.

Their home for the next two weeks is not only rustic and cozy, it's tidy, clean, and as charming as a fawn nuzzling a doe in a spring meadow. They can't get over the loveliness of the setting, the waving tall grasses down to the rocky shoreline, the hilly, picturesque inlet highlighted by small wooden fishing boats in a multitude of colors, which benefit from an old-fashioned winching system to haul them up an impossibly long ramp to cope with the stunning disparity between high and low tides. Émile's statement, "Charm out the wazoo," doesn't duplicate Sandra's choice of words, but she takes his meaning. They've landed not only on their feet but, as near as she can tell, smack-dab in the heart of a summer paradise.

She would not care to survive a winter here, but for the next two weeks, if she's not quite in heaven, she's exactly where she wants to be.

"Like living in a Wyeth painting fifty years ago" is how she puts it.

Sandra has brought basic supplies from home: sugar and tea, coffee, a variety of spices, even a large jar of flour in the event that she succumbs to an urge to bake, which she might. The scent of cookies in this old house should be especially tantalizing. Bulk items that she's not likely to repurchase have been brought along, and she wants to set up her kitchen right away and have that done. Émile prefers to explore, shop later. Their compromise is to stroll on a beaten path through the tall grasses to the shore of Whale Cove, breathe the salt air, relax, then get to work. Exploration of the island will come later.

The trip back into town is also peaceful. The pickup remains in the ditch, and just as they are entering North Head, a police car at full speed swishes past them, cherries flashing. Émile can't help following the vehicle in his rearview mirror.

"Émile," Sandra gently warns him.

He tries his best to keep his eyes on the road.

They don't know where to shop, and while the first store they drop into has a disappointing inventory and high prices, it makes up for that with a convivial air. Lots of laughter and chat among customers and employees. They feel themselves in a different place. After the groceries, Émile stops at the liquor store. He can hardly believe the stockpile of beer, and buys a case, even though he entered for vodka and whiskey. Sandra remarks on his loot as he comes back out.

"Do I put in a call to AA now or when we get home?"

They duck into a bakery, and while Sandra purchases bread, the place triggers a few of Émile's fonder vices. He comes away with a cake, a pie, and a variety of doughnuts. Sandra thinks that perhaps she'll put her summer baking plans on hold, or her husband might return from Whale Cove the size of one.

"Did you overhear what they were talking about?" Émile asks.

"Was I eavesdropping on other people's conversations? Categorically, no," she teases. But she's curious. "What was it?"

"Grocery store, liquor store, bakery, people are laughing. They seem happy. And yet, somewhere in the conversation, a dead man gets mentioned."

"Really?"

"In each place."

"Did he fall out of a tree?"

After lunch, they set out to explore the island. At Whistle Road Émile wants to turn right. Sandra insists they go left. "I know which way the cop cars went, Émile. We'll explore the opposite direction."

He laughs. He's less keen to investigate the unknown fuss than she thinks. He's really more curious about the island, and off they go. Some twenty years ago, a young journalist helped Émile with a case. The island was the writer's ancestral home. When later the detective needed to sequester a young woman from the bad guys, he arranged with the journalist to hide her away on Grand Manan. A ploy that worked. Ever since, he's been interested in visiting the place, a time that's come.

On this opening foray, they're keen on getting to know the lay of the land. Amazing, to drive down to the lower, southern portion of the island and encounter fog, while the sky is as clear as a bell at North Head. South is less hilly and less high. There's a park with a sand beach and fishing villages to which no picture postcard can do justice. They visit a general store in the town of Castalia that's a throwback to another century, and except for the familiarity of the canned goods and other supplies, they've tumbled not only into another world but into another time. The storefront and the first section fail to indicate the size of the place, but once through there they enter into an expansive space. Here they can purchase steaks or the freezer to put them in, a bolt of cloth or electrical wire, penny candies on one side of the aisle, socks on the other, and beyond that shirts, pants, party dresses, and bicycles. A workingman's steel-toed boots over here, toys over there, and, in between, computers and cereal. This is where they will shop in the future, Sandra determines, falling in love with the ambience while appreciating the prices, too. She listens for talk of a dead man, but here the employees are stationed too far apart from one another for idle banter to flourish.

Back on the road, she reads out the names of places they will investigate later: the Castalia Marsh, Woodwards Cove, the Thoroughfare, which is a crossing to Ross Island, underwater at high tide, the villages of Anchorage in Long Pond Bay, and Seal Cove, and Jack Tar's Cove, Deep Cove, and Flock of Sheep. Just south of Flock of Sheep Sandra's eye catches what appears to be the tip of a staircase on a cliff. Nothing looks private, there are no signs, there's room to park, so she suggests an excursion. Émile turns around, and soon they are descending a steep stairway to what looks like a secret, small, and remarkably pretty beach in a wee cove below.

They spy sand on the shore sheltered by rock face on three sides. If this is a public spot where they are free to picnic and swim, nap or read a book, then they have truly landed in paradise.

The little cove is exactly that. A special place that could never be accessed without a stairway. Big boulders shelter the sand from the sea, the waves bursting on them first, then running gently up and minding their manners ashore. The couple is about to make the steep ascent back to the car, determined to return in their swimsuits one day with a stocked hamper and wine, when Émile steps past a boulder and is saddened by what lies at his feet. A dog, a magnificent black Lab, dead on the sand. Flies have alighted, but not many, nor have they been intrusive, so the body washed up in a recent hour, the dog, in all probability, having drowned.

Seeing him bent over, Sandra comes up behind her husband.

"Oh dear," she says.

"Oh dear," he repeats, and straightens.

"What should we do with him?"

"She's a female. Maybe not full-grown, but still about fifty pounds."

"No, Émile, you can't carry it. More like sixty pounds. Your back."

"We can't leave it here. I'm not going to bury it in the sand. It'll be unearthed in the next storm."

They stare at the poor animal awhile. No collar.

"We can alert the authorities," she suggests.

"I bet they have better things to do. In any case, if we leave her for even a little while, the flies and rodents, not to mention the birds, will have at her."

They share a glance, then gaze at the dog again.

"Okay," Sandra says. "I can help. Take it slowly. We'll rest on the way up."

"I was planning on doing that even without carrying a dog."

He has to dig in the sand to get his forearms under the Lab, but soon enough he makes it to his feet, adjusts the dog's weight, and proceeds. Sandra tries to take some of the weight off by putting her hand under the body where it sags between Émile's arms, but in the end he's on his own, and they commence their climb. He doesn't let on that for all his inherent strength, somewhat diminished by his sixty-six years and lower-back issues, the task will probably kill him.

He keeps that prospect to himself as he staggers up the stairs.

The Mounties arriving by aircraft brought in a dog, a German shepherd. A forensics team, also from the mainland, detailed and scrupulously photographed the site, and the detective from Saint John asked Aaron Roadcap to drop by the local station for questioning. Roadcap politely declined, saying not unless he was fed first. Not having the budget to offer the man breakfast, they drove him home to feed himself and arranged to pick him up later in the afternoon for a talk. The detective agrees with Corporal Wade Louwagie that Roadcap is a curious fellow, although he does not seem to be behaving with criminal intent, guilt, or apprehension. He strikes them both as a peculiar person who is more or less an upright citizen.

"If you believe in the myth of the upright citizen. I don't, personally. But just because his old man's a convicted murderer doesn't make him a killer, too," the city detective quips.

His partner from the city whose name is Jack Hopple reminds him that "Bad apples don't fall far from the rotted-out tree trunk."

"That's not how the saying goes," the detective tries to correct him.

"No matter how you say it, still true."

"You're too class-conscious, Jack," the superior admonishes the other detective, although playfully. "Clouds your view of the big picture."

"We had a chat earlier," Louwagie mentions. "Roadcap and me. When we were out here alone. He doesn't believe his father was guilty of that murder."

"Just convicted of it. Sounds guilty to me. Doesn't it to you? Is he out yet?"

Detective Marshall Isler may have been thinking the same thought that Louwagie had entertained at the outset of all this.

"Sorry, sir. He's dead. Died in prison," Louwagie tells him. "Roadcap was a kid at the time." He doesn't know why, he just feels he should stick up for the guy.

A rotund man in his early fifties, with thin gray hair and a thick mustache, Isler jots down a note in a red book slim enough to slip in and out of his shirt pocket. "What can you tell me about our dearly departed reverend? What was he into, besides 'Jesus loves me, this I know'?"

Louwagie's knowledge is limited. He's bumped into him at public events, and has heard nothing untoward about the man. "A bachelor."

"That's suspicious right there," the city detective points out. A bachelor himself, Louwagie fails to agree. The man inscribes a notation in his red book, then inquires, "What else?"

Louwagie says that the pastor's congregation, Presbyterian, seems to be one of the saner groups on the island. He does not mean to suggest that they're all batty, only that a few come across as off-the-wall. Every congregation preaches against alcohol, and perhaps Lescavage did, too, despite being known to take a nip himself.

"Falling down drunk type thing?" Isler asks him and Louwagie says no.

"Let's say that he could drink a lot at times but still hold it. I administered a Breathalyzer once. He barely passed, still, the physical tests he passed with flying colors. Walked a straight line like a train on rails."

"Why did you test him? Random stop or did he give you cause?"

"Zigged when he should've zagged. Said he was reaching into his glove box for something."

"For what exactly?"

The detective, in Louwagie's opinion, is overreaching. He comes across as a man who asks questions to make people think he has an idea, when nothing at all is floating through his head.

"We're going back a couple of years, sir. I'm not sure. Can't remember. I think he said he was reaching in the glove box for his gloves."

"Nobody does that," the detective replies. "Puts gloves in a glove box."

Louwagie doesn't think that that's as profound as the detective apparently believes, but he keeps his peace. He wanders off on his own to sit on a boulder while the detectives do whatever it is they're so brilliant at. While awaiting their report, he reviews for himself what's transpired.

Eventually, the forensic folks concede the obvious, that the open air after a vicious storm doesn't leave much to go on. Much of the blood and ooze washed away. They don't seem terribly anxious to stir the muck and body slime more than is necessary. They will pick up the pieces, and Louwagie is so relieved that this job doesn't fall to him, he believes he can French-kiss each one of them and the snoop dog twice. He knows better than to say so and remains nonchalant about this terrific news. He might not recover if he's required to bag the man's gooey intestines or separate out his organs. The Mountie has already explained that the desiccated vomit on the cairn is his own, not the perpetrator's or the victim's. He's grateful that the other cops seem to understand and not think badly of him.

Then comes the matter of getting the bagged body out. The undertakers nearly killed themselves coming in when one turned his ankle in a small crevice and came close to stumbling right over a ledge. All he was carrying at the time was a light stretcher. They're nervous about trying their luck a second time while lugging the dead man along the edge of a cliff. They can also take routes through the forest, where they are liable to get lost. Lescavage was not a heavy man yet his remains make for an awkward weight. To take the longer path in the opposite direction from the way they came in is infinitely safer, and Louwagie makes that decision and hires two local men to spell them along the trail. Miles with a body between them will be cumbersome and tiring otherwise, and pulling it behind an ATV over rough terrain too damaging to the corpse. The undertaker's van can meet them where they emerge from the trail close to North Head, so that Lescavage, discreetly packed into a body bag, his innards in another, will not be subject to a public viewing just yet.

All are agreed, and Louwagie arranges with his own partner upon his arrival, and the two city detectives, to escort the corpse and its entourage down from high ground. He will do for him in death what he was unable to do in life—protect him.

As he departs with his grim brigade, he notices that Detective Isler is trying to see if the dog can pick up a trail of a different kind, but if the animal has nothing to go on he doubts that the men will learn a thing. In terms of solving the crime, it's reasonable to suppose that if the killer keeps his mouth shut and doesn't wave the murder weapon around in a bar, and if he hasn't conveniently parked his DNA on a signpost, then he has a chance of being home free. Unless someone has openly been threatening the man or was seen coming up here with him—in a storm, in the pitch-black—they'll have no leads to pursue. They will have absolutely nothing to go on. Likely, that will only focus pressure on Aaron Roadcap, for finding the body while out in a gale at night—two strikes against him—and they'll have to find the mysterious people he says camped out in the storm, if they even exist.

At least, Louwagie is thinking, as he trails the procession across the lovely mountain meadow, that that would be how he would handle the investigation if it was left up to him.

The dog lying dead in the open back end of his Jeep is visible as Émile Cinq-Mars asks a pedestrian where City Hall might be located. Fortunately, the old-timer doesn't glance in the rear. The man with a wizened complexion and a long, crooked, bony finger that he uses as a pointer needs to think twice. In the end he provides simple directions. Driving off, Émile finds the building straight away. Above the door the sign is carved in stone: CITY HALL. He discovers the entry firmly locked. Odd, this being the middle of the day.

"Maybe they take early lunches," he gripes as he straps his seat belt back on.

"Their lights are on," Sandra notices. So they are. The side of the building has a bank of windows well off the ground, all showing the interior lit up by ceiling lights hung from chains, the bulbs covered by stout metallic shades.

"Maybe they don't use the front door for some bonkers reason," Émile grumbles.

He tries the back entrance then, up a short flight of stairs. Again, the door's locked, but this time he hears sounds inside, a muffled clamor, nothing he can figure out, so he knocks. When no one answers he puts an ear to the wood and listens. More rambunctious thumping, like a gathering of boxers working out on heavy bags. Still, listening with his ear to the crack, it's more thunderous than that, yet strangely muffled. He has no clue what's going on at City Hall to create the noise, and his curiosity is piqued.

He believes he's in the village of Castalia. He's not positive of that, either, and no sign is posted to help him out. He strolls around to the far side of the building, out of sight of the parking lot now and no longer visible to Sandra, who's holding down the fort in the Jeep. He's glad she talked him out of his original idea, to carry the dog through the front door and drop it on the first desk in sight. He's done enough lifting for the day without lugging the dead animal around and around this building. The far side does yield an advantage. A window suffers a broken corner, a hole through both panes of glass, likely caused by an errant baseball or a rock. While the windows are too high off the ground for him to gaze inside, here he might better interpret the strange sounds emanating from the room.

This time, he hears a rhythmic grunting to go along with the repetitive thumping. Drolly, he wonders if City Hall hasn't been transformed into a daytime brothel. One keeping a hectic schedule. Curiosity now has the better of him, but there's no way into this edifice. Coming full circle to the front door again, he mounts the stairs. He spots his wife leaning forward in her seat to see what on earth he's up to as he begins to pound, very heavily, on the big wooden door. He bangs it with the side of his fist as hard as he can, even though he knows that the pounding going on inside is much louder. He stops to listen from time to time, then pounds again, less interested in the dog's carcass now or in contacting an owner than he is in uncovering the origins of the noise. About the fifth time that he stops his banging to listen, he hears some-thing. Or rather, nothing. A change. He hears silence. He assumes from this that his pounding has perked up the ears of those indoors. So he goes at it again, harder than ever, both fists this time, a furious citi-zen demanding a voice at City Hall.

Finally, the door is unlocked and creaks open a crack. "What?" a high-pitched male voice asks. He can see a portion of the man. Cinq-Mars is over six two when he stretches, while this man is taller.

Forgetting, perhaps, that he no longer carries a badge, he speaks with an authority that sounds official. "What's going on in there?" And thinks to add, Group sex? before he censors himself.

The door opens a wider sliver, still too narrow for anyone to enter through, although he might make an exception for the man inside, who's as thin as he is tall, about the width of a fishing pole.

"I believe the operative phrase to be," the man lets him know, "that that's none of your concern. Not in this lifetime, nor the next." Good point, and the visitor agrees, but the fact that the other man talks with the door barely ajar, his face in shadow, undermines his perspective, to Émile's mind. He's not inclined to leave just yet.

"This is City Hall. It's a public building!" The retired cop does irate quite well.

At last, the door opens an appropriate amount. The man is not taller than he is after all because he's wearing elevated boots which lift him an extra four inches. He has a thin, pinched nose, scant fair hair that's brushed forward in the front but sticks up in clumps at the back, and he's sweaty. Very dark brown eyes. He's wearing what Émile would describe as a kung fu or judo uniform—a thick short robe tied with a jute belt over white trousers that end at midcalf. While he still can't figure out what could constitute the rhythms he overhead, he's guessing they have something to do with martial arts. Behind the young man is a wall on which rain gear has been hung to dry, and behind that barrier lies an eerie silence. People are probably listening in, so he's not going to get a full explanation easily.

"This is not City Hall," the man informs him, his tone clipped, condescending, weary. "Maybe it used to be. Once upon a time. It is now *privately* owned."

His emphasis on *privately* sounds like a slow incision.

"Ah. I see. Like for a judo studio, something like that?"

"If that satisfies your need to poke your nose in where it does not belong, then sure, something like that. Goodbye!"

"There aren't any signs up," Émile protests. "No advertising."

"It's a *private* building. Why do we need to advertise? The old City Hall name is inscribed above your head, but in stone, which is not easy to remove. Nor do we feel the slightest obligation to undertake the cost of doing that. Anyway, it's part of the original look of the place, so we left it."

"We?"

"We."

"There's a new City Hall, then. I need to find it. I have a dead dog."

"I'm sorry about your dog."

"It's not my dog."

"I'm no less sorry. For the dog. There's no new City Hall. Years ago, long before you interrupted my afternoon, towns on this island were independent, each with its own City Hall. Since then, they've been amalgamated into one. By the province. Now there's only one City Hall for the entire island and this is not it. Try North Head, but I'm really not sure and I am busy, so if you don't mind."

Whether he minds or not, the young man is closing the door on him.

"Kung fu?" Cinq-Mars asks. "Tai chi. Akido! Which is it?"

"Excuse me? It's not any of those. Did you run over the dog?"

"It drowned. Karate!"

The man is still shaking his head.

"Bokator!" Cinq-Mars calls out. He wants to get this. "That's from

Cambodia. Choi Kwong-Do, that's from Korea. Am I getting warmer at least?"

"We're not a martial arts studio. Sir, I'm closing the door."

"You're *not* martial arts?"

"Sir, if you don't leave, I'll have you removed. Don't knock on this door again. You are not welcome here. Do you understand? I'm trying to be polite. I could say this a different way, but you are not welcome here."

"A different way. You mean the *f* word?"

He closes the door quite directly on Émile's face. Rebuffed, Émile turns, and departs the stoop, miffed that he's not guessed the activity inside, but now more curious than ever. "They're not martial arts," he explains to Sandra, forgetting that she possesses no reference to make sense of the comment. "And so much for island friendliness."

"What? Who? Why should they be?"

"Friendly?"

"No, martial arts."

"They pound around a lot and they're private. They wear these skimpy robes with belts. They're secretive, I'd say. Any guesses?"

"I have no clue what you're talking about. Is this City Hall or not?"

"Not." He starts the ignition. "I'm going to that general store again. I bet someone in there can tell me where to go."

"I'm sure they won't be the first or the last people to tell you where to go."

Émile is too irritated to notice the ribbing.

"By the way, don't be too quick to sully island friendliness," Sandra advises him. "I've been sitting here reading license plates. Ontario. Nova Scotia. Rhode Island. New York. Even Quebec, and I don't mean us. North Carolina. Michigan. Missouri. Can you believe that? Missouri. Here. On Grand Manan. So don't blame unfriendly locals."

This gives Cinq-Mars pause. People have come a long way, and from many different places, to make pounding noises not connected to martial arts. As the man said, it was none of his business, but in saying that, he might as well have waved a red flag before a bull. His vacation is cracking up to be all that he expected and yet challenging, as well.

Nothing galvanizes his attention more than people behaving in a secretive, indeterminate way, especially if they're on his doorstep, or he on theirs.

At the general store, Émile briefly waits for the cashier to become free. She seems an affable and mature woman, in her forties, whereas others nearby are quite young and might take the death of a dog to mandate either a maudlin or dramatic response. He need not have been that discriminating, for once he speaks to her, she promptly broadcasts the news to everyone within earshot, then proceeds to ask over a loudspeaker for a "Margaret" to come to the front of the store.

"Who's Margaret?" Émile wants to know.

"A fisherman's girlfriend," he's told. When he returns only a blank stare, she explains, "A bunch of them have black Labs."

Margaret shows up and is told about the dog in the Jeep and immediately falls into a near panic. The very thing that Cinq-Mars was hoping to avoid. "Oh my God, it's not Remington, is it? Is it Remington? Oh my God!"

She throws herself out the front door, running from car to car, so that Émile has to chase her down. He cautions her to take several deep breaths, and she does, clutching her chest, before he opens the hatch to his Jeep. "Easy, now." This seems an impossible instruction for her, but once the hatch yawns wide, she relaxes.

"It's not Rem. Rem's a guy dog. This is a girl dog."

"I explained that to the cashier, but you didn't give me a chance."

"It could be Alex Waite's. He's got a girl dog." She's digging under her apron, which is some bother, then her hands resurface with her mobile phone. Sandra entered the store with him and probably hasn't noticed this kerfuffle, as she remains inside. He scans the windows for a sign of her, but she's elsewhere, probably lost in the store's vast hind room. "Alex," the girl is saying into her phone, "it's Margaret." She is no Peg, this girl, no Maggie. "How're you doing?"

She crosses her fingers while listening to her friend's response.

"That's good to hear. Do you know why?"

Émile hears the man on the other end ask why.

"Before I tell you that, how's Sass doing?"

She's doing fine, he says, but the young man is losing patience.

"Okay, that's good. You know why? Because there's an old guy here with a dead black Lab. Looking for its owner, yeah. It's a girl dog, too. Like Sassie."

Émile waits while she listens to a spiel, and adjusts to being referred to as an old guy. The girl's expression grows sad. "Okay," she says. "Okay. I'll tell him. Okay. Yeah. That's too bad, yeah. Yeah. You, too."

She clicks off her phone.

"Okay," she says.

"Okay," Émile repeats, encouraging her.

"The dog is Gadget. I know, a bit weird that name. Anyway, it's Gadget, and she belongs to Pete Briscoe. He's brokenhearted, my friend Alex says, because last night Pete was out fishing, only he wasn't really fishing, he was just riding out the storm, but anyway he was out on his boat and at some point, Pete doesn't know exactly when or what happened, but Gadget went missing. Off the boat. Into that wild sea. Alex says that Pete's been bawling his eyes out ever since, that he was on the radio last night telling the other guys about it at sea and bawling his eyes out over the radio. He wanted to search along the shoreline. The guys were warning him off that because it was too damn dangerous and Gadget was either going to make it or she wasn't. So I guess she wasn't. Will you tell him? He doesn't live far from here. You'll probably have to wake him up like I did Alex—those guys had a rough night—though I'm sure he'll appreciate that he can give Gadget a proper grave and that. You know what?"

She appears to be waiting for an answer. Émile asks, "What?"

"It'll be better for Pete in the long run going out to sea knowing that Gadget's not floating around out there somewhere. I sincerely do think so."

Émile assures her that he will take the remains to Pete Briscoe if she will be kind enough to give him directions. "I'm only a tourist. I've got all the time in the world, so that's good, but I don't know my way around."

Sandra chooses that moment to poke her head out from the massive carnival that is the general store. She's only checking on his whereabouts, and pops back inside again.

"Lord God Almighty!" Margaret suddenly exclaims. "Can you believe this day?"

"Ah," Cinq-Mars says, "ah, how so?"

"First Orrock dies!"

"Who's Orrock?" he asks.

"Only the boss and owner of everything! He owns the fish plant, a lot of the boats. He owns the lobster pounds, the salmon-fishing farms, most of the property. I'm told the only thing he doesn't own on the island are the banks, but he owns most of the money in them, so there you go. What difference does that make?"

"I see. But I thought this province was owned by the Irving family."

"Sure it is. But what they don't own around here, Orrock has a hand in."

"And he's passed away?"

"In his sleep. He didn't deserve that."

"Too young a man, was he?"

"Old enough. But he didn't deserve to die in his sleep. He should've been drawn and quartered. He should've been cut up in slices and tossed over the side as fish bait."

"I take your meaning. Not well liked."

"Despised, pretty much. He wasn't sliced up though. Reverend Lescavage, he's like a shiny penny, a lucky one, the sweetest little guy, littler than me anyway, but he's the one who gets sliced. Not in his sleep either, poor guy. At least I don't think so. He didn't get fed to the fishes, but apparently, *apparently,* it was gruesome what happened. The birds ate some of him. What a terrible way for a sweet man to die. Don't you think so? And on our island! A murder!"

Émile Cinq-Mars is grateful that Sandra has stayed inside and is not hearing this, or she might pack them both up and leave. For his part, he has to acknowledge that as much as he is happy to be on the island, and his first impressions are positive, matters are starting to get interesting.

"Now you show up!" Margaret exclaims.

He's momentarily confused. How could she possibly know who he is?

"With a dead dog!"

"Oh . . . right. Right. It's been quite a day around here."

"That's three dyings all in the same little while!"

"Yes, I see," Émile says, and is more glad than ever that his wife is not within earshot to glean that the dead appear to be falling out of the trees on Grand Manan. Then he has an idea. He's amazed that he has solved the identity and the mystery of the dead dog by talking to the right person. This may be a place where any investigation into anything can be supported by local knowledge, rather than with what he's put up with throughout his long career—namely, witness silence. So he says to Margaret, "Listen, I was just down to the old City Hall. To inquire about the dog and what to do. It seems to be occupied by an unusual group."

"Oh them," she says.

"Yeah, them," he says, hopeful. "Do you know what they're doing in there?"

"Well," she says, and for the first time her voice falls to a whisper, as if a secret is about to be conveyed, "they think that we don't know."

"We," Cinq-Mars repeats.

"Us. The people. The town. The whole island, for that matter."

"But you do. Know."

"Of course we do. We even have video."

"Really."

"Yup."

"So what is it? What are they up to?"

"They're learning how to fly. I kid you not. I do not yank your chain. Hey, let's go back in. I'm supposed to be working."

He walks with her across the parking lot.

"Margaret, ah, what do you mean, fly?"

"Not in airplanes," she whispers with that conspiratorial inflection again, and adds once more, "We have video."

"Who does?"

She shrugs. "Oh, I don't know. Somebody. It's been shared, so maybe everybody by now. They sit on the floor and cross their legs and do their meditations and go "Ooommmm," and nobody minds that so much. Each to their own, right? Then they go bouncing around on the floor, banging their thighs and knees on the floor trying to bounce up into the air. So they can learn to fly. They're a bunch of loonies. They believe—we saw a group like them on the Internet—they think they'll fly someday. You know, levitate and like that?"

"How do you think they're doing?" His question is intended less to find out about a group of initiates, most likely spawned by an East Indian cult, than to discover how seriously the locals take them.

Margaret flashes a smile. "Let's just say that nobody's seen anybody hovering above the treetops just yet."

They arrive at the store's front steps at the same moment that Sandra is coming out. She's accumulated more shopping bags and wears a rather sheepish grin. Émile laughs. "No matter," he consoles her. "We're on vacation. This helpful young lady is giving me directions to the home of the dog's owner, then we're off."

ELEVEN

Madeleine Orrock slept during the day.

She made up the king-size bed in the guest room, a place she's never slept in previously and rarely visited except as a child, and then only if she was looking for a place to hide. The moment her head hit the pillow she expected to be down for a fortnight. So much rolled back over her. Her father's death, his inert body, their lives together, all that ancient history, as well as the sea she was tossed upon to arrive here, that bucking boat, a thrashing rain, and as she fell helplessly into slumber— one part mental fatigue to three parts physical exhaustion—a darkness befell her even as the sun rose higher in the sky outside her window. Too tired to get up and pull down the shade.

Whether it's bad dreams or a festering hunger or sunlight that wakes her she doesn't know, but her deep sleep lasts only three hours. Awakening, she considers staying right where she is, at least until dark, though she soon realizes she's utterly famished. She recalls her miserable seasickness on the crossing. She's been running on empty, or at least sleeping on empty.

She thinks about making herself lunch, but once up she's too light-headed, perhaps too lazy. She locks up and strolls into town to hunt for a café. Invigorated by the sea air. Maddy was born on this rock, and the taste and smell of the air is every bit a part of her DNA she believes as is her gender, her height, her skin and bones. Assuming that her arrival is late enough, that the tourists won't be jammed chockablock into the Compass Rose—she's right on that score—Maddy settles into the cozy waterfront restaurant. She's spacey after her half nap and from her lack of nourishment, so it takes a while to detect that others have noticed her presence.

While she might come across as just another tourist to the younger set, older folks among the staff and local customers have recognized her, her name whispered among them. Oh yes. This is part of living here. Being an Orrock, wearing what her father called a mantle but what she knows to be a yoke.

Yes, she wants to call out, not too loudly but quite firmly, I am an Orrock. My father's daughter. Live with it. God knows, I do.

Here anyway, on Grand Manan, she lives with it. Years away, she can forget what that's like, but returning home it comes back upon her like an enemy's sweet revenge.

She's been enjoying her lunch. Now she can't get out of there fast enough.

Spooked on the way home, as well. This time, eyes observe and access her, appraise her, dismiss her, evaluate, condemn, and despise her. Or simply remember her, even though she is incapable of remembering the people who do. That was always a problem for which she found no sympathy. Everybody on the island could identify her by name while she was acquainted with only a smattering of people. She always felt at a disadvantage and exposed, especially during times that are best enjoyed privately. Slipped on the ice? Everybody knew. Kissed a boy? The gossip might as well have been on television. Flew off the handle in a rage for no reason? Every person on the island psychoanalyzed her and most pegged her as either crazy or dim. No matter what she did or which way she turned or where she hid or how she conducted herself, well or badly, she was always on display, and here it is happening again. The added aspect now is that her family is dramatically the subject of conversation today: her father is dead.

Maddy enters the house and immediately recalls, with apprehension, what she has done so many times before, fleeing home even though it was the last place on earth she wanted to be. *What a silly girl I am!* Some things are so hard to outgrow.

Still. She feels sheltered behind that closed door. And recognizes an ancient reprobate of a feeling. On the one hand, she's sheltered and safe. On the other, she's trapped.

Like I'm my own endangered species.

She's surprised, alarmed even, when someone rings the doorbell.

She hopes Simon Lescavage has come over at last, and if not she reminds herself to pay him a visit. He should be able to advise on what to do next with respect to the funeral arrangements. But it isn't him. Plainclothes Mounties are on her doorstep. The two men show their badges.

She didn't know that Mounties ever went anywhere in plain clothes.

"We're from Saint John," the one called Detective Isler explains, as if what difference that makes should be both obvious and respected.

"Do you mind if we step in?" the one called Detective Hopple asks.

"This is about my dad?"

"You have our sympathies, ma'am."

No one has ever called her *ma'am* before. A sign that she's getting older, she supposes. Or maybe Mounties learn to talk that way. "Sure. Come on in."

Once inside, they issue kind words with respect to her father's death, and since they are being considerate, she offers them tea. They both accept, which helps her to assume that this really is a courtesy call. She leaves them in the living room to their own devices while she puts the kettle on, and before it whistles she returns, sitting opposite the two of them. She spreads out her hands to ask, "What's this about? How can I help you with anything?"

"Do you know Reverend Simon Lescavage?" Isler queries.

"Of course. Yes. I was thinking about looking him up. People were trying to find him this morning, but I'm afraid I fell asleep. Exhausted, I guess."

"Understandable," Isler says. Hopple doesn't appear to share that point of view, but in any case, he says nothing. "I'm afraid I have bad news for you then."

She can scarcely believe what they say, and remains staring at them once they finish their summary of the details. Maddy feels horrified in a way that she's never experienced before and only the scream of the kettle's whistle penetrates her mood. Reverend Lescavage has been murdered. That's so hard to fathom. She bounds up to make the tea, and rushes back, her hands shaking.

"I don't believe it," she says finally. "I can't believe it."

"It is a shocker," Isler commiserates. "A troubling case. Exceptionally violent. I think this island is going to have a hard time coming to grips with that. If a killer is loose . . . well, the island's not that big, is it? I certainly don't want to alarm anyone, but there's no getting around it. We're in a frightening situation here."

"My God," she says quietly. "I still can't believe it."

The three remain quiet awhile, as though allowing the news to settle. Then Detective Hopple intrudes on the stillness. "May I ask, ma'am, when was the last time you saw the minister?"

Maddy thinks about it. "Three, four, years ago. Something like that."

The two men share a silent communication between themselves.

"What?" Maddy asks.

"You see, ma'am—"

"Please don't call me *ma'am*. I don't—" She pauses, feels that she must sound rude and senses in her voice her father's curt dismissal of others. "I'm sorry, it doesn't agree with me. It makes me sound *old*, or something."

"Pardon me. Miss Orrock, then," Isler says.

That sounds worse, but she's done with putting her neuroses on display.

Hopple takes over. "What we understand is this. Miss Matheson was here last night, looking after your father. She was relieved of that duty by Reverend Lescavage. The next person to arrive at this house was you. As far as we know. So are you saying that you did not encounter the reverend last night?"

Maddy does not promptly catch on to their line of inquiry. "That's what I'm saying, I guess."

"You guess," Isler says.

"Okay. I know. I came home. I found my father asleep in his bedroom. I was upset, actually, that he'd been left alone. Later, I realized that he wasn't sleeping. He was already dead. I didn't want to wake him, you see."

"I see," Isler murmurs.

"The point is, Simon Lescavage wasn't here."

The detective writes something in a little red notebook which he supports on his broad left thigh. "So you arrived home, found your father deceased, and you didn't contact anyone about that?"

She feels threatened. "That's right, Officer. Not at that time of night."

"Detective is the proper nomenclature, not Officer, just so you know."

"Who gives a shit?"

"Excuse me?"

"I'm sorry. What's this about? Why are you asking me these questions?"

Isler pauses a moment. Then speaks to her in a slow, low voice. "As you know, we're investigating the murder of Reverend Lescavage."

"I'm saddened by his death. I liked him. He was always kind to me. Not many on this island were. I'm horrified, in fact, if you want to know the truth. I'm probably in shock or whatever, but why are you talking to me, asking me these questions?"

"Because you're the last person to have seen him alive."

"I saw him three or four years ago! Nobody's seen him since?"

The detective puts his little book away. The tea is still steeping on the coffee table between them.

"There's no need for sarcasm," Isler warns her.

"I'm not—" Maddy stops herself. She wants to rampage, she knows. She's not ready for anything like this. It's crazy and she wants it to end immediately. She has the thought that her father would never put up with this, that he'd have had the man's badge by now. Both their badges. "It's not my intention to be sarcastic," she says in an even tone.

"You were the last person to see him alive," Hopple says.

Before she can react to that, Isler modifies the statement. "Alleged," he admits. "You're the last person alleged to have seen him alive."

"I did not see him last night. Or yesterday. Or today. Or this past week, month, or year. I could go on. But I did not see Simon Lescavage last night. I trust I've made myself clear. Is that all?"

They can tell that they are no longer entitled to tea.

"One more question," Hopple states. He's a man in his late thirties, with a basic Mountie mustache and a wine mark below his left ear. Maddy thinks of him as nondescript, not handsome, not ugly, not big, not small, not someone she would sleep with in this lifetime. If there happened to be an incidental social component to their lives, if they were members of the same church or golf club, she'd be courteous to him, even friendly. Nothing more than that. Not friends, but possibly, under the right circumstances, friendly.

She goes through all that in her head and doesn't know why.

"Oh sure," she says. Sarcasm creeps out again.

"How did you get here?"

"What do you mean?"

"To the island?"

"I drove up from Boston. That's where I live. I took a boat from the mainland."

"A boat," Isler repeats. "So not the ferry."

"My father was dying. I needed to get here in a hurry. I hired a boat. You can ask the skipper."

"We will. What's his name?"

"Stick McCarran. Know him? He's from Blacks."

"We'll look him up. So you took a boat over, at night, in the storm, and nobody saw you arrive or what you did after you arrived."

"It was nighttime!" she objects, catching his drift.

"I understand that. Nevertheless, you arrived at night, in a storm, when nobody was outside to see you or your movements. Right or wrong?"

"I'm done talking," Maddy says.

"Are you? You won't answer the question?"

"I answered it. You asked it twice. I would like to be left alone now." She doesn't know why she says it that way, exactly. She'd rather invite them to get the hell out of her house, but even after thinking about it a moment she only repeats herself. "I'd really like to be alone right now. My father, you know, did just die." She hates herself for playing that card, but figures that these outside policemen know nothing of her or her family and probably can't imagine how little she cares about her father's passing.

"I understand," Isler says, and rises. Hopple doesn't seem to understand, but he also stands. "Thank you for your time, Miss Orrock. I'm afraid that I have more difficult news for you."

"What now?" She remains seated, looking up at them.

"I've called for an autopsy on your father."

"What on earth for? He was ill and old."

"Yes. Of course. That's what will be confirmed, I'm sure. He was ill. He was old. But you were the last person to see him alive—"

"I was not. I never saw him alive last night."

"Allegedly, then. You are allegedly the last person to see two people alive. Mr. Orrock and Reverend Lescavage. One man unquestionably was murdered, the other is dead. So it behooves me to be thorough, to investigate the cause of your father's death, as well. Merely procedure, Miss Orrock. I wouldn't give it a second thought. Just wanted to let you know."

"Gee, thanks," she says, regretting her tone but helpless to break it off. "Look. I'm sorry that I'm not at my best. Back-to-back shocks. My father's death. Now Reverend Lescavage is gone. Three shocks—you think I might be involved somehow. I—I'm sorry. But I need some time to myself."

"Certainly. No need to see us out, Miss Orrock. We can find our own way."

She has no intention of seeing them out. She's glued to her chair, and realizes that now. They go without her help, and once they're gone Maddy pours herself a cup of tea. Poor Simon Lescavage! The real shocker is that someone out there thinks that she might have been responsible. Probably the townsfolk do. That's the running rumor by now. *That Maddy Orrock, she arrived back in the dead of night and went on a rampage, she did, probably killed her dad then sliced up the minister.*

And what did that cop say? It *behooves* him. Oh lord. She'll have to deal with that man again. The situation will *behoove* her to do so.

Maddy knows that she has a lot to take care of on the island, particularly with respect to her father's various businesses. Something has to be done about them. She only hopes that she can find help with that so she can get away from here, the sooner the better.

She loves this place, Grand Manan, it lives forever in her marrow, but she hates it, too. The crux of the problem is, she hates herself whenever she comes home.

TWELVE

The day is nothing but glorious by the time Sandra and Émile settle onto their front porch, with its grand view of the meadow sloping down to Whale Cove, purple lupines waving back and forth as though in greeting, across to the banquet of hills rising on the opposite shore. Émile fixes drinks. He's having an Italian lemon soda with Skyy vodka, she her usual pink cosmo. They have almonds to munch on, smoked salmon spread and crackers, and the salt air adrift on their nostrils.

"That was some guy," Émile says. She gets the reference. They knocked on the door of the man who lost his dog at sea and he came outside in tears. Peter Briscoe was shaking by the time they opened the hatch, and Sandra helped him to remain standing. But he slumped to his knees the moment his precious Gadget was revealed, then toppled onto the ground, releasing a mixture of guttural bellowing and gasping, a desperate cry. They couldn't take this sorrow, this lament, in part because they couldn't believe it, so over the top. Émile pegged him as an addict of some kind. He and Sandra helped him to get up halfway, then he burrowed his face in the dog's hide and endlessly wailed that he was sorry.

"I'm sorry, Gadget! I'm so sorry!"

He was too distraught to be comforted.

Eventually, he insisted on carrying the dog over to his pickup. He chose the front seat, making the carcass comfortable and saying that he knew a place, a good place, to lay poor Gadget to rest. The fisherman kept wiping tears from his eyes under a thick unibrow, and they both wanted to linger on with him, but there was no point as he wasn't going to speak coherently anytime soon. They patted him on the back, said goodbye, and steered for home.

Cocktail hour brings relief from that emotional morass. Sandra sits nestled in the cushions, her feet tucked up under her on the wicker love seat. Émile occupies the matching chair beside her, his immense legs stretched out toward the sea. The hour is magic, thanks to a crystal-blue sky and the waving grasses, the grand view, and this sense of utter ease. He's gathered that the island has serious, even shocking, troubles, but like the prissy man in a robe and the elevated shoes said down at the fake City Hall, none of it is any of his business.

The peace of their location seeps inside him, as well. While he believes that he may not deserve this, he is definitely ready to take it on, and perhaps he very much needs a time of reflection and recuperation. He and Sandra have agreed to give themselves more time, to see if they can't grasp what ails them, and rebuild their union, yet they must do so with the difficult understanding that it can all come apart in a flurry should they fail. Some dementia undermines them, obscure, rapacious, an internal cross-wiring that's taken away what was once secure and intimate and replaced it with what feels brokered, under-written, a play performed according to another's script. They don't quite feel themselves anymore when they're together, and that tears at both of them, each in his or her own way.

Sandra thinks he's spent too much time over his long career with bad guys and cops, that when he's with her that vulgar dance continues in some subliminal fashion. Émile has an idea that she has spent too much of her life with horses, establishing a relationship criteria with the animals that doesn't translate back to one-on-one with a human being as easily. Up to a point, they agree, one with the other. So here they are, away from cops and robbers but also free from horses, and so far, they're comfortable.

So when two Mounties, one in a tunic, the other in plain clothes, come around the corner of their cottage and intrude on their peace, Cinq-Mars is less than wholly cordial. He gets his back up immediately. Sandra has always liked Mounties because they share an affection for horses—they are the *Mounted* Police, after all—but this intrusion into the only real summer holiday of their lives is more than a bit much. She blames Émile, perhaps with just cause.

"How," she demands, the moment after the Mounties introduce themselves and before they state their business, "did you find us?" As if they are a pair like Bonnie and Clyde, out on the lam for years, retired from gunplay and living off the spoils of their holdups. On this old wooden stoop, she readily imagines a shotgun discreetly tucked behind the screen door, and they'll be dancing ecstatically in a hail of bullets by the next moment.

Or, if not bullets, entreaties. Same difference, to her mind.

The plainclothes guy's name is Isler, and he assures her that he hasn't been hunting them down. "I got a call, from the commander for Eastern Canada."

"Jean-Marc Racine," Cinq-Mars grunts.

"Him, yeah. My boss. I mean my big boss. I've never heard from him before. Never been in the same room. You've got some kind of pull."

"I didn't call him," Cinq-Mars protests.

"But he seems to know you're here," Sandra mentions under her breath.

Émile tries to wave away the comment. "He and I were talking on another subject. I may have mentioned that I was taking some time away. You know, he was shocked. He's never heard me say that. So he asked where."

"And you told him."

Émile shrugs. It didn't seem like such a big deal at the time.

"What's up?" he asks the intruders. He hasn't offered them a drink as yet, as they seem to have arrived on business.

Isler explains about the terrible death of the minister, Simon

Lescavage. "We've just come from interviewing the guy who found the body. His father was a convicted murderer, so maybe it's a family business, but we don't have a thing on him at this point. Only that he was out in last night's storm for no logical reason other than he likes big storms. Also, he says a group was camping up on the cliffs. Evidence shows somebody was up there, and we'd like to find out who, obviously."

"I don't know why you're telling me any of this," Émile says.

"Sure you do," Sandra contradicts him, and he anticipates some edginess between them to come out later on.

"Commander Racine contacted me," Isler says. He lets that hang in the air as an explanation.

Sandra takes up the challenge. "My husband is retired, first and foremost. As well, allow me to state the obvious for you. He's not a Mountie."

The comment is more pointed than Émile realizes, as the two cops seem sheepish now.

"I'm the problem," the other cop, Louwagie, maintains.

"You're not the problem," Isler states, and sighs as though he might not believe what he said.

"What problem? And guys, make it short and sweet. I'm supposed to be taking it easy with my wife here. We're having a drink. It's cocktail hour. I'd ask you to join us, but, you know, pardon my manners, I don't necessarily want you to stay, not until I know what's up."

That's going to win him brownie points with Sandra later on, he's sure.

"Another man has died," Isler reveals, deliberately not answering the question. "Natural causes, most likely. We're having an autopsy performed."

"Why?"

"To confirm natural causes. Primarily to give us a time of death. You see, a young woman came onto the island last night by fish boat. Through that big storm, if you can believe. Her father died sometime during the night. The other man, the one who was murdered, was in her father's house last night. So. She arrives mysteriously in the dark. Two men who were in her house are dead the next day. Suspicious, no?

I've called for an autopsy, since our experts are on the island for the murder anyhow. If we can pin down time of death, that might tell me if her father was alive or dead when she showed up. And it might help us guess when the other man left the house."

"Okay. Makes sense. But what does this have to do with me, and what's Corporal Louwagie's problem that you say is not a problem?"

The two cops again look at one another. Louwagie chooses to admit why he's a liability. "I have PTSD. In recovery, let's say. The brass have let me hide out here, assuming I only deal with drunks, drugs, and arson."

"Arson?" Cinq-Mars asks.

"It's a thing here," the uniformed Mountie explains. "It's how the locals get even when they feel they've been done an injustice. They're not into law and order so much, not in the traditional sense. It's more a case of you screw me and I'll burn your house down, or your car, or your boat, or your dinghy, or your back shed, depending on the level of the grievance."

"Only now there's been a murder. Which suggests a larger level of grievance," Cinq-Mars says.

"When somebody really gets ticked off, the usual practice is to hang the other person off a cliff for a spell. That usually gets the message across."

"Nice," Cinq-Mars says.

"Interesting," Sandra notes. The light is lovely at this hour across the fields, the birdsong and chatter hypnotic. She doesn't want to lose that sense of magic, of equilibrium, of peace, but this talk isn't helping. She really doesn't want to lose her husband to crime fighting once again.

Isler explains, "I'm the I.O. But I'm not stationed here, I'm out of Saint John. I can come in once, twice a week, tops. So Corporal Louwagie has to carry the load. This has been a gruesome crime and . . . well . . ."

"I'm not great with gruesome," Louwagie confirms. "The murder was a hell of a mess. That said, I'm handling it. I'm all right. I haven't fallen apart yet."

"Commander Racine thought that since you have this reputation, Detective Cinq-Mars, that you might be willing to back up Corporal

Louwagie while I'm engaged elsewhere. Talk him through it. Suggest. See that he stays on track."

"Make sure I don't come apart at the seams is what he really means," Louwagie says, cutting to the chase.

"Will you?" Émile asks him. "Come apart?"

"I don't think I will. I'm doing all right. The past hasn't totally come back to haunt me, not totally, not yet, but then again . . ."

"Then again what?"

"I haven't tried to sleep yet."

Shit, Cinq-Mars is thinking.

"Pretty gross, what I saw this morning. I can't pretend it doesn't bring up some bad stuff. Things I'm shaky about. I'll see a shrink. Talk about it. It's not good to hold that stuff in."

Shit shit shit, Cinq-Mars is thinking.

"I'm getting the picture," he says. "Corporal Louwagie, are you aware of any cults on your island?"

"Cults? Some of the churches are a bit wacko."

"Outside cults."

He says no.

"Then you might want to check out the old City Hall in Castalia. People in there are showing up from around the continent to try to learn how to fly. I don't mean in planes or ultralights. They're teaching themselves how to levitate. Without much success, I gather."

Louwagie is still staring at him without any sign of comprehension, while Isler's chin is wagging up and down.

"So you think people who think they can learn to levitate might be out in a storm at night," Isler says.

"Trying to marshal the forces of nature, or some such. Maybe hoping a lightning bolt will strike their collective ass and shoot them off the ground."

The plainclothes detective removes a red book from his shirt pocket and jots down that note. He looks at Émile then. "So you're already helping and you just arrived on the island."

"That's the limit of my support," Émile lets him know.

"Émile," Sandra says sharply. If he's declining their request for

assistance, she guesses that he's doing so on her account. She knows
that this might not be the best motivation in the long run.

"No. Look. I've not had a summer off my entire life. I want that.
Specifically, I want this summer. So, gentlemen, I don't care what's going
on with your investigation. I'm not interested in being an informed
party. Tell Racine not to call. If you want my advice, let Corporal
Louwagie go with this as far as he can, and if he can't, get somebody else
in here. Just don't call me. That's final. Guys, been a pleasure. Nice meeting you both. Now if you don't mind, I'm going to sit here awhile and do
nothing but listen to the birds and drink vodka until the fish boats return and the sun goes down. If that's okay with you. Or even if it's not."

Sandra knows that her husband possesses the ability to make it
known to all and sundry when he will broach no further argument, and
people always get that. These two policemen get that now. She gets it,
too. Whatever point she might raise will fall on deaf ears, and for once
she is quite happy with that. No blame falls on her for his decision.
Émile has spoken. He is not going to be on this case. Nobody, not even
Émile himself, she can tell, doubts that for a second.

"Thank you, sir," pronounces Isler. "I'm sorry for our intrusion."

"Thank you," Louwagie says, and his voice conveys that he refers to
more than tolerating the visit. He wasn't given a ringing endorsement,
although he did receive exactly the feedback he wants the brass to hear.
He does not know if he can take whatever is coming in the deep dark
of the night, when the trembles may overtake him. Yet, time has gone
by, and he does want an opportunity to find out. It's time to give this
up or get on with it. To decide if he is healthy enough for this line of
work, and if not, to face that fact.

The men depart, the couple gaze off across the meadow and sip their
drinks, and after about five minutes go by, Émile hazards to say, "Where
were we?"

Sandra touches the back of his hand tenderly. "Right here, Émile,"
she says. "We were right here where we are right now."

The first of the fish boats, with a bright green hull, eases its way
back into Whale Cove at the end of a long day's work.

PART 2

THIRTEEN

The sun has set beyond the distant hills to the west, the sky on the horizon turning a brilliant crimson that reflects on the sea between Grand Manan and the mainland. The tide is rising as Aaron Roadcap departs his cabin on the steep slope of Dark Harbour, waves rolling gently across the long flat plain of the sand-and-rock shore. Unlike the previous night, when he embarked to relish the storm in solitude, on this peaceful night he seeks companionship, and walks down a trail to the waterside, then up a separate path that draws him back into the thick trees of the cliffside. He carries on past the shacks and ramshackle cabins of his neighbors. Enough light lingers in the sky to make out the rocks, stones, and hollows along the path, and to avoid patches still muddy from the downpour.

Roadcap is strikingly handsome, with a waviness to his black hair, which he wears just a bit long around the ears and at the nape of his neck. His shoulders are classically broad, and on the hottest days of summer, out in the shallows cutting dulse with his shirt off, not only do the women giggle and make no bones about their admiration of his pectorals, his six-pack, his waist, his tush, the men let loose a few catcalls as well. They laugh, but their overt mockery perhaps is feigned. Their admiration differs from the women's only by being tinged with envy.

He takes longer strides up a steeper embankment to gain the tumble-down cabin he's heading for. The roof overhanging the long porch is tinged with moss. Chairs face the sea and branches have been cut away to clear the view. Four men sit out tonight, their voices muted in the hush of the evening. At the near end, a woman wearing glasses knits, and at the far end, her young daughter sits in a huddle on an old rocker above her terrier, her legs pulled up, her chin resting on her knees. She fiddles with her fingers, bored among the adults, but perks up as Roadcap arrives. Steps he climbs at the end of the balcony aren't rotted yet, they only look that way. They're often damp and usually bereft of sunlight under the canopy of the forest, the humidity having stained them green. They're slippery. The porch repeats the same look—damp, sturdy enough to warrant sitting upon without being in immi-nent danger of skidding down the cliff. Not a place where anyone wants to arrive gussied up. Which is of no account, as the regulars on hand tonight and those who habitually show up rarely step out of their work clothes.

Pulling up the first free chair he comes to, Roadcap sits between Angela and the others. He leans back and gives a wink down the aisle to Della Rae, whose happy grin sails back to him across the porch.

"Guess we yakked about the devil too loudly in our haste," the man called Frank attests. He has the grubbiest appearance of the bunch, having not washed up since coming off the beach where he cuts and collects dulse. Grime streaks his forehead. Not unlike the latest arrival, the others have cleaned up and look half-decent. "Ears burning there, Roadcap?"

"Is that what drew me down to this hell pot?" he jousts.

"Cops drive in, cop cars go back out all day," the man known as Chip says. He's exaggerating. About sixty, he's a scrawny man, wizened. Three days growth of white whiskers skim his jaw. His fingers have been purpled and made gnarly by time, bad weather, and long stretches of work out in the sun and during cold winters. "If I get a chance, maybe I'll take your cabin over."

"I'm not selling," Roadcap replies. He knows what Chip's getting at.

"Who's buying? Thinking about taking it over, that's all, once you're outta there, doing time for this or that. Confiscating. That's what I had in mind. Said nothing about buying."

A few men chuckle, although Roadcap appears less amused. Plump Angela peers over her glasses to see how he takes the ribbing, finds that he's all right, then goes back to swishing her needles around.

"The Mounties didn't book me yet," Roadcap reports. "So the cabin stays with me. Beer for sale, Angie?"

"Cooler's half-full, Aaron. Your money's about as good as the next man's. Maybe better."

"No discount for the better, I suppose."

"Nothing much changes, hey?"

Roadcap helps himself from a cooler that's flooded with melting ice and twists off the cap. He drops three loonies into the tray on the windowsill and doesn't take change. That's what she means when she says his money is better than the next man's, as the next man rarely tips. He takes a long pull on his Moosehead and sits down again in the same chair, and this time the terrier shoves itself up from its nap. With some difficulty, he stretches his old bones, then waddles down to say hello to the newcomer. Roadcap leans forward and gives the dog's floppy ears a vigorous scratch.

"Why they interested in you at all?" Chip asks. Everyone turns to take in Roadcap's reply. "If they was looking for me, I'd understand that more."

"You heard about Lescavage?"

No one answers, and the quiet is strained and holds a portent. Even Della Rae is looking down the porch at him, interested in the adults' conversation now, and Roadcap, as if summoned, looks up.

"Don't jump to conclusions, people. I didn't do it. I happened to find the body, that's all."

They continue to stare down at him until a weathered blond man whose name is Kai finally says, "Jesus, Aaron."

Angela puts her knitting down. "You can say that ten times over and tack on a Hail Mary to boot. You found the body? We heard it was gore city. The reverend got cut up, they say. What's supposed to be on the inside of him was outside."

Roadcap resumes patting the dog's lovely soft ears. He sees a flea jump and takes his hand away then.

"Brutal," he concurs. "Yeah."

Frank, the last man in the row before the girl, declares, "Holy Mother of Crap."

Everyone seems to agree. They join in a mutual silence.

Roadcap breaks it. "You want me to talk about what I saw. Dish up the gore city details. But that's not going to happen, so how about we change the subject? There's a kid sitting around out here."

"Who, me?" Della Rae asks.

"Yeah, you. What are you now anyway, seven?"

She sighs with some elaboration, pokes out her tongue, and wags her head at the porch roof, as if she's heard this joke before and found it tiresome then. Secretly, she's tickled to be the center of attention.

"I'm two and a half, okay? So there."

Kai asks, "How old are you really, kid? No, seriously, I forgot."

"I'm nine! Okay? Got it? Nine? Christ, you're gonna ask me again tomorrow."

"Don't take the Lord's name in vain, Della Rae," her mother trumpets in a singsong voice.

"You do."

Men on the porch say "*Oooooo*" to mark her lippiness.

"Never in vain, dear," Angela disagrees. "In anger, sometimes. In tribute, on occasion. In exasperation, quite often. But never in vain."

Della Rae wags her head at the porch roof again.

"Let's hear it for all that's holy," Chip proposes. "I mean, isn't it the fuck? Lescavage gets sliced up. His belly fat is cut right out. All his disgusting squirmy stomach rope is lying on the ground. What do you think he did to piss somebody off that much?"

"Could be there's a madman on the loose," Angela says. "Could be he didn't piss nobody off. Could be this is what you call a random act of violence."

"My ass. He pissed somebody off."

"My mom's right," Della Rae argues. "I mean, lookit here. There's three or four madmen sitting right on this porch. Any one of you freaks could've done it."

She smiles and giggles all on her own, and while the men pull faces, they are pleased to have been singled out for her notice.

"These guys don't think that's so funny, Della Rae," Roadcap tells her, even though that might not be the case. "Know why?"

"Why?" Della Rae leans forward to get a better look at him.

"Because it might be true."

They give out a few hoots over that.

Chip has a position paper he wants to put forward. "I might be a loon, sure. I'll cop to that. Nobody's ever accused me of being fucking sane. But I want it known that I ain't the nuttiest loon in this saloon." His rhyme tickles Della Rae, and she laughs in a quick burst. "That's all I ask for in my life, that no man and no nine-year-old girl think I'm the worst of the bunch."

"Yeah, that's not asking for much," Angela agrees.

"You're the pick of the litter there, Chip," Roadcap says, and everyone is smiling and being agreeable for now.

"Maybe second-worst?" Della Rae asks, and the men "*Oooooo*" again.

Their round of amusement sputters out, and it's left to Hollister, who's a short, stocky man with thighs the size of fat tree stumps and hands like fishnets, who's not spoken all night, to take them back to where most of the men want to go with their talk in the rapidly failing light.

"Shit, man," he remarks, his voice a deep baritone. "You're a Roadcap. Taken in for questioning. I mean, you? After what happened to your dad, you couldn't've been too happy."

"Just doing my civic duty, Hollis." He resumes giving the dog attention.

"Fuck that shit," Hollister tells him.

"How about we change the subject?" Aaron Roadcap suggests.

"How about we don't?" Hollister retorts. "I mean, get off the shitbox, hey. Lescavage, he was all right. Okay for a preacher. I went to some of his funerals. He did all right. He made sense. He came around here. Married us, buried us. He didn't ask no questions. Hey, he didn't deserve nothing like what happened, not from the shithole I'm sitting over."

They were quiet awhile and then Angela said, "That was his first big mistake."

"What was?" Frank asks.

"Coming around here."

Others chuckle lightly but Hollister wants to keep the talk serious. "Come on. Get real here. Somebody cut him open? Can you imagine that? Imagine that. Right here on Grand Manan. What the fuck? Who does that?"

Roadcap takes a long pull, then says, "That's what the cops want to know. If anybody has an answer, they want you to talk to them."

"Fuck that shit," Hollister says again.

"They're not looking straight at you?" Frank asks, looking hard at Roadcap, who shrugs.

"They'll look at everybody. They have to. It's their job. They're going to ask if Angela didn't do it. Or Hollister. Or Frank. Or Chip."

"Or you," Chip counters.

"Yeah. Or me. Why not? I'm not immune."

"Don't let them railroad you, son."

Roadcap enjoys another swallow, then shoots a glance at Frank. He sincerely wants to reassure him. "You can take that to the bank. I'm not going to let that happen anytime soon."

The men are thoughtful awhile and return to their drinking and their quiet. Chip gets another beer for himself and one for Hollister, who pays him when he brings it over. Angela eyeballs the coins in the dish. Sufficient, just short on tips. She's asked herself before and does so again: How can she get these guys to tip, if not on a daily basis then at least weekly? Either that or she'll raise her prices, and she knows they won't like that. They'll boycott for a month. They'll return eventually, but a month without their contributions will be hard to bear.

Della Rae gets up and crosses the floor. She's so quiet that Roadcap doesn't notice her coming until she taps him on the shoulder. He smiles, then lets her slide over a knee and she snuggles into him as he tucks an arm around her. The other men are watching, and in a way they are marveling, although this is a sight they have seen for years. They've heard Angela's admonition before, but she feels that the matter bears repeating. She doesn't even bother to look up from her knitting to say it, either.

"That's a privilege Aaron has earned, gentlemen. Don't none of you other guys get your ideas."

They always have ideas, everybody knows that. Ideas can't be helped, but rules are rules, and they not only understand the edict but accept that its repetition is undoubtedly necessary.

Kai rises and drags his chair with him. He fits it in closer to Roadcap's. He leans forward to speak very quietly to him while the child is on his lap, although the others, if they strain their ears, can hear, too. Della Rae observes Kai as he talks, while growing sleepy.

"This changes things, Aaron. Don't it, you think?"

"What does?" Roadcap asks.

"You know what I mean."

"The preacher being dead? What does that change?"

"Not Lescavage," Kai says, and Roadcap understands him now.

"Orrock."

"Don't it change the way the wheels turn? Hell, don't it change the dirt we walk on? The rain that falls? I swear to God, I hear the fucking whales talk about it when they come up for air. The tide might not come back tomorrow, they say. We had a day to get used to the idea, but I can't. You?"

Perhaps the girl's sleepiness influences him, but Roadcap stifles a yawn.

"I suppose it changes things somewhat," he says.

Kai leans farther in. "Any suspicion on you, get out from under that,

Aaron. Get me? You don't need shit like that. It can muck things up. Now's the time for action. Right? Am I right?"

Rather than answer, Roadcap asks, "Who made you my adviser in chief?"

Straightening in his chair, Kai prepares to stand and move away again. But he has more to say. "Just remember who your father's best friend was, Aaron. Remember that before you go forgetting who your own friends are. You always think you don't have none. That's not the only thing you're wrong about. Some of us, we have your back."

The two men stare each other down, then Roadcap makes an infinitesimal gesture with his chin and Kai understands to lean back in again, this time to listen. Roadcap leans in also, so that they're close together, with the girl between them.

"Any time you're with me, out on the flats or wherever, don't be at my back, Kai. Just don't guard my back ever. Don't stand behind me. Stay out in front of me where I can keep an eye on you."

"Aaron, don't talk like this."

"Stand where I can see you at all times, Kai. Take this as a solemn warning. And yeah, you're right. You couldn't be more right. What happened today. Orrock's death. That changes everything. Just so you know."

"I think we understand each other," Kai says, loudly enough for everyone to hear.

"I'm not sure that we do." Roadcap gestures for the man to lean in close again. He whispers directly into his ear, so that even the girl sitting on his lap can't hear. "Don't strike a match in my vicinity, Kai. Nowhere near my property. If anything of mine burns, I'm going to assume it was you who did it, even if it wasn't, and you get to pay the consequences, whether you deserve it or not."

"That's not fair," Kai objects.

"I'm not selling fair. I'm giving away a free warning. Don't strike a match. Make sure nobody else does, either."

The man backs away from their close contact.

"I was a friend to your father," Kai attests. "You should remember that."

"That was then. This is now." He gestures for him to lean in again, and reluctantly Kai does so, but only partway. "Have you never asked yourself why you're still alive? That's why. But that ticket's been punched. Its final destination is coming up soon. Get off that train, Kai. Get out of the caboose. I don't want to hear about your old friendship again. You said things have changed? Right. From now on, only what's happening in the present counts. That's what's changed."

Kai can tell there's no beating down the other man's animosity. He stands and starts to return his chair to its old spot, but instead puts it down and walks off the porch. He disappears along the descending trail. Roadcap doesn't bother to watch him go, and rocks Della Rae lightly on his thigh. It's dark out. He sips his beer, and she closes her eyes in the gloom and curls more tightly into him.

Everybody heard a good chunk of what he said.

They are free to imagine the rest.

Angela says, both emphatically and gently, "Anytime you speak to somebody like that again at my house, kindly take my daughter off your kneecap first. Before any fist gets swung."

The girl seems ready for a deep sleep, and closes her eyes against him.

"So, Aaron," Hollister asks, "is there a war on? Like a war on of some kind?"

Roadcap adjusts the girl's weight across his lap and lets her lean more fully into him. He seems to be contemplating the question. "Let's put it this way," he suggests. "You know what we say when we're out cutting dulse on a good day?"

The query receives no reply.

"Come on, what do we always say?"

Frank takes a stab at it. "I guess that would be, keep your knives sharp."

"Keep your knives sharp," Roadcap warns them.

Hollister utters a little surprised cough, then says, "I hear that."

Nobody dares utter another word as they stare out into the night. At their backs, the moon's rising. Although they can't see it yet, they do see its reflection on the dark surface of the sea.

FOURTEEN

Madeleine Orrock is not accustomed to being disorganized. She is also not accustomed to housework, and doubts that she ever did any in this home while growing up, other than to keep her own room tidy to blunt her father's commentary. He entered her bedroom only when it got really messy, so that was sufficient motivation to clean up.

Yet her second morning on the island finds her both disorganized and doing housework. She knows that other matters ought to take precedence, in particular the funeral arrangements, which have been thrown to the wind with the demise of her local minister. Now she's not sure which way to turn and is intimidated about going back on the street to ask anyone. She needs to get over that, and overcome an internal lassitude that's settling unnaturally upon her, so she undertakes the vacuuming, hoping that a dose of physical activity will jump-start her synapses and firm up her resolve to broach what is necessary.

She's just put the machine away and is staring out the front window when her father's housekeeper comes up the walk. She recalls that her name is Ora, with an *O*, as the young woman is proud to say. At times in her life she's introduced herself as "Maddy" and thought to interject, "But I'm not mad." She was never wholly confident that she was justified to utter the line, as it might be untrue. Ora, on the other hand, breezes through life correcting the mental spelling of everyone she meets, first thing, wanting the world to know that she's nobody's aura.

Maddy has the door open before she's halfway up the steps.

"I've got cookies!" the housekeeper exclaims. She has a way of mounting stairs that seems cumbersome, even oafish, although on a level footing she's not that way. Her grin is wide and bright and perhaps that's what has Maddy glad to see her. Either that or she's finally in the mood for company. "Lo and behold, hang on to your silverware, I've got muffins, too!"

Unlike yesterday, this time Maddy lets her in.

Nervously, they wander into the living room together and Ora Matheson agrees to sit, although that feels odd to her and she makes a point of saying so. "I never thought these chairs were built for a bum like mine. I mean, a poor girl's." She finds that her anatomy fits quite well, and squiggles around some. "Of course, I thought if I sat in one during working hours and your father caught me, this is before he got sick, he'd swat me with a broom. Maybe the stick end. Now I'm scared he still might!"

Maddy offers coffee.

Ora accepts tea. "We can have a muffin! I made them myself."

"With butter?"

"Loads!"

Maddy figures she might as well have tea, too, and allows a pot to steep in the kitchen, bringing out just the cups and saucers first, then the milk and sugar.

"My goodness," Ora says.

"What?"

"Usually, that's me doing the serving. If my mom could see me now, she'd be screaming. She'd want me begging your forgiveness for my unbridled—that's what she'd call it, most likely—my *unbridled temerity!* My mom *loves* big words. All strung together. You should hear her talk sometimes, though she's been quiet lately. I think because she smashed up the truck. Ran it into a ditch. I told her, 'Mom, no biggie, it was already smashed, often,' but I think her pride hurts the most, though her face took some knock. Ugh. Black and blue. I'd say more blacker than bluer."

"I see," Maddy says.

"But you don't want to hear about that," Ora says, and Maddy excuses herself to fetch the teapot.

When she returns they each remark on the beauty of the day and agree that a run of good weather would be nice. They are awkwardly quiet awhile until Ora conveys that she's not sure if she is expected to pour the tea or if Maddy will. "I don't know myself what's right," she says.

"Not a problem, Ora. I'll pour." Still, she lets it steep another moment or two, which is when she realizes that she has her father's knack to make the other person uneasy. She probably takes a measure of her father's enjoyment in observing others grow frustrated with their own unease. She pours, smiles, and simultaneously they take a sip before biting into the muffins. Maddy compliments the chef. "I'm usually not into these things, but these are pretty good."

"Thanks. The cookies—I shouldn't say so, but. The cookies are to die for."

"I'm not into cookies, either, but based on the muffins, I believe you."

They sip and munch and release little smiles.

Then Ora says, "It's been my best-paying job, working for your old man, so a bit of hit in the pocketbook, if you know what I mean, him dying and all, so I was wondering, you know, if you had a chance, as they say, to reconsider."

"Reconsider?"

"My employment. I'm good at doing the cleaning, the washing up, making the beds and all that. I can look after the place for you, while you're here and after you're gone away again, if you go away again. Are you going to sell?"

"Do you think I'd find a buyer?"

"Beats me. Out of my price range. In your range, I have no clue.

Somebody from off-island, I suppose, with the big bucks. You never know."

"Hmm," Maddy ponders.

"Like another professor, like all those professors up the hill."

"Yes," Maddy says, as she knows about them, "the Harvard gang. I teach there myself although I'm not part of their club. They're well-heeled—this house, though, is too rich for their blood. The thing is, Ora, I've already done the cleaning, and there's no washing up to speak of. Right now, I feel the need to do my own housework."

"That's not how rich people behave," Ora scoffs.

"Isn't it? How many rich people do you know?"

Ora thinks about it, then with a sheepish grin sticks up one finger.

"And he's dead now, right?"

Ora agrees. Maddy cocks an eyebrow to claim victory for her point.

"What about the businesses?" the younger woman asks. "Are you selling them, too? I guess you have to, hey? What do you know about salmon or dulse or the fish plant? Too bad your daddy had no sons. Ha-ha, for more reasons than one."

Putting her cup down on a side table, Maddy knows she's about to be mean. The impulse surprises her, as it comes upon her so naturally. At least in this house it does. "Actually, Ora, I know everything there is to know about dulse, salmon farming, the fishery and the fish plant. I was born and raised on this island, don't forget, my father's daughter. You obviously don't know this—he had me working at his side and at sea, hard at work, since I was a toddler."

"Really? I didn't know. I didn't think rich girls—Of course, I'm younger than you, so I never saw you at it, I was too young to be look-ing, if you know what I mean. So, since you know all about the busi-nesses, are you selling them off?"

As she turns away, Maddy smiles, and in a way she is finding her own reactions more humorous than anything else. Still, she asks Ora, "Are you asking for yourself, or for the whole island?"

The young woman bursts out laughing. She needs a moment to control herself. "You're right," she says. "You're right! There's really no difference. Tell me, you tell the world! My mom will agree with you on that. Of course, if you tell *her* something, you might as well send a radio signal throughout the entire *universe*."

Then Ora gazes at her, as though confident that Maddy will answer.

She's almost forgotten the question. "Oh," Maddy says, "most likely. I'll see. I will not be living here, that's for sure."

"You'll go back to your professoring work. Do you think anybody is buying businesses like ours? On this island, like they say, who's got the money, honey?"

"Maybe I'll sell to the Irving family. They own ninety percent or whatever of New Brunswick already. Maybe they'd like a little more."

"They're so rich, they won't live here though. If they need a house-keeper, they already have one, I bet. Or two. Or ten!"

"I suppose that's true." Maddy's glad that her tea is about done and the muffin consumed. She was happy for a spot of company, now she's ready for peace and quiet again.

"So you don't know the *professors* who live up the hill?"

"Not personally, no."

"What does that mean, not personally?"

"It means I know of them, one or two I've met, but I don't know them."

"Oh. Well. Maybe if you meet any while you're here—I mean, they'll talk to you before they talk to the likes of me. Only natural. Unless by accident maybe, an *excuse me* if they bump into me at the farmers' market and nearly knock me down. So if that's the case you could ask them for me, you know, as a favor for looking after your dad, and I think I did a good job with that, to be honest."

If she's finished her pitch, it doesn't matter, as Maddy's lost the thread. "I'm sorry, Ora, ask them what?"

"Oh! If I can be their housekeeper. Do you mind? I'm looking for jobs, see?"

Maddy confirms that if she bumps into one or two she'll be happy to ask the question. She knows that neither situation is likely, bumping into anyone in that group or, if she does, addressing the ambitions of a housekeeper. She keeps that to herself and lets Ora think otherwise.

"Okay, then," Ora says, and Maddy assumes that she's on her way out the door. She's miscalculated. "So, did you learn anything? After what I let you in on yesterday, have you figured anything out at all?"

"What did you let me in on?" She really has no clue.

"Don't you remember? I told you that our job is to find stuff out, about like what the Mounties are up to. So did you? Find stuff out?"

Taken aback by this turn, Maddy recognizes that she's being included in the local gossip circle, as a possible source for more. "I think what I know about the whole thing, everybody knows."

"Yeah. I figured. The Mounties talked to me. I didn't like the old one from the mainland much. Not because he's from away, although that, too, but because he's such a dunderhead, don't you think? Anyway, he's left. He's off the island. Like in that TV show."

"He'll be back, I'm sure," Maddy says.

"Do you think? Ugh. Shit me."

This time she's genuinely curious, and not being merely polite when she asks, "Why? What's the problem?"

"I'm more worried about you than me, of course. Did you like the muffins?"

"They're fabulous. Why worry about me?"

"Oh, you know, I got an alibi. So I'm okay. But you don't, not really, right?"

"Why would I need an alibi?"

Ora is surprised by the question, as though perhaps she hasn't thought of something and that's why it's not obvious to her. "You know. Reverend Lescavage was here. Then the next thing, he's dead. In between, you came here."

Maddy stares back at her. She realizes that she's learning something that hadn't occurred to her before. "Of course, you were here, too, Ora, and so was Reverend Lescavage, then the next thing is, he's dead."

"It's that old one, from the mainland, that's the cop I don't like."

"What's your alibi, then?" Maddy feels her heart rate tick up a notch. Her palms perspire. She doesn't need more trouble, and understands that she has no precious alibi to prove her whereabouts. She arrived in a storm, in the dark, while the electricity was out. Anybody seeing her out a window at that hour wouldn't know who she was. Though she figures, and thinks this through at lightning speed, nobody can accuse her of anything, either, a fresh arrival on the island, whereas this somewhat dippy girl, who really knows what she is up to or what's going on with her? She definitely had contact with the deceased *before they died*.

"Oh, a good one, my alibi. I went over to my boyfriend's house. He'll vouch for me for sure. I told them I didn't think you did it."

Maddy looks off toward the edge of the carpet, then looks back at her. Her voice is quite low now. "Excuse me?" she says.

"I vouched for you. Sure I did. I said, just because you hated your father and never came to see him the whole time he was sick, that doesn't mean you had anything to do with it. I told him your father knew he was going to die."

"Wait. Wait a minute. What do you mean, 'do with it'? Do with what?"

"Your father. That policeman, the old one, he said it. He said it was a curious thing that a man dies in one house and the only person reported to be with him then gets murdered himself. So he asked about me."

"About you."

"Yeah, because I was there, too. Here, I mean, in this house. Like you said. So I gave him my alibi. I was with Petey. Do you know Petey? Petey Briscoe. He remembers you, he says, but maybe he was too young back then for you to remember him. Anyway, he has his own boat now, Petey does. He fishes. So Petey vouches for me and then the dunderhead starts asking what he really wants to ask. I could tell. That bit about me needing an alibi, that was all for show, I think. He really wanted to ask about you."

"Me," Maddy says. She feels her blood pooling in her heels.

"Yeah. But don't sweat it, I vouched for you. I told him it had to be a coincidence. He's a stubborn old mule, though. He keeps asking his old mule questions. I told him what your father knew and that seemed to satisfy him somehow, get him out of my face anyway."

"Ora, what do you mean?" Maddy asks. She makes the effort to remain perfectly calm. "What did my father know?"

"Only two things. That's all. At the end, your old man was sure of only two things in this world. One was, you were on your way home to see him, and the other was, you know, that he was going to die. So that's what I told the copper. Was that wrong? It helps with your alibi, don't you think? That you were on your way to see him, and your old man knew it, and he knew that he was going to die."

Maddy falls still awhile.

Ora bounces up. "Okay! No jobs here! Feel free to let the house go all messy! Don't do the dishes! Don't vacuum! Then you'll have to hire me again! Remember. I don't come cheap, but I'm worth it!"

Out she goes, and Maddy remains alone and tired on the sofa, contemplating life on this island that she so loves. Why did it always grate against her here, why did life's capricious and renegade nature always find a way to seek her out for special attention while she was here when all that she really ever wanted—*all* that she ever wanted—was to be left alone?

FIFTEEN

Initially, to Émile's chagrin, but very much to Sandra's delight, they discover that once a week the village of North Head is animated by a lively, open-air market. Folks who might otherwise never say boo to one another arrive from every island nook to barter, converse, and frolic. As reluctant as Émile has always been to devote a minute, let alone precious holiday time, to shopping, the atmosphere of the market is enchanting and gathers him into its eclectic fold. Soon he's indulging a secret pleasure to his heart's content, as the people watching is terrific. All the better that the milling throngs embody a motley mix of haberdashery, of varied cultures and interests.

Old-timers, now done with their lives at sea, and older women devoted to grandchildren the rest of the week but released to their own joys for a morning, come by. Kids high on the jukebox of colors and talk and indeterminate noise run loose and shove and holler. Scatterings of young women push baby carriages. Other folk—not all, but some in distinctively peculiar dress—who hail from an island hamlet known as Dark Harbour, broker trinkets and knitted clothing and show a propensity for jocularity and sly, ribald chatter amid dour men sharing flasks. And girls flaunt their tresses as various jumbles of both talkative and taciturn adolescent boys check them out while pretending a greater interest in passing cars. They all converge and meld as though swept along by a tidal bore.

Émile discovers a coterie of vagabond seniors, who live modestly, the majority in trailers and vans, who park themselves on the island for the summer and drift to Florida come fall. Snowbirds who are not well-heeled, but they've adjusted to their circumstances, having figured out the means to make their wandering pay and enhance their latter years with adventure. They also sell items to the tourists, such as polished walking sticks for the Grand Manan trails, shawls for the cool sea air, bric-a-brac souvenirs, jewelry made from beads, stones, and beach glass for the ladies, and spiffy hats for the men. A former schoolteacher sells potions and a former plumber barters the world's best glue. Émile buys a walking stick for twenty bucks that he knows costs no more than two bits' worth of varnish to produce and is happy to do so. He's charmed by the instrument and also by the spry old guy in his eighties who sells it to him.

All around, voices are merry and the time happily festive.

Émile catches sight of Sandra tucking purchases away in her bag, including foodstuffs and books, knickknacks and clothing accessories. He's happy that she seems so delighted. If he's not mistaken, she's bought fudge, and he's especially glad about that. The warm sunny day contributes to the mood, but the potpourri of wares, the wild mix of people, a seasoning of sixty-year-old transplanted hippies from another time and weathered local fishermen, perhaps also from another era, market gardeners and craftsmen and tourists from every which place, kids and old folk combined, everyone under the influence of good cheer, puts an exclamation point on the fun of the hour. Sandra sees him noticing her and smiles back.

She hopes that he didn't see the fudge, a surprise.

"Hello there," a voice addresses Émile Cinq-Mars. He expects another hawker in his ear when he turns, but the man is not standing behind a stall, and anyway seems too well dressed. An ascot, for starters, with a monocle tucked into the chest pocket of a pinstriped vest. Like him, he's a buyer, not a seller, or at least someone who's wandering through, and he's vaguely familiar. The man issues a reminder. "Yesterday. Car crash. For want of a better word."

"Right," Émile recalls. "You drove that poor lady into a ditch."

The fellow, who's thin and nearly as tall as Émile, knows instantly that he's kidding and laughs him off. "My mission in life," he adds. "Drive anyone not behind the wheel of a Mercedes right off the road. Claim my proprietary rights to all asphalt surfaces."

"How'd she get on at the hospital?"

"None the worse for wear. Apart from her nasty abrasions. I, meanwhile, was nearly talked into an early grave. Once she gets going, hold on. I hit the martinis pretty hard after I got home. I'm surprised to make it out this morning." As he speaks, his white eyebrows are animate. Thin to nonexistent on top, his hair gathers in a longish wave at the base of his neck. His narrow visage is rimmed with liver spots. He exhibits an air of good humor, intelligence, and, Cinq-Mars concludes, money. "Sir, I must say that I want to thank you. Yesterday you came along at an opportune moment, as our dispute was at risk of becoming acrimonious. You took charge and found a solution. I was about to lose my cool. I was only trying to help but making a royal botch of it, and the truth is, you did both the lady and me a good turn. As I told my wife, whoever that masked man was, he's done this sort of thing before."

"Guilty," Cinq-Mars admits. "Cop. Retired."

"Ah! I thank you, for the loan of your expertise, Officer. Professor Jason DeWitt, sir. Pleased to make your acquaintance once again."

"Émile Cinq-Mars." At that moment, Sandra comes over, and he adds, "My wife, Sandra, whom you met yesterday."

The dandy tips his cap and repeats his own name for her. "I have a summer home on the road up to Seven Days Work. You're visiting?"

Sandra shares where they are staying and he points out that they're "practically neighbors," inviting them up for an afternoon cocktail on a day of their own choosing. "It's the only constant in my life. Late-afternoon drinks overlooking the sea the moment the sun dips below the yardarm. You've no doubt heard about our murder. Wretched business. Having a policeman come visit will be reassuring, and informative, I might imagine."

In other words, Émile interprets, in a manner of speaking he's being asked to sing for his supper. Or for a drink. He accepts the man's card and promises to call, although Sandra wants to know, as they move off, "Are we going?"

"House on a cliff, up high. We might. For the view."

"I'm game if you promise to talk about more than murder."

"Solemn vow. I am not interested in this island's body count."

"You can be induced."

"My will is nothing if not strong," he quips.

Returning to their Jeep, Émile takes the bag from Sandra as it has some weight. He tramps along with it over a shoulder while his newly acquired walking stick in his opposite hand stabs the pavement. He's feeling like an alien in a new land, and enjoying the sensation. At the car, a closer inspection of her merchandise confirms the fudge.

"Émile!" she admonishes. "Get your nose out of there this instant!"

Another purchase though, a secondhand book, instigates his curiosity. "Seriously? You? Numerology?"

"It caught my eye."

"Hunh."

"Oh, don't make a federal case out of it. Something for me to dillydally with over the summer."

"What federal case?"

She wants him off the subject. "What's next for our day, Émile? What are you up for?"

He brandishes the polished, curvy walking stick, thick yet light and gnarled with knots. An object of exquisite beauty. "Look at me. Put my boots on and I'm set for a hike." That's what lured them to this island, the magnificent walking trails across the cliffs overlooking the sea. "What say you?"

She was hoping he'd suggest it.

———

Coming away from the flurry of the market, the solitude of the trail feels all the more pronounced. Keen early risers have gone ahead, while others wait to have lunch before embarking on the trek, so in between those groups they have the path to themselves. They've studied trail maps and guidebooks, and know they will be led over the top of Seven Days Work, with its astral views of the Bay of Fundy. Rising straight from the sea, it can be scaled from its base by only the most skilled and daring of rock climbers, and only then with strategy and care. The sheer, towering rock face exhibits the geographic ages of the earth—the planet's oldest exposed rock is present here—and from the top a stunning view. Then comes Ashburton Head, followed by the Bishop.

"Wait a minute," Sandra stops to say, snagged by a thought. On her left, a peaceable meadow is lit by wildflowers and graced by a following breeze. To her right, the waters of the bay sparkle far below.

"What is it?"

"That murder took place along this trail."

"No problem. The scene's clean by now," her husband assures her.

"Then it's not the murder that's made you keen to hike?"

Émile expresses mock alarm. "Sandra, since when are you so suspicious of me? Perish the thought, okay? We've talked about this trail once a week for the past three months. Besides, it's a beautiful day and I'm keen to hike."

"Okay. All right." She doesn't sound convinced.

"What do I care about a silly murder? Am I the investigating officer?"

"Not yet."

"No *yet* about it. I'm not interested." To drive his message home, he resorts to French. *"Pointe finale."*

She's not swayed. "You protest a little too much maybe" is her final note.

Early along the trek, they encounter Pete Briscoe. Well off the trail, he spots them first, throws down a shovel, and literally gallops through the tall grasses to intercept them. He says he's burying his dog in a spot he can find again in the future, thanks to a stand of nearby pines. They're both inclined to leave him to his ceremony although he seems anxious to talk.

If they introduced themselves a day ago, their names are forgotten now, so each of them revisits the ritual.

"I'm glad to run into you again, Sandra," Pete Briscoe says. "You, too, Émile."

Cinq-Mars quashes a smile. The way he came across the meadow makes his phrase quite literal. "Why's that?"

"To thank you! I don't think I did. I was a wreck yesterday. But thank you. For finding Gadget, then caring enough to look for her owner. That was really great of you. Not many tourists would take the time out of their day to do something like that for a poor man like me. I was hoping to say a proper thanks."

"We have animals ourselves, Pete. Dogs. Cats. Horses galore. We know that losing one is difficult."

"I was drunk."

Cinq-Mars doesn't know if the man is trying to excuse himself or explain his grief, although either way there is no need. "I see."

"Hungover when we met. The day before, drunk. At sea. In the storm. I admit it. That storm was all I needed. So me and a lot of the boats spent the night on the water, and some of us—I was one of them—partied the night away. Not much else to do. I don't know how it happened, but it was my fault. I was drunk and I know better than to tie one on out on the water. How Gadget went over the side, I don't know. A wild night, I should've made sure she stayed below or in the wheelhouse. I lost my best friend and it's my fault. The truth is, I have to face that fact. I do. That misery. I wasn't at my best yesterday. A man should say thank you for what you did and I plumb forgot. Not forgivable, but I hope you will anyway."

Émile is feeling mildly embarrassed listening to the discourse. The more assurance he offers, the more Pete Briscoe protests. He gives up trying and accepts the other man's supreme and eternal—apparently—thanks.

"You're welcome," he says.

"You should come up to the Whistle," the fisherman suggests, an invitation.

"I've read about it. A lookout?"

"Walk or drive up to the top of Whistle Road. People get together at sunset, before and after. Have a few pops, you know."

"I see."

"But that's not the whole point of it, the drinking. Only a part. There's no bars on the island, see. We drink in our houses and we drink at the Whistle. Watch the whales swim by, watch the sun go down, tell a few stories. Oh, I tell a lie. We go through a lot more than a few stories. A ton! Our talk is better than what's on the boob tube, that's a home truth, so come by, the both of you, listen in. You'll enjoy yourselves."

"We might do that," Cinq-Mars tells him. Sandra gives him a look, as he seems to be accepting every invitation that's coming his way, not his usual nature.

"I gotta get back to burying my poor pup. It's hard to find a place that's not solid rock up here."

Sandra speaks up for the first time. "I thought you buried Gadget yesterday."

Pete Briscoe turns back, nods. "I planned to," he concurs. He tightens his forehead in thought, which effectively binds his unibrow into a single line of fur. "Too upset. I couldn't bury a penny yesterday if you dug the hole yourself and all I had to do was drop in a coin. So nope. Had to get a better hold of myself, you know? Do it the right way. Do what's best for Gadget."

"Why up here?" Émile inquires. Briscoe won't notice, but Sandra detects the suspicion in his voice.

"Do you know a more beautiful place on earth? Wouldn't mind my own ashes tossed off this cliff, when the time comes. When I'm out in the bay, what do I see but Seven Days Work? In fog, Seven Days Work comes up first on the radar. Now when I see this cliff, I'll see Gadget. I'll know she's up here, having a romp. She loved the boat, but she loved running here the most. Rabbits! She never cared for fish, they scared her, but she loved chasing rabbits. Now she's free to, all day and all night long."

He seems set to blubber again.

"It is a beautiful resting place," Sandra agrees.

"The oldest rock on earth, they say. Grand Manan was at the equator when the Americas, and Europe and Africa, were all one continent. Did you know that? Seven Days Work was at the middle of the earth at the dawn of time. Different planet then, hey? Now we're flung off to nowhere. Gadget will lie here. At the middle of the old world, on the oldest rock in existence, with the best view a man or dog can see."

A speech worthy of a funeral, a good point of departure. The couple voice their good-byes and carry on with their hike.

They are quiet along the trail for a distance before Émile compliments her. "Good question," he remarks.

Sandra has no clue what he means but thinks about it for another forty yards before she mentions, "I didn't ask any questions."

"Even better."

She thinks about that as they cross over a stony patch and pick up the worn trail again. "What do you mean, Émile?"

"Without actually framing it as a question," he explains, "you asked how come he's burying his dog today and not yesterday."

Accustomed to her husband thinking things through on different levels, she tries to do the same, but nothing surfaces. "So?" She takes his hand. They walk side by side before the trail narrows once more.

"Anytime a man leaves where he is, to run over and speak to you when there's really no need, that means he doesn't want you to be where he was, he doesn't want you to know what he was doing. Which is fine. People do private things. And yet, you saw him yesterday. He was distraught, but that motivated him to bury his dog yesterday, like he said he would do. The state he was in, nothing was going to prevent that. What or whom he's burying today is beyond me. Not his dog though. Gadget's in the ground already. Maybe up here. Or elsewhere. She's already in the dirt."

Sandra can't help but look back over her shoulder, but the bluff where Pete Briscoe has been digging is out of sight due to the gentle contours of the land. "Should we go back? Spy on him?"

Émile laughs. "Listen to you. Detective Wife."

"Well. It could be serious, no?"

"And none of our business. If somebody is reported missing, we'll know where to look. I'll suggest Pete to the authorities. But if someone is being buried, chances are, he or she is already dead. Nothing we can do. And yes, I'm kidding. If I thought for one second that he's burying a person, I'd intervene. Still, you saw him yesterday, and today. He's not the kind of man who hides his emotions or even tries. He's nervous today. He doesn't want us to know what he's up to. Mischief, I'd say. Is he a man out burying his neighbor on a whim? Or even his neighbor's goat? Not likely."

"Then what? Best wild guess."

"A picture of an old girlfriend, who left him ten years ago after an aging rock star got her pregnant and she wanted to keep the baby. He's finally done with her emotionally. Your turn."

"Hmm. A souvenir from a current love affair that he needs to keep secret because the woman is his mother's best friend and twice his age."

"More to his mood. You win."

Sandra keeps thinking it through seriously. Often she chides her husband for his investigative instincts, but this stuff excites her, too. "He's hiding something he stole, or a time capsule, or he's digging for buried treasure, or concealing a secret. You're right, though. Even if I don't know any killers, to my knowledge, I'm pretty sure he's not one. At least, he hasn't killed anybody lately."

"There you go. You could be the detective."

"Hardly."

They separate again in order to stroll in single file, and give themselves over to the sea breezes and the sun as they walk across the back of Seven Days Work and gain the promontory known as Ashburton Head. Émile switches his walking stick from hand to hand as he tromps along. The constant pace and the mesmerizing clarity of light and the newness of the experience, the terrain and the astonishing vista transport him through time. He may as easily be a wandering minstrel in Elizabethan days, or a shepherd on a Greek isle centuries ago, or a man hiking across the Holy Land on his way to pay taxes to the Romans some millennia back. Except that he walks on happily.

By a small creek, he stops. A mood, a thought, takes hold.

Sandra wonders what it might be.

He has to think it through himself, and ask, "Can we stay here a moment?"

She's content to do so, as there's much to see. They are not looking straight down at the water, but across a meadow and then through trees, yet the bay is visible to them and Sandra spots flashes of white moving in tandem, far off, which she takes to be whale spouts.

"What Pete said," her husband remarks, and his tone is reflective, even reverential, in a way that he can be sometimes. For all his hard-core life as a big-city cop, he's nurtured a spiritual side. "It might not be true to the nth degree, but close enough. This is old rock. Among the oldest on the planet. Not the whole island, but Seven Days Work. Upheavals, ice ages, tidal erosions, whole continents breaking apart and scattering, oceans both disappearing, then intruding. All that. This rock on which we're standing has experienced *all that*. Eons and eons. We can look at great mountain peaks, yet they're babes in time compared to this rock."

"It's something," she agrees. It's almost too much to take in, think-ing of its survival through time, not dissimiliar to contemplating the lives of stars.

"And here the rock stands," Cinq-Mars continues, "part of an island where people are dissecting a murder. After all this time," he scoffs, "we're infants. We haven't learned to get along."

"Sad. But what's on your mind, Émile?"

"Sometimes I regret my career. A life devoted to chasing down the bad guys. Dealing with death and destruction day in, day out. There's so much more to grapple with in the universe than just our human wasteland."

Sandra wraps two arms around him and hugs, so that he's supported by his two legs, his wife, and his mighty walking stick. "You did good, Émile. You did good."

He concedes as much, although to a lesser degree than she might prefer, and they resume their march.

They leave Seven Days Work and cross the back of Ashburton Head.

Émile does not expect to identify the scene of the dreadful crime that has befallen the island. Had this been his handiwork, no sign of it would exist once he and his people concluded their investigation. Police, then, are less thorough here. The most telling evidence that they've landed at the minister's last stand is a ribbon of yellow police tape knotted to the branch of a bush. Long strands of tape that previously sequestered the scene have been torn away and removed, but not untied, so telltale indicators remain. Sandra sees them, too, a second piece and a third small ribbon, and slows down to suit Émile's shortened stride.

Émile Cinq-Mars can't help it. He knows better than to tempt himself, and yet he has to look around.

Sandra is not cross. She expects no less, and doesn't interfere with or admonish his embedded professional interest. This is her man, after all, and she is not about to change him. She permits him to peruse the crime scene on his own, letting him get his famous *feel* for the place beyond what's visible. She sits while he wanders in a great circle, almost disappearing from her view back into the forest, and she knows that he's done only when he returns to her side. She's spread out part of their picnic to nosh on before continuing the hike. Émile sits on the grass with cheese and pear slices between them, and sips from the cup of red wine he's offered. Before them, a stand of trees lines the edge of the cliff, and beyond that is the deep blue of the water below the lighter vast blue of the sky. If this place was not heaven before, it is now—now that an investigation occupies his mind.

"No secrets," she instructs him. "Tell me what you see, Émile."

"They missed it," he says. "I'll bet you anything they didn't see what was right before their eyes."

She knows what a brazen remark it is. That attitude often got him in hot water with colleagues. Not only is he claiming to be attuned to clues that other policemen didn't notice, but he's brash enough to surmise how they've conducted the investigation, what they've observed and concluded and missed. All this from taking a brief stroll around an empty meadow.

"Okay," she encourages him, although her invitation is partly a challenge. "I'm not saying that I doubt you. I'm not that foolish. Just tell me how the heck can you reach that conclusion from looking around at grass and rocks?"

What he says next surprises her more than anything he's confided in the past about his professional life. "I know," he admits. "I know. It scares me, too."

She goes quiet again, waiting, aware that his intention is not to show off. He told her one time that people, mainly other officers, prosecutors, and attorneys, usually want him to explain every drip and dribble of how he has entered into his conclusions. He always resents that approach to his work. He learned over the course of his career to back up his conclusions with the force of logic and evidence, and to expect that people who want to know what he knows also want to know how he got there, how he leapt to the right conclusions. Often, that is material that he cannot reveal. He often does not know exactly how it works himself. Intuition, he's convinced, is a powerful force when treated with respect and properly nurtured. But try to explain that to a superior officer, or even a cadet. Try to explain that the mind has a core brain so rapid that it has no language, because speech is too slow, and communicates through impressions to the person with a mind able and willing to translate those impressions into ideas. What is commonly called intuition, Cinq-Mars credits to that core rapid-fire brain within everyone.

"Way up behind us," he says.

"Where you were walking?"

"I went up to get an overview."

"Your famous feel for the place."

"But I found a clue instead."

She looks around behind her, to the perimeter of where he patrolled.

"I don't see anything," Sandra admits.

"I'll take you up in a minute. I saw grass that's been trampled, probably while it was wet. It hasn't popped back yet. So I followed that line. I came upon a site where someone may have been having the same problem as our new friend-for-life, Pete Briscoe. You remember what he said about trying to dig in soil that wasn't solid rock just below the surface? Six, ten inches down—in places, sometimes less, sometimes more—this is solid rock."

"Not to mention the oldest on earth. So?" she asks.

"Not the best or easiest place to bury a dog. Or, for that matter, a human being. The departed minister was to have a grave dug for him up there. Or, more likely, he was asked to dig his own grave. In any case, the digging commenced, but once the digger hit solid rock, and tried again, and again, fruitlessly, that part of the job had to be amended. That's when he was tied to a tree instead."

"How do you know he was tied to a tree?"

"People in town said so. I happened to overhear them."

"Oh. Okay, smart guy. Aren't you the brilliant detective."

"But they missed it, Sandra. They missed that he was supposed to be buried up here and never found. Lescavage was supposed to disappear. Becoming a public spectacle was a second, and therefore the less preferred, option. Something about him being a public spectacle might compromise the killer, and that's why the killer wanted him underground. That might even be why he had his stomach cut out. To change the dynamic. To fool people. Also, because the killer panicked, I think, once his first option dissolved. That's going to be a key element to this case, that he was supposed to disappear completely but the killer panicked. The unknown facts of the case have the potential to unwind against the killer. If the cops ever get on it, that is."

"You'll have to tell them, Émile."

He releases a long, slow breath. "I'm not investigating this murder, Sandra."

He seems particularly determined. "Okay. You don't have to be," she says.

"Okay," he says.

"But you can still tell them."

"They'll think me an ass."

They continue with their lunch. Sandra knows her husband too well and she thinks to ask, although he's given her no indication to do so, "What else, Émile?" With him, there is always something else.

He glances at her almost guiltily. As though to have his synapses

this far away from her and involved with a whole other agenda consti-
tutes a form of marital cheating. He's not thinking of some lover he
doesn't know or a fantasy he's willing to indulge, he's simply gone off
into the ether, into the passionate embrace of an idea.

"Oh, Sandra," he moans unhappily, "I really hate to say this."

He needs encouragement, which she provides. "Just say it, Émile."

He really does hate to reveal what he feels compelled to impart, so
instead says something else. He asks a question. "Why do people come
to a high promontory like this in a storm? Not for the weather. It's miserable wherever you go. You can stay put and get just as wet. Not for the
view. There is none in the rain at night. What advantage, in the midst of
a deluge, does high ground provide? Other than salvation from flood-
ing, or a better chance of a lightning strike, I suppose."

Nothing comes to mind for Sandra. "Tell me," she says.

"Radio signals," he replies.

He thinks that this might end the discussion, but she's not been
fooled.

"Come on, Émile, what is it that you don't want to tell me?"

He looks at her first, a hazard in a moment like this, then away.

"I think I know who committed the murder," he tells her very quietly, and she can tell that he sincerely regrets having to say so.

Sandra looks around at the scene, at the lovely waving grasses, the
trees, the shining vista. She looks at the dirt and the rocks and marvels
that such inert objects could impart to her husband their secrets.

"So you're on the case," she says, "whether you want to be or not." So
much for our vacation, she's thinking. "You have to be."

"No." His tone is quite emphatic, which surprises her yet again.
"I can't be. To prove it will take local knowledge, which I obviously don't
have. And even if I did, I think it might be extremely difficult at best,
and more likely impossible. Not being on the case, I have to keep my
mouth shut, because of course I might be wrong. And if I reveal only
part of what I know, that could be destructive. Better to let things
evolve on their own. A little knowledge can wreck things, and that's
all I have. A scant tidbit of knowledge. I'm better off assuming that I'm
wrong. It's not my job to get an innocent person into a whole shitload

of trouble with only second-rate cops on the case. So I'm staying out of it."

"Pointe finale," she says, really to tease him. Émile nods in agreement. She's still not sure, and as she packs up the remains of their picnic, adds, "We'll see, Émile. I also have intuition, and I don't believe that you're done with this yet. You're trying too hard not to be. That won't work."

"I don't know what it is exactly, San, but I'm determined to stay out of it. That surprises me, too. I just believe it's the right thing. Let the local boys handle it."

He wanders off for a sheltered pee. On the way back, he studies, not for the first time, the cairn where someone has been sick, probably upon seeing the body as the rains would have washed it away had the person been sick earlier. So, best guess, not the killer's vomit or the victim's. If a policemen lost his appetite for life here, he feels empathy for that man or woman, and thinks no less of him or her, and, rather, in a strange way, thinks more of that person. The sight that instigated this illness, a glimpse of the eviscerated victim, must have been savagely ugly. Photographs would have been taken. Although he's not on the case, not by a long shot, Émile accepts that he will find it hard to resist the temptation to examine them should anyone offer. He hopes that no one will.

"Why, Émile," Sandra wants to know upon his return, "are you so convinced that the police didn't see what you did? You haven't spoken to them about this in any great detail."

"The footprints in the grass give them away. We can see where the investigators tromped through here, and none of their footprints goes high enough, up to where there was an attempt—three attempts, I'd say—at digging."

She has another issue to broach. "If you think you know the killer, who is it?"

"Remember the last time you had too much knowledge?"

Another time. Another place. She knew too much and was kidnapped. "Different situation, surely."

"True. You're in no danger here. But you might meet the person in question. Are you sure that you won't accidentally tip off that person about my suspicions? How could you not? Or treat that person differently than you would otherwise, which, in a way, is the same thing? On top of all that, you know me. I need to keep things inside. Let the kitty out of the bag too soon and it never grows up to be a cat."

"That's not a saying!"

"I just made it up."

"Émile Cinq-Mars. You're a—"

"A what?"

"A piece of work." A notion occurs to her. "A seven days' piece of work. There. I just made that up."

Happily enough, and feeling a close bond following the intimacy of their talk, they depart the crime scene and carry on across the edge of the sea and sky. They don't know that they are both thinking more or less the same thing. Émile said, "Let the local boys handle it," and he's hoping that they can. Sandra, on her part, is hoping that they will.

SIXTEEN

Officer Wade Louwagie pulls up his squad car outside the old-fashioned General Store so popular with tourists, in particular, and island folk, as well. He is on his way to interview the group that has rented out the former City Hall, to check if they were up on the cliffs the night of the murder. The day is turning into a warm one. He hasn't had much to eat and is feeling light-headed, even faint and strangely distracted, so he stops to pick up a sandwich and a cold Dr Pepper.

He chooses the egg salad.

"I guess it would be stupid for me to say the sandwiches are selling like hotcakes today, but they are, so really I should say the sandwiches are selling like sandwiches, since that's what they are, but they don't usually sell out so quickly, so we have less choice to offer now, because they're selling like hotcakes. You see?"

He doesn't. The cashier, Margaret, scarcely takes a breath, and the cop is hard-pressed to follow her logic. "I'm fine with the egg," he manages to say.

"You're kind," she assures him.

He pays, thanks her, and is about to leave when she declares in a voice that's almost defiant, her arms emphatically crossed under her modest bosom, "I'll let you kiss me in the back room, Mr. Policeman. Nothing more. A nice kiss. In the back. That's my offer."

Now he knows that he's truly lost in this conversation. The best that he can muster in return is, "What?"

"A kiss. Don't you? Kiss girls, I mean. I do. I mean, I kiss boys, not girls, but you get me. That's my offer. In exchange."

Something is being bartered here, but he has no clue. He's gone from light-headed to dizzy, and he's dizzy enough that he's nervous about it now. Sometimes island girls just turn his crank and he's come to believe that they do it for a lark, to make fun of him. This one is more puzzling than any.

"In exchange for what?" he asks.

"You know."

"No," he contends, "I don't."

She beckons him closer and cups his left ear while he stares down at the slight, yet mesmerizing cleavage of her breasts, revealed now as she leans in to whisper. "For information. About the murder. The gossip. You know. Tell me stuff. The lowdown on the hoedown and I'll give you a nice kiss. That's fair, no?"

When they both retreat, she's smiling and he has no clue if she's serious, half-serious, or having fun with him to the hilt. She looks like she's about to burst out laughing, so he dares not take her up on it. He'd be the butt of jokes. Louwagie marshals his shoulders back, as though to summon a measure of dignity.

"I'm an officer of the law, ma'am. I don't partake in gossip."

"Partake! Oh. There's a word. I'm only kidding anyway. You know that, right?"

He does now.

"You know how it is. People come in here all day and they want the scoop. What can I tell them? What's, you know, public knowledge? What's okay to pass on? I mean, a murder, come on, geez, we don't have those around here. We burn each other's cars and boats, houses— sometimes we might dangle somebody off a cliff for a few hours—but we don't do anything serious. This is *serious*. People want to know what's up. Should we be worried? I never lock my doors. What for? Should I now? Should I?"

Louwagie yearns for a customer to walk through the front door or to come out from the vast array of goods in the back and rescue him, at the very least interrupt. No such luck. He's still thinking about how her breasts glow at the edges of the fabric of her blouse and blue bra and he's imagining what that kiss in the back room might be like if that were ever possible and not just another infernal tease. He hates being a cop sometimes. Young women tease him so freely so often that he must come across to them as easy pickings.

"I'm sorry, ma'am—"

"Ma'am? Ma'am! Come on. Do I look like a *ma'am* to you?"

Yet she's still grinning at him, despite her tone, looking as pleased as punch.

He tries to smile back. Everything is a joke to some people. Even he is.

She helps him out. "It's Margaret. I've told you before, but you never take it in. What's wrong with you? You look like you're going to fall over. I have a boyfriend, but, you know"—she waves a hand in midair—"we're kinda shaky. I mean, I'm always kinda shaky with boys."

"No wonder," he says, the first bright remark he's managed.

She gets what he means, too, and laughs off the tease. Indiscriminately offering kisses to cops could cast any relationship upon a rocky shore. "Oh that," she says. "I was only kidding, right? So, what can you tell me about the murder? Much? Anything? Not gossip. Not that, just, you know, what you're allowed to say so I can turn it into gossip. Ha-ha."

She doesn't laugh, she just says, "Ha-ha." Then she laughs at her own remark and so does the officer. With a tip of his cap, he's quietly heading out the door. An escape.

Something happens on the way back to his squad car. At first, he's not convinced that what he's feeling will amount to anything. That it's merely another dose of whatever has been ailing him on this day. He's less certain as a wave swamps him. His right knee buckles, he almost goes down, as if he's been shot. Then he feels remarkably dizzy. He's not eaten all day, but that shouldn't be enough to do this to him. He makes it to his vehicle and puts his sandwich bag on the roof of the car and stands there, tenuously upright, both hands against the roof, as though he's being frisked. He stays that way awhile, as if under arrest. He knows he has to open the door but that doesn't feel possible at the moment. He has to get into the car and drive away even though it feels out of the question. He has to interrogate some people, but he has no clue what questions to ask. He's afraid to get into the car. He's scared to death to drive. He thinks he'll drive straight into the sea. Off a bridge or some such. He stares at the steering wheel and fears getting into the car more and more every second. A wave is coming over him again and this time it won't disperse. He has to do it though. He has to open the door and get in. He must overcome his condition. He *has* overcome his condition, why is it back on him now?

Corporal Louwagie puts his hand on the door latch.

Holds it there awhile.

He hears another door slam behind him.

Checks over his shoulder.

It's Margaret. "Are you sick?" she asks. He can't reply. He can't speak.

He has to get in the car first.

He opens the door.

He looks in the car. He just looks in. He can't imagine sitting in there. And then he topples over.

He's on the ground and he's ashamed of himself and he knows he can't let this defeat him, but he panics. He fears that he's already finished, beaten by this disease, and the girl, Margaret, is by his side and he would like that, to kiss her in the back room, but he can no more tell her that than he can get in his car, and he struggles as she paws him, tries to stand while she tries to get him to stay down, to relax, to stop fighting as he claws at the car to help get himself back on his feet, and he wants to say, *I'm having an episode,* as if that will explain everything when the phrase has never explained anything, but that's what the doctors say, and he tells her, "I'm having an episode," and just saying that, getting the words out, admitting it, helps so much.

It's miraculous how much it helps. His breathing relaxes.

"What can I do?" she begs. "What can I do?"

He wants to kiss her.

He has his wits about him though. He knows better than to say what he really wants. "Help me stand up straight. Don't let people see me. I don't want anyone to see me."

Together they get him properly on his feet. He hangs on to the open door.

"Now what?" she pleads. "Oh my God oh my God, what's wrong?"

"Please. I don't want anyone to see."

"Cars are coming, but."

"The back room," he says.

"What?"

"Take me in there. Can you?" He doesn't say, You don't have to kiss me, but he wants to say just that. He says, "I need time," which makes more sense.

They start off. "Oh my God," she says along the way. "Oh my God. What happened to you?"

"Don't let anybody see me."

"Nobody's going to see you!" She suspects that a few people will.

Margaret guides him up the stairs and into the store. What she calls the back room is all the way forward, really just in the rear of the older front section. It's a private space for employees to hang out and for the storage of surplus supplies like cigarettes and coffee and candy. He's able to sit and accepts a sip of water from a paper cup that she hands to him. She stands over him.

"Can you . . . go back . . . and close . . . the door?"

"The door?"

"The car door."

"Oh. Yes. Sure. Stay here. I'll be right back."

They both know that he's not going anywhere.

While she's gone, his head spins less. His feet feel far away, and when he looks at them, he contracts the toes inside his boots as though he's squeezing mush. He squeezes them just to experience the odd sensation. He breathes heavily now but more evenly and senses that he's coming back to some sort of equilibrium. Out the corner of his eye he spots a door ajar. He knows that he should not look, but he does. He sees the edge of a toilet in the enclosure. Seeing that toilet in that small room causes him to reel and he panics, and when the girl comes back he is on the floor, moaning and clutching his chest, and she rocks him where he lies, and when another girl comes in she screams at her to take care of the store, "Take care of the store! I got this!"

She's got this.

She rocks him. Back to life, in a way. She knows when tears are on his cheeks that he's probably getting better, so rocks him less. She'll let him come out of this in a way of his own choosing. Keep his stupid male pride intact. He comes to his knees, then props himself up onto the chair again, and sits there, silently wringing his hands.

After a while, she whispers, "What happened?"

"I had an episode."

And she says, "I don't mean now. I mean, what, what happened to you?"

He wants to kiss her. Maybe that's what happened this time, the make-believe suggestion of a kiss. He says, "Do you mind—I'm sorry. This is crazy. Do you mind closing that door over there?"

"The toilet?"

"Yes. The john."

"Sure. Why?"

He doesn't want to say. Then thinks that he should. "It's a memory." Then he says, "Somebody else saw me."

"No biggie. I'll tell her to keep her mouth shut. And she will. Just like I will. If she doesn't do what I say I'll kill her, and that'll keep her quiet for sure."

She's always joking, this woman. He can't keep up.

She goes over and shuts the door and comes back and sits opposite the policeman. That's when he tells her about the child's head in the toilet bowl and what that did to him, how it wrecked him for life and that's why he got shuffled off to Grand Manan, to recover.

"But today, you saw something just as bad."

Even though he recoiled initially, and his stomach heaved and he was paralyzed by dread, her statement helps him understand what has laid him low. A delayed reaction. A whiplash effect.

"What I saw on the ridge," he admits, as though he has something to confess, "was nearly as bad. A reminder anyway. But it wasn't the worst."

"What was the worst?"

"Looking at the photographs they took afterward. I don't know why."

She leans into him, speaks quietly. "You have to sit here and take care of yourself, Officer Louwagie."

"Wade," he tells her.

"Okay. Wade. Nobody's going to know. Okay? It's our secret."

He holds so many secrets so tightly to his bones. He feels a certain ease in having one that at last he can share.

SEVENTEEN

Returned to the sanctuary of their summer cabin, Émile and Sandra Cinq-Mars enjoyed a peaceful late-afternoon nap. The timbre of birdsong lulled them to sleep, and as they awaken, the scent of sea air wafts through the open windows, a magical stimulation of the senses. Rising with some minor muscle soreness brought on by their long trek, Émile reconfirms that he's glad not to be on the job. Glad also not to be running down the murder that's presented itself locally, like some kind of devilish, or at least impish, temptation.

He wants no part of it.

This is so much better than that. Just lying around.

Besides, the time has come for drinks.

The high that routed the storm brought with it warmer temperatures, and the day progressively heated up. They choose to occupy the shady side of the porch to imbibe. To combat the heat, Émile opts for a long vodka tonic, while Sandra fixes her favorite cranberry cosmopolitan. A few salty snacks and mixed nuts come out. Sandra tucks her legs in under her on a comfy wicker divan and opens her newly acquired, nearly antique book on numerology, while Émile is content to stare out at the grasses and the bay beyond, observing a dalliance of warblers and thrush, goldfinch and pine siskin. Way off to the right a dog romps freely, literally bounding into the air as though its abundant happiness is all but impossible to contain.

Sandra observes, "We've had quite a day, Émile."

Although she contends that he always has some other level to achieve in any talk, Émile has detected a pattern that's similar in her. Whenever she utters what might sound to be nothing more than a casual observation, a way of breaking a silence, such thoughts with Sandra inevitably instigate the onset of a trail worth traveling, as if her life is perpetually littered by bread crumbs. Émile conveys a soft utterance and waits for her to say more, then smiles to himself when she does so.

"Taking care of horses . . . putting in a hard day's work is satisfying, you know? Get all the chores done, the animals exercised, watered, fed, brushed, put to bed. And yet the prize for that long day's work—which *is* hard, and you can never ask the horses for a weekend off—the prize is always to get up in the morning and realize that you have to do it all over again."

"Whereas here, we don't know what tomorrow brings."

"My sentiment exactly. I like this. I love it. I could get used to it in a hurry."

"Mmm," he concurs, although vaguely.

"Horses are demanding," she imparts from long experience. "Seven days' work and the next week begins. Only it never ends."

He agrees again, yet with only a slight grunt.

For her part, she knows that he is thinking of something and so delays speaking, hoping that he'll come out with it. He doesn't always. Émile prefers to keep contrary thoughts to himself.

This time though, he declares his position. "Ironic, in a way. Today I bitched about devoting my life to criminals. Chasing them down really means being tied to them by a kind of umbilical cord. I wasn't complaining exactly, and you're not either, but I was reflecting on what a shame it is to devote one's life to criminals. You have a similar thought—namely, that the care of horses takes up the bulk of your life. Both the better part of your day and ultimately, let's face it, the better part of your life. You'll notice a similar theme running through here."

She does. "Careers are demanding, no matter what they are. Even though we've been lucky enough to choose ours, and to have enjoyed them, a career can still have a shelf life. Comes a time to move on."

No grunt this time, which she extrapolates to mean that he's not quite ready either to agree or disagree, but he's taking her ideas deeper into his consideration.

"So, individually," he begins, "our lives have been changing, right? Yours and mine. Maybe I'm just being hopeful here, but perhaps our couple troubles stem from that, when really we should count ourselves fortunate. We're both seeking a change. The trick might be to find out what we're looking for and track it down together."

A different prong to the discussion altogether, and Sandra muses that she may have been apprehended by her husband's famous penchant for speaking at cross purposes to help foil a culprit's gambit. Yet she puts that notion aside. He's right, of course. They have to talk about this, get down to the root of the matter.

"I'm not sure about anything being a trick, Émile. I take your meaning. I take your intention. But we can't be facile if this is going to be real."

"Expressed poorly, then. But . . . you do take my meaning?"

"We need to go over what we do next. No criminals for you. No horses for me. Is either possible? If so, what else is there? Dogs and cats?"

He laughs, and sips his vodka tonic. "Why not? Go save wildlife. A zebra in Africa one week, some kind of lizard in Brazil the next. Then off to the Rockies to rescue Bigfoot from an avalanche. Exciting, no?"

"Haven't you had enough excitement for one life?"

He surprises her. "What I'm feeling right now, with this view and this drink and the company of my lovely wife, is as relaxed as I've ever been. I'm skeptical that this is real, but I like it. As the kids used to say, I can dig it."

"Speaking of digging," Sandra asks, "what *was* that fisherman up to this morning with his shovel?"

He laughs again. "Maybe you should do the detective work from now on, San, and I'll take care of creatures. The change might do us both good. I could become a bird-watcher maybe."

"Okay, now, here's a subject!" She springs this on him, and her sauciness is evident before she explains a thing. "Speaking of what suits us both. Old story, but we've noted that your libido is not what it used to be."

"Now what?" He isn't really perturbed, knowing that she's always delicate around the subject.

"Hear me out. It's understandable. You're older. But I was thinking. Why wait for nightfall, when you're tired, to try? Doesn't that defeat the purpose? I know you want to meet me halfway on this."

"All the way, I'd say, is what I *want*," he teases.

"So then, I was thinking. You know what some people call 'nooners.' We could have . . . cocktailers. No pun intended. It's just a suggestion. No pressure whatsoever. But a drink, a romp in the hay, a sleep, then dinner, then a quiet evening. We could try it, Émile. Not now. That's pressure and unfair. But we could try it. You might like it. The way our life is set up here, by the sea, could be the ticket."

The idea has merit, although he's not sure about one thing and says so. "Why not now?"

She smiles in return, and something might develop, but the sunny disposition of their day is clouded by the sound of a car, not a vehicle in the best running order, pulling up in front of the cottage. Sandra goes down to the end of the back porch and peers around the side wall. A tall, astonishingly long-legged woman uncurls from an older Porsche. The visitor neglects to turn the engine off at first, and leans back inside the small frame to eject her keys. When she stands upright again, she catches sight of Sandra around the corner of the house and smiles. A perfunctory greeting, the smile fading immediately upon being summoned. Sandra notices that the young woman appears under duress.

"May I help you?" Sandra calls out.

"I'm looking for Émile Cinq-Mars. The detective."

Mentioning his old profession is a warning sign, but Sandra invites her around to the back.

Émile is on his feet by the time the visitor appears. She scales the short stairs and arrives with her open palm extended, stepping past Sandra to shake his hand. She's a handsome woman, though not a conventional beauty, her features strong, and she carries her height with confidence. She then retraces a step and offers her hand to Sandra. "My name is Madeleine Orrock. How do you do?"

"Miss Orrock," Émile says. He has a handle on whom she must be.

"I go by Maddy."

"I'm Sandra, and of course my husband, Émile. What can we do for you?"

"Can we talk?" the tall woman asks. "Sorry to intrude. I'm a bit shaky. I've just had news. Sir, it was suggested that I come to see you."

"Who by?" Émile inquires.

"The police," she states.

Sandra takes a deeper breath, glances at her husband, and offers Maddy a drink. The woman declines until Émile insists, then she opts for a vodka tonic like his. She's ushered into a wicker chair and Sandra volunteers to make the cocktail. Émile sits on the love seat closest to her. He doesn't mean to inflict his incisive stare down his imposing long beak but does so in any case. Force of habit. She seems ready to bolt, he projects, so breaks off his penetrating gaze.

"What police?" he asks. "Louwagie, I presume."

"No," she says, "no. This one came to see me on his behalf. Officer Louwagie is taking some downtime, this other officer told me, but they both thought that I should be informed right away."

"Informed?"

"That was the question I asked. Informed? So, expecting to be *informed*, I invited the officer into my house, where he proceeded to interrogate me."

Sandra hears this last line as she opens the screen door with her hip and places her guest's drink down on the small oval table beside her. Maddy takes a sip at first, then a gulp, and Sandra asks, "Should I leave?"

Maddy begs her to stay. "This isn't private. I mean, it *is*. I hope you don't tell anyone about this, but I've interrupted, I've intruded. Please stay."

Sandra agrees after receiving her husband's subtle nonverbal accord—he is the person this woman has sought out, after all—and Émile continues. "You were interrogated. About what?"

"You two are visitors. You have no reason to care."

"We heard about a recent murder. Is this related?"

"No, sir. At least I presume that's a coincidence. My father died two nights ago."

"You have my sympathies. I'd heard. The police told me. An autopsy is to be conducted."

"Normally, no one bothers with the death of an old man. Not here. But because of the murder, a visiting medical examiner is handy."

"What's become of that?" Émile is forming an impression of his visitor. Her intelligence is apparent, and she probably keeps herself together and controlled. Something's upset her, and he doubts that she's accustomed to being in a state. He imagines that her life normally goes along swimmingly.

"Do you know who my father is?"

"Should I?"

"He owns this island. Or he did. Hell, I guess I do now."

"Owns," Cinq-Mars repeats, both a leading question and a criticism.

"Okay, an overstatement. I'm *understating* it if I say that not much on this island was bought or sold without my father raking in a cut."

"I see. And he died of old age?"

"I thought so. I drove in from Boston because he assured me left, right, and sideways that he was on death's door. Honestly, I didn't want to come. We had that kind of relationship. Anyway, I was hoping against hope that he might say something. He insisted that he wanted me here. I came, hoping for a deathbed confession. Or apology. Or something.

"You drove through the storm."

"I did, yeah."

"As we did, actually."

"Really?"

"On a different errand entirely. How did you find your father when you got here, Maddy?"

"I arrived too late. He was already dead."

"Again, I'm sorry for your loss."

"Yes. Well. Nobody else is. Truth be told, it's not much of a loss. You'll find that out sooner or later if you take this case, so I might as well tell you now."

Sandra and Émile exchange a questioning glance.

"Maddy, there may be a misunderstanding. I don't know why you're seeking me out."

"Officer Methot—Réjean Methot—he suggested it. He said that you already said no to investigating the murder of Reverend Lescavage, but he also said that you might be my only hope. Things aren't looking too good for me otherwise."

Émile laments, "I'm still in the dark here."

"Sorry. I'm rattled. Making no sense. Okay, I arrived home. My father was dead. I've been told that he was being looked after by his housemaid. She was relieved that night by Simon Lescavage. That's what she told me anyway."

Up to this moment, Émile is feeling that he might be in the company of a soft loony, someone who is bright and privileged from whom he might need to extricate himself early on and perhaps with difficulty. Now the parameters are beginning to interest him.

"The same clergyman who was killed."

"That's him. When I arrived home, he wasn't there. My father was neatly tucked in his bed with two nickels on his eyelids. The bedcovers smoothed out. He seemed peaceful in death. As though he passed away quietly."

Émile sips from his own drink. He wipes a bead of perspiration from his left temple. Now that he's gotten over his concern that she might be a trifle daffy, he sees that she's not only smart but credible. He doesn't feel he's dealing with someone who's trying to put something over on him. Though if it's true that a policeman directed her to him, he needs to have a word with that man.

"What was the agenda for this so-called interrogation? What did Officer Methot want to know, essentially?"

"Honestly, I think he wanted to know if I killed Simon Lescavage."

"Really?" Émile is surprised. He recalls that the two officers on the island had not been given laudatory reviews. One was dismissed as being of lesser intelligence, the other a basket case. "Did he indicate why he might think that way?"

"I arrived here during the storm. By boat. With the power on the island off. That's held against me as if I'm responsible for the rain and the power outage. I was home alone. That's also held against me. Apparently, the whole point of my arriving in a storm was to do away with people when no one was around. They think I was the last person to see Reverend Lescavage alive, since he was in my house. He left before I arrived. How do I prove that? No witnesses were out on a night like that one."

"The slimmest, barest of threads. Only natural they'd ask questions, given that you and the minister were in the same house on the night that he was killed, even if it was at different times. They don't know that for certain. Are you sure that the officer is accusing you of anything? Not just asking the necessary questions?"

All three persons on the porch know that he's coddling Maddy Orrock now, patronizing her, and both Émile and Sandra see that she does not take it well.

"It gets worse, sir." Her voice is strident. "Much worse."

"Go on."

"The autopsy on my father has confirmed that he apparently did not die of natural causes, as everyone, including myself, had assumed. He died of suffocation. My father, apparently, was put to death. He was murdered. And, while an endless line of persons known and unknown would've liked nothing better than to do that to him, I am, apparently, considered to be in that line and also, quite probably, close to the front. Or first in line. So I'm a person of interest in the death of my father, and, since he was last seen in my house, of Reverend Lescavage, too."

"Did you kill your father?" No longer humoring her.

"Please. Of course not. He was dead when I arrived. Would I have, if I had the chance? I'm not the type. Could I have? Yes, in the sense that I had the opportunity if—*if*—I arrived earlier, but I still don't have it in me. Did I have motive? I'm inheriting a fortune that was coming my way anyway, so the most I can be accused of with respect to motive is impatience. The whole thing is preposterous, except that I know this island. Once the word gets out—and it will—that my dad was murdered, *everybody*, and I mean everybody, will believe it was me."

A quiet lingers on the porch, then Sandra says, "That's dreadful."

"And how—" Émile begins a question, then checks himself to make sure he is not being impolite. "Not that you are not welcome, you are perfectly welcome, but how have you come to arrive on my doorstep?"

She understands his query. This is an out-of-the-blue visit for her, as well. Less than an hour ago she'd never heard his name.

"My father and I," she explains, "did not have a good relationship. You've gathered that. Yes, an understatement. Still. He's my father. So having him die, I haven't known what to think or how to react or even what it is I feel. I have to concede that I'm feeling more than I expected. I'm being hit with a few things that go back a long way."

Both Émile and Sandra can understand that, and encourage her with nods.

"This policeman arrives. He essentially accuses me of murder. Or *suggests* I did it. Holy shit. I mean, what? *What?* And I learn that my father was suffocated and that's like, *what?* Why? You know? God, he was going to die anyway, why would anyone bother?"

"Good point," Cinq-Mars murmurs.

"I'm not proud of this, sir, and it surprises me. I kind of came apart. You know, with the cop in my living room. Got all weepy and frantic and angry and, in the end, indignant. The Orrock in me came out. I questioned who these plebeians are to dare challenge anything I say. Not my best trait. I fell apart. I had the shakes. I still do. Fuck. Excuse me. I haven't slept much. I think he felt sorry for me, this cop in my house accusing me of murder. I doubt if cops are supposed to be that sympathetic. Maybe he liked me or something."

She digs out a Kleenex from the front pocket of her tight jeans, swipes away a few sniffles, then resorts to her drink to moisten her throat. They wait. They both know that when she says that the policeman may have liked her, she means that he was attracted.

"The thing is, and this is ironic, and so goddamn baffling in a way, I wanted my father . . ." This time, and for the first time, she chokes up on mentioning him. "I wanted my father to be here, because he'd know what to do. He would know how to deal with this mess and with this person and with the police and with everything. Even with his own funeral, and I don't have a clue how to handle that."

They see for themselves that the stresses of the last two days are resident inside her, suppressed and managed, but liable to burst out and seize control. She is a strong woman despite that, which they see as she effectively pulls herself together again.

"I was angry at myself, more than anything, for wanting my father alive again so he could take charge of the situation. Anyway. Tears and tantrums later, the officer told me about a retired detective who has declined, he said, to help out with the investigation of the murder of Reverend Lescavage. He suggested that I talk to you. He couldn't help me out. He has a job to do. Throw me in jail, I guess, I understood the gist of his job to be. He said if I need help—which is obvious—then maybe I could ask you to investigate my father's death. That's why I'm here. To ask for your help. I can pay you, God knows. I imagine I'm wealthy now, so that's not an issue."

Cinq-Mars gives her speech some thought, nods, and mulls things through. He shares a glance with his wife but doesn't want to hold that look for long. He starts out by saying, "Maddy, you have to understand that I'm taking a break—"

"Émile," Sandra interrupts. This time he's obliged to hold her gaze a longer time, give her take on the situation more weight. She can't see a way around the circumstance that's presented itself. If he thinks that she should devote her time to rescuing wildlife, if he figures that that's in her DNA, then there's no time like the present. As well, he is who he is, she knows it, and the situation is a call to action. "You can't say no."

He may be able to argue against her point of view, but decides without any fanfare that that will not be worth the effort. The young woman now appears quite hopeful when he faces her again.

"I cannot accept payment."

"I know how this sounds, but money is nothing to me, sir. I'd feel better about imposing. You're on holidays, like you said."

"The thing is, I'm not a *private* detective. Or a detective for hire. The difference is this. If I investigate what's going on, I'll be interested only in the truth. That may save you from further difficulty, or the truth may reflect badly on you. Do you see? You may know your innocence in the affair, but I do not. If I am in your employ, charged with getting you off, I would be hired, essentially, to prove your innocence even if you're guilty. I won't do that. If the truth sets you free, if I help you out, when everything is over I'll submit an invoice, enough to purchase a future trip for my wife and me. Perhaps enough to pay for this one. Such as it is. We'll see. Should the truth put you behind bars, that is what I'll deliver when the time comes, if I discover that that's how things should go."

She understands. "I'm not afraid of the truth. I'll be so grateful if you take this on."

"Mmm." He's not wholly committed as yet. "Let me ask you a few questions first. Direct questions, Maddy."

"I'm a big girl. Shoot."

"Why *did* you arrive in the middle of the night? In a storm?"

"I drove from Boston. The weather slowed me down. I called my dad. I told him I wouldn't make the last ferry. He arranged for me to come by private boat. Today, I had that skipper load my car onto the ferry and I drove it off, then all this happened. Anyway. My dad didn't want me to wait for the morning ferry because he didn't think he'd live long enough to see me. That he wanted me to visit at all, you understand, was a first. Enough to make me curious enough to come, ASAP. I wanted to hear what he had to say."

"About what?"

She reflects on the question a moment. His tone demands more than a simple answer, that she go to the grit of the matter.

"Not just about why he was such a bastard. I was secretly hoping he'd beg me. You know. For forgiveness. That was a fantasy. I warned myself to put no stock in it, but I'm human. Realistically, I wanted him to say something about my mother. He never told me much. Almost nothing. I always felt that there was something he'd held back from me. I wanted to know what."

"What happened to her?"

"She was thrown off a cliff."

"Really. When?"

"When I was a child. She was thrown off Seven Days Work onto the rocks below. The man who found Reverend Simon Lescavage's body, his name is Aaron Roadcap, his father threw my mother off Seven Days Work."

"Why?"

Maddy lifts her shoulders and shakes her head at the same time. She holds the pose, as though this is the mystery of her life. "That's what I wanted to talk to my dad about."

"What can you tell me about Mr. Roadcap, the younger? What does he do?"

"Do? He lives in a tar-paper hut over in Dark Harbour. He cuts dulse."

"Dulse," Cinq-Mars says, although he knows what it is.

"Yeah, the seaweed we harvest around here. The Bay of Fundy brings in nutrients from the sea with our huge tides and takes all the dirt back out to the Atlantic, day in, day out. That's why the whales are here and the fish and that's why the seaweed is so rich in nutrients. We cut and ship the dulse as chips. Also, my dad owned a small plant that pulverizes dulse. He shipped the powder to health-food nuts around the world, but mostly to California and Scandinavia. He's pretty much cornered a monopoly on that. Anyway, Aaron Roadcap cuts dulse and lives in squalor, as near as I can tell."

"Is there anything else you can say about him? Did he have a quarrel with Lescavage, for instance?"

"I wouldn't know. Down through the years, we've met from time to time. Awkward. The thing about him is . . ." She stops a moment, as though to reconfigure this insight, then forges on. "A couple of things, really, apart from living in squalor, are strange."

"What's that?" Émile asks.

Maddy looks at him, then glances over at Sandra, almost as though to suggest that she is more likely to understand this part. "I hate to say it, but he's as handsome as a god. Seriously. Literally. And the other thing is, he's no dummy. He's smart, and he talks well. He doesn't talk like some dulse-cutting drug user."

"Do dulse cutters use drugs?"

She shrugs. "The fishermen do. A lot of fishermen do, so why not those at the bottom of the totem pole? Only makes sense, really. Who wouldn't, if what you do all day is walk in tidal pools and harvest seaweed? Pretty boring."

"A simple enough life," Émile remarks, which the three of them understand is not the same evaluation.

"The policeman," Maddy notes, "implied that my arrest is a distinct possibility. Maybe imminent. I'm feeling a bit desperate. I have to bury my father, defend myself, and deal with the judicial system and with the fallout on this island. I hope you can help, sir. I really have no one else I can turn to. My dad is dead and my only friend here, really, was Simon Lescavage."

Émile's been noncommittal, but he's forthcoming now. "You won't be arrested. It might take one call, it might take two, but that's not going to happen." The evidence is circumstantial, at best, but a local cop might grasp a straw and run with it. Émile is connected to everyone up the ladder, and if the investigating officer doesn't see that it's in his best interest to tread slowly, superiors the cop has never met will educate him otherwise. Émile is confident of that. His connections will be powerful in this instance.

"You can do that?" Maddy asks, already impressed but, as a woman of the world, suitably skeptical.

"He can," Sandra assures her. "He will. If you're innocent, you can't have a better person in your corner."

What Maddy says next impresses them both, especially the wary detective.

"Innocence, as you must know, is in short supply on this planet. I'm not painting myself as lily-white or squeaky clean. But I did not kill my father, nor did I have the opportunity, nor would I have had the will even if I'd had the opportunity. Nor did I have the inclination to do so—*it never occurred to me!* It occurred to someone, apparently. And cut up the one adult I ever admired? Do that to him? Me? I'm sorry, but that's preposterous. That's strictly maniacal. I might be screwed-up, I know that much about myself, but I am not a homicidal maniac. The problem is, I was home alone, which isn't much of a defense."

Impressed, Cinq-Mars sits back in his chair. He's on the case. His wife doesn't mind, has even insisted on it, so he's in the clear on that account. The case is more complex and intriguing the more he learns. The day has been grand, but the days ahead show a different promise, and he's rising to that challenge, and perhaps, to that pleasure.

"Émile will help you sort out what happened to your father and to the Reverend Lescavage," Sandra promises. "I'll help you with the funeral arrangements. I'll be happy to have something to do while he's occupied. I won't say it'll be fun, but we can keep each other company."

Maddy Orrock seems to want to decline the offer, but she really can't bring herself to do so, and nods both consent and thanks. Sandra wears a smile right through the censor of her husband's glance. She guesses that he wants her to tread cautiously. On that, she doesn't give a hoot.

"Our conversation has kept you from your drink, Maddy," Émile points out, "and me from mine. Let's drink up slowly—while we do, tell me about yourself. This will mark the beginning of my inquiry. I need to learn a lot quickly. I won't grill you, but please say whatever comes to mind. What I need to acquire right now is what I do not have, and that's local knowledge. Talk. Free-flowing. Never think that anything is too incidental. It'll all help."

That conversation is proceeding and their drinks are finished and renewed when they hear the dull buzz of a cell phone vibrating on a wood surface inside the cottage. Sandra hunts it down so that Émile can continue his fact-finding mission, and brings it out to him. She's already answered and exchanged a few words, and the look on her face is one of apprehension. He reads the caller's ID off the smartphone, excuses himself, and walks off the porch and across the back lawn. Where the tall grasses take over, he converses for some time before returning to the porch. He finds the women sharing a peek at Sandra's book on numerology. She's written down her guest's birth date and full name, with which she intends to experiment with her new hobby. The two women look up as he arrives back, and each sees that his visage demonstrates some evident disquiet.

"Maddy, you're a prof at Harvard," Émile says.

"Sociology. Born and raised on this island, yet my specialty is the sustainable development of big metropolitan centers. Go figure, hey?"

"Up the road from where you live, another Harvard professor resides."

"Oh, a few Ivy Leaguers are on the island. Summer people. Harvard's well represented, oddly enough."

"But one professor in particular. His name is Jason DeWitt."

"I know him."

"We met him ourselves yesterday. Again this morning. In fact, he invited Sandra and me up for drinks. Are you close friends?"

"Casual acquaintances, let's say. If we pass in the street or a corridor, we nod. Unless he corners me."

"Corners you?"

"I find him overly affable. He seems to think that everyone he meets is a bosom buddy. In Boston, he introduced me one time to a friend of his *as if I was also* a friend of his, and as if the other friend and me were now inseparable for life. If you've met him, then you know that Professor DeWitt makes himself difficult to ignore. We're neighbors here, although I'm not around much. Academically, we're in different fields. Why?"

"I'm sorry to tell you this, as it may invoke a certain bad memory, but this afternoon, our Professor DeWitt went over the side of Seven Days Work."

Sandra is dumbfounded, but clearly Maddy Orrock is stunned and in some dismay. "That's impossible. I just saw him. When did this happen? Just now? Oh my God, what's going on? What happened? I mean, did he trip and fall? Was he pushed? Did he jump?"

Émile responds initially with a soft utterance under his breath. Then reports, as though to himself, "Apparently, on this island there's a fourth option." He speaks up, explaining himself and dismissing his comment at the same time. "Around here, some people hope to fly. Exactly what happened remains to be determined. Apparently, a fisherman out on the water saw someone drop off the cliff and called it in. The professor's body was recovered on the rocks below."

"I don't believe this."

"What is it?" Sandra asks.

Maddy's voice falls to a frail whisper. "I went to see him this afternoon. A courtesy call. I guess I was looking for support. That means I was probably one of the last people to see him alive. Maybe the very last, unless someone killed him." She looks up at Cinq-Mars, staring into his eyes, imploring him. "Honest to God, it wasn't me," she insists.

Cinq-Mars nods and touches her hand in sympathy. He knows what everyone does, not just cops, that that's what people say, particularly the guilty, when accused of a terrible crime. He's sympathetic, yet in no position to take her at her word.

PART 3

EIGHTEEN

Émile Cinq-Mars digs out Corporal Louwagie's business card to buzz his mobile phone. The officer invites him over. His home isn't far away, but is tucked into a wooded community off the beaten path in North Head. A challenge to locate. Cinq-Mars finds a modest, charm-free bungalow clad in the vinyl typical of New Brunswick dwellings, this one pale yellow with green trim, and a brown roof in urgent need of repair. Overall, the house and yard are due for a sprucing up. At the roof-line, a crop of weeds thrives in the gutters.

He rings the bell and waits.

Neighbors have kids, yards that sport swings and basketball nets and a general mess of toys. Louwagie's home shows only the accoutrements of chores: a lawn mower, a watering can, a stepladder pitched on its side. He's almost feeling sorry for the man even before he answers wearing a long, forlorn face.

"Detective," Louwagie says. "Good to see you. Come in." His expression is far less cheery than his words, which are delivered in a lifeless monotone.

"Émile is fine. I am retired."

"Are you? I'm hoping you're back on the job."

Cinq-Mars finds that his initial impression has merit, for when they sit in the living room, four bottles of liquor stand upright between them on the coffee table. A rum, a gin, and two vodkas, one Russian, one Finnish. None is open. He knows what this means.

"Did you just buy these?"

"Confiscated the lot. A year ago. Off kids. Kept them tucked away in the garage until now."

A secret cache, just in case.

"So you're contemplating a long leap off the wagon."

"Or I'll follow our professor off a cliff. Look, I can drink in moderation. One drink, maybe two on the weekend."

"You mean glasses, not bottles." He knew enough to take all contemplations of suicide seriously. "But I'm seeing the good news here. You haven't started in. You're fighting this. What's going on?"

They're talking, but Émile notices that the other man scarcely seems to notice his presence.

"The shrinks call it an episode."

"What do you call it?"

"Fucking scary shit."

The man's as angry as he is frightened as he is depressed.

"You've been sober awhile?"

"Seems like forever sometimes. Or maybe it was only yesterday. I'm not that kind of an alcoholic."

"There are kinds?"

"I'm into panic-button booze. I'm free to drink in moderation—seriously, I am—until a bender sideswipes my ass."

"Okay. Let's get this over with. Either take a long drink, in which case your career and most likely your life are over and done, or I'll open the bottles and pour them out. We've got a murder case, looks like a multiple-murder case, to investigate. I can't do that without your able assistance. Or I get somebody else in here. I can make that happen with a call. Don't ask me to prove it, just decide. Either this stuff gets flushed or your life does. I've got enough to do. I'm not playing nurse-maid here."

Tough love. The way to go in some circumstances. Murderous in other situations. Not quite a roll of the dice, but not far off it either.

"Fuck you, too," the cop says.

"Whatever. Your life. Your call."

Louwagie appears to be thinking the matter over. When he nods, it's the slightest gesture. Émile knows to jump at the chance, and takes all four bottles through to the kitchen, uncaps them, then lets the liquids gurgle away two at a time. He turns on the tap to disperse the scent, too, in case the poor guy sticks his nose down the drain later on to inhale the fumes. The waste of good booze bugs him, but he's cheerful enough—he can afford his own. When he returns to the living room, Wade Louwagie hasn't budged. A good sign.

Émile remains standing. "Tell me this doesn't mean you're over the side."

"I'm hanging in. A tiny speck inside my brain wants to find out if this shit will pass."

"Curiosity keeps you alive. Okay. As good a reason as any. Corporal, I know what the Mounties want from you. To stay on the job, get back in the saddle, ride that horse. It's all bullshit, of course. They're Neanderthals that way and because you work for them, you have my sympathies."

At least Louwagie seems to cheer up a tad, hearing that.

"I won't ask you to take a full load. We'll keep you under wraps. We'll travel together, you can guide me around. You can give me access here and there and I'll give you the pleasure of my company. That's what you need right now, company. I'm not saying you want it, only that you need it. But I won't depend on you for much, so relax about it. Maybe we'll tweak your curiosity. Bolster your life force that way. Stay upright, Wade, see what tomorrow brings. Before this, you were okay. You can get back to that again. Maybe more easily this time than last. We'll see. Okay?"

Louwagie seems more present now. "So you're on the case? What changed your mind?"

"Your idiot partner. I'm going to brain him. He sent Maddy Orrock to see me. She was persuasive."

"You're working for her then. Everybody here works for the Orrocks, sooner or later."

"I'm on the side of truth, to see where that leads. As far as getting paid for my services goes, I'll figure that out later."

"I'm a wreck."

"I noticed. We've been through this."

"I'm spaced-out. I feel strangely remote."

"Remote?"

"To myself. Somehow, I'm far away. From here. From now. I don't think I can help. I should stay out of your way."

"Yeah, that'll work. You'll be drunk by midnight or dead by morning. Look. First things first. Lescavage was killed. I need to visit his house, and I need to see the crime-scene photographs. I can't do either without you. Are you in?"

"Don't show me those photos again."

"Again? You were there. Almost first on the scene. You went back to the pictures after that?"

"You think that set me off? Maybe. I haven't been right since. I got through the scene, but not the pictures. Weird."

"Maybe not so much. One is actual, real. The photos aren't. They can get inside your head in strange ways. I've seen it before. Was that your vomit up on the ridge?"

Louwagie nods.

"You should've let yourself upchuck again, looking at the pictures. Don't hold that shit in."

"You sound like my shrink."

"We're riding together now. So I am your shrink. Can we get going?"

"The manse first?"

"You got it."

"Sure. Why not?"

Émile's not going to coddle this guy, but on the way out he permits himself to give Louwagie a double tap on the shoulder, to comfort him.

To help buck him up. He likes the fight in his new partner. Not opening a bottle—that took some inner demon-fighting strength.

Louwagie drives in Émile's Jeep. He's wearing casual civilian clothes anyway, and Émile is just as happy that the man doesn't have a gun on his hip. They don't bother with his squad car, and stop at the police station to pick up the photographs and keys.

"House first," Émile dictates. "If I look at those pictures now, they might affect my observations."

On the way over to the Reverend Lescavage's village manse, the younger man doesn't have a word to say, his eyes off to the side ditch, his mind probably further afield. Émile has driven by the manse several times without realizing that it shares a connection to the small white church next door, the one with the bent steeple. Located far enough off the property it seems to be only a neighbor to the church and the tidy graveyard at the rear. Émile notices how it differs from what's familiar to him back in Quebec. He's been inside a few rectories in his day. In every instance, there was no mistaking the home as being a priest's residence, often priests plural, whereas this one evokes the Protestant style to blend in with the community and not be segregated by any ecclesiastical countenance. Catholic to the core, he still isn't sure how he feels about that.

Louwagie unlocks the front door and they step inside. Light falling through the windows onto the lovely patina of the old and warped pine floors and onto the dusty wooden bookcases somehow accentuates the silence of the cottage. Compared to the Mountie's home, this one benefits from a charm the other dwelling can't imagine.

"Where'd you get the keys?" Émile asks.

"Pardon me?"

"Did you take them off the minister's body?"

"Oh. No. He didn't have a set of keys on him."

"Seriously? Didn't that strike you as odd?"

"Lots of people don't lock their doors around here. The church lent me this set. The extras are for the church, the vestry, and the church hall."

"Trusting. If he left home without his keys, do you see them lying around here? His church keys, for instance? Did you see them before, up on the ridge?"

"Never did. Don't now."

"Which raises the possibility, no?"

Louwagie needs a moment to think about it, then nods. "Maybe somebody took his keys off him. Like I said, he might not have bothered with keys."

He's surprised that Émile doesn't move much. He's been informed of the man's fame, his reputation as a phenomenal detective, one who's busted biker gangs and gone up against the Mafia and come out on top, intact anyway, and who was assigned to felony crime through most of his career yet wound up solving murders on the side with a success rate rivaling anyone in Homicide. The Mounties who came out from the mainland warned that this guy was connected to police departments, including his own, at high levels, so no matter what—whether he got involved or not—he was to watch his step as long as Émile Cinq-Mars was on the island. Which intrigues him, despite his misery and depression. He wants to see how a so-called great detective operates, and is surprised when the man scarcely moves.

For his part, Émile tends not to explain himself to anyone, but in this situation feels sympathetic to the man's plight, to his mental condition, and helps him out. "Get a feel for the place. That'll tell you about the life that was lived here. That'll tell you as much or more than any goddamn scrap of evidence."

"A feel," Louwagie remarks. Neither a skeptical nor a trusting comment. He's willing to be educated.

Eventually, Émile browses through the man's papers and books, with an emphasis on what he's been reading and writing lately. The Mountie sees him smile.

"What?" Louwagie asks.

"I know these books," Émile reveals. "Read them myself. He took an amateur's interest in cosmology, in the origins of the universe."

"He was a minister. God created the universe in seven days."

"You believe that?"

"Not me," Louwagie states. "I think most clergymen know better, too. This other stuff is way over my head. The science. Religion or science, one or the other is the same mystery. Both are wasted on me. The world wasn't created in just seven days. Nor was that cliff at the end of this island. But they might as well have been, for all I know."

"If you take the time line as metaphoric—I've long assumed that you have to be an irrational dope not to take it that way—one becomes similar to the other." Émile looks up. "His sermon for this Sunday. You caught me smiling when I was reading it. Let me run this through out loud. They might be his last words."

Cinq-Mars clears his throat and picks up the man's handwritten sheets.

"'Believe in God or don't believe in God,'" he quotes, "'but that's not the question. Whichever way you step out the door in the morning, start by believing in yourself.'"

Émile smiles again. "He might've been addressing you, Officer Louwagie.

"Then our preacher adds, 'If you really understand what it took for you to come into being, for a visible universe to burst into creation, for gasses to coalesce and condense and stars to form and atoms with their protons and neutrons and electrons and dense nuclei—an atom, by the way, is composed mostly of space—and those atoms fly through stars and space and time that to our puny minds is endless, a length of time that might as well be eternal in terms of our ability to conceive of it, and through all that nothingness these stray wild atoms and their cohorts land on planet earth, to be vegetables and minerals, monkeys and fish, yes, fish, and spend time in the body of Christ and in Buddha and in the bodies of various village idiots and tyrants to arrive, for now, for a brief blink in time and space, in your body and in mine—if you took into account merely the human cost, in disease and illness and the striving and migrations and war and building up and tearing down, and if you were to ruminate on the sheer accident of two people, one male, one female, abiding together at a fluke moment in time when conception is ready and able and willing to take place, then you might begin to grasp how impossible *you* are, and how silly you are to *ever* believe in yourself. But if you can believe in yourself, then you might begin to appreciate that belief in God is not so far-fetched after all, for we know nothing from nothing of dark energy and dark matter and what makes an atom tick or why two of them out of infinite billions partner up and travel together, along with countless billions of others—with *these* billions but not with *those* billions—so in the end all we have, all we can have, thanks to science, if I may say so—I, of all people, a man who stands before you stripped of his faith—thanks to science and thanks also to Scripture, ultimately, all we have is belief and nonbelief. Knowledge? Pursue it, by all means, with honesty and passion. Know that knowledge is a mug's game, which is to say that it is forever boundless, like the faith of certain individuals, like the ignorance of others.'"

Enjoying the homily, his voice lowering as though he's starting to read it only to himself and not to his audience of one, Cinq-Mars takes a seat.

"'Ultimately, you will believe what you choose to believe or what you cannot help but believe, but if you believe in yourself, then know that that is ludicrous, and no less ludicrous than another man's belief in God. I believe in neither. Neither in myself nor in God, although I am an imperfect man, and in my weakness and decrepitude I confess before you that I have a belief, and my belief is in you. In all of you. In this cloud of life and humanity before me. People have come to this island in recent years who believe that one day they can leave by flying off it though a process of vigorously flapping their knees and thighs. Ah, you laugh, but don't you see? Your simple understanding that you must row, sail, or power a boat, or swim, or hire an airplane, or die in order to depart Grand Manan, is so elegant in its simplicity that I can only acknowledge that I believe in you. That belief, perhaps, dooms me, for out of it I may yet crumble and come to believe in myself, and out of that impossible and absurd error in judgment, I may yet believe in God again. Although I doubt it, pun intended.'

"In the margins," Cinq-Mars points out, "the preacher reminds himself to wait for a few chuckles to die down before proceeding. Then he continues, 'In the meantime, I pray for you, my dear congregation, to be safe upon the sea and safer still upon the waters of life, and I pray for you to be loving and caring, for nothing good ever arrives from a contrary direction. That alone makes me ask if God is not on one side, evil on another, but I'm having none of it. As your pastor, I can only say that my nonbelief may disturb us all, but out there in the universe, I sense indifference. And *that* is the crux—there's a word for you, with embedded meaning—the crux of the matter.'"

While listening, Louwagie wandered somewhat aimlessly around the room, idly glancing at objects and artifacts from the man's life. He manages his first faint smile as Émile concludes the completed portion of the sermon. "They say he's been packing them in lately. I don't attend his church, but some who go to mine have slipped off to hear him talk. Kind of ironic that talking about losing one's faith from a pulpit puts more people in the pews."

"Curiosity for some," Cinq-Mars acknowledges. "You can always draw people out for a crash. For others, perhaps they relate."

They carry on through the rooms without conversing, Louwagie assessing the other man. Émile asks him about dulse, which he's coming across in various packaging in the house, as chips, as flakes, as a powder, and in a sundried form.

"What does this stuff taste like anyway?" Émile asks.

"Try it. You probably won't like it."

"Really?"

"An acquired taste."

Émile nibbles on a chip.

"So?" Louwagie asks him. "What does it taste like?"

He thinks it over, nibbles some more, and concludes, "Iron."

"Loaded with the stuff."

"Rusty iron," Cinq-Mars adds. "You're right. I don't like it."

When they return to the front door to leave, the younger man sums up, "I guess we got nothing here."

"Not true," Émile contradicts him.

"How so?"

"I've discovered that Lescavage was popular through delivering an unpopular point of view. He made fun of the meditating flyboys and girls. He lived an uncomplicated life, yet he was a curious fellow and a thinker. He was clearly modest when it came to material possessions, always a good sign for a man of the cloth. And one more thing that a good detective might bring forward as raw evidence."

"What's that?"

"That," Émile says, and points.

Louwagie takes a look, then steps across the vestibule and lifts up a pair of rain pants tossed into a corner of the entry closet.

"The water stains on the floor look fresh enough," Cinq-Mars explains. "Most likely, he went out in the storm wearing rain pants. To go over to Orrock's place, perhaps? Then he came home and tossed them. But when he departed again, he left them behind. What does that tell you?"

The Mountie does find this curious.

"It was still raining. It poured the whole night through," Louwagie recalls.

"First, it tells us that he came home. Then he left and did not expect to go far, so he dispensed with the rain pants. Nothing nearby is all that nearby, so if he was going back out into the rain, it was to go no farther than a car. His car—I presume the Jetta outside is his—is still here, so he was being picked up. Someone he knew, a friend perhaps, took him away and he ended up rather dead."

"In slices," Louwagie adds. He feels a change in himself, a charge, a movement away from depression and a budding excitement coming on. He speaks quietly, but nonetheless remarks, "Interesting."

Progress. Émile catches the return of a smidgen of the man's life force.

"Now let's find a place to study those pictures," Émile suggests.

"Don't say *us*," Louwagie reminds him. "Whatever you do, keep them out of my sight."

NINETEEN

The day's been long, and Émile feels a comfortable fatigue wash over him on the precipice of evening. Or is it the alcohol? Drinks with Sandra take an edge off, and they dine out in Whale Cove, a short jaunt from home, enjoying a meal worthy of a fine restaurant in any world capital. Out of respect for where they are, both opt for the halibut, and following a shore walk afterward they return to their cabin arm in arm. The gulls salute, rather than serenade, their stroll.

Émile decides to go up to the Whistle to check the place out.

"I want names," Sandra decrees. "Full names. And birth dates."

She means for her new hobby, her interest in learning numerology. Émile notes that she doesn't ask to go, too. Either she has surmised that he wants to do this on his own or that she's too tired. His wife seems perfectly at ease—and looks so beautiful and content in the dimming light on the porch—that Émile feels no guilt for this momentary abandonment. He has work to do. He decides to walk up the hill. The talk of drinking at the meeting place, and given that he's already had a few, squelches any impulse to drive, and Sandra may want the car. An effort is demanded, and he arrives looking forward to the downhill trek in the dark later on, when he's done here.

He's early, but not the first to show up. That designation falls to a white-haired couple from Delaware, according to their plates. Cinq-Mars and the couple stand at a height, the drop before them steep and dramatic. They exchange smiles, content to stand by for a sunset that promises to be spectacular. In the interim, whales swim by the island on their way deeper into the Bay of Fundy, and the three are thrilled when the great mammals break the surface before deep dives.

"There's some dispute," the man from Delaware contends, and he has a way of twitching his cheeks as he speaks that's alarming, "about whether it is correct to call a group of fish a school."

"I've always used a school of fish," Cinq-Mars tells him, not sure that he wants to be a party to this conversation. He was enjoying the peace of the Whistle. "I like it. All those studious minnows wearing glasses and reading books. I suppose they have computers now, too."

The man doesn't seem to notice his whimsy. At least the woman smiles. "Some contend that *school* is a corruption of *shoal,* that really it's a shoal of fish."

"I prefer *school,*" Cinq-Mars maintains, deliberately cross now.

"Whales as a collective can be a shoal, or a fleet, or a gam, a pod or a school even, or a mob. I like mob, myself."

Cinq-Mars has his back up without much cause—*tourists!*— forgetting that he's a visitor himself. He isn't going to agree with this man on anything. "I prefer herd."

"Can it be a herd?"

"I've heard," he tells him, and he's being honest, "that it can be a herd."

Outgunned, outmaneuvered, the rigid man from Delaware with the popping cheeks and stern brow gazes out across the water and the hills beyond. His wife shoots a glance at Émile, interested in the fellow who performed an impossible sleight of hand, defeating her husband at being a superior prick.

The Whistle lies not at the very crest of this ridge, but on the downward slope to the sea. Once upon a time, a fog whistle blew from this point, and while it is now gone the name remains. The three tourists lean their thighs against the wood balustrade as they take in the view.

A car bounds up and over the crest toward the threesome.

The man from Delaware seems less relaxed now, somewhat uneasy as the new car parks right in behind his own by the side of the road, leaving little room to squiggle out. He heaves a sigh, as though to designate the newcomer as a dolt, and no doubt assumes that he can ask him to move later on. The new arrival is a diminutive man whom Émile finds familiar, although he can't immediately place him. He comes straight to the balustrade, takes a long and satisfied gaze, and breathes in deeply as though inhaling the view, then digs a pack of smokes from his pocket, bangs the pack to shake one out, and lights up.

"You don't smoke, I bet," he says.

"Used to," Émile acknowledges. "Quit. Long ago."

Most smokers usually say "Lucky" to that, but this one says, "Can't understand it. Neither why nor how. We've met."

He grins broadly then with an undeniable sparkle, and Émile places him.

"You're Raymond, from the ferry."

"I'm Raymond from the ferry," he agrees. "I hustled you into your car while you wanted to stand by the railing, enjoying the view. Happens every trip. There's always a troublemaker in the group." That sparkle again. He isn't being critical.

Suddenly, the man from Delaware spies more trouble for himself. Evenly spaced, about a half minute apart, six pickups broach the hill and swing down toward the meeting place. The vehicles park in the middle of the road and on both sides, so that the American couple may have to walk home now. Any exit for their car is blocked. The man appears sullen.

Fishermen and their companions tromp down the hill and a pair of flasks are passed. Émile and the couple from Delaware are included in the offering, but only Émile indulges himself. A smooth, peaty scotch.

Over the next ten minutes, sixteen more cars park and empty out. Even walking away from here will be a challenge.

"I built this barrier," Raymond tells Émile at the cliff, then asks, "Know why?"

"I presume so people won't fall off. You mean you built it personally?"

"Personally, yeah. But for two reasons."

"Should I be able to guess?"

"I don't mind telling you why," Raymond says with a laugh. "If you can guess, that might be a bit of an insult."

"Then I'd rather not guess."

"One you got. We look after our own. If somebody is too drunk or stoned or getting off on some shit, you know what I mean, he has to stand on this side of the barrier and watch the pretty sun go down. We take our precautions."

"Makes perfect sense. And the second reason?"

"So that one among us can lean back and look the other way, back up the hill."

"Okay." Cinq-Mars ponders this. "Someone is looking uphill why?"

"That's what might've been impolite to guess. So that no Mountie can surprise us. We'll see him coming. He won't bust us for drinking, unless he's got a burr up his ass, but he might bust some of the young guys for their M&M's and whatever else they put down their gullets, or suck into their lungs."

"Then that makes total sense," Cinq-Mars admits. "I commend you."

"Like I said," the man confirms, "we look after our own."

This time, that smile of his seems less friendly.

He cocks his head a little, a further indication.

"So you know who I am," Cinq-Mars surmises. "What I do."

"You've landed on a small island. There's consequences to that." Raymond sips from the flask, then passes it along to Émile, who does the same. "Everybody's got a job to do in life. I'm not holding your work against you. We got people falling off cliffs now where we never did before. I mean, you gotta go back in time for that kind of thing. We've got a bit of a history for *hanging* people off a cliff, just not for letting them drop. Which is different. We got a man of the cloth being sliced up for crow food. That cannot be justified. We need somebody to come in here to undo the wrong. Tidy this shit up. Make it right. I guess that's you."

"I appreciate the understanding."

"Just don't break up the party. Now that would be a crime against humanity."

Cinq-Mars sees Pete Briscoe walking toward him. More cars are coming over the crest, until finally they must park on the other side of the zenith.

"I was invited, Raymond. I'm here to join the party."

He grins broadly again. "Yeah. Right. Like I said. Everybody has a job to do."

"Raymond," Émile says, testing the waters as the sun reddens in the west and a cooling sea breeze picks up, "all these people come here. How long do they stay?"

"Everybody keeps their own dance card."

"That couple over there, see? First car in. Does that mean they're last out?"

"Remember, I'm the one who shoos folks off the boat. Do they want to leave?"

Émile speaks up to address the couple from Delaware. "Do you two want to leave?" He knows the answer before asking, as their misery is obvious.

They can enjoy the beauty of the evening, the whales below and the crimson setting sun across a vast horizon. All these people, though, so many cars, the alcohol, the laughter, the flirting women and intemperate men, the size of these muscled fishermen, their off-color language, the unmistakable waft of marijuana, this is neither a suburb in Kansas or Delaware and they want to go home. First the woman nods yes, then the man.

Raymond whistles—a strikingly clear and loud trill. Everyone looks up. Everyone, absolutely everyone, stops talking.

"This car here, first in, the Impala, wants out."

A movie scene. An unbelievable one at that. Car doors are opened and slammed shut, then the vehicles skitter into ditches and up the other side, back up over rock surfaces, buckle up closer to one another, spin their tires up a bank, veer this way, then that. Two dozens engines roar and whine and the pickups budge an inch here, a few feet there. Many back up, some are pushed into an alternative position, and, not unlike the Red Sea parting for Moses, the pair from Delaware are granted a sacred path home. Men and women provide hand signals, the spoken word is at a minimum, and the couple makes the turn around on the edge of the cliff and picks their way back up the hill in their vehicle to say good-bye to the Whistle just as the sun dips below the highest hill on the mainland. Then they're gone. Cars jostle and shimmy around and suddenly they're back in place and, as quickly, everyone is back at the cliff's edge, yammering away as though they'd never been interrupted.

People on this island, the wily old detective takes note, know how to get along. They know how to get things done.

He's reminded of that opinion a half hour later when, in faint light, a man comes over the hill to join the group, perhaps having parked on the other side of the crest, or he was dropped off there, yet looking as though he just walked the entire perimeter of the island twice around. He possesses a wildness to his countenance that causes others to check him out.

Cinq-Mars takes note. "Who's that?" he asks his new friend Raymond.

People seem aware of the fresh arrival, and many chatting a moment ago are rendered mute by his approach.

Passing a flask on, not his own this time, Raymond squints to make a positive identification. "Aaron Roadcap, the guy who happened to find the minister's body not too far from here."

Cinq-Mars is intrigued, as much by the respect, or fear, the man instigates in others as by the man himself. "Maybe you can introduce us."

"Trust me, Émile," Raymond counters, and forces a smile, "he knows who you are."

Having seen this gathering in action when charged with moving a car, Cinq-Mars doesn't doubt Raymond's statement. He's intrigued. He's been charged with investigating people who are intricately connected and intimately familiar with one another, so much so that it's hard to believe that anything, let alone a murder or two, or three, can go unnoticed on this island or remain unsolved for long.

While he senses that Roadcap has been informed of his presence at the Whistle, and has come here specifically to see him—no logic to the thought, pure conjecture and intuition—the man does not approach at the outset. He remains close enough that, given the social interactions at the Whistle, engaging with him is inevitable. Émile is convinced that Roadcap's purpose is to talk to the off-island, non-Mountie, retired cop who's mysteriously taken over the biggest murder case in island history. Or is it the second-biggest, as Roadcap is the son of a previous killer? He notes a sea change to the environment. Large groups have formed into smaller entities. Voices lower across the board. Women are especially quiet—they don't say much at all. People still return to the pickups and come back again with more beer, but otherwise the tenor on the cliff has changed. A sense of anticipation wafts in the night air. People are expectant.

Without detecting the genesis of a different movement, Cinq-Mars is suddenly brought up short, for he and Roadcap, still apart, have been isolated together. Everyone else has magically moved off, as if a modest form of teleportation shifted the crowd twenty feet away without disturbing the air yet successfully segregating the two men. Émile can imagine being thrown off the cliff at that moment, and among the three dozen witnesses none will have seen a thing. All will deny that he was ever there. The thought creates a tinge of fear in his gullet. His senses are alert. He looks down and looks up again, and Roadcap is beside him, beer in one hand, leaning his posterior back against the rail fence, staring west. No barrier between himself and the sea.

The sun is long gone. The last glimmers of red light are fading.

Émile stands on the opposite side of the fence, protected by it.

He wonders if he says nothing, and merely waits, what the man will say.

Finally, Roadcap twists his neck to look at him.

"Cat got your tongue?"

"Admiring the view."

"What's left of it," he says. Then adds, "I found the body."

"I heard. I know which one you mean," Cinq-Mars tells him.

Roadcap concedes this with a nod. "There've been a few."

"What's your interest?" Cinq-Mars asks him, deciding to be forthright.

"In what?"

"In me."

This man has authority among his peers. Cinq-Mars can see that. This is not an idle meeting or an exchange provoked by insecurity.

"I know how wrong the police can be sometimes. Dead wrong. They have the power to destroy an innocent life. I want to keep tabs on how things pan out."

Cinq-Mars dwells on that a moment, although really he's trying to hold to a sense of this man. He looks like a fisherman, except that he's strikingly handsome, more like a girl's dream fireman, and lives in a sketchy neighborhood. Yet the very tone of his voice exudes intelligence, which anyone might expect, yet a sophistication to his manner and speech is surprising. Maddy told him to expect an educated mind, but to the degree that he is willing to permit it within himself, Émile finds himself spellbound. Part of that he puts down to the night, the vanishing crimson horizon, the beauty of the sea, and the reaction of others, but part of it cannot be measured by anything in his previous experience.

"You're talking about your father," Cinq-Mars says.

"What do you know about him? See, that's unexpected. I'd want to keep tabs on something like that. What you know, let's say, or what you think you know."

"You're surprised that I've done my research."

"You know what they say."

"Tell me."

"A little knowledge can be a dangerous thing. Yet I'm surprised you know anything about us."

Yes, Cinq-Mars acknowledges to himself, knowing what he knows about police work, it is surprising if a policeman is aware of anything.

"What can you tell me about your discovery?"

"Nothing I haven't told the Mounties."

He thinks about that answer. He has a hunch. If he can relate to this man and detect the depths of an uncanny intelligence in him, then Roadcap may well be able to do the same with him. What he might say to a local policeman or a relatively local Mountie from the mainland, and what he might be willing to impart to him, could provoke two very different lines of inquiry. He has some trust building to do, perhaps years of distrust to tear town. None of that can be accomplished or even broached with so many ears nearby, and he isn't sure that the other man, with his manner as much as anything, isn't suggesting as much. Pete Briscoe, for one, eyes them closely, and Cinq-Mars can tell that he wants to get closer to this confab, that he resents giving them so much space. Still, the whole of the Whistle is a small area, and others, ears straining, eavesdrop.

"Any thoughts on Professor DeWitt?"

"I don't run in his circles," Roadcap stipulates. "Didn't really know the man, although I met him. Maybe he jumped. Not many around had much to do with him. I never heard that he had much to do with us."

If Émile had to qualify the man's reply, he'd mark it down as being careful. Plotted. Circumspect. Indeed, if he doubted the man's mind, he might conclude that he was coached by a legal representative, that this governs the quality of his response. Since he does not doubt the man's mind, Cinq-Mars concludes that he coached himself.

"You harvest dulse for a living. A little bird told me that."

Roadcap nods, sips from his beer, and sweeps the neck of his bottle to indicate the bay. "The beauty of this place never leaves me. I'd rather cut seaweed from a rock than sit in a chair all day."

An acknowledgment that he has options in life he's dismissed.

"Perhaps I could watch you work someday. I know nothing about dulse."

He's asking for a private interview, which the other man has anticipated.

"I'm out on the flats at Dark Harbour, the low side of any tide."

Just like that, they've agreed to meet again, and privately.

Roadcap briefly rubs one eye, then the other, an indication of weariness.

"All right," he says, confirming that. "Short and sweet. I'll see you around."

He walks back up the hill again and a man Cinq-Mars assumes is his driver traces his steps. Moments later, he hears an engine start up, a pickup by the sound of the growl. Raymond wanders closer to him again, and conversations regain their currency around them.

"Quite a place," Cinq-Mars mentions. "The Whistle. This island."

"It is," Raymond agrees with some conviction. "What's going on, nobody needs that. Nobody's for that. We're all every one of us against it."

Cinq-Mars accepts the sentiment as intended. He doesn't bother to say that while it may be true, somebody thinks differently and favors the killings, given that one or more people, jointly or in collusion, caused two murders and possibly a third to occur. The oddity of the case is that one killing was precipitated by a knife's rapacious blade, one by suffocation, and a third death, a murder or not, from a fall. Cinq-Mars has seen the photos of Lescavage's death, a grotesque killing, yet not a crime of passion in his deliberation, for the knife's stroke was straight and therefore swift from the apex just under the center of the rib cage down almost to the hip bone. Then, while the victim would have been roiling in the horror of that incision, strapped upright to a tree trunk, a matching slice was ripped down the opposite side of his solar plexus, the third line of a triangle. The swipe across the belly was more savage in a way, less precise. It might have occurred first, causing the man's intestines to spill out. Possibly three murders. With that kind of disparity in method—blade, suffocation, a fall—he has to think that more than one person is responsible for this havoc. Raymond's claim that nobody wants what is happening derives only from one man's wishful thinking.

Studying the photos, Émile had consoled Louwagie. "No big surprise that you got sick."

Anyone who witnessed the scene in person, and that would include Aaron Roadcap, or through the photographs, knows that a person capable of extreme horror is on the loose. No fanciful island serendipity about how people on the island aren't like that is going to will that fact away.

At the outset of his investigation, Émile accepts that whichever person he is talking to at any one moment might be the person capable of such butchery.

TWENTY

In early morning light, Émile and Sandra repeat the walking tour at their end of the island. They have no plan to do the whole trail, as Émile intends to examine the ground where they spied Pete Briscoe shoveling. Still, the stroll provides the joy of birdcalls and pliant sea air and soon they rhapsodize about a return trip to Grand Manan one day, which might include a boat ride out to view the puffins, an excursion on a lobster boat, another to be up close and personal with whales. Émile wants to investigate the salmon farms to make up his own mind on their pros and cons, sick fish being a major con, and he wants to visit a weir to learn more of how it operates. Sandra teases him that all he really wants is a net *that* big, for criminals, not herring. She has a point, for the genius of a weir is that the fish find their way in easily enough but can't find their way out because they keep swimming in circles in one direction only. How great would it be if criminals marched their way into prison, and even though the door remained wide open they couldn't use it, because they kept marching in a circle around the yard.

They speak also of spending a whole glorious day sitting on a beach—but only after this nasty business is behind them. They kiss, a pause on their walk to commiserate with each other for failing, once again, to have a holiday.

"Don't worry about it, Émile," Sandra says.

From a precipice, they observe a fish boat motor out, gulls surrounding it in a feverish cry for scraps. They earn a few, as a crewman culls the bait box and tosses wastage into the sea. Then the truly rambunctious bickering begins.

"I imagine they're company," Émile ponders. He's mesmerized by the scene, the richness of the color, the example of proud, tenacious work. "Like barn cats to a farmer. Lonely work. Must be. The gulls are company, I suppose."

Locating Pete Briscoe's spot is not difficult. They had certain pines to pinpoint, and that proves easy. Ascending a rise, they see where holes have been dug, then backfilled, the surface smoothed over. Rain, sunlight, and vigorous grass will conceal Briscoe's labors over time, but they've come early enough to be successful archaeologists.

Émile has brought along a garden spade nicked from the shed by his cottage in order to scratch the earth. He digs a patch separate from Briscoe's handiwork to give himself an idea of what the undisturbed terrain looks like when turned over, its texture and density. He can then revisit the other man's excavations and sort out any differences. Going deeper, he will be able to determine the limit of Briscoe's foray. His theory works, for in a couple of the old holes Briscoe soon struck solid rock. When Émile does find a deeper hole, nothing is in it.

He tries elsewhere.

No luck.

In all—and Émile walks a wide berth to confirm that he's missed nothing—Briscoe dug eight separate patches. Only in one is anything found, and Émile would rather not have made the discovery—a long stool has been left behind.

"He was going to the bathroom?" Sandra asks. "That's why he was digging?" By itself, that makes no sense.

"Can't be. Who walks a mile into the woods when there are public toilets in town? If he came here with a shovel it wasn't to dig an out-house. His waste is incidental."

"Nothing's here. You only have one more to dig."

Nothing shows up in that hole either. He hits rock eight inches down.

On the walk back they puzzle it through. The consensus between them is that Briscoe might have buried something. When spotted by Émile and Sandra, he opted to dig it back up again. Still, that fails to explain the need for eight separate holes. Sandra proffers the habit of squirrels, who bury their precious nuts then fail to remember where. The critters hope that enough of them bury a sufficient quantity of nuts that they're bound to sniff one sometime by digging around. Émile quietly takes that in, and Sandra needs time before she grasps that he isn't being his usual pensive self. His mind has gone off somewhere.

"Émile? What is it?"

"He could have been burying something," the detective explains. "Or he could have been digging something up. There's a third option."

Given his general parameters, she can't think what that might be.

"At the crime scene, somebody tried to dig a grave. Okay, that's my conjecture, but somebody was digging for some reason and didn't get very far. Here, the digger had some success and some failure. There are holes where the earth remains soft enough and deep enough under the surface, where Briscoe could have gone deeper. Then there are holes that hit solid bedrock."

"What does that imply?"

He doesn't want to say. "Suppose somebody had that problem orig-inally. A grave can't get dug when it's necessary. So Lescavage is strapped to a tree instead and savaged. Now suppose that somebody wanted to do such a thing again. What would the killer think to find out before committing to a second time around?"

Sandra gets it. "He'd want to make sure he could dig a grave. So Pete Briscoe was experimenting? Making plans? Émile, is he your killer?"

Émile cocks his head from side to side, makes a face. "His alibi has holes. I haven't gone over it carefully, or tried to break him down. Those aren't the questions foremost on my mind at the moment."

"What are?"

"Why the hell was Pete Briscoe up here shoveling if he's not our killer? What other explanation might he have? If so, what was it he didn't want us to see? What did he feel so strongly about that he has since removed the evidence? And if he is probing for an easy-to-dig burial ground, who does he plan to inter? I don't believe he came all the way up here only to shovel his own shit, although apparently he did that, too."

Back at the cottage, they enjoy a simple lunch of salmon sandwiches and chips, followed by cherries and cool lemonade. Émile then absconds with the Jeep and heads to the primary general store on the island. The young woman who works there found a dog's owner quickly, and Wade Louwagie let on that she subsequently helped him out when an "episode" shattered his nerves. She knows stuff, Émile is certain. She knows people, their place and their histories. He needs to acquire local knowledge and Margaret of the General Store strikes him as a bountiful source.

Confirming that, she knows who he is this time and what he's been up to. Island news is making the rounds only a whiff slower than the speed of light.

"So I heard you're, like, famous, like a Sherlock Holmes–type guy."

"Not by a long shot." He wants to explain that he doesn't think of himself as particularly bright, merely diligent, with a missile's guidance system for the truth. That might take time and still not be understood. "Our Corporal Louwagie could use a hand at the moment, so I'm pitching in."

"You can say that again, poor guy."

"You were kind to him."

"Maybe too kind. He might have ideas now."

"Would that be so terrible?" he asks.

The hint of a blush slips onto her skin, even as she shrugs. He studies her. Sometimes even the most humble of people exude a warmth and honesty that transcends the usual quagmire in which humans perpetually bathe. She is one of these, spry and witty and cogent, and probably a real tease in her way to any boy who's not prepared for cleverness. He cannot say if Margaret's a gossip—she may or may not be—although she is a bona fide gatherer of gossip, he imagines, given that her workplace is a hub for the island sport. He's hoping that she discriminates between information that is truthful and what ought to be held up to the light.

"Any chance that you can take time off for a chat?"

"My boss is a stickler."

"I see. I don't mean to impose, but when is your next break?"

"Of course . . ." she says, and lets her voice trail off in a telling way.

"'Of course . . .'" Émile encourages her.

"If you think that I could say to him that this is police business."

"It is. Let him know that. If you prefer, I'll tell him myself."

At that, she takes his hand as though he's a pupil and she his teacher guiding him to the principal's office, in this case her boss's. She knocks.

A voice shouts back, "Open!"

She shoves him through the door ahead of her, hanging back. When Émile utters the phrase, "police business," she repeats it for her boss's benefit, which prevents Émile from getting to the point.

"What police business?" the boss inquires. He seems pleasant, not a pariah.

"I need to ask Margaret a few questions."

"About the murders?" He's more than surprised. He almost takes umbrage. "She doesn't know anything."

"About the island," Cinq-Mars counters. "She can help me out on several fronts. I need to talk to her precisely because she's not in any way associated with the murders. I don't want this conversation with anyone who might be even remotely involved."

He understands, and changes his tune. "About the island, Margaret knows everything. What she doesn't know, she can invent and still be right."

"Police business," Margaret repeats, as if she's won a prize.

"All right," the owner allows, "take her away. Just bring her back in one piece, if you don't mind. The truth is, I don't know what I'd do without her."

Outside, Cinq-Mars suggests a walk by the seaside.

"Too close to the fish plant. Do you love the stinkeroo of dead fish?"

Good point. Instead, they head off along a footpath by a brook. A few bugs assail them, but nothing serious.

"What do you want to ask me? My boss is right. I know nothing about those murders. My gosh. Not me."

"This is touchy, Margaret. Let me explain it to you carefully, because I need your fullest cooperation."

"You have it. Of course! I'm cooperating."

"You know the people who live here. I don't. I want to ask you about certain people. I don't want you to think that someone is therefore under suspicion. No one is. I just need to start putting together how certain pieces interconnect and how certain people fit with others. I don't want you to talk about what I say because, misinterpreted, if you make the wrong assumption, you could ruin a good person's reputation."

"I get you. Don't worry about me, sir. I know when to keep it zipped. But thank you. That's a compliment, and I thank you."

Émile is momentarily lost.

"You're saying out loud that you trust me. I appreciate that. Fire away."

He does like this girl. Smart and able.

"Who," he wants to know, "is Aaron Roadcap?"

First, she needs to lean against a maple, let her neck and head droop, and release several breaths without appearing to draw any back in.

"Isn't he just," she says, looking up and straightening again, "the world's most handsome man? He's so beautiful. You should see him with his shirt off. I have. Only when he was on a beach, you understand. Okay. I have not been all around the world, I've hardly been off this island. But oh my God, isn't he the world's most handsome man? He is so frigging cute! I just want to die whenever he walks in, which isn't close to often enough. He should take his shirt off more often. I have a boyfriend, but I wouldn't if Aaron clicked his fingers in my direction. Anytime he visits the store I need to go pee after."

She makes him laugh. She won't bore him, this girl. "The thing is,

Margaret, where I come from, girls also take into account what a man does, what his place in the world might be. Sometimes it doesn't mean so much if a man is handsome if he's not also, let's say, as an example, a movie star. Or just a good guy."

"I know what you're saying," Margaret attests, and Émile believes she does. "He picks dulse. Aaron Roadcap wades in the cold waters off Dark Harbour with his shirt off on a hot day and picks dulse. He's not a banker. He's not even a fisherman. He's one step above shining shoes for a living, not that anybody around here makes a dime doing that! I can't believe that anybody on earth can't shine their own shoes."

"You do understand me," Cinq-Mars confirms, hoping to get her on point.

"He lives in a hovel. How can an attractive man live in a hovel? Probably with rodents for pets. Or maybe he has a cat, I don't know. I wish I knew. I would gladly visit his hovel to find out. But the thing is, what you need to understand is, Aaron Roadcap is not *just* a dulse farmer." She resorts to a conspiratorial whisper, and checks around to see if anyone else is listening. But they occupy these quiet woods on their own.

Émile Cinq-Mars is wholly confident now that he has come to the right person to fortify his local knowledge.

"Go on," he says, encouraging her.

TWENTY-ONE

If he stuck to a logical list of priorities, the cult's gaggle of levitating devotees would not be next to interview, but as he's in the vicinity and following no such list, Émile Cinq-Mars knocks on their door. Besides, he bears a grudge against them, still miffed by the lack of civility he experienced when he showed up with a dead dog. If he can in any way disturb their afternoon, that success will only elevate his.

He thinks it might make him so happy, he'll positively float off the ground.

For this encounter, the group's leader and resident doorman at the old City Hall does nothing to ingratiate himself or his band of spiritual neophytes. He's still wearing his high-rise boots, suitable for a clown. "Not another dead dog story." The man is expressionless. "Do we have an epidemic on our hands?"

Today he's not sweaty, and his motley crew seeking to defy gravity must be on a break or enjoying nap time. They've gone quiet, wherever they might be.

Cinq-Mars is equally as superior. "You're the only person on the island who doesn't know who you're talking to right now, or why, or what's at stake."

Arms crossed, a hip buttressed against the doorjamb, the tall, skinny, waiflike sentry with a skin tone that eschews the sun—perhaps Dracula-like he ventures out only at night and, unlike the drinker of blood, only during storms—blows a bubble with chewing gum. It pops, and his tongue slips it back into his mouth again. He asks, "Who are you supposed to be? King Kong?"

The detective figures that he probably deserves that, and tells him, "I'm an officer of the law investigating a rash of murders on this island."

The lie, he justifies, is a minor one, a question of time and circumstance. The fib is working, as the guy seems less blasé. "You're a cop. A cop who the last time he was here didn't know that this isn't the real City Hall. Are you sure you've got your story straight?"

Cinq-Mars figures he's owed that one, too.

"Like I said, you're the only person on the island who hasn't heard of me. Best advice? Take this meeting seriously."

The man concedes an inch, at least. "I can't help with any murders."

"Let me be the judge of that."

"Officer," he says, giving his brow a wipe as though overcome by the lassitude of the age, "shouldn't you show me your badge or something?"

Rather than do the impossible, Cinq-Mars stares him down.

"Okay, okay. Look, we're not exactly integrated with island life. People don't know us, we don't know them. I don't know you or anybody else, so don't take it personal. Truth is, me and nobody who comes here can help you."

"Your group was on the ridge the night the Reverend Lescavage was murdered."

"How do you know?"

"Who else would be silly enough to be out on a night like that?"

"That doesn't answer my question."

"I'm not answering questions. You are."

At an impasse, perhaps a crossroads, the two men glare back at each other.

"There's a slow way to do this," Cinq-Mars advises him. "Most find it mildly uncomfortable. Some come undone. Another way is easy. Which do you prefer?"

"The quick," the man said. "Of course. The easy."

"Good answer. Let me in. I'll ask, you'll reply. Afterward, I'm gone from your life and you probably won't remember I was here."

"Unless you arrest me for murder."

"There's that."

The man holds the door wide open, and Émile Cinq-Mars steps inside. His nostrils twitch from the scent of incense. Patchouli. A few sticks smoke nearby. His host takes him through to an antechamber off the vestibule, where they sit under the image of a white-bearded guru with long white tresses seated in the lotus position and smiling idiotically, in Émile's opinion, like a dolt in love with his daily enema. He desperately wants to say so but correctly holds his tongue. The skinny fellow squats on an exercise ball behind a small table being used as a desk. If he crosses his legs on that thing and keeps his balance without rolling away, Émile will be impressed. But the man keeps both feet steadily on the floor.

"Fire away," the fellow on his ball says. He bounces slightly.

"My wife is studying numerology."

"Seriously?"

"I don't know how serious it is."

"I mean, seriously, you're going to talk about your wife?"

"I was going to explain why I want your complete name and date of birth. Now, I'll just ask you to tell me." Cinq-Mars has armed himself with a notebook picked up at the General Store, and he writes down the mystic's name: Geoff Samuel Brown. And his date of birth: February 9, 1986. The man volunteers as well that he's from Pawtucket, Rhode Island.

"Is she going to find out the murderer using numerology?"

"I wouldn't put it past her. If you knew my wife, you wouldn't either. What were you doing up on the ridge the night of the murders?"

Don't give him a chance to confirm or deny his presence there. Stick with the assumption as being a bald fact and see how he bears up.

"We were out in the storm."

"Obviously."

"I mean, we were out there *because* of the storm. No storm, we stay home."

"I'll repeat my question. What were you doing?"

"Being with God. You?"

"You believe in a thunder god, do you? Or is it a rain god? It wasn't the goddess moon."

"No harm to remind the soul how fleeting life is. Have you ever contemplated such a thing? No. You wouldn't. A cop. A storm such as the one that recently swept through here has power, great force, yet that *appearance* of force is less than a mosquito's piddling fart compared to the power loose in the universe. Have you contemplated such a thing? This is where our minds diverge. We remind ourselves how small we are in comparison to that mere puff of nature, which helps us begin to grasp how infinitesimal we are compared to a force of infinite power."

Cinq-Mars nods. He says, "Good."

"Why good?"

"I was hoping you weren't trying to get struck by lightning."

"Maybe we were."

"You jest."

"So do you. There wasn't any lightning when we went up there. Not at first."

"Were you trying to fly?"

The man straightens in his seat, then tugs on tufts of hair at the nape of his neck. This seems a studied reaction, to Émile's eye. Then Geoff Brown arrives at a decision and appears determined not to answer the question. In a way, Cinq-Mars is impressed, as any answer will put him at a disadvantage.

"Did you see anything while you were up there? A man was murdered on the ridge. For the sake of this conversation, let's say that you didn't do it—"

"I didn't. We didn't."

"If you had, would you admit it? You see what I'm getting at. Let's say that you didn't kill the minister. Did you see anybody or anything up on the ridge that might pertain to this investigation?"

"Flashlights," the man admits. "They were a bit far off, but we saw them."

"How many?"

"More than one. Hard to tell otherwise. So two, maybe three."

"In what direction were they coming from, and what direction were they going?"

"They came from North Head. We assumed they were following the trail. We saw them over Ashburton Head. Then we saw another man—one flashlight—coming up from the other direction. He saw us, too. After that, we were on our way."

"Why would you say that you had nothing to contribute to this investigation if you saw all that?" He doesn't give Brown a chance to answer, and presses on. "When did you see the dead man?"

The silence floats in the room like smoke hovering at eye level, though Cinq-Mars imagines the other man's mind buzzing. "Never said I did," Brown replies.

"Come on. You left early. You packed up in a flash. Something spooked you."

"The man who came up the trail spooked us."

"Why?"

Geoff Brown passes his right hand over his face to give his left eyebrow a scratch. Émile doesn't recognize the gesture and is not sure how to read it. Only later will he think that it occurred while the man was making a decision to tell the truth.

"We saw lights. We valued our privacy. A couple of volunteers from our group went to investigate. To intercept. A significant hike. They found a dead man. Obviously slaughtered. They brought us back that news. Then while we were considering what to do, the other man came by. I mean, who walks out of a storm of that power? Besides us? And now the cliffs were crowded. We were, as you say, spooked. That made us think that maybe we'd better leave before we were blamed. We have no pull on this island, no friends in high places. Few friends period. We didn't know where the storm walker guy came from. Maybe he was with the others and had just circled around, so he might be a murderer. That was a definite possibility, which put us in danger, right? Safety in numbers, though. Even if he was just an innocent bystander, like us, then he might tell others that we were up there. So we left in the dark before anybody could identify who we were. How did you identify us, anyway?"

The question warrants a smirk from Cinq-Mars, and Geoff Brown understands. What other large group would be out in a storm for the fun of it? Boy Scouts? They'd be prepared, they'd head home early. Essentially, Geoff Brown had confirmed the identity of his group for him.

"Did you know the victim, sir? The clergyman?"

The way he casts his glance down instantly betrays him. He can't deny it now, and seems to understand that. "I met him a few times. Like you, he seemed to enjoy making fun of us. Apparently, not that I was there, he frequently mentioned our group in his sermons. Not with much affection. Very little Christian kindness. Or even respect."

"How do you know?"

"That he spoke about us? He told me. Anytime we were mentioned he sent me a copy of the sermon. Always with a request for comments, but we didn't bite."

"Why do you suppose he did that?"

"Honestly?"

Usually when someone brings up the matter of honesty, it is because they intend to lie. Cinq-Mars, on a hunch that this could be an example that disproves the rule, nods.

"He had trouble with believers. He baited me so that I might bait him back."

"Did you bother?"

"Once at the grocer's. Once rather loudly at the farmers' market. The talks were heated and I am ashamed for losing my equilibrium. That's all he wanted, I think. To show me and others that I'm not as enlightened as I might pretend. He didn't need to go to all that trouble, truth be told. All he had to do was ask."

He didn't sound like a man who'd had it in for the minister.

"One more quick question."

"As long as you don't mean a trick question."

"Maybe it is. Why do you wear tall boots when you're tall to start with?"

He studies them first, the six-inch heels and the five-inch soles. He smiles, as though to concede that they look ridiculous. "When I take them off, my normal height seems small. That provides me with two advantages. One, I feel small, so my natural height is no longer a point of pride. I'm helped to feel humble. And two, I feel that I should be higher, as though I'm sinking when I should feel as though I'm—"

He stops.

"Flying?" Cinq-Mars coaxes him. "Levitating?"

"I feel as though I'm sinking when I should be elevating my consciousness."

"Good save," Cinq-Mars opines. "I hope you won't be offended, or mind my saying so, but you might be a lesser kook than I first imagined."

That wins him a smile.

"I'll need to speak to the others, specifically to the two men who saw the body, then to everyone in your group."

"Not two men," Brown corrects him. "One man, one woman. The woman is still on the island. The man, I'm afraid, is deceased."

Cinq-Mars stares down his imposing beak at him. "Don't tell me," he says.

"Professor DeWitt," Brown admits.

"And what can you tell me about that?"

"Nothing. We're in shock. That's why no on is here today. We don't understand it. Honestly, he gave us no indication. I'm sure it was an accident. Had to be. Unless—. Did someone kill him, too?"

Cinq-Mars is unsure of his own response. He proceeds slowly. "What is it, Mr. Brown, that requires you to be here today? Why aren't you with the others? What are you protecting? You're obviously guarding the place."

Geoff Brown from Pawtucket raises an eyebrow and purses his lips briefly, nothing more. Cinq-Mars is being informed that that is none of his business, and a murder investigation doesn't change that opinion.

He rises. "Thank you," he says. "I'm sorry for your loss. And I hope you get off the ground soon."

"Sure you do," Brown says.

At the front door, while being ushered out, Cinq-Mars surprises him. "I agree with you, by the way. I find that especially true in my profession. If you think about it, you might understand why."

"What's that?" Brown, tall in his shoes, is stumped by his comment.

"Always good to remind the soul how fleeting life is. Thanks, Mr. Brown."

He hates it when he comes to respect someone he's previously dismissed, but he imagines that he'll get past his umbrage with himself soon enough.

At the height of his powers as a big-city detective, Émile Cinq-Mars wouldn't have done this, and he wonders if he's being lazy, hazy, or caving in to a pending old age. Perhaps, after a long career, he's finally being efficient with the public purse. He'd normally line up witnesses and suspects in an order that permitted his investigative prowess to step along a path taking him from pillar to post logically. Later, should he find it possible to connect the dots with a thread, the line might show circles closing in around the culprit. Perpetually tightening. He never minded crisscrossing the city daily, or getting stuck in traffic, or missing a meal because of a zany schedule. What mattered more was to proceed along a preconceived, virtually ordained, pattern. On this job, he is not dipping into any public purse, so even his willingness to be efficient makes no sense, yet he's finding that he prefers to interview people according to their proximity, not according to any plan. Pending old age is the answer he selects. What else accounts for the shift? That, and saving on gas money, which is now a personal expense.

So the next person he seeks to interview is Pete Briscoe. He's closest.

His mental preparation with respect to Briscoe has been half-hearted, in part because he doesn't really expect to find him in. Don't fisherman fish? They're in fishing season, the man should be out on the water. He's surprised when he finds him puttering outside his house, packing his pickup before heading down to the waterfront. Mildly cross with himself for not performing his due diligence on this guy,

Émile warns himself to be circumspect, to make this an initial fact-finding tour only. He can always bring a keener focus once he has his ducks in a row.

The man greets him warmly. They no sooner shake hands than Ora Matheson pokes her head out from behind the screen door onto Pete's porch. "Petey? Going yet?" Then she sees Cinq-Mars. "Oh. Hello."

Not as a question, Cinq-Mars looks at Briscoe, who shrugs. "Girlfriend," the fisherman states, an explanation neither requested nor required.

Ora bounces down the steps. "You're him, aren't you? Tall, with a big—" About to say *nose*, she censors herself, something that Émile determines is uncommon for her. To bring attention to what is already an attention grabber crosses a line that she recognizes as a social barrier. Émile now knows how complete strangers are managing to identify him so confidently. "I mean," she says, "you're tall. Petey told me you're so tall."

Briscoe is embarrassed. Cinq-Mars couldn't care less.

"Yes, I have a massive honker. So did my dad, and his dad, and so on, going back who knows how many generations. I wear it with pride."

"Oh my God," she says, "it is *huge*!"

"Ora," Briscoe snaps back.

She checks in with him, then looks at Cinq-Mars. Then makes a comic face, as though to suggest that some people are too uptight to suit her, although nothing's to be done. "Aren't I the stupid mutt," she says.

Catching them together is unfortunate, he thinks initially, yet Cinq-Mars quickly calculates an alternative strategy to take advantage of this development.

He addresses Briscoe. "You're not fishing."

"On my way. Crew's on the dock. I'm not late, but I will be."

"Oh, you can give the great detective—we heard you're a really great detective, that you sent the Mafia packing—we can give him the time of day, Petey."

"I suppose," Briscoe says.

Cinq-Mars is adding up what's been said about him lately and understands that his reputation has probably ignited and is now a brush fire. By dusk, he'll have been responsible for solving the Jack the Ripper crimes, and in a week he'll have been credited with arresting twenty of the world's worst serial killers and uncovered that Osama bin Laden remains alive, living on the dole in Wichita.

"He's trying to register for health care," he says, but the young couple has no clue what he's talking about, and can only glance at each other.

"You were Mr. Orrock's housekeeper?" he asks, returning to seriousness.

"He was a slime bucket," Ora claims. "You know? Really. There's no excuse to treat good people the way he treated good people. I had to stand my ground with that man. Always trying to feel me up, he was."

"If you'd've told me that, I would've throttled him myself," Briscoe brags.

"Do you know who did?"

"What do you mean? Who? Who what?"

Émile's hoping that this ploy works, knowing that it could easily backfire. Telling these two that Alfred Orrock was murdered will not merely ripple across the island and have an effect—in this community, it will be a tsunami. Shake people up. More talk might surface that way. The murderer will be surprised by what is common knowledge, and might show a hand unwittingly. Or not. Risk forms a big part of the strategy.

"Alfred Orrock was suffocated to death. People are going to gossip, I should warn you, about whether or not his nurse did it."

"I was never his nurse."

"Housemaid, then."

"I looked after him, but I was never his nurse. I stood my ground on that."

"His housemaid. You were there, though. That's the thing. The night he died."

"When I left him he was alive!"

"That may be true. I'm betting that you have no witnesses. Am I right?"

She starts to utter the Reverend Lescavage's name but stops herself. That's not going to do her any good.

"He was alive when I left him."

"Then the minister showed up and he was killed, too. A busy night for somebody."

"Wasn't me!" She's vehement about it, he'll give her that.

"Of course not," Pete Briscoe says.

Cinq-Mars grants them that. "He did tick you off, though, didn't he? Feeling you up and being mean. You can see why people might talk. What they might say. They'll think you despised the man. Not an overstatement, is it? People might say you'd had enough. A moment of rage, it wouldn't take long, and suddenly he's not breathing anymore. All you have to do is adjust the pillow and call up Lescavage to come on over, then if he puts up a fuss about the dead guy, off him, too. Or have your boyfriend do it."

"Hey! You shut up now!"

"Why? I'm only pointing out what people will imagine, what they'll say. The inevitable, don't you think?"

Funny, Cinq-Mars notices, that the man is hot to defend himself when he is rather tepid about protecting his girlfriend when she's accused.

"What were you burying up on the ridge the day I saw you, Mr. Briscoe?"

"My dog."

"Why dig eight different holes?"

"What?"

"Where's your dog now since she's not there? What have you done with her remains?"

"Petey?" Ora asks, perturbed by the expression on her boyfriend's face.

"I moved her. I dug her up again. Moved her."

"Pete?"

"Never mind, Ora!" he barks. "A personal-type thing."

"Eight holes?"

"I had trouble finding her again is all."

"That's not what it looked like to me."

They're still outside in Briscoe's yard. Cinq-Mars wouldn't mind going inside, talking within that confined space, which would be cooler, undoubtedly. Any moment for that shift has passed. He won't be invited indoors now.

"What did it look like to you?" Briscoe asks him, and then to the surprise of both men, Ora asks exactly the same question, word for word. The look on her face suggests that she's defending the honor of her man.

"I saw that digging site as an experiment," Émile says, "a trial run, if you will. To discover where to dig your next grave."

"What are you talking about?" Ora interjects. "Petey? Petey, what's he talking about?"

"Bullshit," Petey explains. "He's talking bullshit, Ora."

"I figured. Smart-ass detective, my royal ass."

Perhaps by the end of the day, his island reputation may yet be mud.

"You'll be going now," Briscoe says.

Cinq-Mars decides that he might as well. He drives comfortably to North Head. Along the way he sees Briscoe's pickup make an appearance, hanging back. Two can play at that game, and in North Head Cinq-Mars pulls over and Briscoe, with Ora along as a passenger, goes on by. He watches Briscoe unload at the docks with Ora's help, then they kiss, then Ora heads off on foot alone. Briscoe greets his crew. Émile reminds himself to talk to that crew one day soon. They launch a dinghy to go fetch the fish boat, and while they do that, Cinq-Mars starts up again, and intercepts Ora down the road. He slows, and drives beside her while she walks.

"Need a lift?"

"I'm not gong far."

"Hop in anyway. Escape the heat."

She thinks about it and mops her forehead, then climbs in.

"Which way?" Cinq-Mars asks.

"Straight on except for the curves."

They don't have much to say to each other. Émile is not interested in

developing a relationship that has to be advanced by his constant probing. His questions pertain only to the island, to what growing up here
was like, to how anybody can ever eat dulse, let alone every day.

"It's healthy! Loads of iron."

"Maybe that's why it tastes like iron ore."

"Dulse chips beat potato chips hands down. Eat too many potato
chips, they'll kill you. Eat too much dulse and you're Superman. Feel
like him anyway."

Turning down the sloped driveway to her home, which sits in a bit
of a gulley, they are met in the yard by a woman he recognizes. She had
the traffic incident with Professor DeWitt, in which she ended up in a
ditch, later the hospital. Ora's mom is coming across to see him. As he's
rolling down his window, Ora gives her an earful about who he is.

These women might be helpful someday. They might never trust
him, but he feels that his cause will not be advanced if they fear him.
The woman's first words are, "Detective Big Shot."

"I'm just trying to help out, ma'am."

"Ma'am. Ma'am! Nobody's called anybody *ma'am* around here since
sharks wore bikinis."

He doesn't know for sure, but assumes that that means never.

"So the guy who nearly ran me down went over the cliff. You better
not try to pin that one on me."

"Mrs. Matheson, is it? Same as your daughter's last name?"

"She's not somebody's doorstep drop, no."

"You say," Ora interjects.

"All that wailing was for you, my dear, not some figment of my
imagination."

She's got her there.

"What are you driving Ora around for? What's she done?"

"Aw, Mom."

"Just saving her some walk time, Mrs. Matheson. On my way home
anyway."

"Home? Home! You mean you live here now?"

He smiles. "Temporarily. I used the wrong word. I was on the way to
the rental cottage where I am temporarily residing."

The woman seems satisfied that she's won the day, and Cinq-Mars backs up, careful to avoid the big DULSE FOR SALE sign, underscored by the word SPECIALS! He carries on home. He's happy to arrive, to put his feet up and have a drink. He tells Sandra so. "Good to be back in the rental cottage where I am temporarily residing."

What? Some bee is in his bonnet about the case, she assumes.

TWENTY-TWO

Following their customary evening stroll, Émile and Sandra Cinq-Mars pile into the Cherokee and drive to the Orrock mansion. Maddy's in the front garden snipping flowers for the funeral that's two days off, and also to brighten the residence. Delighted to invite the couple inside, she's demure through a tour of the house as Sandra gapes, particularly impressed by the views, while Émile strikes a removed and solemn countenance. Like Maddy, he's of two minds with respect to the place. For him, the home is also a crime scene.

Émile inquires about her relationship with the late Reverend Lescavage and what she knows of how he got on with her dad. Both accounts are skimpy, bereft of substance, until she opines that the minister was probably her dad's only male friend over the last twenty years.

"Friend."

"I'm not saying he was a good one. Dad needled him and Simon took it as a cross to bear in life. They were like that since day one. But they tolerated each other's company. They could get philosophical without the reverend feeling he had to stick to the company line, if you know what I mean. As for my dad, ladies came and went in his life, but male pals were rare. Men either worked for him or were in competition with him or they plain didn't like him. I thought he had no friends except for Simon, until this week."

"What changed this week?" Émile asks.

"The skipper who brought me over here? Sticky—that's the name he goes by—Sticky McCarran, he and my dad were close, in a way. Friends? Maybe not. An employer/hired-hand relationship, but he actually thought my dad was an okay guy. Just misunderstood." She did a pantomime of rolling her eyes while saying this, as if even now the idea is too ludicrous to be entertained. "Anyway, they got along. My dad bullied the minister. He probably controlled Sticky, but I doubt if he's a man who can be bullied."

"I'd like to speak to him."

"Sticky? I can give you his number. He lives in Blacks. He tells me he's usually fishing. Best to get him at night, I think."

Later the women convene to discuss the funeral arrangements which are not to be in Reverend Lescavage's church anymore. The elders there haven't been able to scrounge up a replacement, temporary or otherwise, and worshipers plan to fan out to various second choices among the island's multiple denominations. A difficulty lies in divining how many people might show up for the funeral. Refreshments afterward seem appropriate. Potentially, the island's entire population will be interested, yet some people might think a boycott an appropriate gesture. Hard to gauge, as Maddy isn't in touch with the locals. "I used to have friends here. No more. Like me, they had the good sense to leave."

"You say that, and yet to me, this island is paradise," Sandra mentions.

"Yeah, it's a great place to visit. I own it now. I ought to know."

The statement, Sandra knows, is far more bitter than boastful.

As the women chat, Émile sits in Alfred Orrock's bedroom and listens to the walls speak. If only they were more articulate and didn't mumble so. He thinks what the room's few visitors before him have already asked themselves: Why would any man require so much space to sleep in? Empty space, too. If he himself ever slept in such a room, he'd add a writing desk, a comfortable chair or two, a library. Heck, as a rich man, he'd put in a pool table, then a bowling lane. To sleep in this vast surround confounds him, although he supposes that it's somewhat like sleeping under the stars, without the requisite mosquitoes or any threat of rain. If he lived in such a room, Cinq-Mars decides, he'd invite a few cows in to create an atmosphere around the campfire, then install a campfire.

While his initial impressions are idle, Émile does try to confront the psyche of this man. So much space, just to dream in. He might have been claustrophobic. He lived on a tightly knit island where he was disdained, yet had a sky and a sea to gaze out upon, and obviously he enjoyed the view, confirmed by the plethora of large windows. Gazing out over the dark bay, Orrock would have seen bountiful stars on a clear night. And the airliners out of New York bound for Europe which typically trace a flight path straight up the Bay of Fundy.

Orrock bullied the Reverend Lescavage, but the latter nurtured an interest in the universe and its origins—might Alfred Orrock have shared that passion, or been jealous that such a pursuit found favor in another man? A man he bullied and dismissed? Yet he needed the more timid man in his life, this foil, his only friend. To Orrock, all men must have appeared to him as pipsqueaks, their interests ridiculed, with the possible exception of members of the Irving family, who own virtually the whole province. Most people, Émile concludes, struck Orrock as trivial. They slept in small bedrooms. Hence his lack of companions. The parish minister in his humble abode had impressed him in some other way, as did the fisherman he permitted himself to befriend for no other reason, perhaps, than he lived off the island. The fisherman brought him out upon the vast blue sea. The minister—from what Maddy said, they were old and familiar disputants on philosophical matters—took him for a ride upon the vast array of the unknown.

Émile speculates on whether the restricted geography of the island did not contrast sharply with the man's yen for distance, for the infinite, that in being stretched between the two realms he found no comfort, no happiness in life.

Cinq-Mars entertains a notion that perhaps Orrock bullied the

minister not only because he could, but that he also hated his need for
another's company, for discourse, for a friend. Lescavage may have
permitted the dynamic because he recognized Orrock's motivation. If
so, then the deceased minister was indeed someone willing to live his
faith, or his non-faith, in that that he was willing to be punished in order
to lend his abuser a measure of kindness.

Still, Cinq-Mars can't figure out who killed Orrock, or summon a
reason why. Did Lescavage do it? Why not allow a dying man to die
naturally? Why help him along?

The question is no sooner asked than a curious and compelling
answer arises, a new possibility. That the bullied man had had enough
and killed his oppressor may be a likelihood. Certainly it's feasible,
although such a shift in a long-standing dynamic is rare in the world. Or
Lescavage could have killed Orrock because he was bullied into doing
so. That fit their customary dynamic. Given Orrock's pleasure in power,
his control over his island world, his penchant for vast spaces, the sea,
the sky, he might have wanted out from his circumstances, from the
tedious, painful, prolonged business of dying. He may have wanted to
be off to the infinite unknown.

He who controlled his world may have chosen to control his own
death.

Suffocation killed him. Not an easy thing to do, mentally, and difficult enough morally, but simple to accomplish physically. The killer
wouldn't need to even look at the victim. All he had to do was place a
pillow over the man's face and lie on it.

Cinq-Mars holds the pillow in his hand, the probable murder
weapon. Fluffy. Down-filled. The housekeeper could have done it. The
minister had opportunity. In theory, so did the daughter. Orrock was
sick enough, frail enough, that any stranger seeking shelter from a storm,
or anyone who wanted to move in the dark while the storm rendered
him or her invisible, could have done it. Which made everyone on the
island a suspect. And whether the minister did it or not, or if he merely
discovered that the man was dead, the question remains: what happened
to the Reverend Lescavage?

Standing in the vacuous emptiness of the patriarch's room, Cinq-

Mars reflects that the answer lies neither in how nor even by whom, but in why. Find out why someone wanted a good man dead, he believes, and the case is solved.

He has more people to talk to. More knowledge to gain.

Émile Cinq-Mars is up at the crack. A habitual early riser, Sandra stays under the covers. Outside, woodland birds and seabirds make their presence evident, yet they seem less than raucous, perhaps in deference to the idyllic beginning to the day. Soft light casts a warm radiance upon the shoreline cliffs, the rocky beach, and the swaying grasses close by the cottage.

Coffee and a bite of toast and he's out the door.

Before retiring the previous night, Émile put in an overdue call to Sticky McCarran. What he learned interests him, although how the mystifying tidbit he gleaned fits into the overall jigsaw puzzle of this case is beyond him. Sticky was out on the water the night of the murders, ferrying Maddy Orrock across to the island. Cinq-Mars wanted to know if he had seen or heard anything unusual while crossing the bay. He didn't want to lead him in any one direction, and purposefully chose not to mention that he was interested in radio communications, exchanges among boats that night, or ship-to-shore messages or vice versa, or anything that came across as odd or inexplicable over the airwaves. He planned to ask the Coast Guard the same question, and listen to any recordings that might have been made, if they let him, but someone familiar with the usual chatter on that radio frequency and familiar as well with the principals at sea might be a superior resource.

On that account, he was correct.

"A fish boat was anchored below Orrock's house," Sticky brought up.

"Was that unusual?"

"Any day or night, it's a bit weird. It's not a smart place to anchor off. The current is strong, harbor traffic is frequent, you might not be seen, and the waves can be lumpy even on a calm day, not to mention the obvious."

"Please," Cinq-Mars said, as he didn't know, "mention the obvious."

"That shore's a shipwreck waiting to crush you."

"Weird, then," Émile summed up over the phone, the receiver cocked between his ear and shoulder while he scribbled notes, "but not totally out of the question. Is that what you're saying?"

"Nope. Not saying that."

"Okay, what are you saying?"

"In a storm, it's beyond ridiculous to anchor there. Hell, you're only a short hop from the harbor. If you don't want to risk going in, and I admit, it's not easy in those conditions, like a camel through the eye of a needle, then stand farther off, you know? Or go around to the lee. Or get inside Whale Cove. The last thing a skipper should do if his brains aren't up his arse is anchor off close to that shore. If your anchor drags in those waves, you're on the rocks before you can react. Totally out of the question is what I'm saying, but somebody was there anyway."

"We don't know who," Cinq-Mars presumed.

"Sure we do. It was Pete Briscoe."

Cinq-Mars listened to the silent air over the telephone a moment.

"You got close enough to identify his boat?"

"He didn't have enough sense to stand off elsewhere, but he had enough sense to reduce the chance of a collision in the dark. He left on his AIS."

"Sorry. What's that?"

"AIS. Automatic identification system. More of us keep them on board these days. AIS is a device that transmits your boat name, type, speed, and position to other vessels or shoreside and receives the same data back. I never saw Pete's boat, not in that downpour. The radar was fuzzy, at best, but the AIS let me know it was him and showed he wasn't moving. Except for the wave action. Otherwise he wasn't moving."

Suspicious enough. "He was below the Orrock house. Did you hear from him, maybe over the radio?" He wasn't leading him before, but was leading him now.

"Later. Yeah. Normally, I would've hailed him, but I was making harbor. That took all my concentration. Yeah, now that you mention it, I did hear him over the horn later on. Not that I paid much attention. By then I was moored in North Head, trying to catch a little shut-eye. A bad night, so the radio stays on, you know, in case there's trouble and you need to pitch in. I heard Pete having difficulty, nothing life-threatening. Not for him, anyway. Dog overboard. Yeah, that was weird enough. This was more weird: he said he was conning the shoreline for his pooch."

"Why, Sticky?" He wanted to say his name at least once, and did so. "What's so weird about that?"

"Because he still wasn't moving. I checked. I had him lined up on my AIS."

"Couldn't the others see that he wasn't moving?"

"It's a relatively new device. Fairly expensive. More of us have one, but it's not the first device put on a working boat. With those who had one, some had troubles of their own. Others weren't paying attention, or didn't give a hoot. I was safe in the harbor. Easy for me to listen in."

"So Briscoe wasn't moving but more or less saying he was."

"Exactly what he was saying. That didn't sound like the truth to me. You know, no skin off my nose particularly. He sounded drunk anyway."

When he was ready to sign off from the conversation, Émile offered up a mild platitude. "Good of you to talk to me, Sticky. And good of you to help Miss Orrock to cross over to the island that night."

"You know how it goes. She pays well. Anyhow, I got to drive her Porsche onto the ferry after that. Took it for a swing around town first. That made the trip worthwhile by itself. I didn't take her across because it was a good thing. I don't deserve the compliment for that."

"Okay, so you did it for the money. And the chance to drive a Porsche. Still, not everybody would've bothered."

"I didn't do it for the money, although I got paid. Well paid."

"What, then?"

"I didn't, one hundred percent, absolutely for sure, know that Alfred Orrock was going to die. If he didn't, if he survived the night even, I didn't want to face him in the morning after turning down his daughter the night before. I'm not that big a fool. That's one thing."

"Sounds like there's another thing."

"You bet. If Alfred dies, who replaces him? I'm thinking to myself, the daughter, no? I didn't want to be in the bad books of somebody who generates most of the extra work for a man like me on Grand Manan. It was just good politics to do what she wanted, that's all I'm saying. Just good business. Nothing to do with kindness. I billed her to make sure she knows that, while she can count on me, I don't come cheap."

Cinq-Mars accepted that. He understood. He doubted that even Maddy was aware of the power now at her fingertips. "Thanks, Sticky," he said, and signed off.

This morning, he's off to see a man on the island who, if he doesn't actually have power—and Cinq-Mars is convinced that he does—challenges the power of others. He drives across island through the hilly woods to Dark Harbour.

Having checked the tide tables, he's arriving early. When he turns down the steep rocky road to that strange hillside habitation, men and women are out in the shallow waters, at the edges of sandbars, bent over and working. He spies them from a great height. The road grows only more bumpy and becomes rockier and increasingly narrow, virtually daring any novice to proceed. Soon it appears impassable to Cinq-Mars. He's glad to be in a Jeep but doesn't want to wreck the undercarriage either. Émile parks, partially pulling up an embankment, and sets out down the hill to the sea on foot. Twice he almost stumbles over himself on the descent. The trail turns into a virtual donkey path wet from hillside streams. He passes by ramshackle huts where dark-eyed kids peer out at him through the doors' ripped screens. Not much color distinguishes the shacks, although a large number brandish junkyard artifacts on their mossy porches, usually for the sake of an artistic impression. Flies buzz and mosquitoes pester, and Cinq-Mars makes his way down onto the beach, where he finds relief.

The flat portion is wet, and he removes his shoes and socks to proceed, carrying a set in each hand. The sand is so cold he begins to hop along.

Water spilling from the Labrador Current chills this bay, and his feet redden quickly. He meets three children first, and perhaps they're supposed to be working, but they are so obviously in a mood for play that no one seems to mind. He asks if they know where Aaron Roadcap is.

They look at him as though he just asked where to find the ocean.

One boy points in the general direction of eight men. Under the sun's bright glare, and given the similarity of everyone's clothing, recognition is difficult. Nor can he concentrate very well, his feet seizing up. He knows he didn't plan this properly.

"Is he in the first group or the second? It's much deeper, isn't it, where they are?" He's trying to be cheerful. The fact that he can't recognize Roadcap even at a distance confirms the suspicions of each wild child. Here's a man who can't be trusted. Here's a man who can't stand in cold water without constantly raising one foot, then the other, to try and warm them on the opposite calf. Silly ninny. Here is someone we call a stranger. Someone we've been warned about. An evil outsider. So they clam up and Émile can't really blame them. He asks again, with a bigger smile, but perhaps that broad grin kills his standing once and for all among these kids. Their defiance is as evident now as their pride. They stay glumly, emphatically silent.

It's as if they are defying him to keep both feet in the water at the same moment.

He can't. His feet are freezing. He says goodbye.

Walking on, he picks out Roadcap in the second group of dulse harvesters, and rolls up his pant legs to wade into deeper, colder water.

Now his calves scream back at him.

The working adults wear black hip waders, and he's guessing that under them they have on multiple warm socks and cozy long johns. Approaching them, he must look like an idiot, an idiot who wants to holler.

He's hoping either to go numb soon or perish.

Seeing him, Aaron Roadcap straightens up. His grin widens the closer the former cop gets to him. By the time Émile is at his side—off the sand now, in among the rocks, the frigid water is up to his knees—Roadcap is enjoying a good laugh.

"Ah, are your feet cold?"

"You mean these blocks of ice? Are they my feet?"

He holds one foot up to the warmer air, like herons do. Then, unlike any heron, he squeezes his shoes and socks under an armpit and, with his hands free, grabs the toes to pass along some warmth.

"Let's get you back to shore. I presume you came out here to talk to me."

"And to learn about cutting dulse, but maybe that can wait."

"It can. Your feet? Maybe not so much."

Over the last forty yards across the sand flats, Cinq-Mars excuses himself, dispenses with pride, and runs.

"Be careful," Roadcap warns when he arrives back onshore himself. "Your feet might be mistaken for lobsters, they're so red. They might end up in a pot."

"At least they'd be warm. Somebody, please. Put them in a pot."

Roadcap chuckles while he removes his hip waders. Not only does he have socks on, Cinq-Mars finds out, but shoes, which have a thick sole. Émile is thrilled to plop himself down on the sand and put his socks and shoes back on. Then in silence they walk off the beach. Where the forest meets the edge of the sea and climbs the face of a high, steep slope, Roadcap locates a trail invisible to the visitor. They enter into that darkly shaded enclave. The two clamber along a narrow trail, ascend a short wooden ladder at one point, and scramble on through the woods and across exposed mossy boulders until they land at Roadcap's rough-hewn home.

What Margaret at the General Store termed a hovel. She was right, too.

They settle into chairs on the porch and the visitor scrunches his toes inside his shoes to try to warm them that way, grimacing.

"Coffee or whiskey?" Roadcap asks, and pops back up again.

"It's so early," Cinq-Mars objects.

"Single malt? There's no clock on the good stuff."

"I wonder if I might prevail upon your hospitality," Cinq-Mars negotiates.

"Both? No problem."

"One for my inner warmth. The other so I can press the cup against my toes before I drink from it."

Roadcap laughs easily and goes inside while Cinq-Mars gazes out at the serene beauty of the ocean from this treetop aerie. A woodpecker lands on the banister and gives him the eye, as if to request his photo ID, then flies off, and in a moment Roadcap returns, the screen door banging shut behind him. He's carrying the whiskey and four mugs. No glasses here. They'll drink whiskey and coffee from tin mugs adorned with bright portraits of curious cows.

"Coffee's perking. It'll be a couple of minutes."

"Sorry to impose."

"I felt like a break. My head's not in it today. Mr. Cinq-Mars, can we come to a mutual agreement?"

"Sure thing. On what?"

"I'm not going to prison for something I didn't do."

Cinq-Mars waits for him to pour, then takes a sip. Good whiskey. He thinks it might be impolite for him to check the label, but in any case it's smooth. Irish, he thinks, and raises his glass in salute to the drink itself.

"How about," Cinq-Mars responds, "you don't get anywhere near a prison for something you didn't do?"

"Sounds about right to me."

"All this in deference to your father, I suppose."

Roadcap makes a deflecting motion with his chin and shoulders.

"I agree," Cinq-Mars says. "Let's not repeat past mistakes."

"Agreed. If you don't mind, I'll be skeptical about you to the same degree that you're suspicious of me."

"Am I? Suspicious?"

"Bound to be. It's not a problem. I understand. But I need your assurance in principle."

"Agreed. Tell me, Mr. Roadcap, where did you study?"

"Study what?"

"You tell me. You went to university. You grew up here, yet you talk as though you learned the language somewhere else, which suggests that you went away somewhere, at least for a spell. University is as good a guess as any. Makes sense. Other than your clothes, which are related to your occupation and this environment, you give off an educated air. Yet, you didn't have a mother for most of your life and your father was in prison. University, then, from that point of view, seems unlikely. I'm not going to put you in jail for anything in your background, Mr. Roadcap, but you must admit, it's intriguing. Where'd you go?"

Roadcap thinks about it, then decides to see to the coffee. Cinq-Mars hears wood crackling in the stove inside. No electricity here. No coffeemakers. This will be a cup made the old-fashioned way, and when it arrives, it's all he can do not to forget the whiskey. The coffee is so good, he doesn't use it on his toes.

"McGill," Roadcap stipulates, after he settles into his chair again, stretching his legs out. "In Montreal. Your city. Most folks from here choose a school from the Maritimes. I went elsewhere."

"Why?"

"I think you already explained why." Roadcap sips the hot coffee, then washes it down with a whiskey chaser.

Cinq-Mars feels that he can get into this life, although realistically for no more than a day or two. Perched on a dark cliff overlooking the sea and living in a tree house, essentially, has its wild, organic appeal. Back to the primitive. More than anyplace he's ever visited, he senses that here he's on another planet. "How so?" he asks his host.

Roadcap displays a contemplative disposition when he sips. "I'm from Dark Harbour. If I'd gone to a Maritime school, which most do from this island, people from here would have let my story run loose. Dirt-poor dirt and a murderer's son to boot. I wanted out from under that, let's put it that way."

"Yet you returned here after graduation, if you graduated."

"Most of us do. Graduate and return. Look out to sea. You'll spot a dozen boats at any one time and most of the men on board, skippers and crew both, have degrees in English literature. It's just how it goes. There's no work after we get those degrees. Anyway, we prefer the work we do, to the work we don't have."

Cinq-Mars believes that the coffee and the whiskey and, perhaps especially, the forest musk and the sea air are giving him a high. He could fall asleep and check himself off as being content in life.

Instead, he asks another question. "You mentioned the fishermen.

Does that life not appeal? Hard work, certainly, but so is cutting dulse. If I was a young man on this island, I'd rather fish."

"You're fishing now, aren't you?"

"Lifelong habit, asking questions. Pete Briscoe is a fisherman. He owns his own boat. Wouldn't you aspire to do that work?"

"Pete Briscoe is not a fisherman."

"Excuse me? How do you figure that? Are you saying he's a bad fisherman?"

"He works the salmon farms. That's not fishing. I know, a lot of money is changing hands. Most of it went into Orrock's pocket, but still, it's lucrative for everyone. I don't get along with those guys. They don't do much, really. Take amphetamines, fix a net, call it fishing. Fishing is dangerous, but what's the main cause of death on the boats? Storms? Hazards on board? Nope. It's crack cocaine, baby. Not the wild sea. Not the scary work. Just crack, that's the number one killer in the modern age."

Cinq-Mars needs time to absorb that opinion. He keeps falling into a fondness for this man who's illusive and difficult to comprehend. Could he really be someone who doesn't fish, or fish-farm, because he's disappointed in the culture? If so, he's a more complex individual than probably anybody knows.

"I still think it's remarkable that you managed to do it, however you did it. Go to university, I mean. Who raised you?"

Roadcap seems reluctant to answer the question, as if hoping that Cinq-Mars will settle for a shrug. The detective can see why women make remarks. If he stares at him long enough, he feels as though he's been lulled by the man's beauty. It's astonishing, the jawline and the intelligence embedded in his dark eyes, and the striking details of his eyebrows and chin and forehead. The strength of his perfect nose. Émile conjures what life must be like for this man. He himself has been stared at for his immense beak, but people stare at this man for his total lack of common imperfection. He should be on a billboard advertising cigarettes. Men and women both would find themselves taking up smoking again without knowing why. Émile gives himself an inner shake to overcome the lassitude he's feeling in his bloodstream and doesn't take his eyes off the handsome fellow until the other man relents.

"Did you see those kids out on the flats?" Roadcap asks him.

"We spoke."

"Believe it or not, they're picking dulse today. At the end of the day, they'll make somewhere between fifty cents and a buck fifty. When I was their age, I also picked dulse. Except, even back then, when we made less per pound, I'd take home twenty to twenty-two bucks a day. If I was having a bad day, I'd stay out longer until I made quota, even if it meant swimming in that cold water to cut dulse. I saved up. Made money. In university, I came back here every summer and paid my own way. On fish boats, or working the weirs, or picking dulse. Those kids out there, officially they're home-schooled. Unofficially . . ." He lets his voice trail off.

"I can't imagine what that means," Cinq-Mars admits. "Are you saying they're not schooled at all?"

"Unofficially, you are sitting on the front porch of Dark Harbour Elementary School. They're home-schooled, only it's not at home. It's by me, right here. In the off-season, I'm their teacher. I don't get paid for that, but others schooled me and raised me. This whole community—this hamlet, if you want to call it that—parented me. We've developed the ways and means of living off the grid, you know? Not just the electrical grid. We slip through the cracks and sometimes it's not by accident. So," Roadcap concludes.

"So," Cinq-Mars repeats.

"You have something on us now. We'll find out what kind of cop you are."

"Mmm." Cinq-Mars understands, and resorts to the whiskey. Then he says, "I'm not sure what kind of cop I am. At least not anymore. But I've never been a truant officer and I don't suppose I'm going to start today."

"Good to know," Roadcap states, and the two share a smile, then salute each other with their glasses, as though the day, and their talk, is as good as that.

Émile breaks the ambient quiet. "Two questions on the tip of my tongue. Perhaps your answers might alleviate my suspicions. Maybe not."

"Ask."

Cinq-Mars had talked to Margaret, down at the General Store, who knows things. He knows things, too, now, even before he asks his questions. "Who do you sell your dulse to? I mean, is it Orrock? Did he come here personally in a truck and hand out cash? Do you deliver it to him in a wheelbarrow? How does the system work?"

For the first time, Cinq-Mars notices that his host is uncomfortable.

"We dry the dulse in the sunlight, which lightens the load. Then we pack it and carry it up to our own vehicles, and drive it into his plant, where some of it is turned into chips, some is pulverized. Tourists pay more to have a nibble, but we don't really have time to sell it ourselves. Orrock buys in bulk."

"Not anymore. He's dead. Is that an issue?"

Roadcap twists around in his chair a little. "We're hoping the company keeps going somehow."

"Any competition? Other buyers?"

This is a question Roadcap is apparently unwilling to answer. His protracted stare out to sea seems hard, unreasonable. He has literally to shake himself to return his attention to the porch. "Some say so. People have gone up against Orrock from time to time, but if someone controls the market, if someone has the foreign buyers in his hip pocket, then anybody else coming along doesn't have much of a chance."

"But others have tried."

"It's futile."

"And others might seek to steal away the foreign buyers."

"Anything's possible. Not my lookout."

He knows Roadcap is lying. "Interesting," Cinq-Mars notes.

"What was the other question on your tongue?"

Cinq-Mars doesn't want to lose this man's confidence, such as it is. He's glad that he does have a second question and that this one is less intrusive. "About your going up to the cliffs in a storm. Is that a secret? Or do others know that it's a habit of yours?"

While he thought that he was asking a more straightforward and nonthreatening question, the man appears to have qualms.

"What is it?" Émile asks, encouraging him.

"I'm having trouble answering because it's not clear-cut. Do I advertise that I have this predilection for storms? No. Is it anybody's business? No. Is anybody likely to see me? Maybe once in a blue moon, but they're not likely to think it's a habit."

"So that answers that, no?"

Roadcap shrugs. "Look. I've had girlfriends. Tourists, sometimes, summer people, and island girls, too. When I'm in a relationship, do I share stuff about myself? It happens. On this island, we understand something. That a secret doesn't mean a secret for life, except— maybe—in the rarest of circumstances. A secret is something we hold for a good long time, that's all, then we let it go. And once it's let go, it finds its way around. It's not a wildfire. We never know when or how long it will take. Eventually, on this island, what was a secret one year becomes common knowledge down the road."

Cinq-Mars has a more pressing inquiry to get to, but he's interrupted by shouting. He's unable to decipher the loud, confused outcry from far off, a bit higher up the cliff, although the expression on Roadcap's face is one of swift alarm.

When Sandra Cinq-Mars awoke that morning after her husband's departure, she hurried through breakfast to be dressed and ready when Maddy Orrock arrived to pick her up. They had an early appointment with a pastor who'd agreed to do the funeral. The Reverend Robert Unger receives the pair into his humble vestry, and after a few minutes Sandra perceives that his distracted, somewhat batty persona conceals a perfectly competent man. He's podgy in a way that lets her feel at ease—given her work around horses, she's probably stronger than he is, despite his greater mass—and his hair, she decides after some careful evaluation, is best described as orange. The pastor's schedule is a busy one, as he's preparing to bury his best friend, the Reverend Simon Lescavage, and is acting also as a representative of Jason DeWitt's family.

"One tragedy piled upon another." The professor's remains are to be dispatched home to Boston.

The funeral is about flowers and protocol, seating arrangements, and a choice of hymns. "You understand," the pastor assures her, "that my remarks will be kind. I will also acknowledge Mr. Orrock as a man of authority. His will was formidable, his reach extensive. He never tried to please everybody all the time."

"Or anybody ever," Maddy interjects. The pastor chooses not to hear.

The ground they must cover is quick and simple when presented by someone who goes through the ritual repeatedly, and afterward they agree to coffee, as their host already has a pot perking. Especially good coffee, they find.

"He was too brainy, our Simon," the Reverend Unger attests, off in his own thoughts. "He refuted my opinion on that, but he was too brainy for a simple man. Too many high-and-mighty thoughts in his head and not much of an outlet for them. Except for his sermons, but his homilies passed people by, I think. But . . . it's the savagery I cannot abide. Why must we be brutes? Simon asked me that question once. 'Why must we be brutes?' Safe to say, he was speaking of the human race in general. But it's the specifics . . ." The reverend loses himself in a vision of his friend's death, of that horror. He adds quietly, "Why must we be brutes?"

He seems to be addressing Sandra directly, but she's at a loss and doesn't wish to respond with only a faint notion. She lowers her head.

They wait there, in the quiet sadness of the room, before taking their leave.

Roadcap, in his thirties the more agile of the two, lights out from his house along a narrow ascending footpath, kicking up stones and thrashing through undergrowth. Cinq-Mars can't keep up, then stops trying, recognizing that nothing good will come from turning an ankle or breaking his neck. He measures his pace and keeps a keen eye to the ground to secure his footing. The best that he can hope for is to keep Aaron Roadcap in sight, and in that mission he is successful.

They run in the direction of a commotion—outcry, shouts, a scream. Some sort of chaos.

What's ahead comes into focus through the trees. A fire. He sees it first, then smells the smoke. He assumes that a house is ablaze, but cutting through a thick stand of pines and skirting around an immense boulder, he recognizes his own vehicle on fire. The Jeep. His heart pounds. Carrying on for another twenty yards, he stops, as though he can't trust his vision unless he does so and takes a good look. His breath is short, a bit painful. No doubt now. That's his own Jeep Cherokee going up in flames and thick black smoke.

Arriving back upon the rocky road, he finds that a brave brigade of men and women who want to fight the fire is being held back. Roadcap has taken charge. People are being pushed away in case the vehicle explodes. Smart.

"Gas or diesel?" Roadcap shouts out to him. Cinq-Mars delivers the bad news. Gas is far more likely to explode, making this a dangerous situation.

People know it's his Jeep, so when he joins the fray to help push everyone farther back, he's obeyed with less reluctance. Anyway, they all realize that it's too late to save anything now.

The interior is gutted. The seats have been incinerated, the roof linings are in flames. The engine compartment has not been touched, but it's a risk to fight the fire up close. Men are discussing it and weighing the odds, and Cinq-Mars steps up alongside them. They debate the wisdom of smashing windows out, which might fan the flames with more oxygen, and yet, as a result, the interior might burn itself out more quickly, sparing the engine and therefore the likelihood of an explosion. No one knows what will happen, but the consensus is to smash windows. Roadcap looks at Cinq-Mars, as though requesting permission.

"Go ahead. She's toast anyway. Stay safe."

Yet there is no way to stay safe except to run. The cliff dwellers are worried about the potential for a forest fire if the vehicle explodes. Such an eruption could destroy their homes and possibly the entire hamlet.

Four big rocks are located, and one person at a time races to the car and hurls his rock. The windows dent and splinter but don't give way easily. A number of throws from close in are required, then there's a surge of flame as the first window shatters and the rock goes right through onto the front seat. The men decide that that's enough, no further risk need be taken. After this initial flurry, the fire does go hotter, but it also appears to be exhausting its fuel supply and petering out.

Roadcap, who took several runs at the Jeep, is breathing heavily. "Follow me," he says.

Cinq-Mars is glad to discover that they're not running this time, although his companion takes long strides through the woods, then quickens as he nears a home. He dashes up steps onto a porch and bursts through the front door. When Cinq-Mars falls in behind him, Roadcap is coming back out again.

"He's not here. He's gone."

"Who?"

"Your arsonist. The guy who burnt your Jeep."

"How do you know? Why'd he do it?"

"That's what he does." The younger man flexes his shoulders, not to suggest that he doesn't have an answer; rather, that it's obvious. "Somebody paid him to." He seems ready to burst off again when he casts a glance at Émile's face. Then he taps Émile's elbow. "Sorry about your Jeep," he says.

"Yeah. Thanks. So am I. But it's replaceable."

"You're right, by the way. In your suspicions."

"Meaning what?"

"There's competition in the dulse business."

"And what part do you play in that?"

"We have other problems right now. Do you have a cell phone on you?"

"Yeah. Why?"

"I think you should call the cops. The Mounties."

Cinq-Mars endorses Aaron Roadcap's suggestion with a nod.

Sandra just loves stepping into this old house. She lives in an old one herself, but this cottage gets boarded up for the harsh winters and accommodates only summer guests, so it secretes a persona of sea breezes as the curtains lazily breathe out and in, and exhibits a patina not only of time and summery days but of a tranquillity, earned and nurtured and made to hold amid the tumult of the modern world. She loves it here.

She imagines that Émile will be home for lunch, and although it's officially his turn, she elects to prepare it. Noon is still a couple of hours off, but if she can have the salad ready to be tossed and the cold cuts lined up neatly, when he does arrive, it'll be a speedy presentation. She might take a stroll down to the water or into town after that, wherever her mood takes her.

In the kitchen, she hears a sound, then another. Sandra smiles. She knows it's not Émile. Being in the back of the house, she would have heard him drive up and probably seen the Jeep by now, so what she's listening to are the grumbling conversations old wood gets into sometimes. A floorboard creaks. A crossing beam seems to groan under its breath. She detects a faint snap. As though these old seaside cottages breathe with the coming day, fueled by sunlight. Yet another sound does disturb her, seems a trifle loud. Too specific. Expecting only a quiet place to sit on a beautiful day, she pokes her head into the living room. Sandra utters a surprised murmur, mingled with a sharp intake of breath, before a man's hand prevents her from screaming as she's thrown down upon the old pine floorboards.

In Émile's estimation, Aaron Roadcap is deliberately keeping his distance and protecting himself from further questioning by maintaining a protective buffer. It's not as in the old days, when, if he wanted to question a material witness, he could exercise his authority to do so. Now, he remains at the mercy of such people and their whimsy. For the nonce, Roadcap has chosen to go mum.

He thinks about calling Sandra. That will be a difficult discussion. To reveal that the Jeep burned would be bad enough if they were home, but accompanying the report will be the observation that they've again been able, largely at Émile's behest, to run their time away into the ground. Danger lurks once more, damage has been done, and rather than broach that conversation, Émile elects to procrastinate. He knows that he's being a coward, but it's better, he argues with his angels, to let Sandra enjoy her morning in peace before breaking the ugly news.

With any luck, he might discover that today's misfortune is merely random.

Not that he believes it for a second.

They wait for Corporal Louwagie to show up and make an official report—Émile will need to make an insurance claim. Once again, he reminds himself that this isn't like the old days, when he could have damaged a department issue and checked off a few boxes on a form and been done with it. This is all on his own dime now. The Jeep Cherokee, saved from any explosion, is nevertheless destroyed. A more noble soul might think to file down the passenger compartment, pry in new seats, lay fresh carpet, replace the roof and wall linings, and pretend that the smell of smoke and charred metal is dissipating. For his money, this is one for the junkyard, although it has served him well. Better for someone to pilfer the engine and the transmission. Heck, even the tires have survived, with the possible exception of the spare, which may have melted in its rear bunk. The metal is still too hot for him to check. The Jeep's a stinkpot now in the literal sense.

Standoffish initially, the denizens of Dark Harbour are sympathetic as they peruse the sad remains. This is not normally how tourists are treated here. Like tourists anywhere, they may be privately scorned from time to time, but for the most part their business is appreciated and the natural friendliness of islanders surfaces first. Sometimes disputes are resolved by burning cars, but not a tourist's car, and rarely even in the summer, because that's just bad for the island's reputation. Even when it comes to arson, a standard of etiquette is followed. You wrong me, I burn your dinghy. I wrong you, you burn my shed. Okay, we're done, let's move on. But this, in the wake of murder, is out of line, out of character, and this poor man deserves to be comforted, increasingly, by the minute.

Cinq-Mars is ready to make a break for it from under the welter of so much heartfelt commiseration and kindness when Louwagie finally shows up, saving him.

Roadcap breaks from the small crowd that he's put around himself as a protective moat to greet the Mountie first. More polite, Cinq-Mars needs a little more time to extricate himself from his band of new friends. When he goes over, though, Louwagie separates from Roadcap and speaks to him privately.

More commiseration. "I'm really sorry about this Émile. Any ideas?"

"Ask him."

"You think Roadcap did it."

"He was with me. So no. Nor do I think he was involved, although that's conjecture. I'm pretty sure he has something more than a good idea who did it."

"All right. I'll get to him. First, let me ask you a couple of questions."

"Such as?" He's surprised by the man's initiative.

"Have you pissed anybody off in particular?"

"Not to my knowledge. At least not royally. I supposed I've pissed off half a dozen people by now. But I can't point a finger, no."

"Okay, then," Louwagie says, and turns to examine the charred wreck again. Émile is guessing that the man is done, that he has nothing more to ask, only to be brought up short by his next volley. "Was anything in the car stolen? Or, if you don't know that yet, was anything in the car worth stealing?"

Cinq-Mars just stares at him a moment.

"The fire could have been a cover," the Mountie states, as if in his own defense.

Of course he's right. Émile's just surprised that he hadn't thought of it, and that Louwagie has more potential to be a detective than he'd noticed.

"It could have burned," Cinq-Mars tells him.

"What could've?"

"My notebook. My notes on this case."

Louwagie checks out the Jeep again from their safe distance.

"Or somebody might have stolen your notes. And now knows what you know. Burned or stolen. We may never have an answer to that one," he remarks.

"Not unless it shows up elsewhere. Can you do me a favor? Police work."

"Name it."

"Follow the money. It's an ancient adage. Orrock was nothing if not rich. Find out what is in his will. I can't rightfully ask, because the only person I know who might have a copy is, in a manner of speaking, my client. You see the dilemma. You have both the legitimacy and the authority to ask to see a copy. People might think so anyway."

"Okay. I'll do what I can. Right now, I'm going to arrange for a tow. I'm taking the Jeep into evidence."

"It's not doing me any good now."

"I'll give you a lift back to town."

"Thanks. I appreciate that."

"I'll talk to Roadcap later. Away from here. From what I know, Émile, this is not the place to get into anything with that man."

"Are you saying that was my first mistake?"

Louwagie smiles first. "Who said it's only your first mistake?"

The Mountie is showing signs of life. Émile enjoys that as Louwagie walks off to put in a call over his two-way radio. He steps away before the local folk drift back to his side to comfort him some more.

He calls Sandra.

He thinks he's misdialed when a man's voice answers.

His brain reminds him that he speed-dialed, that her name is up on the screen.

"Yeah?" the man gruffly bellows for a second time.

He's suddenly slammed by desperate fear.

"Sorry, I was trying to call my—"

"Your wife? She's not here."

"Where—"

"Oh, she's probably crow meat by now up on Seven Days Work. If you hurry, if you go real quick, you might make it before the seagulls peck out her eyes."

The line goes dead.

"Louwagie!" Cinq-Mars yells at the top of his lungs. His voice causes the entire community gathered around the incinerated car to look up and the officer to swivel swiftly around. And then, for he's thinking now at an impossible speed, as if putting his strategy together at the speed of light, Émile yells, *"Roadcap! You, too!"*

The two men come running on the double without a clue why. The timbre of his voice and the intensity in his eyes are the sole signifiers they need to grasp that this is bad.

TWENTY-THREE

Cinq-Mars is quick to dispatch Roadcap, two of that man's Dark Harbour cronies, and the wife of one of them up Whistle Road in a jalopy driven by the woman. She insists because it's her car. Émile and Louwagie rush to tackle Seven Days Work from the opposite direction, via Whale Cove, stopping first at Émile's summer cottage. He sprints inside and is back out in a jiff. He hoped to find his wife there. A note. Some explanation. Evidence to deny, confirm, or vanquish this desperate strait. Nothing awaited him but empty rooms, the turned-up corner of a rug, and a spot of fresh blood the size of a quarter on the floor.

"Let's go!" he shouts before he's even slammed the door shut, and they're off.

The road ends and they must tramp, as he and Sandra have done, on foot.

This time, the striking views provoke his tears. His eyes blurry, he stumbles. For a second time, Louwagie makes a good impression on him, forging on without stopping to help, leaving it to Cinq-Mars to pull himself together and catch up.

He's glad of that. The man has his woes, but he's capable in a crisis when his forlorn demons fall away. Good to know.

Down hilly paths into pastoral meadows and up the opposite banks into another clearing, then a quick jaunt through the woods, pacing themselves but going hard, fast, and it's back out under the sunlight and over a stream and across a broad rock outcropping that resembles a giant tortoise's shell. He stops once, and hates this, but he must lean over, hands on his knees, to catch a breath. He'd love to be superhuman and race ahead, but he can't, he needs to breathe. Louwagie, younger, faster, also takes a breather, although his recovery time is quicker and he carries on ahead of Émile. The ex-cop does a calculation. Six good deep breaths, then one more, and he's back in pursuit of this singular hope, this wish, that he's not too late, that somehow, whatever madness runs rampant here, Sandra lives.

Émile speaks to her as he runs. Speaks to his God. Prays. Moans. Weeps again and flings himself down a hillock in a renewed fury of will and aggression, and he will not think the worst and he will not stop. He sustains the pace and a hundred yards on he passes Officer Wade Louwagie. The younger man's chest heaves in exhaustion and pain.

He slows down through a stretch of cooler woods, grateful for the arbor's shade, and just before the bare sunlight breaks again, he stops. Émile breathes deeply, staying upright.

Louwagie stops beside him.

"She's got to be alive," Émile says.

"Yes," Louwagie concurs. Émile glances at him. The cop wants to say more, to be more encouraging, but he can't talk. He has no breath. Émile touches his shoulder, and the man places his opposite hand over his. They say more that way. Then press on, falling into an improvised scamper, a half run, half high-speed walk.

Roadcap warned that more than two paths connect to Seven Days Work. A network of trails like arteries pump hikers in and out of the space. Any avid walker knows the maze. To monitor every route is beyond their scope, and only the two main trails leading to roads and possible exit vehicles are covered. If a criminal is foolish enough to assume that Cinq-Mars is coming up from Whale Cove, as he's doing, leaving the exit via the Whistle free, he'll be caught. Slim chance of that. Cinq-Mars runs and knows that this is not as it has always been for him in the city. He cannot call out uniforms from multiple stations and summon the SWAT team. This is simply all he can do for now, and all he can do for now is run.

He's frightened that he's being lured to the precipice. *She's probably crow meat by now up on Seven Days Work.* Like Sandra, he's in the hands of his enemies, whomever they might be. They're pulling his strings, they're in charge. And why would they guide him here if not to enjoy his agony when he finds his wife eviscerated? His darkest thought, yet he fights to cling to a fervent hope. Killers don't normally volunteer information about their crimes, nor guide authorities to the scene. That helps him to believe what he wants to believe, what he insists on believing: that Sandra is all right, that whatever is going on, *this is not that*, and whatever this is, *you'll come through. Sandra!*

Reaching another clearing, with stupendous views across the bay under a brilliant sun, Cinq-Mars discerns that he was right to send Roadcap on this mission. Although the younger man has had to cover twice the distance he has, he's now in sight. He's fit. He's still running, a jog, but a quick one, while Cinq-Mars brings his hands back down to his knees and works to breathe. He vomits. He has to. His breakfast rising up through his diaphragm and gathering with his fright and panic and need. A spasm so violent it tears his lungs out of him, and now Louwagie is back alongside him, a hand on his back, advising him. "Breathe, Émile. Just breathe. We don't have any brown bags up here. You've got to breathe steady. Breathe."

Cinq-Mars points. Louwagie sees Roadcap then, too, and knows what this might mean. They've covered almost the full distance between the Whistle and Whale Cove and still no sign of Sandra. A cruel wild-goose chase? Louwagie, then, sees Roadcap stop dead, and he has seen them, too, but he is viewing something else or has heard something or someone and now waves his arms. The sweetest signal. He's jumping up and waving his arms.

"Émile!" Louwagie cries out, breathless himself, needing to breathe deeply himself. "Has he found her?"

Pure adrenaline now, Émile runs on. For moments at a time, he's partially supported by Louwagie's strong hand. He's puffing and spitting and his heart is all but bursting from his chest, giving out. He slows when he sees her, or at least sees where Roadcap is headed, and that lump hanging on a tree trunk might be her. A flash of color, a blouse perhaps, blowing in the breeze. He slows, not knowing how she will be found, a photo of Lescavage assailing his brain, not knowing if she is even the one strapped to a tree, waiting to be found. But who else?

Dead or alive? The question an intruder that occupies the whole of his being now. Dead or alive? *Alive! Alive! Alive!* he shouts out to himself. He assails the sky, all hope, and still no evidence to be seen.

Cinq-Mars stops twenty yards off. Louwagie is at his side. Roadcap's men are far behind him, trying to run but really only staggering along, clutching their sides. Roadcap, though, is by the tree, which curves outward from its base, where a limp form hangs out over the edge of an impossibly high cliff. Cinq-Mars stares. He waits. He can't breathe. His heart has quit.

Then Roadcap waves him on, shouts, *"She's here! She's alive!"*
ALIVE!

His body's more battered than he realized and it's all he can do to hobble on. An ankle is twisted, his hips rebel, and his tongue is lolling out of his mouth, bloated as he gasps for air. Rocking from side to side in a spasmodic motion that he can neither understand nor control, he pulls up next to his wife where she's lashed to the trunk, and collapses in a heap, nearly toppling off the edge into the ocean below.

"Émile!" she cries out. *Her voice!*

He's sliding off the edge when his fingers snare a root and he secures a toehold on a jutting stone.

"I got this!" he calls out, though the root is bending and the stone feels as though it's crumbling. "Leave me be! Get her off! Get her off!"

"Oh God, you're a mess," Sandra says, and he laughs, and squirms in an attempt to help himself back up and not slide off the edge that slopes downward into the sea. He carefully cranes his neck around to look up at her.

"Sandra."

She's weeping. Her cheeks are wet.

"I'm sorry," he says.

"Don't be."

"Get her off!"

Louwagie and Roadcap try to unknot the twine that binds her, multiple wraps, but it's impossible. Roadcap pulls out a knife. Although the policeman confiscated one of his, he rarely goes anywhere without one, never knowing when he might be enchanted by a low tide or a beautiful flowering of dulse.

"Careful," Louwagie warns, whispering, the danger implied but not stated. Roadcap nods. The Mountie has wrapped an arm around Sandra, but her body leans out over the edge of the cliff, with little surface at her feet to land upon. If released suddenly, she might be hard to catch. A simple trip and she'll sail clear the whole way down. At least Cinq-Mars is easing his way back up to safety, and finally he shoves himself to his knees. "Steady" is Louwagie's warning to Roadcap, but a knife stroke suddenly releases more twine than expected and Sandra bursts from her restraints, crying out, falling torso-first onto the sloped grade of the cliff. Louwagie deflects her collapse but loses her from his grasp. Her knees hit next and hard, but her torso is bending over the ledge and she's looking down hundreds of feet to the surf below when Louwagie clutches a thigh in the crook of his elbow. Émile lunges for her also and snags her belt, but his momentum pushes her down closer to the edge. He's lost his foothold, and his handhold now barely sustains him as he overlooks the sea. Louwagie further secures his grip on her thigh, but it takes yeoman strength to clutch the tree trunk with his fingertips and keep himself on solid ground.

One simple slip, and all three will slide over the cliff.

They shout to one another in combined chaos and delirium and panic.

Roadcap is the only one left with free hands and a secure purchase, and he sorts out the situation on the fly. They have but seconds. He comes around behind Louwagie and tells him what he's about to do. He'll pull Louwagie back while the policeman maintains his hold on Sandra. That will give the Mountie an instant to improve his grip on the tree trunk. If his fingers slip—and his grip is tenuous—the three will go over the edge. Louwagie wants to argue, but there's no time for that. Roadcap positions himself behind the tree to provide full purchase, and he's able to heave. He's strong. He has Louwagie wholly in hand and all three persons are yanked back and in the same instant, Louwagie reconstitutes his grip on the tree and improves his footing. Exactly as Roadcap instructed. He's steady now. He's confident now. He's fully stretched out between the tree trunk and Sandra's thigh and can do no more, but he's holding firm. Émile is staring straight down the cliff into the waters below and sliding farther. An endless fall is imminent, and while he resists what overcomes him, he feels eternity's touch right up his spine. He's familiar with danger, knows the calm that takes over at such moments, knows his brain is firing at lightning speed, but in this instance, among all his near-death experiences, he is obliged to do nothing more than not move. He wills himself not to move even as his body slips farther off Earth's most enduring rock.

Way below him, a pair of seagulls glide. Effortlessly free. He sees that. He thinks of that. Their white wingspans sharp against the dark rocks and water below. The gulls give the distance, his long plummet, definition. He will pass them by on his way down. Sandra's voice snaps him back from the brink of shock.

"Émile."

"Sandra," he says.

They say nothing more than that, but everything they know and believe and all their love is communicated. He has her clasped by the waist and hangs on.

"Quiet, everybody," Roadcap commands.

They obey.

"Émile," Roadcap says. "You're the problem. Your weight is too far forward."

So he came to rescue Sandra and now might send them both to oblivion. "I'll let go. Nobody's going down with me."

"Émile," Sandra says, breathless.

"Be quiet." Roadcap's voice is controlled, if not calm. "In a moment, on my command, I need you to release your wife very carefully. Very slowly. You think you're holding her up. She's holding you. Your weight is the problem. I'm going to get a grip on you. Wait for my command."

Cinq-Mars is in an awkward position. Roadcap must hook a foot around the base of the tree, stretch his other leg out so that he's almost doing the splits, and crook that ankle in front of Émile's knee. Then he grips him by his leather belt and the waistband of his trousers, and when he has as good a hold as he's going to get, as good a hold as Émile has on Sandra, he says, quietly, emphatically, "Ease off on her, Émile. Starting now. Let go."

With all of eternity before him, he must let go.

Facing downward, his feet on higher ground, Émile does what he's told, loosening his grip on his beloved. She remains in Louwagie's firm clutch. He puts his left hand down when advised to do so, grips a rock with his right hand when that's the instruction. Then Roadcap asks him to do a kind of flopping motion. "Like a seal. From your knees, then your hips, up through your torso. Only flop yourself back up toward me. I've got a hold on you. I won't let go. Give it a try."

He does this awkward flop on his belly back an inch. He's thrilled by that inch. Ecstatic, even. The second attempt yields no progress, and on the third he slides downward and everyone yells in unison. Sandra screams his name, and Émile is again staring into the abyss. Blood rushes to his head. He's petrified now. His fingers and arms are straining. Oh to be younger, stronger than this. But that thought, an admission of defeat and dejection, is what he needs to steel his resolve. He can find it in himself to do this.

Roadcap is stretched out in agony now, his legs strained to the breaking point. He's barely able to maintain his handhold on the man, and grunts as he breathes.

"Émile," he says, and they all hear the desperation in his voice. "We've got to time it right. Coordinate. When you're up in the air for a millisecond, that's when I have to yank you back. Knees first, Émile. Not your hips. Knees first. On my count. One. Two. *Three!*"

They gain an inch or two. Panting in pain now, Roadcap wastes not a second's time. "Again! One. Two. *Three!*"

Another inch, but this time Émile has a solid grip with both hands and a toe.

"I got this!" he calls out. I got this!"

That news allows Roadcap to alter his position, and he squiggles back. He keeps his handhold but straightens his legs to lie parallel to Émile.

"Nice and easy. Crawl back."

He does so. Backward. Crab-like, slow and meticulous. He's halfway to where he can stand when Roadcap leaves him on his own. Roadcap grips the tree trunk as Louwagie does and leans way forward. All he can grasp is Sandra's hair.

"This might hurt," he warns her.

"Who gives a—"

He yanks her straight back and she screams, if only from the shock, and so does Émile in sympathy and alarm. But she is safe now, and grabs hold of the tree trunk on her own. Louwagie has come back part-way with her, and now is free to pull himself to safety. Roadcap helps Sandra around to the secure side of the tree. Émile works his way back up the rock face, and all four slump in a pile upon the ground.

They just lie there.

Louwagie is bent, as if mangled between the couple, and keeps them from colliding into each other in a dangerous way as they attempt to move. Émile says, panting, "Sandra, what was that about?"

"Just hanging out," she pants, "by the seashore. Ouch, my hair."

Lying on his back, Roadcap chuckles.

"Okay, you two," Louwagie interrupts, pawing at the earth and trying to straighten his posture without getting up. "Enough wisecracks. Who did this to you, Mrs. Cinq-Mars? And how? Why? What can you tell us?"

When she tries to answer she only gurgles at first. She coughs up dirt.

The four silently and simultaneously agree that it's time to sit up. Save for a scrape on her forehead, Sandra is physically sound, although the carnage her nerves have endured emerges as she tries to explain.

She was brought up to Seven Days Work with a hood over her head in an all-terrain vehicle.

"Those things aren't allowed up here," Louwagie takes umbrage, then realizes that that's the lesser crime of the day.

"Narrows down the field," Roadcap mentions. "To me, they're like motorized mosquitoes. Truth is, we don't have a million of them on the island."

"Everybody's a detective," Cinq-Mars murmurs from his seat on the ground.

Louwagie likes the thought, though. Basic processes of elimination can pare down a short list to potential miscreants.

"Which way did they leave?" Louwagie asks.

"Neither left nor right. I could've seen them," Sandra tells them. "The sound of the machine went back straight behind my tree."

The three men stare behind them into the forbidding forest, where a network of walking trails fans out like a spider's web.

Roadcap proves to be the optimist among them. "There's only a few ways to get in and out on an ATV."

"Maybe they came across hikers who can provide a description," Louwagie adds.

"Did they say anything, sweetie?" Cinq-Mars asks. "Why they did this?"

She nods yes but can't answer just yet. Her trauma and the adrenaline of her rescue rebounds across her nerve endings. She fights to pull herself together, and Cinq-Mars, who's recuperating also, who suddenly feels so light-headed he could fly, stretches his arm behind Louwagie's back and holds her hand. "Next time," Sandra says, "I go over the side. That's what they said. That's their message. This was a demonstration. Next time, they shove me over. That's what they told me to tell you."

Émile blows out a gust of air.

"All right," he determines, and attempts to rise to his feet. He benefits from Louwagie's helping hand as the Mountie's getting up also, and stretches once he's on his feet. His lower back is an old lament that's been behaving all summer—after the cross-terrain gallop and these gymnastics he's doomed for a relapse. "I'll get you off the island."

"Émile," Sandra states, in a tone he finds worrisome.

"What?"

"Don't give me that crap. We've been through worse stuff than this." The two men look at him as if he ought to be arrested for what he's done to this woman. "I know your arguments. It's not what I signed on for. We don't know whom we're up against. We don't know the odds. We don't know how it'll play out, so we might as well err on the side of caution. Blah blah blah. Cry me a river."

"That's about the size of it. Sandra—*think*—we don't need this. Not our fight."

"Oh, Émile," she says, and again he's not happy with her tone.

"What, San?"

"Didn't you see me tied to that tree? I believed they were going to throw me over! I was terrified, Émile! Saying my prayers. You'd be proud of me for my sudden switch to religion."

She makes him laugh, she makes him cry. "So?" he asks.

"When you were sliding off the edge, you didn't see me scared out of my mind? This is our fight now, Émile. This is *so* our fight."

He blames her life on horseback for her competitive fire.

It's taken all this time, but the men who came with Roadcap finally arrive. They collapse into the tall grasses thirty feet away, panting and gasping.

"All right." Émile relents, and will say nothing more about beating a retreat. He's back on the case, and back in charge. "No arguments on this one point: when we leave here I'm taking you to Maddy Orrock's. At least she has locks on her doors." He turns. "Mr. Roadcap. I need to talk to you. Walk with me."

Way in the distance, not over the water as yet, as their views are to the east and northeast, but to the west over the hump of the island, the heat and high humidity of the day are bringing on storm clouds. Cinq-Mars doesn't take the younger man too far, as the conversation will remain a secret only if the man so chooses.

"If you recall, we came to an agreement," Cinq-Mars reminds him. "You don't get jail time for something you didn't do. I was less clear on my side of the bargain in that, what I get out of it. I didn't know. Now I do."

"Okay," Roadcap says, studying him.

"Here's the deal. Tell me what you know. No further negotiations. Thank you. Really, I can't thank you enough for saving Sandra and me. Sandra especially. To say that that's appreciated is so much an understatement, it's ludicrous. I'll show my gratitude when I can. Right now I need answers. No more keeping your cards so damn close to the vest."

"All right," Roadcap responds, a tentative acquiescence.

"You didn't like my asking you about dulse. Why not? What makes you uncomfortable with that? Before you go back into your shell, please remember that I saw my wife tied to a tree overlooking a cliff."

"Is that a threat?"

"Should it be? What makes you uncomfortable about dulse?"

Roadcap looks down, then away, internally hemming and hawing through a possible response. He seems to decide on a course to follow, and looks up.

"I'm Orrock's man," he says.

Not an answer Émile expects. He actually takes a step back, then has to retrace the movement. "What does that mean?"

"I operate the dulse trade for him, on the home front anyway, the supply end. He takes care of—sorry, *took* care of—the distribution end."

"I picked you as a man who might try to take it away from him."

"You're wrong in that."

"Okay. Tell me, how does his death change things?"

"To be decided. The winds of change are blowing. There's been competition lately, long before his death."

"Who from?"

"We don't know."

"We?"

"Orrock. Me," Roadcap explains.

Cinq-Mars is skeptical of that response, distrusts it. "How can that possibly be true?"

"How? Whoever is involved knows who they're up against. I don't mean me. I mean Orrock. They've done a helluva job of staying on the down low. Haven't shown their faces. They haven't made a move that risks their own exposure. My guess, they're setting things up, and when they make a move, it'll all be over. That, at least, is the plan."

"And you don't have a suspicion?"

"I have a suspicion. More than one. I draw blanks when it comes to proof."

"I'm all ears."

Roadcap takes a second to line up his opinions, then proceeds. "The timing of when things started to go wrong might be a clue. People who cut dulse for me started bickering about prices. I didn't think much of it at the time, it's normal, only Orrock started hearing from his distribution end about price, and I was hearing from my supply end about price, and that all occurs more or less at the same moment. Me and Orrock, we both get suspicious. So I kept my ears to the ground."

"And?"

"That's partly why I was on the cliffs the night of the big storm. The cult goes up there in a storm. I go for my own reasons, but because I do, I've encountered them up there before. They're trying to obliterate their minds in the wind and the rain, use the power of lightning or the storm to fly, or some harebrained stupidity. I went up there specifically to spy on them, because I know they race to get there in those conditions. They'd mark that storm down as perfect."

"Okay, so you're not quite the Daffy Duck I took you to be. But why spy on them? What's the interest?"

"Because. We had issues cropping up from both our supply and distribution ends, and that time exactly coincided with the arrival of the cult on the island. With my ears to the ground, that's all I came up with. That, and checking out their parking lot one day. I noticed a lot of American plates. Including, notably, California. That state is our biggest customer by far. But that's all I've got on them. Coincidence."

"Coincidence is good," Cinq-Mars notes. "Always a thread worth following. Okay, who else? You said two."

"Maddy Orrock."

"Seriously? What's her line? Do you have more evidence on her?"

"Less. But she comes in here every few years like a tide. Then fades away again. Every time she comes and goes she leaves her father in a crappy mood. He didn't trust her much. His own daughter. He told me she might be out to get him. Orrock was a wealthy man—from various sources. The salmon farms dwarfed what he made on dulse, but dulse started him out. It's still the backbone, not just the original component that put him on the map. Dulse is as steady as the tide when it comes to making money. That's really all he cared about, making money. And dulse was the one business he could own outright without the bigger boys being involved, you know who I mean, without the really big fat cats also having a bite. That meant something to him and maybe, maybe, not just for the steady cash. Maddy? Not so much. He was skeptical of what she was playing at, and, you know, she lives in the States. She knows the business. Grew up with it. She might be forming her own distribution network. After all, she's always hated her dad. She's been my big fear, anyway, that she'll take over, either over me or instead of me."

"Control the distribution, you control this trade, is that the idea?"

"Totally."

"What's your degree from McGill?"

Although Cinq-Mars wants to hear the answer, his technique in an interview is to keep the person off guard. Allow no one to anticipate the next question or know what the last one was meant to reveal.

"What? Why? Biz admin."

He said it so fast, Cinq-Mars can't be sure. "Business administration? You?"

Roadcap doesn't confirm that right away, as if he already regrets mentioning it. "Orrock," he says, then stumbles. "Orrock . . . I know that everybody is down on the man, but Orrock put me through school. Financially, he helped people who helped me when I was growing up. He pointed out to me what my opportunities on the island might be. He believed in me. He set me up."

"Maddy Orrock," Émile brings up, "comes in like a tide. Attracted much?"

The man from Dark Harbour receives the inquiry as a challenge, straightens his shoulders only for a moment before he relents. "Sure. Why not? Although she's always hated me. Through school and that. For good reason. My father pushed her mother off a cliff. So the story goes. My dad told me that Mrs. Orrock fell, and him I believed. Not the cops. Not the courts."

"Strange, isn't it?" Cinq-Mars proposes. "Your father throws Orrock's wife off a cliff, or that's how the courts ruled, yet he takes care of you while you were growing up, then trusts you to manage the business most dear to his heart. How do you figure that?"

The question provokes a sorrow, opens an old wound, which Cinq-Mars can see. In thinking it through, Roadcap has to deal with variant emotions along the way. Émile is patient.

"I believe he was never sure. My feeling is that he had doubts, that maybe his wife neither fell nor was she pushed. He might've had an inkling that maybe she jumped. So looking after me was a kind of guilt thing, on account of my dad. But there you go. I don't know. I've never known for sure. And now he's dead."

Cinq-Mars touches a hand to the man's shoulder, then suggests that they move on. "I want to get Sandra away from here. After that, I've got work to do."

"Émile. I know you don't trust me a whole bunch. That's okay. I don't trust you, either. Big deal. I'm saying you shouldn't trust Maddy all the way. She's paying you, and that puts you in a jam."

"She's not. Paying me. Who told you that? I told her that I won't be hired, in case I have to convict the one who's signing the checks. If I help her out, I'll send a bill. If I put her in jail, it'll be hard to collect on my invoice. I won't bother trying."

"Well," Roadcap decides, and Cinq-Mars is impressed with him once again, "you don't have to bill me. I'll help any way I can."

"Thanks. As far as trusting you goes, I just trusted you with my life. Nobody would've said boo if you let me drop."

"I thought about it," Roadcap says, but under the surface he's smiling, which Cinq-Mars can spot in his eyes.

They shake hands in a formal way, a moment that falls naturally upon them at the outset, until both men suddenly retreat, as though realizing that the circumstances oblige them to remain wary of each other. They return to the group. The sky may be darkening in the west, but the meadow glows with light—to Émile's eye, lit by both the sun and Sandra's relieved smile.

TWENTY-FOUR

Mild consternation arises when a motor disrupts the peace of the meadow and forest, blotting out the symphony of an easy breeze through the leaves and the ocean's wash a great drop below them. Émile Cinq-Mars gazes across the bay, as if a fishing vessel has floated into the sky. He's been fooled by an ATV, its muffled roar echoing off a string of trees along the shoreline, and seeing it bound over a hillock he responds with a moment's elation. His wife's abductors are either unbelievably stupid to have returned or so filled with remorse that they feel compelled to surrender.

No such luck, he notices seconds later.

"I called him," Louwagie explains. "He can take you out."

The vehicle is driven by his constable, Réjean Methot, and while Émile's fantasy is dashed, he's delighted to see the second Mountie. He can use the ride out, and make good use of the time saved.

He grouses, "Ah, you couldn't've called him sooner? Spared me a heart attack running in here?"

Louwagie finds his complaint amusing.

"What?" Cinq-Mars barks back.

"Émile, I did call sooner. Back in Dark Harbour. This is how long it takes to fetch the machine, get organized and out here ASAP. Or would you prefer we'd left your wife dangling over the edge until now?"

Cinq-Mars concedes a grin. Once again, the Mountie has shown capability under pressure. He gathers that they've both been afflicted with a kind of giddiness after Sandra's rescue, and Louwagie, having found a person tied up and eviscerated in recent days, is relieved down to his toes to have located the next victim high, dry, and alive, albeit tied up and emotionally distraught. Sandra, he notes, is coping well. Better than he is. As if, as she implied, she's experienced this sort of thing before.

The ATV is a two-seater. Sandra can settle onto Émile's lap, and Louwagie is content to walk out. The retired detective nixes that arrangement.

"Wade, can't you drive this thing instead?"

He can, but that doesn't seem fair to his officer, to make him walk out.

"Obviously, Réjean can give us a lift," Émile explains, "but I need you to drive me around after we drop Sandra off. Not just because I don't have a car."

"Why," Sandra asks, "don't you have a car?"

As shaky as her condition may be, his wife doesn't miss a beat. Nor can she be she fooled easily. She catches a glance between Louwagie and Roadcap and knows that something's up. Yet how much grief can she bear? To let her know that their car has been incinerated, that the two of them have been attacked not once, but twice—*and before noon*, Émile wants to say, although there's no logic to the thought—is more than he's willing to get into at the moment.

"Later on that one. Let's just say that the roads on this island can be risky."

"Oh, Émile." Better to have her annoyed with him for reckless driving than frightened more deeply by the truth. At that moment he has a sudden notion—he appreciates the range and capabilities of his unknown adversary. He and Sandra have been simultaneously attacked on two fronts, which took planning and manpower, expertise and co-ordination. Daring, too, although his gut feeling tells him that since neither attack was necessary, except to bolster his resolve, they were instigated by fear and possibly panic. Who, then, has he managed to scare?

As well, these provocations were *ordered*. Given that they took place at the same time, different people were involved in each incident, so the actions were either independent of one another—highly coinciden-tal, therefore unlikely—or one and probably both required people to *follow instructions*. Both events were meant to *threaten*, unlike Lescavage's murder, where there had been no known threat, only the execution. Émile is familiar with a modus operandi from his days dealing with violent biker gangs. Those gangs never—*never*—made threats, at least not any they meant to carry out. If and when they killed someone, they did so without the victim being alerted ahead of time. If they did issue a threat, that meant they had no intention of carrying it out. If these people operate in similar fashion, and he suspects they do, then he and Sandra are probably safe, for the perpetrators did nothing with their opportunity to inflict serious harm. All this tells him that whoever organized the day's threats controls underlings—someone has a gang—but that individual is neither foolish enough nor powerful enough to have ordered them killed. Nor were the underlings willing to do more than threaten—in the greater scheme of things, a car fire and strapping someone to a tree, with one of the most impressive views on earth, caused no one bodily harm. And the events were in keeping with island tradi-tion. Here, rough boys might be cajoled into doing such things as long as a line was not being crossed. Sandra had fallen, initially, getting cut in the scuffle, but she was never punched or bruised. Émile gleans from this that when a murder needed to be committed, at least in the killer's mind, the perpetrator operated alone, without help, unable to order anyone to either carry out or aid and abet so ruthless a crime. He con-siders that today's troublemakers may not have connected their actions to the murders. They might even have been hoodwinked into thinking that something else was at stake.

Having hunted professional killers and organized gangs all his life,

Émile Cinq-Mars can detect when he is dealing with amateurs. Not that amateurs, he reminds himself, aren't equally as dangerous and lethal. With their spotless records and obscure motivations, at times they can be more difficult to root out.

"As I was saying, Corporal, I need you with me. I may require the loan of your authority. Remember what I asked you for? About following the money, the will? Ask Réjean to look into that when he gets back to town. I need you with me."

"You think it's that important right now, the will?"

Sometimes, in the greater scheme of things, go by hunch, and sometimes go by the numbers. Following the money will fulfill both obligations, as it is both by the book and a wholesale hunch. Still, Louwagie's question stands as a good one, for which Émile doesn't have an equally good answer. "Who knows? I want to find out if Orrock anticipated anything. He controlled so much. Did he control his succession? If so, how? I'm grasping at straws here, but somebody is turning the wheels in this scenario and somebody else is greasing them. If there's something about power and money to be found out, I need to find that out. Better quickly than too late."

"Sure thing, Émile. I don't mind driving this thing. Hang on. It'll be bumpy."

"Try bumpy," Sandra pipes up, "when you're tied up and gagged with a hood over your head. That's how I got here. Now *that* is bumpy."

The others must walk. They do so knowing that the western sky is threatening, that they might only just make it, or get soaked, before leaving the ridge. One man, though, Aaron Roadcap, lags behind, as though he doesn't fear, and possibly might welcome, the storm. As if it means nothing to him to be out on a cliff in weather or to be struck by lightning.

His wife in his arms and on his lap, Émile hangs on for the wild ride. He loves the intimacy of the moment, her cheek upon his shoulder, her mouth by his neck, the weight of her jostling on his thighs. Safe for now, they speed away, bouncing under the sun. He finds her soft, involuntary grunts when they hit the bigger bumps hilarious. He'd love to kiss her and for their lips to linger awhile, except that the act would either be hilarious also or knock out their front teeth.

They might even swallow their tongues.

While Louwagie may have claimed the ability to drive the ATV, he's showing no particular expertise, and seems adept at finding every rock and hole embedded along the route. He slows down, in Cinq-Mars's opinion, when he should be gunning it, and speeds up when it's time to take care. The officer seems to know that he's flubbing this performance, but insecurity breeds self-consciousness, which breeds a whole new generation of tactical errors. Yet they survive, and make it off the ridge in one piece, though admittedly with loosened joints.

They pile into Louwagie's cruiser. Émile and Sandra sit in the back together behind the protective mesh, not wanting to let go of the other's hand for an instant.

"Maddy Orrock's house," Émile instructs the officer, only to have Sandra nix that idea immediately.

"I want out of these clothes. I'd burn this blouse if I didn't like it so much. I also want a shower, for obvious reasons." When her husband gives her a look, she tacks on, "Émile, he put his hands inside my bra. That's all he did, but Jesus Me. Apparently, he had a job to do—he couldn't have restrained himself? I want this fucker caught."

She so rarely swears.

"Get used to it," she says, and Émile takes her meaning.

"All right," Cinq-Mars instructs the Mountie, "our cottage first. Let Sandra shower and change, then up to Maddy's." He'd rather get to work, but he isn't going to deny her anything for a while, and maybe not ever again.

After calling Maddy Orrock to update their arrival, he rings Sandra's mobile phone, not for the first time since her abduction. On the first occasion, her abductor answered and told him to find her on Seven Days Work. On the second attempt, the phone just rang. The phone was reported off-line on the third call, and he receives that notice again. "Sorry," he tells her now. "If your phone shows up again, it'll be because it landed in a lobster pot."

"You think they tossed it. If it's in the sea, I'm hoping it went down with a boat and those fuckers were on it."

Language, Cinq-Mars is thinking, but he has to let this phase play out.

Louwagie waits in the car as the couple enters the cottage, and Émile stays downstairs while Sandra goes up. He's pretty sure that the spot of blood on the floor is hers, but he knows better than to tamper with evidence. A few minutes later, though, when he's stepping around the spot, he gets annoyed, and in a fit of pique, he finds a cloth and wipes it clean. Nobody's bringing out a forensic team to test a blood spot that's probably from his wife's forehead anyway, so what difference does it make? He stands in the room then, listening to the shower upstairs and to an echo of the tumult that occurred here earlier, this violence against his wife that really was directed against him.

And gauges a violence of his own, latent in his bloodstream.

The terror she must have felt. He's suffering a kind of emotional whiplash, fiercely angry now, and all that tempers his rage is his own contrition for bringing it upon her. He knows he should keep her safer. Since his retirement, it seems that she's been exposed to more risk than ever.

Waiting, Émile wanders out to the porch, where he finds notes on the table that Sandra inscribed in doing exercises in numerology. He's not terribly interested, but with his work in limbo for the moment he tries to figure out what she's been up to. Without having her references, her calculations resemble secret code, and he tries to break it without cheating, without checking her book. He idly passes the time this way when suddenly, straightening at first, then bending his shoulders over the pages, his interest clearly piques. Sandra finds him in that posture, hunched and concentrating. She's dressed in a yellow print dress, looking pretty, still fluffing her hair with a towel.

"How did you find these birth dates?" he wants to know.

"The Reverend Unger. He's a doll. I mean that literally, by the way. I think he's a porcelain doll."

"Everybody's names. Middle names, too." He's impressed.

"You need the full name for numerology. The minister showed me how to check birth and town records for local people online. But Maddy already knew a lot of them, the names anyway, and she helped, too. Why?"

"It's curious."

"Why? Don't tell me you're interested in numerology. *That*, I won't believe."

"I believe in local knowledge. This is local knowledge."

"How so?"

Rather than answer, he smiles. "Let's get you up to Maddy's. I've got to track some people down."

She's willing to go right away, but first she has a question. "Émile? When this started, remember? You said you knew who did it. Or thought you did. How's that panning out? Were you right back then? Or not?"

His reaction, and the scratch he gives his protuberant nose, strikes her as more humble than his usual investigative cockiness. He's willing to take himself down a peg, although only a single peg. "I said then that local knowledge is key. It still is. As far as naming names goes, I have to keep an open mind. If I believe too much in my first instinct, I might miss something, or condemn the wrong person, or miss the best path. I might prove myself right, or trip up and be wrong, but as I said, I have to keep an open mind."

"Could be that our lives are at stake. Certainly our Jeep's life is. So get on it, boy. Stop all this pussyfooting around."

As if he's the one who just took time off for a shower and a change of clothes.

They wait at the roadside in Louwagie's cruiser while Sandra goes up the long walk, and only when Maddy answers and sends out a cheerful wave does Émile give the nod to get moving.

Going down the eastern seaboard of the island to Woodwards Cove, he and Louwagie have no view of the western sky, the height of the island blocking it off. For all intents and purposes, this is a fine sunny day. They know better, and expect rain, but Émile, in the shotgun seat, not having to drive, can appreciate the seascapes, the picturesque coves, and the rocky shore as they travel on. Then they're off the main highway and heading down a gravel road to Pete Briscoe's house.

He's home.

Warily, he greets them through the screen door.

"Can we come in, Pete?" Louwagie inquires.

"That's okay. The place is a mess. I'll come out."

He's putting on a shirt as he does so.

"What's going on?" Briscoe asks. The door clicks shut behind him.

"Just getting up?" Cinq-Mars probes.

"Changing my shirt. Hot day. I got sweaty is all. How're you guys doing?"

"Top-notch," Louwagie tells him. "You?"

"It's all good," Briscoe says. Once his buttons are done, he tucks the hem into his jeans. "So what's going on?" he presses them again.

"If you don't mind, I want you to show me your dead dog's grave site," Cinq-Mars replies.

"I mind." Briscoe understands now that this is not a particularly friendly visit. "Why?" he asks.

"That's really not your concern, Pete," Louwagie informs him. "Detective Cinq-Mars has his reasons and that's all that's necessary here."

"That makes no sense to me," he argues. "You're supposed to be the law here, Wade. You're the Mountie. He's what? Retired? A mainlander."

"I'm also a mainlander, Pete. Mr. Cinq-Mars is helping me on the case," the Mountie explains, but Cinq-Mars is done with being delayed.

"Where's your dead dog buried?"

"What's it to you? Seriously, it's a private place. I'm not going to take you there. Maybe I can't even find it. In the woods. You know."

"I don't know," Cinq-Mars attests.

"You saw."

"I didn't see. I saw you. I didn't see your dog. What's her name again?"

"What do you care really? It's Gadget. What do you care?"

"We're the ones who get to ask the questions, Pete," Louwagie explains again.

Cinq-Mars supposes that Louwagie is being the caring and attentive cop, if not entirely the good cop. He can work with that.

"You get to answer," Cinq-Mars warns Briscoe. "If you don't, we drag you in and make you."

"Make me what?"

"Stop wasting my time. You're in deep enough without wasting my time. That only makes things worse. You haven't guessed that?"

"You come here, ask me where my dead dog's buried, and you're saying *I'm* wasting *your* time. You sure you got that straight?"

Logically speaking, he has a point. Émile isn't going to concede anything today. "Where, Mr. Briscoe, do we find your dead dog? This is the last time I'm asking politely. Next time will be at the station where I speak to you privately."

Briscoe's defiant. "I can take you."

"Does that count for something? This isn't a wrestling match. You can dump that little fantasy in the trash for now. So, do we go down to the station?"

Louwagie helps out by extracting a pair of handcuffs from his belt. Briscoe can't believe this shift in his fortunes and fidgets on the porch.

"Okay. Look. It's nearby, all right? Between the house and the water. What's the big deal? It's above the tide line. It's legal that way. It's just not my property, see. That's why I'm reluctant to tell you. It's not my property."

Cinq-Mars looks over the lay of the land. He already has Briscoe dead to rights on several counts. "Then why," he asks him, "did you put Gadget on the front seat of your pickup? As if you were going to cart her some distance? You can't drive toward the water from here. Putting her in the truck didn't help you."

"I changed my mind is all. I planned to bury her someplace else."

"Why did you change your mind?"

"I just did," Briscoe maintains.

"Where's your shovel?" Cinq-Mars asks next. A new tack. Always keep the man you're interviewing off guard. Not only will he not know where you're coming from, he'll soon be disoriented and confused as to which questions are important and which are, in the vernacular of the sea, red herrings.

"What do you mean by that? What shovel?"

"Haul him down to the station," Cinq-Mars tells Louwagie. "Save us time and trouble."

"What do you mean?" Briscoe protests. "What shovel? I don't have a shovel."

"You buried your dog with your bare hands?"

"No, I—"

"What? I saw you up on Seven Days Work with a shovel!"

"I borrowed it. All right? I borrowed a spade, if that's what you mean. It wasn't my shovel."

"Who from?" Louwagie asks, exercising a patient voice as counterpoint to Émile's aggression. "Where is it now?"

"What do you care? It's only a, you know, a spade, a shovel. I'm not being a hard-ass, but seriously, what do you care?"

"Ask one more question," Cinq-Mars warns him, "one more, and we haul you in. You won't enjoy it. I will. You won't."

If Briscoe is a legitimate tough guy, his threat is meaningless, even laughable. The tough guy would already have won this contest of wills. Cinq-Mars doesn't believe that Briscoe is the tough guy he pretends to be, and he's sure the man has virtually no clue what he might be in for. Which gives him a huge advantage.

"Where's the spade you had up on Seven Days Work? Who'd you borrow it from? Where is it now? We want to know," Louwagie stipulates, less patiently now.

A long, low rumble is heard from beyond the nearest hills, and a darkening of the sky comes into view on this protected lowland.

Pete Briscoe's eyes skip back and forth between the two men, as though he's trying to choose his safer fight. "I returned it," he admits.

"To whom?" Louwagie presses him with mock sarcasm.

Briscoe hesitates.

"Pete," Cinq-Mars adds, "word to the wise. If you're arrested, I'll interrogate you night and day. My wife was abducted a few hours ago.

She's safe now, thank God, but I'm after anyone and everyone who had anything to do with that. You want to exonerate yourself if you can. I'm pissed now. You don't want to go toe-to-toe with me while you're hand-cuffed to a steel bed for hour after hour. Or do you? Do you?"

"I don't know anything about that! I had nothing to do with that! I don't know about your wife. I didn't do nothing!"

"Sure you did. You said so yourself. You borrowed a long-handled spade. I saw you digging with it."

"I'm allowed to borrow a spade. Holy mackerel! This guy makes no sense!"

"You know what?" Cinq-Mars asks. Then warns him again, "Don't answer with another question."

Briscoe doesn't know how to respond and so keeps mum.

"I know what you were digging up on Seven Days Work."

He sighs, as though this talk is torture. "Of course you know. I was trying to bury my dog."

"That's a lie and a half. That's a whopper. I'll remember it when we're together in our interrogation cell and you're strapped to the steel bed. I'll remember how you just lied to me for no good reason. I might go into that room with a hammer."

"Pete," Louwagie reminds him, "you just told us you buried Gadget nearby."

"Oh yeah," Briscoe says. "What was I doing, if you think you know?"

"That's a question," Cinq-Mars points out to him.

The fisherman goes silent then, and Cinq-Mars stands more closely in front of him, staring down his lengthy beak at the much shorter man.

"You weren't burying a damn thing. Certainly not your dog. You were retrieving that long-handled spade from the murder site. That was your job for the day. Admit it. Don't tell me another lie. You took the shovel away from the scene of the crime, where it was up by the forest, and so the cops never saw it. You carried it away and took it to another location. What were you doing with it? Don't answer, because that might come out as another question and you'll be sorry then. You were wiping the blood off it, Pete. Wiping the blood off."

The pupils of Briscoe's eyes have grown huge, but Louwagie is also perplexed, and intrigued. He's evaluating the fisherman under different light. He assessed him as a possible material witness, not someone who committed a serious crime. Now he's not sure. He doesn't know where Cinq-Mars is going with this, but he can tell that Briscoe is busting to elude him.

"Pete," Émile goes on, "you were tampering—this is a serious crime by itself—you were tampering with the evidence. You wanted to get the blood off. After I went by and we saw each other and you came running to me with some cockamamie tale about burying your dog a whole day late, after that you did more than just wipe the spade through the grass to get the blood and the tissue scrapings off. You started digging to make it look good. Because I saw you there. That's the only explanation for what you were doing up there. So—and be careful now, because I'm about to ask you a question and I don't want another question in return, and trust me, you don't want that, either—where is the shovel now, Pete? Who did you return it to? Who did you borrow it from? Don't take your time with this. For your sake, because you're already in serious trouble for tampering with the evidence, just answer the questions."

As straightforward as the path has been laid out for him, Briscoe still doesn't know how to take the first step. Instead, he tries to get around Émile.

"I had nothing to do with any murder. You can't think that. That's crazy."

"Except to tamper with evidence."

"Yeah," he agrees. "Okay. Maybe that. But I didn't *know* I was doing that."

Cinq-Mars backs off a moment. He goes over to the porch railing as another, yet still distant, thunderclap rolls across the sea.

"I'm a big-city cop," Émile says to him, looking out toward the water now with Briscoe at his back. "You've heard the stories about me,

I'm sure." He looks back over his shoulder to see if he'll respond, and Briscoe does nod yes. Émile turns, intertwines his arms over his chest, and leans his butt against the railing. He decides to make use of his exaggerated reputation. "Do you think I cracked the Mafia apart in my home city and took down the Hells Angels by being Mr. Nice Guy? Tell him, Officer. He listens to you. If he comes down to the station, you won't interfere with what I do."

"I'm not interfering," Louwagie says. "Sorry, Pete, but this is serious business, murder is. Things aren't normal anymore."

Cinq-Mars likes this, the conviction in his voice, the logical explanation to deter Briscoe from assuming that the old guy is mere talk, no action.

"You won't protect him," Émile states.

"I'll go home, sir. Leave you two alone."

That's when Pete Briscoe confesses although he might not know it. "I borrowed it from my girlfriend. Okay? The spade."

Cinq-Mars stares him down. Briscoe's a challenge, as his near uni-brow somehow gives him a place to hide his eyes by tilting his forehead down a few degrees, as if his mind and his reactions are hiding in the bushes. Yet Émile has much confidence, gained from long practice, in the ferocity of his gaze, and when the man's eyes do quick little shifts, from holding his look to measuring the mountain that is his nose, and then feeling self-conscious about that, tries to regain a hold on his eyes again after it's too late, the former cop has him right where he wants him.

"Never make me wait this long again for an answer. Understood?"

Briscoe appears to accept this altered structure to his universe, and nods.

Cinq-Mars asks, "Where were you the night Orrock was killed?" Keeping him off guard again, going on to a different subject altogether.

"Killed?"

Cinq-Mars scarcely moves, but ever so slightly his pupils expand.

"Sorry, that's not a question. I thought he died is all. Old age."

"Killed," the older man confirms. "I told you that already. This is not news."

"I just forgot."

"Who can forget that? Selective memory? Now answer my question."

"I was out fishing."

"Not possible," Cinq-Mars states.

"Sure it is," Briscoe protests. His voice is weak and his eyes scurry around.

"You're not a real fisherman."

Cinq-Mars can tell that the man is trying to ask a question but has to warn himself not to do so. "Sure I am," Briscoe says at last, but he clearly has his doubts.

"You're a fish farmer. That's different."

"Yeah, it's different. There's more money in it. A better life, too."

"I understand," Émile says, and there's genuine sympathy to be gleaned from his tone. He knows that old ways sometimes change and people adapt. "What it means, though, is that you weren't fishing that night. Because you don't fish, do you, Mr. Briscoe? You don't fish, and I know exactly, very precisely, where your boat was moored. Under the Orrock mansion." Pete Briscoe so much wants to ask a question that Émile takes pity on him and answers it himself. "You left your AIS on. That's how I know. I'll give you credit. You didn't want anyone to crash into you. Where you were moored, that was possible, even probable, if anyone was making harbor that night. So at least you exercised good seamanship, I'm giving you credit for that. You weren't out fishing and you weren't out at the fish farms. You were moored where you had no business being moored, and you weren't on your boat, because why would you moor there if you wanted to stay on your boat? You'd have gone into the harbor. On to a safer place. The question is—and remember, I don't want you wasting my time, so answer right away—where were you, Pete?"

Pete has begun to cooperate, and Émile needs to keep bringing him along, to help him feel more at ease divulging secrets. Once he says something to implicate himself or others, there will be no turning back. The whole shebang will come out. Louwagie at that moment moves over to an Adirondack chair on the porch and sits down, and both

Cinq-Mars and Briscoe observe him do so. They'd both like to be that comfortable, that free. Louwagie looks up, waiting to see how this plays out.

"Here," the young fish farmer answers.

"Who with?" Cinq-Mars fires back.

"Ora. We had a date. We arranged it, see."

"Where was your dog all this time?"

This part hurts him. "I took Gadget in the dinghy. In the waves, in the storm, she put her paws up on the gunwales at the wrong time. She might've been able to stay in the boat, but she loved the water, and when she lost her balance, she kind of leaped. She half jumped, half fell into the waves. After that, I stayed out there looking for her."

"Looking," Cinq-Mars says.

"She was black, and there was no light in that storm. I saw her for like ten seconds then lost track. The waves moving me around, moved her around. We separated really quickly. I stayed out there looking for her, but I never saw her again until you showed up in your Jeep."

Cinq-Mars crosses his arms, removes the fury of his gaze from Briscoe to give him some breathing room and enough latitude to fall overboard himself. "Why risk it, Pete? Coming ashore. Why bother anchoring your boat?"

At first, he shrugs. He doesn't want to say. Then admits, "For sex. What else? Been a while. I was horny as—Ora was always with Orrock on account of he was sick all the time. She never got away. When she did, I was usually out at the fish farms. It was building up, you know? So we made a date. Then that damn storm blew up. That wasn't going to stop me, was it? Ora wasn't going to be stopped, either."

"Why anchor off? Enter the harbor."

He doesn't want to say. Then relents. "I get paid by the hour. For the fish farm. If I get caught out in a storm, I get paid for that. If I'm seen in the harbor, no pay."

"You quit trying to save your dog and came here instead, just to get laid."

"No! It wasn't like that. I came ashore. I was hoping Gadget would swim ashore. Or, if she was out there trying to get to me and the dinghy, and she could see me, then she'd follow me and come ashore. After I landed, I walked up and down the water's edge looking for her. I don't know for how long. For a long time."

"Yeah, but Pete, you were on the radio."

"That was later. I needed people to know I was out there. To get paid."

"You've lied to me again. You told me you were here in your house. Now you say you weren't here at all. You were all alone on the shore. Walking up and down where not a soul saw you. Not even your dead dog."

"Yes. Okay? I lied. I told you the truth this time."

"You didn't see Ora that night," he continues, and Briscoe responds with silence. "Why won't you say so?"

"I'm not supposed to," he replies, and at that Louwagie and Cinq-Mars share a glance. They've got him now. Cinq-Mars has been looking for men in the hire of a boss, and Briscoe has let on that he is one of them.

Very slowly, Cinq-Mars asks, "Pete, you're not supposed to what?"

Briscoe dips those big eyebrows right down, so that his eyes are totally concealed. When he raises his head again, he chooses to cast his gaze out to sea. "I'm not supposed to say."

"Where was Ora, Pete? As I've warned you, I am willing to take you in. We can go on all day and night like this and play by nobody's rules except my own. You understand that, right? I'm not a cop. I don't have to follow the law. I have no boss to keep me in line. Not a soul."

Involuntarily, Briscoe checks with Louwagie, who makes a gesture with his lips as though to say that he doesn't get it, either, but whatever the man is saying is how this will play out. Briscoe bites his lip a moment.

"You're going to tell me anyway, Pete. I know that. Corporal Louwagie knows it. More important, even you know that. Tell me now rather than later, Pete. That's my best advice. At this stage, you want to be helpful."

The man seems to accept what he's being told, but he attempts to lay out the ground rules for his capitulation. "It wasn't Ora," he contends.

If that's what he needs to believe, Cinq-Mars will let him. "Of course not, Pete. Who could ever think such a thing? Where was she? If she's innocent, and, like you, I presume that she is, the truth won't hurt her. It'll only protect her."

Briscoe takes a deep breath. "She was here. Where she was supposed to be. Waiting for me. Except I let her down. I was looking for Gadget instead."

"How do you know she was here if you weren't?"

A simple man's emphatic shrug. "She told me she was. We talked on our phones. And then, she was still here when I came by in the morning. Only she was asleep."

"Then you had sex." Cinq-Mars doesn't believe that a man who'd just lost his dog would do that, but tests Briscoe anyway.

He's shaking his head. "Too tired," he says. Then he looks out to sea again. "Too upset. I forgot about sex. I just forgot."

Having stepped away from him to give him a sense of space, Cinq-Mars now moves closer to him to choke off whatever his exit plan might be, and asks in a low, commanding voice, "Okay, Pete, tell me, who asked you to fetch the shovel?"

He can almost hear the man ask "What shovel?" Briscoe has learned to swallow that response. Now whenever he's confused or needs time, rather than ask a question, he opts for silence.

"Who was it, Pete?" Cinq-Mars presses him, no longer permitting any maneuvers. "Who wouldn't risk going up to Seven Days Work to fetch it herself?"

His eyes go wide when Cinq-Mars infers that it's a woman, and he insists more vehemently than ever, "It wasn't Ora."

"I didn't think so, Pete. I still don't think so. But you need to tell me what I already know. Who was it, Pete, who sent you for the shovel?"

Louwagie stands again, and also comes closer. The two men, both much taller than the fisherman, stand firm against his desire to elude them somehow.

"Pete, I've seen the photographs of the crime scene, of Reverend Lescavage's body. He was a nice guy, wasn't he? Were you a member of his church?"

Briscoe wags his head no.

"You bumped into him from time to time. In the winter, everybody bumps into everybody else, right?"

He nods yes.

"Quite a guy, by all accounts. Terrible what was done to him. Precise parallel incisions, like this." Cinq-Mars traces two lines over Pete Briscoe's stomach to form the top of a triangle meeting just under the base of his sternum. "Most likely cut with a sharp knife. A knife anyone who cuts fish would use. Or anyone who cuts dulse for a living would carry with him. Then the bottom of those two lines are connected by another slice of a knife."

Briscoe nods to indicate that he understands.

"The thing is, Pete, the center portion of that bottom slice, right here"—and Émile shows on the man's own stomach a slice the length of his hand that cuts below the belly button—"was messy. From a more blunt instrument. Something less sharp. Corporal Louwagie didn't notice this detail because he's a sensitive soul, and such an ugly scene, that kind of horror, doesn't interest him at all." Briscoe looks at the Mountie as though he's willing to sympathize. "I, on the other hand, studied the photographs. The middle part of the lower incision wasn't inflicted by a sharp knife, but by a dull blade, and the shape of it, and the fact that it was rammed into the body several times in the violence of the moment, suggests the business end of a spade. Possibly a long-handled spade. Whoever sent you up to the ridge, Pete, sent you there to retrieve the murder weapon. The person couldn't find it in the dark on the night in question, couldn't risk hunting for it later. Whatever sick story you were told—and you're gullible enough to believe it, aren't you?—that story was a fib. Tell me who, Pete."

While his eyes dart between the two men, they also seem to bear inward, and he's rabbit-like now beneath his furry unibrow, trapped and panicky.

"Name her, Pete. Tell me what I already know. Name her."

"You keep saying 'her'. But I keep telling you, it wasn't Ora. No way."

"I know that, Pete. So name her. Name who it really was. Remember? You didn't want to tell me that you didn't see Ora until the morning.

Because, you said, you weren't supposed to tell me that. Somebody wants you to tell the other story, that you were home with your girl. I know you're supposed to be Ora's alibi. Who says she needs one? If you want, if it helps you, it's the same person anyway, just tell me who coached you on what to say or not say. Who told you to lie? Who sent you for the shovel? Pete?"

TWENTY-FIVE

"Head to Ora's house," Cinq-Mars instructs the Mountie as they buckle up inside the RCMP cruiser. His voice is sharp, not tense, but directed, on edge, as though he's ready to pounce.

"Shouldn't we bring him in? Petey boy's involved."

"A lot of people are involved. That's the kicker. Someone has control over them. Someone is in charge now that Orrock's dead. Leave Pete to marinate awhile. That'll only help us later."

"You have strange methods."

"Notice the results."

"Trust me. I'm taking notes."

"You're a good cop, Wade. I've found that out."

"When I'm not planning on shooting myself." Something's on his mind and Cinq-Mars lets him take his time. "I don't believe my superiors are even close to being right, the way they treat PTSD."

"But?"

"But today, I don't know what it is, I'm glad to be busy."

Cinq-Mars dwells on that awhile. "It's like the work we do," he

postulates. "No such thing as one size fits all. You can follow a procedure, you can go down a checklist, but if you're going to catch the bad
guys, you will have to break from procedure. Even break from what you
think. Sometimes you have to escape your premonitions, even your
faith. You need to get at things a different way each time if you're going
to do it right. I should write a book."

"You think it's the same with PTSD?"

"In a way. Never mind different strokes for different folks, even the
same person might need a new approach for no other reason than it's a
new day. It's all tricky business."

"That's what makes it so tough maybe." He's not driving with any
urgency, sticking to the speed limit. Émile would prefer that Louwagie
pass the guy ahead of them, but supposes he wants to set a good example
for the tourists. They take his picture so often, being a Mountie, he probably doesn't want to burst their bubble with bad behavior on the roads.

"Everything's a challenge, Wade. This case is a challenge. In the end,
you just have to believe."

As they arrive in North Head, a wrecker is pulling Émile's burned-
out Jeep into town. To think that he gave it a fresh coat of wax before
embarking on this trip.

"Now that's one sad and sorry sight," the Mountie observes.

"Pull up beside him," Cinq-Mars requests, and the officer does so at
the next stop.

Cinq-Mars rolls his window down and informs the other driver,
"That's my car."

"Too bad for you. I'm glad it's not mine anyway." He's a jolly-looking
fellow with an impressive handlebar mustache. His hair and whiskers
are a shiny gray.

"Hide it."

"Excuse me?" Someone behind honks, with a rather extreme gentle-
ness in deference to the police cruiser, but both drivers ignore him for
the moment.

"Whatever garage you're taking it to, stick it behind a building, or a
school bus. I don't want it visible."

Given that he's hearing this from a man in the front seat of a Mountie's cruiser, the tow truck driver agrees.

Quietly, Cinq-Mars remarks to Louwagie as they start off again, "I don't want Sandra to see it. The shock. I'll tell her later."

"Good plan," Louwagie concurs. "But Sandra's tough." He's driving on when his fellow Mountie raises him over the two-way. The lad's been hustling, having completed the hike off the ridge and tracked down the lawyer responsible for Orrock's will, as he was instructed to do.

"Ask him how," Cinq-Mars directs.

Louwagie does so, and the man replies over the airwaves, "His daughter told me who his lawyer was. Orrock chose a woman in Blacks."

Typical of the man that he trusted no one on the island, and possibly no man anywhere, with his final instructions. Cinq-Mars is a little miffed with himself that Maddy will have discovered a police interest in her father's will. He should have advised the Mountie to exercise greater caution.

"Pull over," Cinq-Mars tells Louwagie. "Let's hear this first."

His partner's information sounds like gibberish to the Mountie, and he doubts that Orrock was in his right mind when writing his will. Thoughtful, Cinq-Mars declines to speak on the matter. "Drive on," he says instead. "Let's go."

They wait while three cars in a row pass them by going in the opposite direction, their turn signals blinking away, then the Mountie makes an aggressive left onto Ora Matheson's property. A police car showing up on anyone's lot creates a stir, and Ora, on her front porch, ceases taking in the wash. While it may or may not be dry yet, she's hurrying to beat the rain, and the moment that Cinq-Mars clamors out of the car, a thunderclap rumbles both near and loud. Her mother is across the yard—to call it a lawn gives it too much credit and usually results in a chuckle, so her mother often will call it a lawn just to draw down the laugh. Grass is less apparent than weeds. Bare patches abound. Mrs. Matheson rushes to pack the dulse she's hung out to dry in the sun, and she finishes up her work before seeing to the arrivals. At this stage, she can't afford to let her product get wet.

Louwagie signals Ora to carry on with hauling her laundry off the line, and she smiles. Her mother, then, is the first person to go over to greet the men.

"Are you here to buy dulse?" Hers is a husky voice, a match for her stocky form. An immense handwritten sign by the road advertises dulse chips by the pouch or the pound, and invites tourists to take a kilo of "pure dulse" home. "Do your blood a favor. Add some flavor." The line might have originated as a jingle.

Émile declines, and smiles. "I've tried it once and didn't take to the stuff."

"It's an acquired taste. Try again." She has an open bag in the pocket of her navy hoodie, and offers him a chip. She beams while he savors the crunch and evaluates the strange taste.

"Well?"

"Still tastes like rust to me," Cinq-Mars says, but the remark fails to throw her off her game, and she continues to beam.

"I'll lay odds that no man really enjoyed his first ever sip of whiskey or beer, either. Not if he's honest. Or his second. Even his first smoke. Once you're used to it, you can't get enough. You'll see."

"I guess folks can acquire a taste for just about anything."

That's a less friendly remark than she expected, perhaps less friendly than he intended, and her smile changes to a frown.

"What do you want?" Mrs. Matheson asks him.

"What's in your pocket?"

She's confused, which was his intention. "This? Dulse."

"The other thing."

She checks again. "Twine."

"You carry it around with you?"

"For when we hang out our dulse to dry."

"My wife was tied up with twine. So was the Reverend Lescavage."

"Lots of people carry twine."

"I'm not sure they do. What do I know, I'm a newcomer."

"You said it. What do you know?"

"You seem to know that my wife was tied up."

"What? No. I don't know what you're talking about."

"You say. I say that I know enough to ask Corporal Louwagie to arrest you for the murder of Reverend Lescavage."

The suddenness of his remark takes even Louwagie aback. He anticipated a more roundabout approach. Mrs. Matheson thinks he's joking. When she sees that he's not, she snaps back, "You have no proof."

Cinq-Mars returns her volley. "Interesting response. No expression of shock, dismay, or surprise. No protestation of innocence. No mock alarm. No capitulation, either, I'll grant you that much. All you want for us to go on is the burden of proof."

She looks from him to the Mountie, then back again, and whereas Pete Briscoe indicated at least a vibration of fear, this woman shows only defiance. She stands square to him. Hands on hips, her stance combative, she looks ready to brawl. She might be able to whip him, too. While he has the advantage of height and male strength, he also gives away about twenty years. He's further disadvantaged by minor pains and stiffness, and she's a workingwoman. With respect to muscle and sinew, there's nothing soft about her.

"I didn't understand one effing word you just said just now."

"That's okay," he replies. "As long as I understood it, that's all that counts." Ora is walking over, Cinq-Mars is closely observing her as she comes right up to him, initially, then turns back to face her mom. "I'm really only talking aloud to myself anyway," Cinq-Mars concludes.

"What's going on?" Ora asks brightly. "How are you?"

Cinq-Mars counters her smile with a grimace. "We need to borrow a shovel," he says. "A long-handled spade, in particular."

"Oh sure! I'll get it."

Her mother interrupts her retreat. "Ora. Don't." She's sharp, then softens her tone. "Sweetie, don't bother. I lent it out. It's not there any-more."

"Sure it is. You lent it to Petey. I know. He brought it back, Mom."

The three of them are silent and follow Ora's walk across the scruffy yard to a garden shed. She unlatches the door, sticks a hand inside, and retrieves a spade. The first drops of rain commence and more are heard in the leaves.

"So you have your shovel," Ora's mom spits out. "We're going to get soaked out here, so maybe you should be on your way. Just altogether piss off."

Cinq-Mars smiles as though she's a secret comedian. He waits for Ora, then takes the shovel from her. "Thanks," he says. To the mother, he offers advice. "One thing at a time."

He places the shovel with the end of the handle resting on the ground and examines the spade. He looks at Ora's mom, then back at the shovel. He then places the blade close to her face for an instant, and she backs off to one side, not liking that. As if addressing only Louwagie, although he knows full well that the women can hear him as plain as day, he says, "Mrs. Matheson was in a bit of a crash. A fender bender, really, except that she landed in a ditch down the road from here. At the time, I couldn't figure out how the steering wheel inflicted her particular wounds, especially because, even though she was bleeding a little, the cuts didn't seem completely fresh. More as if the accident opened old wounds, so to speak."

"I see," Louwagie says, but he doesn't, not really.

"I couldn't see how her injuries corresponded to an impact from the steering wheel or even a dash. I looked inside the vehicle, and frankly, Mrs. Matheson," he says as he turns to face her once again, "there was no blood."

"Big fucking deal," she remarks. "I bled after."

"Mommy!" Ora says, genuinely shocked by her language in public.

"Indeed. As you see, Wade, her scrapes and her lesions and her scabs perfectly match wounds that might be caused if a shovel like this one, or, what the heck, this very spade, got slammed across her face so that she was hit by the concave side."

He places the spade next to her face for a second or two again before Mrs. Matheson reacts and bumps it away.

Confused, Ora asks, "What are you talking about? What does this mean?"

"I'm sorry to say, Ora," Émile fills her in, "that it means that after ordering Lescavage to dig his own grave up on Ashburton Head, he was able to surprise your mother and use the shovel to smack her across the face. After that, Mrs. Matheson, you had a battle on your hands.

Didn't you? You're bigger, stronger, more fit than the reverend, so in spite of your injuries, or perhaps because of them, you ripped the spade back from him again and in the ongoing battle you thrust it right into his belly. More than once. He ran then. Probably not quickly. In mortal peril, he ran for his life, and in the storm and the dark you couldn't locate him. In the confusion, you dropped the spade. I imagine you as somewhat dazed yourself, perhaps disoriented for a moment or two—you took quite a wallop—so he was able to make progress away from you. Maybe he hid in the tall grasses. But you tracked him down, didn't you, Mrs. Matheson? Poor guy, in the storm he probably couldn't tell a straight line from a circle. I suppose he was in pain. Moaning, groaning, that sort of thing. Am I right? He made it away from the original planned gravesite, although still in the vicinity. Maybe he'd gone as far as he could go, and you just tripped over him. That I don't know. Your idea to bury him wasn't going to work, was it? It had been a good one, for who was going to find him up there? Yet now you had a further fight on your hands. And blood, from the moment you thrust the spade into the minister's belly. What to do? You're bleeding yourself, with this man howling at your feet, his guts hanging out. You had to be quick to finish the job. Strapped him to a tree, with twine, and sliced him up, I presume to make it look like a madman's job. Or maybe you had some further torture to inflict for reasons of your own. Or you actually are mad. Then you ran off. Trouble is, in your haste, you forgot the shovel behind. Maybe you didn't think it was important. How could you find it in the dark anyway? Too risky to go after it yourself the next day when you reconsidered. Still, best to have it found. Out of the picture, so to speak. So you sent Pete Briscoe to retrieve it. He buried it. Then he had to dig it up again because you figured your own blood was on it, too. Couldn't risk it being found. You brought it home instead, because as killers go, you're a raw amateur, aren't you, Mrs. Matheson? I'll be interested to hear what cockamamie story you devised for his sake."

"You're insane," Ora accuses him, but she seems shocked, and isn't ranting. "Why would my mom do such a terrible thing? Reverend Lescavage was at Mr. Orrock's house. Anyway, wouldn't he defend himself?

If she did it—*And she didn't! That's impossible!*—how did she get the reverend to go all the way up onto Ashburton Head? Drag him by the hair? Why did he go? Anyway, why would she do it? You're supposed to be smart, but that's dumb. Wade! Tell him. This is crazy!"

But Wade Louwagie offers no comfort. Neither does her mother.

"Why did she do it?" Cinq-Mars repeats, as though to give the question legitimacy. "How did she get Lescavage to go up there? These are good questions, Ora. You have a right to ask. She's your mother. She and I are going down to the station before the skies open up, where we will have a long chat about questions like that. Afterward, I'm pretty sure we'll have your answers. Now, Officer, arrest this one, please. Let's take her in for questioning."

"Mommy! What's happening! What's going on? Mommy!"

As frantic as her daughter has become, Mrs. Matheson declines to console her, and readies herself instead for some form of hand-to-hand combat with the Mountie. Louwagie is not backing down. Cinq-Mars steps between the combatants, though, and before Mrs. Matheson can deal with his height and his reach, he clutches both her wrists in an iron vise, and before she can react to that leans over and whispers a few words in her left ear. The Mountie and Ora are watching, as though enchanted themselves. Mrs. Matheson instantly goes passive, as though hypnotized. When Louwagie tucks her head down to aid the now-handcuffed woman safely into the back of his cruiser, she meekly complies. Ora suddenly storms the car, but Cinq-Mars places his hands on her shoulders, both to stop her in her tracks and as a gesture of sympathy, even of comfort. The young woman will have none of that and shoves his wrists outward to get his hands off her. She's standing her ground but is no longer charging, and Cinq-Mars takes that opportunity to slide into the cruiser's front seat. As the car drives off, he spots her in his side mirror as she follows the vehicle up the drive to the highway, which runs by the yard at a higher elevation. She doesn't go far before she stops, crumpling, as if from a blow to the stomach. Poor girl. This will be devastating, even more so once she's over the shock. As the car turns onto the highway, he sees her in full scream, but he cannot hear her over the cacophonous beat of the rain, which at that instant commences to pound the car's rooftop, and the girl topples over onto the bare dirt of her driveway as the rain throttles up.

From the cruiser's rear seat, Mrs. Matheson looks back at her fallen daughter. Then she turns around, and her eyes commence to blink rapidly.

TWENTY-SIX

Former Detective Sergeant Émile Cinq-Mars of the SPVM (Service de police de la Ville de Montréal) steps away from the police cruiser in front of the Orrock mansion and indulges in a deep breath, one that falters into a weary sigh. He lingers as he casts a protracted gaze across the vista prepared from the beginnings of geological time. The stately home stands in the foreground, the Bay of Fundy its backdrop, and oh, what his vacation might have been. The air is clear, crisp, still scintillating from the electrical storm days ago that traipsed across the bay to maraud the province of Nova Scotia. Low in the western sky, the sun has not yet changed its hue. Folks soon will be gathering at the Whistle to drink and be merry, watch the whales break the surface of the sea under a reddening sky. A rapt crowd will have plenty to discuss. Returning from his prolonged interrogation of Mrs. Grace Matheson, Cinq-Mars looks exhausted, drained. Yet his work is not done. The more difficult task to his day lies ahead.

Louwagie peels away from the curb, executes a U-turn, and delivers a honk on his way down the hill. Émile strolls up to the house where Maddy Orrock and his wife await. He has good news and bad to relate, and even as the doorbell rings he isn't sure which is which, or where to begin.

He'll have to muddle his way through what comes next.

If one thing has both surprised him and made an impression, it is that he expected to require local knowledge to dent the case. The opposite proved true. Only breaking the case gave him the local knowledge he sought. Then, like Fundy's tide, it surged, quicker than any rider on horseback.

When Maddy Orrock answers the door, Sandra's right behind her. Alerted by the Mountie's farewell honk, they'd seen Émile come up the walk. The husband and wife embrace, each comforting the other for the travails of their day. Sandra can tell immediately how fatigued he is, even how old he feels. As they settle into the living room and Maddy offers coffee, Sandra speaks with a different suggestion, as Émile might be too polite to ask. Knowing her husband, having seen this weariness before, she feels an indeterminate portent in the air.

"Whiskey," Sandra requests. "Émile will have a coffee and a whiskey."

He smiles, and chooses not to contradict her.

Sandra has chosen to sit tucked in beside her man. As the libations are presented on the table at their knees, they separate slightly to accommodate their movements. Maddy sits in one of the two wing chairs opposite. She's wearing Bermuda shorts and a light print top, somehow looking younger because of it. Émile notices some ancient scarring around an ankle, and realizes then that's he's looking down. He's sagging, his head too heavy to hold up. The effort to raise his glass helps him raise his chin up, and he studies the whiskey's color in sunlight reflected off a glass cabinet.

"*The New York Times* has changed its tune," he mentions.

Sandra neither loves nor hates his non sequiturs. Sometimes she bristles, other times they tickle her funny bone. Unschooled in Émile's style, Maddy falls for his line.

"How so?" she asks.

In this way he's allowed to talk, to clear his throat, to settle in and to shape the tenor of the conversation without broaching the subject at hand.

"The spelling of *whiskey*. The Americans and the Irish slip in an *e* before the *y*. Scots and Canadians—and, the Japanese, who are making good whiskey now—dispense with the *e*. For a dog's age, the *Times* insisted on the American/Irish spelling. They've reformed. They will spell the word according to its country of origin when a particular whisky, or whiskey with an *e*, is being discussed. This one, by the way, is *e*-less. You can't slip a Springbank by me without my being aware. And thank you. It's delicious."

She served one for Sandra and herself as well, and collectively, silently, they toast present company.

"Grace Matheson," Cinq-Mars announces, "Ora's mom, has been arrested for the murder of the Reverend Simon Lescavage."

As the woman is barely known to her, Sandra doesn't react, other than to look over at Maddy to see how she takes the news. The younger women seems thoroughly perplexed. "I don't understand. Why? How? Did she kill my father, too?"

"It's a long story, Maddy. Let's settle in. The whiskey, then, is a good idea." He takes another sip, which prompts the others to do the same. The women then ceremoniously put their glasses down as though to encourage his long story. Émile cradles his own glass in both hands, wishing that he could stay silent awhile and just drink.

"Prepare yourself, Maddy. The turns to this tale may stun you. Since I don't know that for sure, it may be that I'll only be confirming certain aspects for you. I mean to say that you might want to steel yourself for a shock or two."

"My God," she says very quietly. Already seated back in her chair, somehow she sinks deeper into its hold. "That's some preamble."

Another sip, another deeper breath, and he begins. "First, to let you know, your father was suffocated to death by the Reverend Simon Lescavage."

He waits for the violence of the news to subside. Knowing that he's going to continue, Maddy, stunned, says nothing.

"He was a gentle man," Émile continues. "Not a stakeholder in anything that would precipitate such a crime. He was one of the few friends your father had. So why would it be him? The answer lies in your father's nature, which is not news to you. He did have a few select male friends, but he permitted others into his life only if they let him lord it over them. Captain Sticky McCarran, for instance, was a friend, but he also owed your father, and Sticky relied on him for extra income. Not always legitimate income, but that's another tale. Your father was friends with Simon Lescavage in part because he was able to lord it over him intellectually. I don't think your father appreciated the minister's loss of faith. He preferred berating him and ridiculing him for his religion. Then, when the preacher agreed with him on all that, Alfred Orrock had no way to humiliate him further. A problem. By then, they were friends, so he could still be mean to him whenever he liked. He found ways."

"Some friendship," Sandra comments.

"That's how they were," Maddy recalls. "But why . . ."

"Why did he kill him? Your father chose to die under his own terms. He was not one to surrender to anyone's will, not even to the will of death. He'd had enough with being weak and sickly. But suicide? Even an assisted suicide? He couldn't bear people celebrating that he'd done himself in. Instead, he coerced the reverend to do it. An assisted suicide, but done in secret, in a way meant never to be revealed."

"How was he coerced?"

"Your father made up two wills, Maddy. The one in your possession—"

"That will gives fifty thousand dollars to Simon. He killed my father for money?"

"As you'll hear in a moment, he offered to give the money away. I think the cash was meant to intimidate him, to make him look bad and to help keep him quiet. He could never confess because people would think as you did now, that he wanted the fifty grand and wasn't willing to wait for Orrock's natural death. No, you see, he did it so that the *other will*, the second will, would never greet the light of day. The will to be accepted as valid is the one that your father signed and that you will carry to his solicitor, who happens to have both in her possession. The one the lawyer puts into action will be the one that is signed and is handed to her. Alfred Orrock threatened Lescavage with signing one and not the other, and the pastor was under pressure because he knew that you were on your way home, Maddy. The second will, the one the minister took away with him, was worded quite differently. In it, the minister would receive nothing, that's true, but the entire proceeds of Orrock's estate would be divided equally among any and all off-spring whose DNA demonstrates that they are his biological children."

Maddy takes that in, shakes her head, and looks up again. "He slept around. If he has bastard kids, I can live with that. But since that will was never signed, the estate is still entirely mine."

"That's correct."

"I don't understand. You said the minister didn't do it for the money. Then why?"

"DNA would be the requirement in the new will."

"Okay."

"Your friend Simon knew what that meant."

"And I don't, obviously," Maddy infers.

"It leaves you out."

Beyond her head lies the sea. Cinq-Mars sees her face framed by a windowpane behind her, and surrounding that pane is glass that reveals the reddening bay.

"How," she asks quietly, "does DNA leave me out?"

"Your father sired other children. He did not sire you. His second will exposed that fact, and your father believed that it would crush you, after his death. If it came to light. He deeply resented that you didn't love him. That you hardly ever came to visit. That you chose to live your life elsewhere. He swore a vow to look after you throughout his lifetime."

"What vow?"

Cinq-Mars chooses to ignore her question for the moment. "A solemn vow that he lived up to. He did not believe, however, that it extended beyond his life. He was willing to trade away your future if Lescavage did not do exactly as he demanded. Put another way, you were his hole card. He was willing to maintain your inheritance, and your ignorance, but only if Lescavage obeyed him. He asked the pastor to kill him. To maintain your inheritance, to spare you devastating news, the reverend did what he was forced to do. He could not allow you to be crushed."

The report feels like a tectonic shift beneath her feet. Émile can see in her eyes that she's searching inwardly through her past and memories, through time and experience, evaluating confrontations and even the days that were pleasant or joyful, to glean some indication, some validation, for this new universe that she now inhabits. Émile glances at Sandra and sees a query in her expression.

"What?" he asks.

"How do you know what happened that night? No one was here to see."

He concedes the validity of her question. Maddy also perks up, as if hoping that the world will be put back onto its proper axis, and spin in a familiar direction, if his hypothesis can be nullified. Although she doesn't know how to receive his news, if it can be dismissed, her next steps will at least follow a recognizable path.

"I've spent all afternoon and then some," Cinq-Mars explains, "talking with Grace Matheson. She was the last person to be with the reverend before he died, before she killed him. Fact is, so much of what I'm telling you comes through her, from him. So it's not direct, but secondhand."

"And she's a reliable witness?" Sandra inquires.

"Everything she says fits with what I know and what we've discovered."

Slumping down in the chair, putting her head back against the high rest and crossing her arms, Maddy Orrock looks puzzled but still demands whatever comes next. "Go on," she insists. "I know there's more."

"Yes. More. The minister intended to stay here that night, or so Mrs. Matheson says. But he was racked by guilt. He was still a religious man in his bones, no matter the contrary opinion that his doubts inflicted on him. He was never able to leave his church, for instance. Having committed a murder, having been coerced into doing so, despite a belief that he had no choice, despite doing it for your sake, Maddy, he was finding it hard to live with himself. He was in torment, that's my impression. He killed a man and that knowledge overwhelmed him. He felt forsaken, more so as time ticked by. He couldn't stay here and wait for you. He couldn't face you. So he went home."

This time when he takes another sip, the women join him. Adequate fortification in this circumstance is viewed as necessary.

"I'm still following Mrs. Matheson's account, which dovetails with my own investigation. He walked home wearing his rain gear. Once home, he took it off, of course. But then he called Mrs. Matheson. She came to pick him up. He ran out to her car, and because it was such a short sprint, he didn't bother with the rain pants. We checked the phone records. He called her on his landline at that late hour."

Sandra asks why he called Mrs. Matheson, of all people, if he wanted to confess. "Why not his friend, the Reverend Unger, let's say?"

"The fifty grand left to him in the will? In the other version, it goes to Grace Matheson. He wanted to let her know that he was going to give her every penny of what was left to him. The best he could do to ease his conscience. Beyond that, he believed that once Mrs. Matheson took the money, she would not be able to mention where it came from. In his heart, he was making recompense for his deed by rejecting Orrock's blood money. For him, the perfect person to confess to, the only person really, was Mrs. Matheson."

"Every penny," Maddy repeats.

"So she says."

"Then why kill him? Alive, he's worth fifty thousand dollars to her!"

"I'm sure her lawyer will bring that up at trial, if he can talk her into pleading not guilty. Fortunately, we have her detailed confession written out in full."

"The question stands, Émile," Sandra says, taking up Maddy's point. "Why would she kill him? Because he confessed to killing Mr. Orrock?"

"I don't think he went that far, to confess to her, not at that point."

"Then why?" Maddy presses. "She was angry about the will? Upset? Really? How would she get him up to Ashburton Head in a storm? It makes no sense what you're saying."

As tired as he is, lingering remnants of adrenaline still pump through him, and Émile discovers that he needs to stand. While up, he refreshes his drink, starts in again with his explanation, and while doing that tops up the women's glasses. "You, Sandra, helped me out on that part."

"Me?" She's unaware of any contribution.

"Big-time. When we arrested Mrs. Matheson she was ready to fight. I mean put up her dukes and box. Comical, if it wasn't such a serious moment. I leaned down and whispered in her ear, and what I said took the fight right out of her. I only had something to whisper because of you. Your numerology, in a sense, solved this case. Certainly it carried the day with my interrogation."

"Get off it." She's both tickled and flabbergasted.

Émile stands by the fireplace at one end of the room's sitting area. "Not kidding in the slightest. You wrote down people's names and birth dates. I noticed that you, Maddy, were born not so far apart from Mr. Roadcap. I noticed that his full name is Aaron Oscar Roadcap. At first, I thought they were odd names. I haven't met other Aarons or Oscars on this island, only a lot of Peters and Hanks and Mikes. So I looked at them more closely. That's when I saw that his initials, A.O.R., are a reconfigured version of your father's, A.R.O., for Alfred Royce Orrock Coincidence? Possibly. In my work, I look upon coincidence as smoke. You know the rest. Where there's smoke, something's burning."

Maddy decides to sit up now. Her left hand covers her right in a way that suggests she's attempting to quell a tremor. "Are you saying that that bloody Roadcap is one of my father's bastard children?"

He doesn't bother to answer. She knows he's saying exactly that.

"Okay," Maddy says. "Go on. If there's more."

"As I said, brace yourself. There's more."

"Jesus."

"I whispered to Mrs. Matheson while she was in a combative mood that I knew who fathered her child, and the fight went right out of her. The jig, essentially, was up."

"But her name," Sandra says, "is Ora Cynthia Matheson. O.C.M. Not a match."

"It's her first name." Maddy has already figured this out, and seems glum now. "Ora. O-R-A. My dad's initials in reverse. That was your identifier?"

Cinq-Mars nods. "You see, Lescavage knew only about Aaron Roadcap. He assumed the entire estate was going to him, leaving poor Maddy out and thoroughly humiliated. What he did not know was that it was going to be divided between Roadcap and Ora, and perhaps others. Grace Matheson knew about it, though, and the promise of fifty grand wasn't enough to extinguish her greed for her daughter's share of millions, and also business interests, this house, the world that's on their doorstep. Grace always expected that when the old man died, she'd live out her days right here, where we are, with this view, in this house. And she could still have it. All she had to do was get your father's other will back from Lescavage, which she did, and get the minister out of the way, which she did by killing him. Then forge Orrock's signature. He had such a shaky hand at the end of his life, how could that be difficult? Who would notice? Her attempt would be as good as his own. Then she'd switch the wills. She took the dead man's keys, because she knew his key ring included a key to the Orrock mansion—her daughter had told her so, in case the old man ever called, and in need, and Ora wasn't available. If she made the switch, then you, Maddy, would be an unwary innocent, a lamb to the slaughter, as you would take the *wrong one* to the solicitor, thinking you'd be getting at least a large cut of the proceeds, only to find out that your DNA eliminated you. At that point, it would be game, set, and match. You'd be out of luck. Crushed, even. Roadcap and Ora, and really her mother, would control half the proceeds each and fight over ownership of this house. At that point, of course, Ora's mom could buy out Roadcap's share—she'd have the cash on hand through her daughter—then live out her days in her mansion while the cash from Orrock's enterprises flowed in."

"Then why didn't she switch the wills?" Maddy asks.

"You'd come home. You were in the house. She might still have bluffed her way in, except that she was cut up and bleeding. The reverend put up enough of a fight to wreck her plans. Of course, I'm still sure she was hoping to pull a switch on you."

Maddy stands and paces. Émile returns to his wife's side on the sofa, taking her hand in his. They can't imagine what might be going through the young woman's head, and give her time and space. When she does speak, they know that she's still confused.

"Roadcap's my brother?"

"He's not. You're no more related than ever. Your father is his father. But your father is not yours. I don't know if that's good news or bad. Or what's worse. Learning that your father has other heirs, or that he's not your father at all, even though he's left you everything."

"But—" She has questions, which are pressing, but Émile has other ground that he feels is best to hoe first, so jumps back in when she's not quick to formulate what's confusing to her.

"Sandra asked a moment ago how Mrs. Matheson got the Reverend Lescavage onto the ridges. That baffled me also, and held up my investigation, even though I was suspicious of her from the get-go. In a way, she wanted to keep it to herself, not tell me, and if a lawyer was in the room, she wouldn't have. Fortunately, she has few skills as a criminal and is even more inexperienced at being accused. She still hasn't had the sense to lawyer up. 'Shysters,' she calls them. Anyway, I, too, couldn't imagine that she dumped him in a truck, then dragged him through the wind and the rain over that rough terrain to where he died. She finally let it out because she was proud of herself. She buffaloed him."

"She what?" Maddy asks.

"Manipulated him. She knew how Orrock controlled him, so she did the same. He'd lost his faith, and either for that reason or for some other, he hated it when others did well for themselves preaching about faith. Or, let's say, the potential to fly based on their faith. He *especially* hated people preaching faith when he knew they were fakes. He spent his life preaching faith, with honesty, then lost it. Still, it was hard to lose it, and he took that seriously, too. He was offended that an outright charlatan might preach about faith. He felt diminished by that. She knew that the cult was going up to the ridge in the storm. They always did, and she had inside information. She did business with them. She induced the reverend to come out with her to spy on them. He was obsessed with the cult. He'd like nothing better than to make fun of them in his next sermon, as he often did. As well, he was feeling miserable, he'd just killed a man, he was not in his best mind, I suppose, so off he went. Mrs. Matheson said that the pastor was a pushover, always had been, and partly she counted on that. She also told him she had her eye on a tree she wanted to transplant, and needed his help. She could only do it in the dark since it was on public property. That allowed her to take along a shovel. He was thoroughly unsuspecting. Then up there, she pulled out a dulse-harvesting knife and made him dig his own grave. While digging, he told her some of the things I just told you. Some things he'd already related. Trouble is, he hit rock. He was arguing with her, apparently, saying that a shallow grave disrespected his corpse. That animals might dig him up and she'd be caught. All that became moot when he hit solid rock. The oldest rock on earth, as it happens. She didn't believe him. In the dark, she couldn't see. She dropped her guard and checked to see if he couldn't keep digging and while she was doing that he smashed the spade across her face and ran. He'd had it with being a pushover."

"Gracious," Sandra says under her breath. "What some people do for money."

"Follow the money. I'm not the first detective to adopt the motto."

"So we're not related, Roadcap and I. Whew. Am I related to Ora?"

"You're not getting this, are you?" Émile clarifies for her. "I understand. It's an avalanche of information and it's all unexpected. Your father is not your father, so you're not related to anyone."

"Who *is* my father? I don't understand. My mother slept around, too? That's what I don't get. Does she know? Mrs. Matheson? Does she know who my father is?"

This is as deep as he wants to go, but he knows he's going deeper.

"She does," Émile informs her. He glances at Sandra for a measure of her strength to help him get through this.

Maddy waits. She doesn't want to ask. She can't bring herself to speak.

"Your father—" Émile begins, but Maddy interrupts.

"Don't tell me," she says. "Oh God, no. Don't tell me. I know. I think I know."

"Who?" Sandra asks.

They wait in silence.

"Do you want me to tell you?" Cinq-Mars asks the tall woman, who clasps her elbows to ready herself.

Maddy nods.

"Aaron Roadcap's father. August James Roadcap."

Still seated, Émile locks eyes with Maddy. She wavers, and chooses to sit down again. He's glad of that, as there's still more to come.

"August James Roadcap is my father," she says, wanting it confirmed.

"Yes."

"The man who threw my mother off a cliff."

"The man who was sentenced to prison for that."

She nods again, trying to process the news, and rubs her arms. Then she stops, as competing strands of thought twist through her mind. She's noticed the difference in what they said.

"The man who threw my mother off a cliff," she repeats in order for him to confirm exactly that.

"No, Maddy. The man convicted of the crime. The man who threw your mother off a cliff . . ."

Émile hesitates. He needs to know that she's waiting for this. That she'll hear it just once and know it at the same instant.

"The man who did that was the man you used to know to be your father. August Roadcap went to jail for the crime, and never revealed that he knew who really did it."

"Why not?" By asking that question, Émile knows that she's understood him.

"To protect you. And to protect his son. Although he was not his biological son, either, as we know. He was Orrock's. Still. He'd been bringing him up as his own, and loved him."

"He knew? He knew that my father was the real father?"

"I noticed something when I saw the birth dates that Sandra transcribed for her numerology exercises. As Mrs. Matheson related the story to me, your mother was no longer having relations with her husband. Orrock couldn't have cared less, at least according to Mrs. Matheson—one of his many younger lovers. Apparently, she was something of a beauty in her youth. Orrock did care when he discovered that his wife was pregnant. A different deal. That meant not only that he had been cuckolded, because he knew he hadn't had relations with her, it also meant that he was not in charge of his wife's life anymore, that someone had taken advantage of his neglect. He could not stand for that.

When he discovered who it was—Roadcap—he went after that man's wife. He plotted to seduce her, and with his wealth, he did so. Obviously, that marriage was rocky as well, given that the elder Roadcap was having an affair with another man's wife. She got pregnant, with Aaron, and that would appear to have been the end of it. His wife was pregnant with another man's child, now he had knocked up the other guy's wife. Maybe it could have ended there—he'd exacted his revenge. Trouble is, Orrock was never a man to settle for a tie. He bided his time. When the moment was opportune, after the kids were born, he took revenge upon his wife by throwing her off Seven Days Work. His planning was so meticulous that he was able to implicate her lover—your mother's, his wife's, lover—in the crime."

"Oh, Mom, my poor mom, what a miserable life she must've had."

Suddenly, the whole of her body shakes and with some violence. Sandra slides across to her, stroking her forearm, saying soft words. Émile knows as well that it's not just this news, but all of it over the previous days, that has done her in.

What comes on quickly is quelled nearly as fast, and when she's calm again, Émile adds, "She loved you. What you have to appreciate is that she loved you as her child, *and* as the child of a man she cared about dearly. The man she risked everything for. She may have been trapped in a miserable marriage, yet she found love with Roadcap. That man also loved you. He made a deal with the devil and never protested his innocence too strongly. He never accused Orrock. He couldn't have made that stick anyway. He never admitted guilt, either, but the case against him was circumstantial albeit strong enough, and his defense was weak. His case was unnecessarily weak because he kept certain things to himself to protect both you and Aaron Roadcap. The children."

"That's why my father used to walk to Dark Harbour so often when I was young. When . . . when we were both young."

"Your lives were in Orrock's hands, yours and Aaron Roadcap's, and Orrock made a vow to the elder Roadcap, which he kept in exchange for his silence, to protect the two of you, and raise you well. Grace Matheson tells me that he had a claim to fame, that he kept his promises once he made them. In doing so, Orrock reveled in his revenge. He found it sweet. All part of his control-freak nature, of course, but there you have it."

Several minutes go by in silence. It's darkening outside, as this portion of the island is sheltered by the western ridges, so light disappears earlier. Sunrises are brilliant, though. Sandra and Émile come together at one point, briefly embrace, then wait for Maddy to find her balance. She knows everything about her lineage now, but she still needs to talk a few things through. "So my father was Roadcap's, and his was mine. Different mothers, though, right? Right." And finally she concludes, "Holy shit," and sits down again.

Sandra slips away to the bathroom and returns with Kleenex. Maddy dabs her eyes. She attempts to smile, tries to laugh, but nothing works out well. And yet she's recovering.

"I'll tell you one thing. If my *former* father thinks he can manipulate me after his death like he did in life, he can think twice. He can damn well bury himself. He can make his own bloody arrangements. I'm no longer involved in the funeral."

Sandra looks across to Émile as though to seek his counsel, perhaps help change Maddy's mind, but she sees instead his approval of Maddy's statement. Sandra relaxes, thinks about it, then agrees. Why not? Let the bugger bury himself.

"What about our nutty professor?" Maddy asks. "Why'd he go over the ledge?"

"He was involved with those who want to fly. He rented the former City Hall for them at his own expense. He was up on the ridge with the other wannabe fliers when Lescavage was killed. He was one of the first two people to come across the body. I imagine that later he suffered what our Reverend Lescavage would have called a 'loss of faith.' He realized that he was never going to fly. He wrote an e-mail to a friend, who sent it back to the police here, in which, in cryptic, and I'd say cynical, language, he suggested that he might make one last attempt. To fly. I think he jumped off the cliff to see if an act of pure belief, of pure faith, would work. I'm also thinking that he expected it wouldn't. In any case, he didn't fly. Blame gravity. By all accounts, he went straight down. Maybe he lifted off the ground for a second, had a fleeting moment of ecstasy. After that, a nosedive. Part of his loss of faith may have come from his growing knowledge that he was being used."

"Who by?"

"Mrs. Matheson, for one. The fliers, for another. You see, Matheson was using the cult and their American connections, including Professor DeWitt, to set up a distribution network in the States for island dulse. Control the distribution, you control the trade. They were working to set up their own shadow network and take the business away from your father and Roadcap. Aaron worked for your dad. Your former dad. Orrock arranged for him to be raised in Dark Harbour after his father went to prison and later his mother died. Saw to his education. Gave him work and increasing responsibility. Roadcap didn't think your father was such a terrible guy. What he'll think now that the truth is out is another story. He's in for a shock. I'm pretty sure he doesn't know that Orrock was his biological father. Or what he did."

"I guess you'll have to tell him," Maddy says.

Émile continues to look at her without responding, until finally she wonders why and looks back.

"Or you could," he suggests.

She snorts a little, but her condition causes a release of mucus, and she has to clean up with Kleenex again.

When Cinq-Mars continues to study her, she protests. "He hates my guts. I've always hated his. Now? After this? I just took his fortune away from him. Now he has several million more reasons to despise me."

"He thinks you're a tide," Émile says.

"What?"

"He refers to you as a tide. You flow in every few years, then flow back out again. At least in his mind."

"A tide? He thinks I'm a tide?"

"A tide."

She gets his point, that he wants her to think about that, and she does.

"Okay. All right. Why not? I'll tell him. I'll tell him that his father didn't kill my mother. That my father did. But really it was his father who killed her, just not the father he thinks it was and not the one who went to jail. I'll tell him—" Her voice breaks. "I'll tell him that my mother and the man he loved as his father, that those two loved each other. The man and woman who loved us both loved each other." She falters a trifle. "I'll tell him *that*."

She says it with a dollop of sarcasm in her voice, but Émile suggests an alternative slant. "Actually, if I were you, that's exactly where I'd begin. The man he loved as his father was yours, and that man loved your mother so much, he was willing to live out his life in prison, in silence, rather than risk any further damage inflicted upon her child."

Maddy looks up at him.

"I'm just saying," he adds, "it might be a starting point."

Sandra and Émile come together again. Sandra makes a motion to suggest that perhaps it's time to leave. Maddy, though, is agitated by yet another question.

"Why . . . why was Aaron Roadcap on the ridge that night?"

Émile shrugs. "He keeps visiting the scene. Where your mother died. Where the man he thought was his father was wrongfully destroyed. But you're right. That's not the only reason. He was also there to spy on the cult. He perceived that they were helping his unknown rival in the dulse trade, and he wanted to understand them, perhaps to undermine them, or to discover who they were working with. That's one thing. He uncovered that Professor DeWitt was part of that bunch. That alone put pressure on DeWitt, and may have contributed to his fall. What also might have contributed to his fall was the little charade he pulled off with Grace Matheson, pretending he didn't know her when she faked her accident. They put on a real song and dance for whoever might come along. It happened to be me. I'm guessing that he started figuring out why she'd hooked him into that. He went along with it because she told him she was drunk and rammed a parked car, and now needed to account for the damage on her truck. One more drunk-driving charge and she'd lose her license. They didn't know I was a cop. They just wanted a witness, a dupe. I happened to drive by. Anyway, that's what Roadcap was doing. Finding out about the components of the group. Just like Lescavage was doing, I suppose."

Sandra has her own questions. "Who burned our car? Yes, I've learned about the Jeep. Who kidnapped me?"

"Grace Matheson. She arranged it all. She doesn't control people who would go out and kill for her. It's not that kind of gang. She was the only one around willing to commit murder. But she panicked. In a way, just like the reverend panicked in going to her. His downfall was her. She has people she can ask to do things, and she asked a few nefarious Dark Harbour folk to do her bidding for a price. To scare me. To scare you. Run us off the island in the island way. Little chance of that."

"Speak for yourself. I think I've developed vertigo."

Émile smiles. "You didn't budge. She fired you up. Anyway, Louwagie will round the others up. That won't be difficult."

"So, Émile," his wife teases him, "you solved two murders today and a suicide. That didn't take long."

"Three murders," he corrects her, "and a suicide. Going back in time, to the death of Maddy's mom."

As though out of respect for that woman, they share a quiet moment. Émile touches Maddy's forearm and speaks softly. "We'll go now."

"I'll drive you."

"It's a short walk. Don't bother."

She nods. Then says, "I disrupted your holiday. My dad—my non-dad, my used-to-be dad, whoever he is—he kept a Cadillac Escalade in the garage. Way too ostentatious for me. Take it. To replace the Jeep. That's not negotiable, but also, accept it as compensation. We'll get the paperwork done. It's all yours."

Émile is about to decline. It's too much, too generous, and who accepts a luxury vehicle for solving a simple case? Sandra pokes him in the ribs, which Maddy sees, and suddenly Émile agrees. The three laugh at that.

"I'll come by tomorrow for the keys. I don't want to trouble you now. We'll check in with you then."

Émile and Sandra hug her and depart. They walk across the broad lawn to the road and head downhill. It's not a short walk around to Whale Cove, and along the way they stop for dinner in the gathering dark.

In a booth at the Compass Rose, Sandra is musing after they put in their orders. "One thing I don't get still. Pete Briscoe. How bad a man is he, to go fetch the bloody shovel and not tell a soul?"

"He's naïve and gullible. A combination that Orrock and Grace Matheson took advantage of. I was curious about the story she told him. You see, Pete knew that the fliers cult was in cahoots with his boss, Grace Matheson. She invented some story about them finding the shovel and getting their fingerprints on it, then coming across the body afterward and panicking. Of course, it was her own fingerprints she wanted removed. The fliers threw the shovel away, she told him, when actually she did. They were innocent. If I may say so, our fisherman bought it, hook, line, and sinker."

Émile is laughing to himself, and she thinks at first that this has to do with his remark. He leans across the table to whisper something else that's not intended for public dissemination, or even for polite company.

"Something else about Pete. I couldn't really figure out why he dug so many holes. I sent Wade Louwagie back to ask him. He was trying to get the blood and guts off the shovel, as I thought, but it turns out he was also trying to find the right hole to shit in. Some holes hit rock, too shallow. A few were deep enough but contained worms or other creepy crawly things. He's sensitive about where he takes a dump."

She laughs along with him then.

"Also what Wade learned. Pete wasn't looking to protect the spade when he came running up to us on Seven Days Work. He'd cleaned it by then, and never thought it was so important anyway. He was just protecting his friends from being wrongly accused, in his mind. That's why he only looked mischievous up there, rather than guilty."

"He was protecting," surmises Sandra, "his waste?"

"Precisely. We came along at an inopportune moment. He hadn't had time to backfill his business yet, and didn't want us to see what he'd done. So he ran over to us and made up a dog story. Turns out, that slightly embarrassing moment is what did him in. More importantly, that moment helped do Grace Matheson in."

The old sea rhyme comes to mind, "Red sky at night, sailor's delight," for as boats bob in the harbor and the ferry comes in, as tourists disembark, the sky glows a brilliant crimson. A wine for the evening, a darker hue of red, is uncorked and poured. "Let the vacation begin," Émile remarks with a grin.

"Finally," Sandra says, and the two clink glasses. "Let's give it a shot."